'Slaughter tells a dark story th   d
doesn't le
The Times

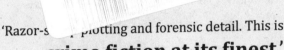

'Razor-s   plotting and forensic detail. This is
crime fiction at its finest.'
Michael Connelly

'Slaughter takes us to the
deep, dark places
other novelists don't dare to go.'
Tess Gerritsen

'Accomplished, compelling and complex, with
page-turning power aplenty.'
Daily Express

'Slaughter knows exactly when to ratchet up the
menace.'
Daily Mail

'Slaughter is one of the most **riveting**
writers in the field today.'
Sunday Express

Also by **Karin Slaughter**

Blindsighted

Grant County police chief Jeffrey Tolliver and medical examiner Sara Linton find themselves dealing with a violent serial killer who leaves his mark in the most brutal of ways.

'Don't read this alone. Don't read this after dark. But do read it.' *Daily Mirror*

Kisscut

When a teenage quarrel explodes into a deadly shoot-out, police chief Jeffrey Tolliver and medical examiner Sara Linton uncover something far more sinister.

'A great read . . . crime fiction at its finest.' Michael Connelly

A Faint Cold Fear

A death on a college campus looks like suicide, but for police chief Jeffrey Tolliver and medical examiner Sara Linton, things don't add up, especially when it involves ex-police detective Lena Adams.

'Slaughter's plotting is relentless, piling on the surprises and twists . . . should come with a psychological health warning.' *Guardian*

Indelible

When police chief Jeffrey Tolliver and medical examiner Sarah Linton take a trip away from Grant County things go violently wrong, and years later the past refuses to stay buried.

'Slaughter is one of the most riveting writers in the field today.' *Sunday Express*

Faithless

A walk in the woods takes a disturbing turn for police chief Jeffrey Tolliver and medical examiner Sara Linton when they stumble across the body of a young girl.

'No one does American small-town evil more chillingly.'
The Times

Skin Privilege

Nothing can prepare detective Lena Adams for the violence which erupts when she's forced to return to her childhood home. It's a case that proves catastrophic for police chief Jeffrey Tolliver and medical examiner Sara Linton.

'Beautifully paced, appropriately grisly, and terrifyingly plausible.' *Time Out*

Triptych

Atlanta police chief Michael Ormewood is reluctantly forced to work with special agent Will Trent on one of the most vicious killings of his career.

'Without doubt an accomplished, compelling and complex tale, with page-turning power aplenty.' *Daily Express*

Fractured

Special agent Will Trent and detective Faith Mitchell must work together to find a sadistic killer who is targeting one of Atlanta's wealthiest and most privileged communities.

'Brilliantly chilling.' *heat*

Genesis

Former Grant County medical examiner Sara Linton, special agent Will Trent and his partner Faith Mitchell are all that stand between a madman and his next crime.

'A fast-paced and unsettling story . . . A compelling and fluid read.' *Daily Telegraph*

Broken

Home for Thanksgiving after a long absence, Sara Linton finds herself drawn into a chilling case, involving detective Lena Adams. Suspicious and resentful, Sara turns to special agent Will Trent.

'Criminally spectacular.' *OK!*

Fallen

With special agent Faith Mitchell suspended from duty, Will Trent and Sara Linton must piece together the fragments of a terrifying and complicated case – before it's too late.

'Slaughter is a fearless writer. She takes us to the deep, dark places other novelists don't dare to go.' Tess Gerritsen

Criminal

Special agent Will Trent finds himself confronting his past when a present-day murder victim bears a chilling similarity to a woman found dead almost forty years earlier.

'Totally terrifying, gripping and surprising, yet layered and satisfying too. Her best book yet.' Lee Child

Unseen

Special agent Will Trent has gone uncover in Macon, Georgia and put his life at risk. And he knows Sara Linton will never forgive him if she discovers the truth.

'Slaughter knows exactly when to ratchet up the menace.' *Daily Mail*

KARIN SLAUGHTER

cop town

arrow books

Published by Arrow Books 2015

2 4 6 8 10 9 7 5 3 1

Copyright © Karin Slaughter 2014

Map on pp ix by Lee Baker

First published in Great Britain in 2014 by Century

Arrow Books
Random House, 20 Vauxhall Bridge Road,
London SW1V 2SA

www.randomhouse.co.uk

Addresses for companies within The Random House Group Limited can be
found at: www.randomhouse.co.uk/offices.htm

The Random House Group Limited Reg. No. 954009

A CIP catalogue record for this book is available from the British Library

ISBN 9780099571377
ISBN 9780099571384 (export)

Typeset by SX Composing DTP, Rayleigh, Essex
Printed and bound by Clays Ltd, St Ives plc

MIX
Paper from
responsible sources
FSC
www.fsc.org FSC® C018179

Penguin Random House is committed to a sustainable
future for our business, our readers and our planet.
This book is made from Forest Stewardship Council®
certified paper.

For Billie, who started it all
(There's a fearful point . . .)

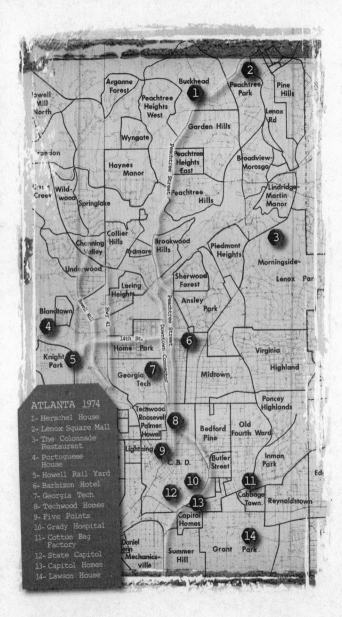

ATLANTA 1974

1- Herschel House
2- Lenox Square Mall
3- The Colonnade Restaurant
4- Portuguese House
5- Howell Rail Yard
6- Barbizon Hotel
7- Georgia Tech
8- Techwood Homes
9- Five Points
10- Grady Hospital
11- Cotton Bag Factory
12- State Capitol
13- Capitol Homes
14- Lawson House

NOVEMBER 1974

Prologue

Dawn broke over Peachtree Street. The sun razored open the downtown corridor, slicing past the construction cranes waiting to dip into the earth and pull up skyscrapers, hotels, convention centers. Frost spiderwebbed across the parks. Fog drifted through the streets. Trees slowly straightened their spines. The wet, ripe meat of the city lurched toward the November light.

The only sound was footsteps.

Heavy slaps echoed between the buildings as Jimmy Lawson's police-issue boots pounded the pavement. Sweat poured from his skin. His left knee wanted to give. His body was a symphony of pain. Every muscle was a plucked piano wire. His teeth gritted like a sand block. His heart was a snare drum.

The black granite Equitable Building cast a square shadow as he crossed Pryor Street. How many blocks had Jimmy gone? How many more did he have to go?

Don Wesley was thrown over his shoulder like a sack of flour. Fireman's carry. Harder than it looked. Jimmy's shoulder was ablaze. His spine drilled into his tailbone. His arm trembled from the effort of keeping Don's legs clamped to his chest. The man could already be dead. He wasn't moving. His head tapped into the small of Jimmy's back as he barreled down Edgewood faster than he'd ever carried the ball down the field. He didn't know if it was Don's blood or his own sweat that was rolling down the back of his legs, pooling into his boots.

He wouldn't survive this. There was no way a man could survive this.

The gun had snaked around the corner. Jimmy had watched it slither past the edge of a cinder-block wall. The sharp fangs of the front sights jutted up from the tip of the barrel. Raven MP-25. Six-round detachable box, blowback action, semiauto. The classic Saturday night special. Twenty-five bucks on any ghetto corner.

That's what his partner's life had come down to. Twenty-five bucks.

Jimmy faltered as he ran past First Atlanta Bank. His left knee almost touched the asphalt. Only adrenaline and fear saved him from falling. Quick bursts of recall kept setting off colorful fireworks in his head: Red shirtsleeve bunched up around a yellow-gold wristwatch. Black-gloved hand holding the white pearl grip. The rising sun had bathed the weapon's dark steel in a bluish light. It didn't seem right that something black could have a glint to it, but the gun had almost glowed.

And then the finger pulled back on the trigger.

Jimmy knew the workings of a gun. The 25's slide was already racked, cartridge in the chamber. The trigger spring engaged the firing pin. The firing pin hit the primer. The primer ignited the gunpowder. The bullet flew from the chamber. The casing popped out of the ejection port.

Don's head exploded.

Jimmy's memory did no work to raise the image. The

violence was etched into his corneas, backdropped every time he blinked. Jimmy was looking at Don, then he was looking at the gun, then he was looking at how the side of Don's face had distorted into the color and texture of a rotten piece of fruit.

Click-click.

The gun had jammed. Otherwise, Jimmy wouldn't be running down the street right now. He would be face down in an alley beside Don, condoms and cigarette butts and needles sticking to their skin.

Gilmer Street. Courtland. Piedmont. Three more blocks. His knee could hold out for three more blocks.

Jimmy had never been on the business end of a firing gun. The flash was an explosion of starlight – millions of pinpricked pieces of sun lighting up the dark alley. His eardrums rang with the sound. His eyes stung from the cordite. At the same time, he felt the splash against his skin, like hot water, only he knew – he knew – it was blood and bone and pieces of flesh hitting his chest, his neck, his face. He tasted it on his tongue. Crunched the bone between his teeth.

Don Wesley's blood. Don Wesley's bone.

He was blinded by it.

When Jimmy was a kid, his mother used to make him take his sister to the pool. She was so little back then. Her skinny, pale legs and arms poking out of her tiny suit reminded Jimmy of a baby praying mantis. In the water, he'd cup his hands together, tell her he'd caught a bug. She was a girl, but she loved looking at bugs. She'd paddle over to see, and Jimmy would squeeze his hands together so the water would squirt into her face. She would scream and scream. Sometimes she would cry, but he'd still do it again the next time they were in the pool. Jimmy told himself it was all right because she kept falling for it. The problem wasn't that he was cruel. The problem was that she was stupid.

Where was she now? Safe in bed, he hoped. Fast asleep, he prayed. She was on the job, too. His little sister. It wasn't safe. Jimmy could end up carrying her through the streets one day. He could be jostling her limp body, careening around the corner, his knee brushing the blacktop as the torn ligaments clashed like cymbals.

Jimmy saw a glowing sign up ahead: a white field with a red cross in the center.

Grady Hospital.

He wanted to weep. He wanted to fall to the ground. But his burden would not lighten. If anything, Don got heavier. The last twenty yards were the hardest of Jimmy's life.

A group of black men were congregating under the sign. They were dressed in bright purples and greens. Their tight pants flared below the knee, showing a touch of white patent leather. Thick sideburns. Pencil mustaches. Gold rings on their fingers. Cadillacs parked a few feet away. The pimps were always in front of the hospital this time of morning. They smoked skinny cigars and watched the sun rise as they waited for their girls to get patched up for the morning rush hour.

None of them offered to help the two bloody cops making their way toward the doors. They gawked. Their cigarillos stopped midair.

Jimmy fell against the glass doors. Someone had forgotten to lock them. They butterflied open. His knee slued to the side. He fell face-first into the emergency waiting room. The jolt was like a bad tackle. Don's hipbone knifed into his chest. Jimmy felt the flex of his own ribs kissing his heart.

He looked up. At least fifty pairs of eyes stared back. No one said a word. Somewhere in the bowels of the treatment area, a phone was ringing. The sound echoed through the barred doors.

The Gradys. Over a decade of civil rights hadn't done shit. The waiting room was still divided: black on one side, white on the other. Like the pimps under the sign, they all stared at Jimmy. At Don Wesley. At the river of blood flowing beneath them.

Jimmy was still on top of Don. It was a lewd scene, one man on top of another. One cop on top of another. Still, Jimmy cradled his hand to Don's face. Not the side that was blown open – the side that still looked like his partner.

'It's okay,' Jimmy managed, though he knew it wasn't okay. Would never be okay. 'It's all right.'

Don coughed.

Jimmy's gut twisted at the sound. He'd been sure the man was dead. 'Get help,' he told the crowd, but it was a whisper, a begging little girl's voice that came out of his own mouth. 'Somebody get help.'

Don groaned. He was trying to speak. The flesh of his cheek was gone. Jimmy could see his tongue lolling between shattered bone and teeth.

'It's okay.' Jimmy's voice was still a high whistle. He looked up again. No one would meet his gaze. There were no nurses. No doctors. No one was going to get help. No one was answering the damn telephone.

Don groaned again. His tongue slacked outside of his

7

jaw.

'It's okay,' Jimmy repeated. Tears streamed down his face. He felt sick and dizzy. 'It's gonna be okay.'

Don inhaled sharply, like he was surprised. He held the air in his lungs for a few seconds before finally letting out a low, baleful moan. Jimmy felt the sound vibrating in his chest. Don's breath was sour – the smell of a soul leaving the body. The color of his flesh didn't drain so much as fill like a pitcher of cold buttermilk. His lips turned an earthy, funereal blue. The fluorescent lights cut white stripes into the flat green of his irises.

Jimmy felt a darkness pass through him. It gripped his throat, then slowly reached its icy fingers into his chest. He opened his mouth for air, then forced it closed for fear that Don's ghost would flow into him.

Somewhere, the phone was still ringing.

'She-it,' a raspy old woman grumbled. 'Doctor ain't never gone get to me now.'

DAY ONE
MONDAY

1

Maggie Lawson was upstairs in her bedroom when she heard the phone ringing in the kitchen. She checked her watch. There was nothing good about a phone ringing this early in the morning. Sounds from the kitchen echoed up the back stairs: The click of the receiver being lifted from the cradle. The low murmur of her mother's voice. The sharp snap of the phone cord slapping the floor as she walked back and forth across the kitchen.

The linoleum had been worn away in staggered gray lines from the countless times Delia Lawson had paced the kitchen listening to bad news.

The conversation didn't last long. Delia hung up the phone. The loud click echoed up to the rafters. Maggie knew every sound the old house made. She had spent a lifetime studying its moods. Even from her room, she could follow her mother's movements through the kitchen: The refrigerator door opening and closing. A cabinet banging shut. Eggs being cracked into a bowl. Thumb flicking her Bic to light a cigarette.

Maggie knew how this would go. Delia had been playing Bad-News Blackjack for as long as Maggie could remember. She would hold for a while, but then tonight,

11

tomorrow, or maybe even a week from now, Delia would pick a fight with Maggie and the minute Maggie opened her mouth to respond, her mother would lay down her cards: the electric bill was past due, her shifts at the diner had been cut, the car needed a new transmission, and here Maggie was making things worse by talking back and for the love of God, couldn't she give her mother a break?

Busted. Dealer wins.

Maggie screeched the ironing board closed. She stepped carefully around folded stacks of laundry. She'd been up since five that morning doing the family's ironing. She was Sisyphus in a bathrobe. They all had uniforms of one kind or another. Lilly wore green-and-blue-checkered skirts and yellow button-down tops to school. Jimmy and Maggie had their dark blue pants and long-sleeved shirts from the Atlanta Police Department. Delia had her green polyester smocks from the diner. And then they all came home and changed into regular clothes, which meant that every day, Maggie was washing and ironing for eight people instead of four.

She only complained when no one could hear her.

There was a scratching sound from Lilly's room as she dropped the needle on a record. Maggie gritted her teeth. *Tapestry*. Lilly played the album incessantly.

Not too long ago, Maggie helped Lilly get dressed for school every morning. At night, they would page through *Brides* magazine and clip out pictures for their dream weddings. That was all before Lilly turned thirteen years old and her life, much like Carole King's, became an everlasting vision of the ever-changing hue.

She waited for Jimmy to bang on the wall and tell Lilly to turn that crap off, but then she remembered her brother had picked up a night shift. Maggie looked out the window. Jimmy's car wasn't in the driveway. Unusually, the neighbor's work van was gone. She wondered if he was working the night shift, too. And then she chastened herself for wondering, because it was none of her business what her neighbor was doing.

Now seemed as good a time as any to go down for breakfast. Maggie pulled the foam rollers from her hair as she walked down the stairs. She stopped exactly in the middle. The acoustic sweet spot. *Tapestry* disappeared. There were no sounds from the kitchen. If Maggie timed it right, she could sometimes grab a full minute of silence standing on the stairs. There wouldn't be another time during her day when she felt so completely alone.

She took a deep breath, then slowly let it out before continuing down.

The old Victorian had been grand at one point, though the house retained no evidence of its former glory. Pieces of siding were gone. Rotted wood hung like bats from the gables. The windows rattled with the slightest breeze. Rain shot a creek through the basement. There was no outlet in the house that didn't have a black tattoo ghosted around it from bad fuses and shoddy workmanship.

Even though it was winter, the kitchen was humid. No matter the time of year, it always smelled of fried bacon and cigarette smoke. The source of both stood at the stove. Delia's back was bent as she filled the percolator. When Maggie thought of her mother, she thought of this kitchen – the faded avocado-green appliances, the cracked yellow linoleum on the floor, the burned, black ridges on the laminate countertop where her father rested his cigarettes.

13

As usual, Delia had been up since before Maggie. No one knew what Delia did in the morning hours. Probably curse God that she'd woken up in the same house with the same problems. There was an unwritten rule that you didn't go downstairs until you heard eggs being whisked in a bowl. Delia always cooked a big breakfast, a holdover from her Depression childhood, when breakfast might be the only meal of the day.

'Lilly up?' Delia hadn't turned around, but she knew Maggie was there.

'For now.' Maggie made the same offer she did every morning. 'Can I do anything?'

'No.' Delia jabbed the bacon with a fork. 'Driveway's empty next door.'

Maggie glanced out the window, pretending she didn't already know Lee Grant's van was not parked in its usual spot.

Delia said, 'All we need is for girls to start going in and out of that house at all hours. Again.'

Maggie leaned against the counter. Delia looked exhausted. Even her stringy brown hair couldn't be bothered to stay pinned on the top of her head. They'd all been picking up extra shifts to pay for Lilly to go to a private school. None of them wanted to see her bussed across town to the ghetto. They had four more years of tuition and textbooks and uniforms before Lilly graduated. Maggie wasn't sure her mother would last that long.

As a child, Delia had seen her father shoot himself in the head after losing the family business. Her mother had worked herself into an early grave on a sharecropper's farm. She'd lost both brothers to polio. She must have thought she'd hit pay dirt when she married Hank Lawson. He wore a suit and had a good job and a nice car, and then he'd come home from Okinawa so shell-shocked that he'd been in and out of the state mental hospital ever since.

There wasn't much that Maggie knew about her father, though he'd obviously tried to build a life between hospital stays. When Lilly was born, he put up the swing set in the backyard. One time, he found some gray paint on sale at the hardware store and worked thirty-six hours straight painting every room in the house the color of an aircraft carrier. On weekends, he mowed the lawn for as long as it took to drink a six-pack of Schlitz, then left the mower wherever the beer ran out. One time when it snowed and Maggie was sick with strep, he brought her some snow in a Tupperware bowl so she could play with it in the bathroom.

'Maggie, for the love of God.' Delia tapped the fork against the frying pan. 'Can't you find something to do?'

Maggie grabbed a stack of plates and silverware off the counter and took them into the dining room. Lilly was already at the table. Her head was bent over a textbook, which Maggie took as a miracle. The last year hadn't been so much the burgeoning of thirteen-year-old Lilly into womanhood as a running audition for *The Exorcist*.

Still, Maggie couldn't give up on her baby sister. 'You have a good night?'

'Peachy.' Lilly cupped her fingers across her forehead in a salute to the page. Her hair was pulled back into a loose ponytail. The chestnut brown fell somewhere between Delia's mousy brown and Maggie's darker hue.

'Peachy sounds good.' Maggie put a plate by Lilly's elbow. She bumped her with her thigh. 'What're you studying?' She bumped her again. Then again. When Lilly didn't respond, she sang the opening lines from 'I Feel the Earth Move,' punctuating each pause with a bump.

'Stop it.' Lilly tilted her head down even more. Her nose was practically touching the book.

Maggie leaned over to set the other side of the table. She glanced back at Lilly, who had been staring at the same spot on the page since Maggie walked in.

Maggie said, 'Look at me.'

'I'm studying.'

'Look at me.'

'I have a test.'

'I know you stole my makeup again.'

Lilly looked up. Her eyes were lined like Cleopatra's.

Maggie kept her voice low. 'Baby girl, you're beautiful. You don't need that stuff.'

Lilly rolled her eyes.

Maggie tried again. 'You don't understand what kind of message wearing makeup at your age sends to boys.'

'I guess you should know.'

Maggie rested her hand on the table. She wondered when her sweet kid sister had learned how to throw daggers.

The kitchen door swung open. Delia's hands and arms were lined with platters of pancakes, eggs, bacon, and biscuits. 'You've got two seconds to wash that shit off your face before I get your father's belt.' Lilly bolted from the room. Delia banged the platters down on the table one by one. 'See what you're teaching her?'

'Why am I—'

'Don't talk back.' Delia dug a pack of cigarettes out of her apron. 'You're twenty-two years old, Margaret. Why do I feel like I have two teenagers under my roof?'

'Twenty-three,' was all Maggie could say.

Delia lit the cigarette and hissed out smoke between her teeth. 'Twenty-three,' she repeated. 'I was married with two kids when I was your age.'

Maggie resisted the urge to ask her mother how that had worked out.

Delia picked a speck of tobacco off her tongue. 'This women's lib stuff works for rich girls, but all you've got going for you is your face and your figure. You need to take advantage of both before you lose them.'

Maggie smoothed together her lips. She imagined a lost-and-found box in the back of a storeroom with all the missing faces and figures of thirty-year-old women.

'Are you listening to me?'

'Mama.' Maggie kept her tone even. 'I like my job.'

'Must be nice to do whatever you like.' Delia pressed the cigarette to her mouth. She inhaled sharply and held the smoke in her lungs. She looked up at the ceiling. She shook her head.

Maggie guessed it was coming sooner than she'd thought. Her mother was shuffling the deck before laying down the Bad-News Card: Why are you throwing away your life? Go to nursing school. Be a Kelly Girl. Get some kind of job where you'll meet a man who doesn't think you're a whore.

Instead, Delia told her, 'Don Wesley was killed this morning.'

Maggie's hand went to her chest. Her heart was a hummingbird trapped beneath her fingers.

Delia said, 'Shot in the head. Died two seconds after he got to the hospital.'

'Is Jimmy—'

'If Jimmy was hurt, do you think I'd be standing here talking about Don Wesley?'

Maggie took a mouthful of air, then coughed it back out. The room was filled with smoke and cooking odors. She wanted to open a window but her father had painted them all shut.

'How did it . . .' Maggie had trouble forming the question. 'How did it happen?'

'I'm just the mother. You think they tell me anything?'

'They,' Maggie repeated. Her uncle Terry and his friends. They made Delia look downright forthcoming. Fortunately, there was an easy way around that. Maggie reached inside the stereo console to turn on the radio.

'Don't,' Delia stopped her. 'The news can't tell us anything except what we already know.'

'What do we know?'

'Drop it, Margaret.' Delia tapped ash into her cupped hand. 'Jimmy's safe. That's all that matters. And you be nice to him when he gets here.'

'Of course I—'

A car door slammed in the driveway. The windowpanes shook from the sound. Maggie held her breath because it was easier than breathing. Part of her hoped it was their neighbor coming home from work. But then shoes scuffed across the carport, up the back stairs. The kitchen door opened, but didn't close.

She knew it was her uncle Terry before she saw him. He never shut the back door. The kitchen was a non-room to him, one of those things women needed that men didn't want to know about, like sanitary napkins and romance novels.

Though the day had barely started, Terry Lawson reeked of alcohol. Maggie could smell it from across the room. He swayed as he stood in the dining room doorway. He was wearing his police sergeant's uniform, but the shirt was unbuttoned, showing his white undershirt. Tufts of hair stuck up from the collar. He looked like he'd slept in his car with a bottle of Jack Daniel's trapped between his knees. Which was probably where he was when he heard about Don Wesley on his radio.

Delia said, 'Sit down. You look dead on your feet.'

Terry rubbed his jaw as he looked at his niece and sister-in-law. 'Jimmy's on his way. Mack and Bud are looking after him.'

'Is he all right?' Maggie asked.

'Of course he's all right. Don't get hysterical.'

Suddenly, Maggie felt the urge to get hysterical. 'You should've called me.'

'For what?'

Maggie was astounded. Never mind that Jimmy was her brother and Don Wesley was his friend. She was a cop, too. You went to the hospital when another cop was there. You gave blood. You waited for news. You comforted the family. All of this was part of the job. 'I should've been there.'

'For what?' he repeated. 'The nurses fetched us coffee. All you'd do is get in the way.' He nodded at Delia. 'I could use a cup, by the way.'

She walked back into the kitchen.

Maggie sat down. She was still reeling from the news.

She hated that Terry was the only way she was going to get answers. 'How did it happen?'

'Same way it always happens.' Terry dropped into the chair at the head of the table. 'Some nigger shot him.'

'Was it the Shooter?'

'Shooter.' He grunted. 'Stop talking out of your ass.'

'Uncle Terry!' Lilly ran into the room. She threw her arms around him and kissed his cheek. She always acted a few years younger with Terry.

Maggie told her, 'Jimmy's fine, but Don Wesley was killed this morning.'

Terry patted Lilly's arm. He gave Maggie a sharp look. 'Me and the boys'll string up the bastard. Don't you worry.'

'Nobody's worried.' Delia came back with Terry's coffee. She put the mug on the table and handed him the newspaper. 'Cal and the others are all right?'

'Sure they are. Everybody's fine.' Terry snapped open the newspaper. *The Atlanta Constitution* had obviously been put to bed before Don Wesley's murder. The main story was about structural changes the new black mayor was making at city hall.

Maggie said, 'Don makes five victims so far.'

'Maggie.' Delia headed toward the kitchen again. 'Don't bother your uncle.'

She pretended not to hear the warning. 'It's the Shooter.'

Terry shook his head.

'They were obviously ambushed. It has to be—'

'Eat your breakfast,' he said. 'You want a ride to work, you need to be ready to go when I am.'

Lilly still had one arm draped around Terry's shoulders. Her voice sounded impossibly small when she asked,

'Is everybody gonna be all right, Uncle Terry?'

'This is still a cop town, sweetheart. The monkeys ain't runnin' the zoo.' He patted her bottom. 'Come on. Eat.'

Lilly never argued with Terry. She sat down and picked at her breakfast.

Terry snapped the paper as he turned the page. Maggie could only see the top of his head, the square crewcut that showcased his receding hairline. He needed glasses. His forehead wrinkled as he squinted at the football scores.

A loud crackle of static came from the kitchen. Jimmy's old transistor radio. A newsman's voice crackled from the tinny speaker. '... reports another officer killed in the line of ...' The voice drained away as Delia turned the volume down low.

Maggie knew her mother was right about one thing: they didn't need the news to tell them what they already knew. In the last three months, four patrol officers had been murdered in the early morning hours near the downtown area of Five Points. They had been in pairs. Nobody patrolled downtown alone. The first two were found in an alley – they'd been forced down on their knees and executed with one bullet each to the head. The other two were found behind the service entrance to the Portman Motel. Same modus operandi. Same lack of leads. No witnesses. No bullet casings. No fingerprints. No suspects.

Around the station, they'd started calling the killer the Atlanta Shooter.

'I put on a fresh pot.' Delia sat down at the table, something she rarely did for long. She was turned in her chair, facing Terry – another thing she rarely did. 'Tell me what really happened, Terrance.'

Terrance. The word hung in the air alongside the smoke and bacon grease.

Terry made a show of his reluctance. He sighed. He methodically folded the newspaper. He put it down on the table. He lined it up to the edge. Instead of answering Delia's question, he made a gun with his hand and put it to the side of his face. Nobody said anything until he pulled the trigger.

Lilly whispered, 'Jesus.'

For once, no one corrected her language.

Terry said, 'Nothing Jimmy could do. He ran twenty blocks with Don slung over his shoulder. Got to the hospital, but it was too late.'

Maggie thought about her brother running all that way on his bad knee. 'Jimmy wasn't—'

'Jimmy's fine.' Terry's voice sounded like he was humoring them. 'What he doesn't need is a bunch of hens squawking around.'

With that, he opened his newspaper again and buried his nose back in the pages.

He hadn't really answered Delia's question. He'd just given the highlights, likely the same details you could hear on the radio. Terry knew exactly what he was doing to them. He'd been a Marine during the war. His unit specialized in psychological warfare. He would draw this out just because he could.

Instead of returning to the kitchen, Delia took a packet of Kools from her apron pocket and shook one out. Her hand trembled as she fumbled with her lighter. She looked calmer once she had the cigarette lit. Smoke furled from her nose. Every wrinkle on Delia Lawson's face came from sucking on cigarettes – the crepe-like lines around

22

her mouth, the sagging jawline, the deep indentation between her eyebrows. Even her hair was streaked with the same smoke gray that came out of her Kools. She was forty-five years old, but on a good day, she looked around sixty. Right now, she looked twice that, like she was already in her grave.

Like Don Wesley would soon be.

Maggie knew her brother's partner was a grunt just back from Vietnam, unable to do any job that didn't require him to carry a gun. His people were from lower Alabama. He rented an apartment off Piedmont Avenue. He drove a burgundy-colored Chevelle. He had a girl-friend – a flower-child American Indian who talked about 'the man' and didn't complain when Don hit her because he'd seen so much bad shit in the jungle.

And none of that mattered anymore because he was dead.

Terry banged his mug down on the table. Coffee splashed onto the white tablecloth. 'Any of this for me?'

Delia stood up. She took his plate and started loading it with food, though Terry was usually too hungover to eat anything in the morning.

She set the plate in front of him. Her tone had a begging quality when she said, 'Terry, please. Just tell me what happened, all right? He's my boy. I need to know.'

Terry looked at Maggie, then looked down at his half-empty mug.

She allowed herself the luxury of an audible sigh before she went to get the percolator from the stove. As soon as she left the room, Terry started talking.

'Toward the end of their shift, nothing going on. Then they get word there's a signal forty-four off the Whitehall

23

spike at Five Points. That's a possible robbery.' He caught Maggie's eye as she came back into the room, like she hadn't been behind the wheel of a squad car for five years. 'They get there, check the place out. Doors are locked front and back. They give an all clear on the radio. And then . . .' He shrugged. 'Guy comes around the corner, shoots Don in the head, then hightails it. You know the rest. Jimmy did everything he could. It wasn't enough.'

'Poor Jimmy,' Lilly mumbled.

'Poor nobody,' Terry countered. 'Jimmy Lawson can take care of himself. Got it?'

Lilly nodded quickly.

'Mark my words.' Terry stabbed his finger into the newspaper. 'This is a race war, plain and simple. You won't read about it in the paper or hear it on the news. We see it on the streets. It's just like I said ten years ago. You give 'em a little power, they turn on you like rabid dogs. What we gotta do today is take back that power.'

Maggie leaned her shoulder against the doorjamb. Her eyes threatened to roll back in her head. She'd heard this speech so many times she could recite it along with Terry. He hated everybody – the minorities who were newly in charge of the city and the traitors who had helped put them there. Left to his own devices, Terry and his cronies would dig a pit to China and throw them all in.

'Who called in the forty-four?' Maggie was momentarily surprised by the question until she realized that it came from her own mouth. It was a good question. She repeated it. 'Who called in the robbery?'

Terry opened the paper again. He folded it into a sharp crease.

Delia stood up. She touched Maggie's arm before she

24

went back into the kitchen. Lilly stared at the eggs congealing on her plate. Maggie sat down in the chair her mother had vacated. She poured herself some coffee but had no stomach for it.

The robbery call had sent Jimmy and Don to Five Points. The heart of downtown. The origin for the street addressing system. The site of Atlanta's first waterworks as well as a red-light district since before the Civil War. Five streets converged there: Peachtree, Whitehall, Decatur, Marietta, and Edgewood. The intersection was near a state university and close to the welfare office where women lined up around the block every day to get their vouchers. Many of them came back at night when all the lights in the skyscrapers were off and the only men around were the ones willing to pay for company.

Maggie could guess what the police response would be to Don's murder. There would be a city-wide crackdown. The jail would be full every night. Johns would be afraid to venture out. That was bad for business. Everybody bragged about never talking to the cops, but the minute commerce was halted, the snitches came flooding in.

At least that's how it usually happened. The Shooter cases were different. Each time, the entire force had mobilized to shut down the city, and each time, the momentum had drained away, the snitches had stopped showing up and eventually, the streets had gone back to business as usual as they all waited for the next cop to be murdered.

This wasn't just fatalistic thinking; the 1970s were proving to be a bad decade for police officers. Atlanta had suffered more losses than most. In the past two years, they'd caught five cop killers, though only one of them had seen the inside of a courtroom. The others had accidents – one guy resisted arrest and ended up in a coma, another woke up in jail with a shiv in his kidney, the other two were checked into Grady Hospital with routine stomach ailments and ended up leaving in body bags.

The fifth one had walked out of the courtroom a free man. There wasn't a cop in the city who didn't spit before he told you that story. Combine that with another possible notch in the Atlanta Shooter's belt and today would be a very bad day for anybody who found themselves on the wrong side of the law.

Terry cleared his throat. He was staring at his empty mug again.

Maggie poured the coffee. She set down the percolator. She straightened her knife and fork. She turned the handle of her mug left, then right.

Terry grunted with disgust. 'You got something to say, princess?'

'No,' Maggie said, but then she did. 'What about their car?' Jimmy and Don had a cruiser. No one patrolled on foot that time of day. 'Why did Jimmy carry him? Why didn't he just get—'

'Tires were slashed.'

Maggie felt her brow furrow. 'The four other cops, were their tires slashed, too?'

'Nope.'

She tried to get the sequence straight in her head. 'Someone called in a burglary, then slashed their tires, then shot Don, and didn't touch Jimmy?'

Terry shook his head, not looking up from the paper. 'Leave it to the detectives, sweetheart.'

'But—' Maggie couldn't let it go. 'The Shooter's

26

changing his M.O.' She had to add, 'Or it's not the Shooter. It's somebody trying to copy the Shooter.'

Terry shook his head again, but this time it was more like a warning.

Lilly said, 'I'm doing a report on the Civil War.'

Maggie asked, 'Were they split up when Don was shot?'

Terry sighed. 'You don't leave your partner. Even you oughta know that.'

'So, Jimmy was with Don?'

''Course he was.'

Lilly said, 'Most of the kids are talking to their grand-parents, but I—'

Maggie interrupted, 'But Jimmy wasn't shot. He was standing right beside Don, or near him at least.' That was the big difference. In the previous cases, both men were forced to their knees and executed, one right after the other. She asked, 'Did Jimmy pull his gun?'

'Jesus Christ!' Terry banged his fist on the table. 'Will you shut the hell up so I can read the paper?'

'Terry?' Delia called from the kitchen. 'The drain's clogged again. Do you think you can—'

'In a minute.' He kept his gaze on Maggie. 'I wanna know what tough girl here is thinking. You got it figured out, Columbo? You see something guys who've been on the job since you were a tickle in your daddy's ball sac missed?'

Maggie figured if she was going to get hit, it was going to be for a good reason. 'In the other Shooter cases, both guys were on their knees. They were shot in the head, execution-style, one after the other. Don was shot. So why wasn't Jimmy?'

Terry leaned over the table. She could smell the whiskey

27

and sweat bleeding from his pores. 'Whatever bullshit thing you've got going with your brother stops right now. You hear me?'

Maggie felt the floor shift beneath her. 'It's not that,' she said, and they all knew what 'that' was.

'Then what is it?' Terry asked. 'Why are you asking all these questions?'

She wanted to tell him that it was because she was a cop, and that the way cops solved crimes was asking questions, but she settled on 'Because it doesn't make sense.'

'Sense.' He snorted. 'Since when did you start making sense?'

'He's here!' Lilly screamed.

They all startled at her sudden outburst. But it was true. Maggie could hear Jimmy's car pulling into the driveway. The Fairlane's muffler was nearly rusted off. The exhaust huffed the same grumbly cough as Delia when she got out of bed in the morning.

Maggie tried to stand, but Terry clamped his hand around her arm and forced her back down in her chair.

She knew better than to fight him. All Maggie could do was listen. The sounds were the same as when Terry had arrived: The car door slammed. Shoes scuffed across the carport and up the stairs. The kitchen door was already open, so Jimmy closed it. He lingered for a few seconds. Maggie could imagine the look exchanged between mother and son. Maybe Jimmy nodded at Delia. Maybe he handed her his hat to make her feel useful.

When Jimmy came into the dining room, Maggie recognized that he probably had no idea where his hat was. He wasn't in uniform. He was wearing green hospital clothes. The shirt was tight across his shoulders. His face was chalk white. His eyes were red-rimmed. His lips were pale below his mustache. There was something haunted about him. Maggie was reminded of the way their father looked when it was time for him to go back to the hospital.

Terry asked, 'Mack and Bud take care of you?'

All Jimmy seemed capable of offering was a nod. He rubbed his hand along the back of his neck. He'd done a bad job cleaning himself. There were still dots of dried blood on his neck and face. Maggie saw a clump of dirt in one of his sideburns.

Lilly clutched her chest. Tears filled her eyes.

Terry said, 'Don't—' but it was too late. Lilly ran to Jimmy and threw her arms around his waist. She buried her face in his stomach and started to sob.

'It's all right.' Jimmy's voice was gruff. He rubbed Lilly's back. He kissed the top of her head. 'Come on. Upstairs. Don't be late for school.'

Lilly released him just as quickly as she'd grabbed him, then ran from the room. Her footsteps pounded on the bare wooden stairs. For just a moment, Jimmy looked ready to follow her, but then his shoulders dropped, his chin tilted down, and he stared at the floor.

He said, 'I don't wanna talk about it.'

'And we don't wanna hear it.' Delia was behind him. She reached her hand up to Jimmy's shoulder, but stopped herself just shy of touching him. In general, their mother's only gestures of affection came in the form of grooming. She used her fingers to smooth creases in Lilly's sweater. She plucked stray hairs off the shoulders of Maggie's uniform. And now, she picked the clump of dirt out of Jimmy's sideburn.

Delia looked at the tiny speck on her fingertips, and Maggie could tell from her mother's expression that it wasn't dirt. Delia clenched her hand and shoved it into her apron pocket.

She said, 'All of you – eat your breakfast before it gets cold. We can't afford to waste food.'

Jimmy limped around the table and took his usual place. He winced every time he put weight on his left leg. Maggie wanted to help him. She longed to run over just as Lilly had and put her arms around her brother.

But she knew she couldn't.

'So.' Delia had already fixed Jimmy's coffee. Now, she loaded up his plate. She used one hand. Her other was still clenched in her apron pocket. 'Anybody need anything else?'

'We're fine.' Terry waved her away.

Delia said, 'The eggs are cold. I'll make more eggs.' She went back into the kitchen.

Maggie stared at her brother because she knew that he would not look back. The faded red spots of blood on his skin reminded her of when he was a pimply teenager. Jimmy had obviously been crying. She couldn't remember the last time she had seen her brother cry. Eight years ago, at least.

She told him, 'You missed *Tapestry* this morning.'

Jimmy grunted as he forked a pile of eggs into his mouth.

She tried again. 'I hung your uniforms in your closet.'

Jimmy swallowed loudly. 'Too much starch in the collars.'

'I'll redo them after work. Okay?'

He crammed more eggs into his mouth.

'Just put them back in my room.' Maggie was inexplicably nervous. She couldn't stop talking. 'I'll do them when I get in from work.'

Terry made a hissing sound to shut her up.

Maggie followed orders this time – not for Terry, but for Jimmy. She was scared she'd say the wrong thing and make it worse for her brother. This wouldn't be the first time. There was a tightrope between them that started to fray every time one took a step toward the other.

In the silence, she listened to Jimmy chew. He made a wet, mechanical sound. She found herself watching the hinge of his jaw, the way it poked out when he bit down. He was like a construction machine scooping eggs into his mouth, chewing, then scooping in more. There was no expression on his face. His eyes were almost glazed. He stared at a fixed point on the wall opposite his chair.

She knew what he was seeing. Gray plaster with a brown patina from all the cigarette smoke. This was the room Hank Lawson occupied on the rare occasions he lived with his family. The minute he got home, he carried down the TV from Delia's bedroom and put it on the buffet table. Then he'd chain-smoke and watch the set until the national anthem started playing. Some nights, Maggie would go downstairs to get some water and find her father staring at the American flag waving across a blank background.

Maggie doubted Jimmy was thinking about their father right now. Maybe he was remembering that last football game. His life before a linebacker turned his knee into oatmeal. Maggie had been in the stands alongside everybody else. She'd watched Jimmy saunter onto the field with his usual confidence. He raised his fist. The crowd

31

roared. They chanted his name. He was their golden boy, the hometown kid who was making good. His future was already set. He was going to UGA on somebody else's dime. He was going to get drafted into the pros, and the next time anybody saw him, Jimmy Lawson would be coming out of a nightclub wearing a mink, with a girl on each arm like Broadway Joe.

Instead, he was sitting at his mother's dining room table with another man's blood on his face.

'Here.' Delia swapped out Jimmy's plate for a fresh one. She added some bacon. Then pancakes. She doused it all with syrup the way he liked.

'Mom.' Jimmy waved her away with his fork. 'Enough.'

Delia sat down and lit another cigarette. Maggie tried to eat. The eggs were cold. The grease around the bacon had congealed. Maggie forced it down because she had questions that she knew she would ask if she didn't stuff food into her mouth.

She couldn't work out how the shooting had happened. The minute some guy approached Jimmy and Don, especially a colored guy, they would've instantly, automatically, pulled their revolvers. It was basic survival. Don had been in Nam long enough to know you didn't let some fella get the drop on you. And Jimmy had been on the job since he was eighteen.

Maggie glanced at her brother across the table. Maybe he'd panicked. Maybe he'd stood there with Don's blood all over him and been so seized by fear that he couldn't do anything but drop to the ground and pray that he wasn't going to die.

Maggie thought about the clump her mother had picked out of Jimmy's sideburn. The piece of Don Wesley's head that was probably in the kitchen garbage on top of the broken eggshells and the plastic package that the bacon came in.

'Time to go.' Terry folded his newspaper. He told Jimmy, 'You get some sleep, son. I'll call you if anything happens.'

Jimmy started shaking his head before Terry finished the sentence. 'No way. I'm not sleeping until we catch the bastard.'

'Damn right we'll get him.' Terry winked at Maggie like it was just him and Jimmy against the world.

Maybe that's why she asked her brother, 'What really happened?'

Terry grabbed Maggie's knee so hard that the pain took her breath away. She cried out, scratching the back of his hand.

He tightened his grip. 'What did I tell you about nagging your brother?'

Pain knifed up and down her leg. Maggie's lips trembled. She wasn't going to beg. She couldn't beg.

'She'll hear it at the station anyhow.' Jimmy sounded more irritated than concerned. 'Come on, Terry. Let her go.'

Terry released his hold.

'Jesus!' Maggie rubbed her knee. She was panting. A shiver ran through her body.

'Stop making a scene.' Delia picked a stray piece of lint off Maggie's bathrobe. 'What happened, Jimmy?'

He shrugged. 'Don went down. I got off three shots. The shooter ran. I started to chase him, but I couldn't leave Don.' As an afterthought, he added, 'I didn't get a good look at him. Colored. Average height. Average build.'

Maggie kept rubbing her knee as she listened. The tendon was pulsing with every heartbeat.

'Cal Vick's gonna have me sit down with a sketch artist.' Jimmy shrugged. 'Not sure what good it'll do. The alley was dark. It happened fast.'

Delia said, 'You're lucky he didn't try to shoot you, too.'

''Course he did,' Jimmy quipped, an edge to his tone. 'His gun jammed. He tried to shoot me, but nothing happened. Lucky Lawson, right?' That was the name they'd given him in high school. 'That's me. Lucky guy.'

Terry obviously didn't like the way this conversation was going. He told Jimmy, 'Get yourself cleaned up. I'll see you at the station.' He made to leave.

Maggie panicked. 'You have to give me a ride.'

'Why's that?'

He knew why. Maggie's car had been in the shop for a week. 'I can't be late for roll call.'

'Then you'd better hurry.' Terry tapped his folded newspaper against her mouth. 'But you keep that slit under your nose closed, you hear?'

Maggie grabbed the plates from the table and limped into the kitchen. Jimmy's utility belt was on the counter. His gun was in the holster.

Maggie easily heard the conversation in the dining room. Terry was making lewd comments about some new female recruits at the academy. Maggie put the plates in the sink. She ran some water so they wouldn't glue together before Lilly could wash them.

And then she limped over to Jimmy's belt.

Carefully, she unsnapped the leather safety strap and slid the revolver from the holster. She checked the cylinder.

Fully loaded. No empty casings. Maggie kept the muzzle pointed down as she sniffed along the firing pin, the top strap, and the cylinder end of the barrel.

No smell of burnt copper and sulfur, just the usual tinge of oil and steel.

Maggie slid the gun back into the holster, snapped the strap closed. She grabbed the railing on the stairs to help propel herself up. She could hear Terry and Jimmy talking baseball, wondering how the Braves were going to do without Hank Aaron. The two men had always had an easy rapport. They could talk about anything – at least so long as none of it mattered.

Like the fact that whatever had happened in that alley this morning, Jimmy Lawson hadn't fired his gun.

2

Kate Murphy sat on her bed at the Barbizon Hotel and listened to the news. Congress had effectively defunded the war. Nixon was finally gone. President Ford had offered amnesty to draft dodgers. Charges had been dropped against the Ohio State National Guardsmen. William Calley was free after serving less than four years for his part in the My Lai massacre.

Kate couldn't bring herself to care. She was out of outrage. All that mattered was that the war was over. Men had finally returned home. POWs were being released. It was never going to happen again. No more boys dying in jungles. No more grieving families back home.

She looked at the framed photograph by the radio. Patrick's smile offered an eerie contrast to the haggard look in his eyes. A starburst of sunlight caught the edge of his dog tags. His rifle was slung over his shoulders, helmet tilted at a jaunty angle. His shirt was off. He had new muscles she had never touched. A scar on his face that she had never kissed. The picture was black-and-white, but in the letter that had accompanied it, he'd told Kate that his normally pasty skin was lobster red – *an Irish suntan*.

Kate had yet to meet Patrick Murphy when she watched the first draft lottery on television. She was in the living room with her family. Cold wind tapped against the window-panes. Kate had a shawl wrapped around her shoulders. Her grandmother had remarked that the whole horrible process reminded her of that carnival game – what was it called?

'Bingo,' Kate had supplied, thinking it was closer to the Shirley Jackson short story.

Instead of numbered balls, there were 366 blue capsules. Inside each capsule was a slip of paper. On each slip of paper was written a number that corresponded to a month and day of the calendar year. All the sealed capsules were mixed together in a box, then they were dropped into a large glass jar that was so deep that the man doing the drawing had to stretch to reach the capsules with the tips of his fingers.

The system was simple: as each capsule was drawn, a draft number was assigned, starting at one and working up to 366, which accounted for leap years. All males born between 1944 and 1950 were eligible for conscription. The month and day of your birth determined your draft number. The lower your number, the more likely you were to be drafted. A second lottery employed all twenty-six letters of the alphabet to determine the priority, by last name, for each date of birth.

September 14th was the first date that was drawn. When it was read aloud, there was a horrible cry from the kitchen. They later found out that Mary Jane, their house-keeper, had a grandson who was born on September 14th.

In the space of a few hours, every boy Kate knew had been assigned a number. No one understood what they meant – when the groups would be called up, where they would be sent, in which branch they would serve, if they were to serve at all. Lower numbers were obviously bad, but how high was high enough to be safe?

Patrick Murphy and his family were asking the same questions on the other side of town. Their TV set was black-and-white. They had no idea the capsules were blue. What they did know was that by the end of the broadcast, their sons had been assigned numbers. Declan came in at 98, Patrick at 142.

Of course, Kate didn't know any of this until much later. She met Patrick in April of '71, a little over a year after that first lottery. Kate was outside Lenox Mall, bored to death as she waited in her car for the tow truck to arrive. Her battery was dead; she'd left the lights on while she was shopping. Patrick gave her a charge. She was aware of the double entendre. So was he. He referred to it incessantly. Kate's irritation didn't stop him from flirting, which was even more irritating, then through attrition somewhat flattering, and then somehow kind of intoxicating, and then it was late enough for dinner, so – why not?

Patrick was twenty-one years old, the same as her. He had a brother already serving. His father was a lawyer. He was studying to be an engineer, which seemed like one of those essential jobs you were always hearing about, like doctor or lawyer or son-of-a-politician. Patrick was none of these. He was a big Irish Mick with a seemingly high draft number who'd just met the girl of his dreams.

They had been together just over fifteen months when he got called up. His father wasn't connected, but Kate's was. Patrick refused to allow favors to be called in. He didn't think it was right. And he was right that it wasn't right, but by then they were married and Kate was furious at her stupid, stubborn husband. She'd refused to see him off for basic training. When they'd kissed goodbye at the door, Kate had held on to him so tightly that he'd warned her she was going to break a rib.

She wanted to break all of his ribs. She wanted to scratch out one of his eyes. She wanted to take a pipe wrench to his knee, a bat to his head. But she had let him go, because in the end, that was all she could do.

She was in love, she was married, and she was alone.

And then September 14th rolled around.

What were the odds?

Kate was helping her parents entertain when she heard the doorbell ring. Mary Jane was in the cellar because someone had asked for wine. Kate answered the door. Instead of party guests, two soldiers were standing on the front porch. Her first thought was how odd it was to see white men wearing white cotton gloves. They were dressed identically. They stood with identically straight spines. Their uniforms were wool, long-sleeved. The weather was unseasonably warm. Beads of sweat dotted their closely shaven upper lips, rolled down the sides of their thick necks.

They both took off their hats in practiced unison. She almost laughed because the synchronization was so perfect. Only one of them spoke. He called her 'ma'am.' Kate heard the words 'regret to inform you,' then she found herself coming round on the couch with all the party guests gone. Their half-filled glasses and still-burning cigarettes were abandoned around the room. The soldiers left her a brochure entitled *Death Benefits*.

'Such a phrase,' her grandmother had said.

'An oxymoron,' her father had noted.

Her mother had smoked a stranger's cigarette from a nearby ashtray.

Kate had no idea where the brochure was now. She didn't really care. She didn't need death benefits. She needed her husband.

Lacking both, what she really needed was to get ready for work.

Kate took off her robe as she walked into the bathroom. She checked to make sure her hair was securely pinned up before turning on the shower and stepping in.

She gasped at the cold spray. The plumbing was menopausal, which was a funny joke considering she lived in a hotel exclusively for women. One minute the water was too cold, the next it was too hot. The stream fluctuated depending on how many women were using identical bathrooms on identical floors. If too many toilets were flushed too closely together, they were all screwed.

Kate stared blankly through the translucent shower curtain as she washed. The view wasn't much: her bed, and the wall on the other side of her bed. She closed one eye, then the other. Her vision was mottled by the green-tinted plastic curtain. She tried to remember what she had liked so much about this place when she'd first seen it. The anonymity? The sterileness? The beigeness of it all?

That hadn't lasted long. Her mother had swooped in with her credit card and her good taste, and now abstract art hung on the walls, a white shag rug covered the awful tan carpet in the bedroom, and Kate's bed linens were more suited for a display window at Davison's than a downtown hotel for single women.

Honestly, Kate preferred the place the way she'd found it.

She turned off the taps and quickly dried herself. The bedside clock had been playing games, flipping ahead almost half an hour while she stood under the water. She would have to stop letting her mind wander. The same thing had happened this morning on the way back from breakfast at the diner. One moment she was asking a man in the street for the time, and the next she was sitting on a bench, staring up at the blue sky, as if she had all the time in the world.

Daydreaming was the old Kate's luxury. She lived on her own now. She had rent to pay. She had to buy her own food and clothes. She could no longer while away the hours reading trashy paperbacks and drinking her father's gin.

Death benefits.

Kate tore away the plastic dry cleaner's bag and laid out her clothes on the bed. From the hallway came the hustle and bustle of girls on their way to work. She thought of them as the first shift – the office girls with their neatly bobbed hair and daringly short skirts. They were young and pretty and still worried about what their parents thought of them, as evidenced by the fact that, as audacious as it was to live alone in the big city, they did so in an establishment that strictly forbade any male guests above the lobby floor.

The second shift would follow in approximately fifteen minutes, older women like Kate who were in their mid-to late twenties. They were all personal secretaries or head tellers. Career gals. Independent. Full of spunk. Kate loved watching them in the elevator. They were constantly checking themselves. Eyeliner unsmudged. Lipstick perfect. Blouse tightly tucked. Hem sharply pressed. Before the car reached the bottom floor, they'd reflexively checked at least three times to make sure that their stockings were straight.

And then they walked across the lobby, heads held high, as if they hadn't a care in the world. Between their shockingly good posture and pointy brassieres, they reminded Kate of ships sailing off to war.

The clock was sneaking up on her again. Kate muttered a curse as she pulled on her underwear. She sat down on the bed and rolled on her pantyhose. She stood up to adjust the waistband. She sat back down to put on a pair of black socks. She slid into the stiff, navy-blue pants. And slid, and slid.

'Oh, no . . . ,' she groaned.

The pants were enormous. She stood up to assess the damage. Even with the belt tightly buckled, the material hung like a deflated balloon around her waist. This must have been done to her on purpose. Kate had given the supply sergeant all of her measurements. She was five feet nine, hardly diminutive, but the legs of the pants were so long that they reached past her toes. A string of curses followed as she searched her underwear drawer for a pack of straight pins that she eventually found in the medicine cabinet.

Kate pinned up the pant legs until the edge just grazed the top of her foot. And then she remembered the shoes. They were obviously designed for men, bulky and ugly, the sort of thing a prison warden or high school math teacher would wear. The heel was too wide. Even with the laces tight, her feet could slip out.

Kate ignored the issue, settling on one problem at a time. Blisters would be the least of her worries if her pants weren't properly shortened. A few more adjustments with the pins and the hem fell just shy of the shoelace.

'Good job.' She allowed herself a smile of relief. Then

42

she caught her reflection in the mirror and was too stunned to speak.

She looked like a new form of centaur: a woman who was a man from the waist down. The sight would've been comical had it not been so jarring.

Kate turned away from her reflection, pulling on the stiff navy-blue shirt. Also too big. The collar scraped her earlobes. The breast pockets were at her waist. The emblems on the sleeves were at her elbows. She flapped up her arms, trying to get her fingers past the long sleeves. Finally, she managed to poke one hand through, then the other. She rolled the shirt cuffs until it appeared she had two large doughnuts on her wrists.

Kate closed her eyes. No crying this morning. That was her promise. No crying until her shift was over.

'Laugh about this,' she coached herself. 'Laugh because it's funny.'

She buttoned the shirt. Her hands were steady. Maybe this *was* funny. Maybe a week or a month or a year from now, she would be telling the story of the first day she put on this ridiculous outfit and tears would come to her eyes – not from the horror, but from the hilarity.

She found the S-shaped metal clips that were designed to hold the utility belt. The equipment was too heavy for just one belt. She had to have one belt looped through her pants in order to support the second belt. Kate hooked one metal clip on each hip. She tried not to think a few hours ahead, when the constant wear would seem like Chinese water torture.

'Silly,' she mumbled. 'The blisters on your feet will take your mind off of it.'

She picked up the thick leather utility belt. This, at

least, looked like it would fit. She pulled the tongue through the buckle, piercing the last hole in the belt, making sure that the metal S-hooks had taken hold underneath the edges.

And then she tried not to think about Virginia Woolf walking into the river with rocks in her pockets to ensure her suicide.

Flashlight on the hook. Handcuffs in the pouch. Radio transmitter clipped to the back. Shoulder mic threaded up to the epaulet. Keychain attached to the ring. Nightstick through the metal loop. Holster secured around the belt. Gun.

Gun.

Kate weighed the heavy metal revolver in her hand. She ejected the cylinder and let the brass blur as the bullets spun around. Gently, she clicked the cylinder back into place, then tucked the gun into the holster. Her fingers were oily from handling the revolver. Her thumb slipped as she snapped the leather safety strap into place.

Oddly, the gun felt heavier than anything else on her hips. She'd only fired the revolver a couple of times at the police academy, and both times all she'd been thinking about was how quickly she could get away from the grabby instructor. Kate wasn't sure she'd cleaned the gun properly. The grip seemed greasier than it was supposed to be. The instructor wasn't very helpful. He'd said that he was against the arming of females.

Honestly, having spent two weeks with the rest of the women in her class, Kate shared the man's reticence. There were a few serious recruits, but many were there on a lark. More than half of them signed up for the typing pool, where they'd receive the same pay as officers on patrol. Only four women in Kate's group had asked for street assignments.

In retrospect, maybe Kate should've paid more attention in typing class. Or secretarial school. Or paralegal training. Or any number of the jobs she'd tried and failed at before seeing a story in *The Atlanta Journal* about women police officers being trained for motorcycle patrol.

Motorcycle patrol!

Kate laughed at her naïveté. If the firearms instructors were loath to train women, the motorcycle division was downright hostile to the idea of women on bikes. The riding instructor wouldn't even allow them inside the garage.

The bedside clock clicked as the numbers turned over. Time had jumped forward again. Noises filled the hallway – the career gals heading out to work. Soft voices. Occasional laughter. The swish-swish-swish of nylons rubbing against slim skirts.

The hat was last. Kate had worn hats before. They were all the rage in high school – pillbox mostly, like Mrs. Kennedy. Kate had found a leopard skin to match the Dylan song. She'd pinned it at a rakish angle that made Kate's mother send her straight back to her room.

This hat would've sent her mother into apoplexy. Dark blue and, as with everything else to do with her uniform, overly large. Wide brim. Gold, round badge sewn onto the center. City of Atlanta Police Department. Inside the circle was a phoenix ascending from the ashes. *Resurgens*. Latin: rising again.

Kate put on the hat. She looked at her reflection in the mirror.

She could do this.

She *had* to do this.

3

Fox sat in his car smoking a cigarette. The windows were rolled up tight. Smoke filled the space. He thought of tear gas. Not for the first time. Not for the last. The needle wouldn't skip on that record. Lachrymatory agents, they were called, which was a fancy way of saying your eyeballs were going to be impaled on spikes. Twenty seconds of exposure was all it took. The gas overstimulated the corneal nerves. Pain, tears, coughing, sneezing, and blindness followed.

Boot camp.

Fox had stood with the men in his unit as they watched the first team get gassed. The exposure was supposed to toughen them up, prepare them for jungle warfare, but what it did was break them down. Grown men screamed like little girls. They tried to scratch out their eyes. They begged for mercy.

Fox had watched them writhe around like worms and thought they were idiots. They had all gotten the same briefing. Sure, it hurt, but you just had to wait it out. Thirty minutes later, you were fine. Thirty minutes was nothing. You could do anything for thirty minutes.

Then it was Fox's turn to be gassed.

Hot tears blistered his eyes. He inhaled needles into his lungs. He panicked. He dropped to the floor. He begged for mercy just like all the worms who had come before him.

That was where the shame came from. Not the crying or the choking, but the begging. Only once before in his life had Fox ever begged for anything. He was twelve years old, and he had quickly learned that there was no use begging, because nobody was going to help you but yourself. So, twelve-year-old Fox had vowed that his begging days were over, and then seven years later, he was at Camp Bumfuck rolling on the floor alongside twenty other grunts like a helpless, pitiful worm.

Should Fox take even a little bit of pride in the fact that he wasn't the one begging the loudest?

A guy from his unit had died from exposure. Undiagnosed asthmatic, the brass had said, but who trusted the brass? Probably they were trying out a new formula on their own men before sending the caustic gas into the field. Wasn't the first time. Wouldn't be the last. War was nothing but a grand experiment. Behind every senseless tragedy, there was some guy with a clipboard.

Fox had a clipboard of his own.

He glanced down at his log.

0546: Exited building. Talked to no one.
0600: Breakfast at diner, usual table, usual waitress: one hardboiled egg, dry toast, black coffee. Read paper. Left twenty-five-cent tip
0628: Walked opposite direction from building, down 14th and around block
0639: Asked unknown businessman for time

0651: Sat on bench outside bank building, stared up at
    sky
0658: Rose from bench, went into apartment building

Now what?

Fox opened the glove box. He saw the pantyhose that had covered his face last night.

Her pantyhose.

The scope of the mission was changing. Fox could feel the shift almost like he was standing on a rug that was being slowly pulled from beneath his feet. This had happened before. Fox would be doing one thing, but somewhere in the back of his brain, his thoughts were mulling over other courses of action. All it took was some kind of lightning to strike. The bolt would hit his skull, and the thing in the back of his brain would jump to the front.

And like that, he had options.

Fox took out his binoculars and used them to find the familiar window. As he watched, the curtains were opened. He smiled at his luck. Sometimes, he missed the curtains. Sometimes, he would look up and his guts would turn to liquid because he had no idea how long ago the curtains had been opened, whether or not he had missed something important.

But today, he saw her open the curtains.

Fox noted a new time in his log: four minutes from now, because he knew that's how long it took for the elevator to arrive on the correct floor, the short ride down to the lobby, the next elevator down to the parking garage, the quick walk to the right space, and bingo – exactly four minutes later, Fox watched Kate Murphy pull her car out of the underground garage.

Christ, she was beautiful. The way the sun hit her face, he could almost let himself forget about her dirty little secret.

Fox rolled down his window to let out the smoke. He put the clipboard on the passenger's seat.

Then he followed her.

4

Terry's anger pushed a low pressure into the car that reminded Maggie of the way she felt when a tornado was about to touch down. Her head throbbed. Her blood felt thick. The hairs on the back of her neck stood at a permanent attention.

They should have been able to have a conversation about what had happened to Don and Jimmy. Two cops stuck in a car; it was normal for them to discuss the shooting, talk out what they were going to do next to make sure the killer was brought to justice. But Terry didn't think of Maggie as a cop and Maggie sure as hell didn't think of her uncle as a confidant, so they both stared grimly out the window and kept their thoughts to themselves.

Besides, justice was probably the last thing on Terry's mind. He wouldn't be thinking about what had happened this morning. He would be thinking about the cop killer who had gotten away with murder.

Last January, Detective Duke Abbott had been shot in the chest while sitting in his parked car behind the City Motel off Moreland Avenue. His partner was inside the motel doing what you'd expect a cop to be doing inside a motel at two o'clock in the morning when he was supposed to be working a shift. Duke was a white cop. Witnesses had seen a black man leaving the scene. By the time the morning paper hit the stands, the city was wound up like an alarm clock strapped to a thousand sticks of dynamite.

Within three days of the murder, they had a suspect's name. Edward Spivey was a mid-level drug dealer and pimp who operated in the vicinity of the motel. A couple of witnesses had identified Spivey as the man leaving the scene of the crime. One claimed he saw Spivey ditch a gun in a sewer grate. The other said Spivey had blood on his shirt.

Terry led the team that had found both the gun and the bloody shirt. For nearly a week, they turned the city upside down looking for Spivey. The suspect proved to be more cunning than any of them anticipated. Instead of running, Spivey turned himself in. He invited a local news crew to meet him on the steps of the station house. He shouted out his innocence. He said the evidence was planted, the witnesses bribed. He hired a fancy lawyer from up north. He talked to any reporter who showed up at the jailhouse. He practically dared the city to send him to the electric chair.

Normally, the city would have gladly obliged, but between Duke Abbott's murder and Edward Spivey's trial, Atlanta had gone through a radical change. The newly elected black mayor had delivered on his promise to bring diversity to local government. Which was good or bad, depending on how you looked at it. Before the transition, a black man accused of shooting a white cop would've gone straight to death row. But then the ballots were counted, and an all-black jury let Edward Spivey walk out of the courthouse a free man. The resulting rift between the police and the district attorney's office made the Grand Canyon look like a crack in the sidewalk.

If Maggie had to guess, she would've said that the only thing on Terry's mind right now was making sure that Don Wesley's killer never saw the inside of a courtroom.

The car jerked as Terry took a left into the parking lot down from police headquarters. The Buick sailed into its regular space. Maggie moved in tandem with her uncle: He put the gear into park. She pulled the door handle and got out of the car. There was a brief moment of relief, then Maggie found herself facing a wall of duplicate Terrys.

Same cropped haircuts. Same bushy mustaches. Same kind of anger flashing in their beady little eyes. Terry's friends all had names like Bud and Mack and Red and talked about the good old days like preachers talked about heaven. They all had multiple ex-wives, angry mistresses, and grown children who wouldn't talk to them. Worse, they were all the same kind of cop as Terry. They always knew better than everybody else. They never listened to anyone from the outside. They carried throwaway guns in their ankle holsters. They kept their Klan robes hanging in the back of their closets.

Maggie couldn't remember a time in her life when Terry's friends were not around – not because of Terry, but because of Jimmy. They attended all of his football games. They dropped by practice to offer the coach unsolicited pointers. They slipped Jimmy cash to go on dates. They bought him beer before he was old enough to drink.

When Jimmy's knee blew out, they had given him a police escort to the hospital.

Maggie had thought that their hero worship would end with Jimmy's football career, but in some ways, they seemed happier to have Jimmy on the job than they were to see him on the field. The day Jimmy had graduated from the academy, the first two rows of the audience were filled with his cheering squad. They all loved him like a son. They mentored him. They told him stories. They offered advice.

And sometimes, if they were drunk enough, they even let Maggie listen.

'Hey!' Jett Elliott banged his fist on the roof of the car. He was so drunk he could barely stand. 'We're not lettin' this one get away with it. You hear me?'

'Damn straight we're not.' Mack McKay shored up Jett with an arm around his shoulder. 'We're gonna take care of this ourselves.'

There were grunts of agreement as a flask was passed around. Maggie pulled her purse onto her shoulder, but she couldn't go anywhere. The wall of Terrys had managed to both block her path and completely ignore her.

Les Leslie leaned against the car. 'The boss already put in a call to California. Three-hour time difference, but they'll get somebody to lay eyes on him.'

He was talking about Edward Spivey. After the trial, the man had moved to the other side of the continent, but no one believed he would stay there for long.

'Oughta fly out there ourselves,' Red Flemming said. 'Lay more than eyes on him.'

Terry slammed the car door. 'Think they'll let us take a noose on the plane?'

'I got two in my trunk.' Jett grabbed at the flask.

Mack pushed him away. 'Fuck off.'

Jett pushed back. 'You fuck off.'

Maggie took advantage of the shoving match and headed toward the street. She didn't want to be around when they really got wound up.

Red held out his arm to stop her. 'Jimmy all right?'

She nodded as she eyed the exit. 'He's fine.'

'He's coming in,' Terry said. 'Wouldn't stay home.'

'Damn right he wouldn't.' Les passed the flask to Terry. 'We takin' care of business today?'

'Hell yeah.' Terry took a healthy drink. 'Gonna put that fucker in the ground. Am I right?'

'You're goddamn right.' Jett grabbed the flask from Terry. 'No trial for this asshole. Only walk he's taking is to the grave.'

There were more murmurs of agreement. Maggie tried to edge around Red.

'Need to keep Jim out of this,' Red mumbled under his breath. Everyone heard him. Nods went around. Maggie was both annoyed and jealous. To a man, they would all lay down their lives protecting Jimmy Lawson.

Terry said, 'You got somewhere to be?'

Maggie realized he was talking to her. She didn't feel her usual impulse to do the opposite of what her uncle said. She started toward the street, glad to be away from them.

The relief didn't last long. She was never going to get away from these assholes. A black El Dorado was pulling into the parking lot. The window slid down. Bud Deacon had his hands gripped around the steering wheel. Chip Bixby was in the passenger seat. He looked worse than the rest of them. His cheeks were more sunken than usual. His lips were a weird blue, probably from smoking too much. Of all of Terry's friends, Chip was the least offensive. Which wasn't saying much.

Maggie preempted the question. 'Jimmy's all right. He's coming in.'

'That ain't right,' Bud said. 'You shoulda told him to stay home.'

She wanted to laugh. 'You think he listens to me?'

'Shut that smart mouth before I do,' Bud warned. 'Is it too much to ask you to be there for your brother?'

Maggie chewed her lip so she wouldn't speak her mind.

'It's gonna be hard for him.' Chip's voice was solemn. Duke Abbott had been his partner. Chip had been inside the motel when Duke was shot. He was also sitting behind Edward Spivey when the jury came back with an acquittal. Two deputies had to hold him down. If one of them hadn't grabbed Chip's gun, he'd probably be sitting on death row right now.

Maggie said, 'Jimmy knows he's not alone.'

'Doesn't matter,' Chip said. 'Something like this happens – you're alone for the rest of your life.'

Maggie didn't know what to say. She'd known Chip forever, but it wasn't like they sat around talking about their feelings.

Chip seemed to realize this, too. He told Bud, 'Let's go.'

Maggie watched the car roll into the parking lot. She quickened her pace again. She didn't want to think about the plans Terry and his friends were making. As a cop, she had a duty to make sure the law was upheld. But she was a cop, and she wasn't going to rat out other cops. Besides, the men were detectives. Maggie was patrol. She was also a woman. No one would listen to her, and even if they did, they wouldn't care unless *The Atlanta Constitution* ran a story on it. All Maggie could do for now was handle what was in front of her, and right now what was in front of her was getting ready for work.

She dug around in her purse as she crossed the street. The brick that was the transmitter for her radio took up half the space in her bag. She clipped it onto the back of her belt, then jacked in the springy cord to her shoulder mic. Maggie checked the dials on top of the transmitter. There were two – one for volume, one for tuning. She could adjust both in her sleep.

Cash from her wallet went into her front pocket. Two pens and a small notepad went into her left breast pocket, her citation book went into the right one. Chemical mace went into her back pocket along with a tube of nude lipstick. Neither one was regulation, but a girl had to protect herself.

She catalogued the remaining items in her bag: a paperback, loose change, a darker lipstick, powder, mascara, blusher, eyeliner. The latter items were not necessary for the job, but necessary if she wanted to keep them from Lilly.

A breeze rustled Maggie's hair as she stepped onto the sidewalk. The sharp pain in her knee was gone. The sensation was more like she was aware that she had a knee rather than that she was about to collapse with every step. She didn't know how Jimmy dealt with the constant discomfort every day. Of course, she didn't know how her brother dealt with a lot of things.

Either Jimmy was lying about what had happened during the shooting or he'd taken the time to clean his gun before leaving the hospital. Considering the half-ass job he'd done of cleaning his own face, she doubted the latter explanation. What was more likely was that he hadn't fired the revolver at all.

In which case, what else was he lying about? Had the Shooter's gun really jammed? Because Maggie had been on the firing range enough times to know what happened when a gun jammed. She'd had it happen herself. She'd seen it happen to others. The sequence was always the same. You pulled the trigger. Nothing happened. You pulled the trigger again, maybe even a third or fourth time, before you accepted that the gun was jammed. The process was like sniffing bad milk or tasting something that was too spicy. You always had to do it more than once. You never believed something was off the first time.

Maggie stopped walking. She looked down at her watch. When the second hand hit the twelve, she mentally walked herself through the Shooter's movements.

Turn the corner. Aim. Shoot Don Wesley. Recoil. Aim. Pull the trigger. Nothing. Pull the trigger again. Run.

Five, maybe six seconds. That was assuming there was no hesitation. And that the Shooter was able to re-aim quickly even though Jimmy had to be moving the moment Don went down.

Maggie started walking again. A second lasted longer than most people thought. The blink of an eye takes around three hundred milliseconds. The act of breathing in and out eats up around five seconds. An average marksman can pull his weapon in under two seconds.

Jimmy Lawson was one of the best marksmen in their

57

division. In five or six seconds, he could easily kill a man.

Maggie turned the corner and almost ran into another cop. He had coffee-colored skin and was wearing a too-tight uniform that made him look like a first-day recruit. His hands went up immediately, another sign that he was new.

She told him, 'Take the next left. Headquarters is on the left, halfway up.'

He tipped his hat. 'Thank you, ma'am.'

Maggie continued up the sidewalk. The man jogged across the street and preceded her along the other side. She'd forgotten the academy had spit out a class of new graduates. There could not have been a worse day for new recruits to start. On top of dealing with the fallout from Don Wesley's murder, they'd have to step over a bunch of flailing newbies who, if past was prologue, would wash out before the middle of the week.

Instead of taking a left on Central Avenue, Maggie kept going straight for two more blocks. The Do Right Diner specialized in bland food and weak coffee, but its location ensured a loyal clientele. The place was empty but for two customers in the back. No one ate here unless they were on the clock, and roll call wouldn't start for another forty minutes.

'Jimmy all right?' the waitress asked.

'He's great, thanks.'

Maggie kept walking toward the back. Two women in various states of undress were lounging across a circular banquette. Torn stockings, micro-minis, heavy makeup, and blonde wigs – these were all perks that came with being a PCO, or plainclothes officer. The women were part of the new John task force, which, as far as anyone could tell, was a moneymaking scheme that kept rich white bankers out of jail.

Gail Patterson winked at Maggie around the smoke from her cigarette. Her deep South Georgia twang played perfectly with her undercover getup. 'Lookin' for some action, mama?'

Maggie laughed, hoping her face didn't look as red as it felt. Her first year on the job had been spent in a cruiser with Gail. The senior officer was gruff and ornery and undoubtedly the best teacher Maggie had ever had.

'I need to bounce.' The other woman downed a glass of orange juice with a loud gulp. Her name was Mary Petersen. Maggie only knew her by reputation. She was a divorcée who had a thing for cops. Of course, that's what they said about all the women on the force, that they joined because they had a thing for cops, so Maggie didn't really know.

Mary's vinyl skirt squeaked as she slid out of the booth. 'Jimmy all right?'

'He's fine.'

'Good. You tell him we're here for him.' She patted Maggie on the shoulder as she left.

Gail waved at the vacated spot. 'Rest your dogs, chickie.'

'Thanks.' Maggie unclipped the transmitter from the back of her belt and sat down. The seat was still warm. She leaned into the soft foam. Suddenly, her eyes wanted to close. Her body started to relax. Maggie had been tense from the moment she'd entered her mother's kitchen.

Gail took off her wig and dropped it on the table, 'You look as tired as I feel.'

'Guilty,' Maggie admitted. 'You look good.'

Gail laughed out some smoke. 'Fuckin' liar.'

Maggie *was* lying. Gail looked like an old whore, which was only partly due to the way she had to dress for work. She was forty-two years old. Her skin was showing wrinkles. Her hair was too black to be natural. There was a heaviness to her cheeks and eyelids. She had a deep cleft between her eyebrows that came from always scrutinizing everything around her.

God forbid if Gail didn't like what she saw. Everybody was afraid of her nasty temper. She had come up when there were no federal grants paving the way for women on the force. She'd fought tooth and nail to get her PCO rank. She was part of the old guard, Terry's group, and like everybody else, she was terrified of losing her status.

Gail asked, 'How's Jimmy really doing?'

Maggie told the truth. 'I have no idea. He never talks to me.'

'Sounds about right.' She kept her cigarette in one hand as she used her fork to cut into a stack of pancakes. 'You ask out that neighbor of yours yet?'

Maggie hadn't come to the diner to talk about her miserable dating prospects. 'What've you heard about the shooting?'

'I heard the killer's not gonna be takin' no walk like Edward Spivey.'

'Besides that.'

Gail studied her. She chewed, then took a smoke, then chewed some more. Finally, she asked, 'Did you know Don?'

'Not really. He was Jimmy's friend.'

Gail exhaled slowly. 'I knew him.'

Maggie waited for more.

'He had a sweet side.' Gail stared off into the distance. 'That's the ones you always have to worry about, the assholes who aren't assholes all the time.'

'An asshole is always an asshole.'

'That's your youth talking.' She put down her fork. 'This job changes you, baby doll, whether you like it or not. You bust balls long enough, you don't wanna come home to a man who rolls over when you tell him to.' She winked. 'You wanna be the one rolling over.'

The only thing Maggie wanted to come home to these days was a quiet house and clean laundry.

'It's when they're gentle that you start to lose yourself.' Gail was suddenly wistful. 'They're all strong and silent, then one day – hell, not even a day, maybe a second, two seconds if you're lucky – this sweet side comes out and—' She snapped her fingers. 'You're a goner.'

Maggie felt slow on the uptake. 'You *knew* Don.'

She shrugged. 'He wasn't so bad when you got him alone.'

Maggie picked at a dried glob of syrup glued to the table. She had always looked up to Gail. She was good at her job. She had a husband who loved her. She was Maggie's idea of what being a successful policewoman was all about.

'Oh, kid, don't be disappointed in me.'

'I'm not,' Maggie lied.

'You know I love Trouble.'

Maggie smiled at the old joke. Her husband's nickname was Trouble.

Gail sighed out a flume of smoke. 'I never see him, and when I do, all we do is fight about money and which bill is gonna get paid first and what are we gonna do about my sister's deadbeat husband and how long can we put off before his mother has to come live with us.' She gave a halfhearted shrug. 'Sometimes, it's a relief to be with somebody who only wants you for one thing.'

'It's your business. You don't have to explain it to me.'

'Damn right I don't.' She reached into her purse and pulled out a flask. All the upper ranks carried booze on them. Maggie watched Gail take a large mouthful. Then another. 'Jesus, I hate it when the good ones die. Fought that fuckin' war and came back here so another American could shoot him in an alley.'

Maggie wondered how many breakfast tables she was going to have to sit around before she got a straight answer out of somebody. She repeated, 'What have you heard about that shooting?'

Gail glanced at the waitress before responding. 'That hippie-dippie girlfriend of his. What's her name, Pocahontas? She made a scene at the hospital.'

Maggie had met the woman once. She had brown skin and jet-black hair that she wore in a long braid down her back. 'How'd she find out?'

'Heard it on the scanner. Don had one at his apartment.'

'I didn't know they were living together.'

She laughed. 'Neither did he.'

Maggie laughed, too, but only so the moment wouldn't turn more awkward. She echoed Terry's words. 'They'll get him, anyway. Whoever did this. Five dead cops. You can only run for so long.'

'They'll get somebody.'

Maggie didn't ask for clarification. There had been

questions about exactly how Terry had come up with the tossed gun and bloody shirt that tied Edward Spivey to Duke Abbott's murder. The shitty part was that the case had been strong without the evidence. Unfortunately, most of the jurors came from Atlanta's ghettos. They had seen too many cops plant too many pieces of evidence to believe this might be the one time that everything had been done by the book.

'Anyway.' Gail tipped her flask into her coffee cup. 'They got all zones called in. Everybody's on overtime. Nobody goes home until it's over.'

'Everybody?' Maggie couldn't begin to imagine how much that would cost. 'They didn't even do that with Duke.'

'Duke was different.'

'They were both cops.'

'Don't play coy, gal. You know it ain't the same. Duke was in a bad place at a bad time. This is Terry Lawson's nephew out on the job, almost taking two in the head.'

'Two?'

'That's the word at the station.' She pointed to the side of her head. 'Don had one here.' She moved her finger to her cheek. 'And one here.'

Maggie could tell they were both thinking the same thing. 'Those are hard shots to make.'

'Just one of 'em's hard. Two of 'em – that far from the target, cheap throwaway gun – that's Paladin territory.'

'It's different from the Shooter,' Maggie said. 'The other four got it once each in the forehead. Point-blank range. Execution-style.'

Gail eyed her carefully. 'You're thinking it's the Atlanta Shooter?'

'Aren't you?'

'The Shooter's still out there. We went balls to the walls the last two times and came up with fucking zero. And the murder this morning, the boys were in an alley when Don was shot, same as the other four victims.' Gail shrugged. 'What do I know? Could all just be a crazy coincidence.'

'Sure.' One of the first lessons Gail had taught Maggie was that there was no such thing as a coincidence.

Gail asked, 'You hear about the tires?'

'They were slashed.'

Gail tipped her lighter end over end, making a tapping sound against the table. 'I know a gal in dispatch says he didn't call it in.'

'What do you mean?'

'Jimmy didn't call a sixty-three.' Officer down. The call was standard procedure when a cop was injured. Gail said, 'Dispatch didn't even know that Don was hurt until they got a call from one of the docs at Grady saying he was dead.'

Maggie looked down. The transmitter for her radio was by her leg. Everybody on the force carried a radio. PCOs, like Gail, kept them in their purses. Patrol wore them clipped to the back of their belts. They were ungainly, thicker than a paperback, heavy as a can of Crisco, and covered in a plastic shell with knife-sharp edges. You either took it off when you sat down or you sat on the edge of your seat to keep from puncturing your spine.

Maggie said, 'They could've been in a dead pocket.' There were pockets all over the city where the radios didn't work. 'They were in Five Points off Whitehall. Reception can be patchy over there.'

Gail's eyebrow went up. She worked in the area. She knew the dead spots.

What she didn't know was something Maggie had just realized: Jimmy's transmitter had been missing from his belt this morning. She could see it clearly in her mind's eye. Keys, nightstick, handcuffs, revolver.

But no transmitter.

'Hey, kid?' Gail tapped the table with her lighter. 'You in there?'

Maggie looked at her watch. She thought about her earlier experiment. Five seconds. That was a long time. Even longer if Don was shot twice. Jimmy had maybe seven or eight seconds to respond. Or not, as the case might've been.

Gail knocked on the table again. 'Am I talking to myself here?'

Maggie looked up. 'Where'd you work last night?'

'Not at the Five, if that's what you're asking. I was off. This is for today.' Gail indicated her skimpy outfit. 'I'm bait for the johns. Zones Two and Three are lending their umbrella cars to round up the pimps. They're hoping to shut down business.'

'That should bring out the snitches.'

'Yeah, but when?' She took one last hit before stubbing out her cigarette. 'All it's gonna do is waste time. Same with the reward money. We already got a million leads from the last two shootings. Bunch of women turning in their husbands and boyfriends, trying to get that five thousand bucks.'

Maggie had run down enough false leads to know the truth behind her statement. 'How is shutting down the streets wasting time? It worked with Edward Spivey.'

'Did it?'

Maggie shrugged. Terry had gotten Spivey's name off a snitch by using the same tactics. There had to be some worth in that.

'Lemme lay it out for you,' Gail said. 'We're looking for some working gal who saw something in the Five last night, right? We're hoping maybe she'll give us a name?'

Maggie nodded.

'So, this is how day one goes down: Our boys are gonna throw every pimp they can find into the slammer. Lock up the pimps, then the girls spend all day getting high and sleeping.'

Maggie nodded again. That was exactly what had happened the last time.

'Day two rolls around: The pimps bail out, they beat up the girls for being lazy, the girls rush into the street to make up for lost revenue.' She lit a fresh cigarette. 'Which brings us to day three: Our boys come in and lock up the whores.' She spun her lighter on the table. 'It's a revolving door, in and out, in and out – day four, day five, however long it takes, they're gonna keep up this giant pissing contest until finally, somebody turns snitch so that everybody can get back to work.'

'That's what we want, though. We need somebody to talk.'

'Yeah, but does that seem like the smart way to do it?' She leaned across the table. 'What did I get up to, five, six days? Meanwhile, whoever killed Don Wesley's already melting the murder weapon in a vat of acid and getting the hell outta town. Or worse, hiring some fancy lawyer from up north who thinks he's gonna take a walk.'

Edward Spivey again. Everything they did today would

be cast in the man's shadow. Maggie asked, 'What's the faster option?'

'We find out the name of the pimp who's running girls where the murder went down, then we get the pimp to set up a meet with his girls so we can talk to them. You know how it is. Them whores won't take a shit 'less their pimp tells 'em to. And most times, he charges some freak to watch it.'

Maggie almost laughed. 'It's that easy? Just go to the pimp and he'll let us talk to his girls?'

'It's easy if we do it. If the boys do it, then we're looking at our very own Tet Offensive.' She shrugged, like it was a foregone conclusion. 'Chicks are better at de-escalating the situation. You know that.'

'Yeah,' Maggie said, though this was a lot coming from a woman she'd seen crack open a suspect's head with her Kel-Lite.

Gail asked, 'You ever break up a fight between two guys?'

'Sure.' Maggie did it at least five times a week.

'They don't stop beating the shit out of each other because they're scared of you, right?'

'No.' Sometimes, all it took was the sight of her squad car to break up a fight. 'After the first couple of punches, they want somebody to stop them before they really get hurt. I'm just the excuse.'

'Correctamundo,' Gail said. 'So, why go through all this trouble and drag it out with our boys banging up their boys and their boys banging up ours when we gals can just talk like semi-reasonable people?'

'What gals?'

'We gals.' She indicated the space between them.

Maggie tried to think it through. 'How do we know they're not lying?'

'How do we know the snitches are telling the truth?'

She had raised a good point. 'Have you told this idea to the bosses?'

'Yeah, Mack and Les and Terry and them all fell to the floor and kissed my feet for being so damn brilliant.'

Maggie grinned at the joke. 'Five Points. A million girls work that area.'

'We're not talking Five Points. We're talking Whitehall. And not just Whitehall, but the section near the C&S Bank where Don got shot. Them whores working that strip are older bitches. Most of 'em are shootin' coke and horse eight balls. Not much life left. Which makes this time sensitive.'

Maggie knew 'older' meant around her own age. 'Okay, so we need the name of the pimp who owns that corner. Do you have any sources who might talk?'

'Sure I do. But I got some bad blood on the street right now. Might've been too hard on a coupla whores got in my way.' Gail tapped her cigarette in the ashtray. 'You know me, kid. Never met a bridge I couldn't burn. I know who's got the information. Just might need some help pryin' it out.'

Maggie felt her toes start to tingle. She was walking along the edge of a very steep cliff. 'I'm not a detective.'

'So what?' Gail stared a challenge into her. This was how Maggie got roped in every time. She wanted Gail's approval too much. 'Lookit, go a couple of steps out. I get the name from a source. Then what? Pimp ain't gonna talk to me. You know how those bastards are. They wanna talk to some pretty young thing still got her tits where they're supposed to be.'

Maggie felt her stomach pitch. Gail had obviously given this some thought. 'You think I can just stroll into some pimp's lair and he's gonna talk to me?'

'Listen, sweetheart, forget what I told you when we were back in patrol. If there's one thing I've learned from being PCO, it's that sometimes it's okay to use the fact that you're a woman.'

Maggie wasn't so sure about that.

'Not like you gotta do anything after that except sit back and watch.'

Maggie knew what she was saying. Give Terry the name, then let the guys take care of the problem.

Gail jammed her cigarette into the stack of pancakes. 'Listen, this is a yes-or-no question. You wanna say yes, meet me at the Colonnade Restaurant around two. You say no, and the guy who murdered Don, almost killed your brother, gets away with it again?' Gail shrugged. 'That's on you.'

5

A large crowd of cops gathered on the front steps of police headquarters. The squat, ugly building was clad in white marble that had been mined from the Tate quarry in North Georgia, the same place where they cut blanks for tombstones. Fittingly, the men all seemed to be talking about death. Even from a distance, Maggie kept hearing Don Wesley's name. Most of them had probably never met him. She could tell from the numbers on their collars that they were from different squads though they all seemed to have the same dark sense of purpose. This was the third instance where a killer had reached into the heart of the police force. The panicked determination that had marked the last two manhunts had evolved into an outright bloodlust.

Nothing brought cops together faster than a common enemy.

And Atlanta had a lot of cops. The city was divided into seven police zones, including the airport and Perry Homes, a ghetto so dangerous it required its own separate police force. Each zone had a corresponding precinct. The downtown zone, Zone 1, used the bottom floor of the headquarters building for roll call. In practical terms, the location was ideal, but it was never good to be this close to the brass. Terry and his friends were always complaining about running into the police commissioner in the men's toilet. She guessed they couldn't decide which part of him they hated more: that he was new or that he was black.

After months of open hostilities, Mayor Maynard Jackson had finally managed to push out the old chief of police. Commissioner Reginald Eaves had taken over around the time of the Edward Spivey trial, which made a bad situation unbelievably worse. Eaves didn't seem to care. He was on a mission to break the white power structure that had controlled the Atlanta Police Department since its inception.

Suddenly, Terry Lawson had a problem with cronyism.

Maggie could understand her uncle's anger, even if she didn't share it. The good-ol'-boy system was great so long as you were one of the boys. When Terry's group first joined the force, black cops weren't even allowed in the station houses. They had to hang around the Butler Street YMCA until they were called out. They were not allowed to wear their uniforms unless they were on the job. Most of them didn't have squad cars. They were only allowed to arrest other blacks and could not take statements from or interview white people.

All of that had changed, of course, but men like Terry embraced change only when it suited their needs.

The first thing Commissioner Eaves did was clean house. In the span of a month, six assistant chiefs and over a hundred supervisory personnel were demoted to the lower ranks. Eaves handpicked the men who replaced them. A lot of new bosses want their own people, but because the old structure was entirely white and the new one was entirely black, people had problems.

Lawsuits followed, but none of them had yet been settled.

Next, Eaves implemented a new testing system to formalize promotions. Before it was all about who you knew, but Eaves wanted to make it about *what* you knew. It was a good idea, but when no black officers could pass the test, Eaves appointed a board of examiners to give oral tests. No white officers were able to pass the oral test.

Lawsuits followed. No one knew what the outcome would be.

Other than the color of his skin, the biggest complaint that Maggie heard about Eaves was the color of his blood: he didn't bleed blue. The mayor had met him when the two were in law school. Eaves had never been a real cop. He'd never worked the streets. Outside of headquarters, no one saw the commissioner unless they were watching the news or spotted his fancy Cadillac rolling down to the Commerce Club for lunch.

Primarily, he communicated through daily bulletins that were read during roll call. Which created another reason to hate the new boss: Eaves was obsessed with paperwork. He implemented new rules about appearance, how to address the public, when to use force, and, most importantly, how to fill out the forms required by the federal government in order to keep the grant money rolling in.

This part was especially important for the female officers. The only reason they were in uniform was because the federal government had bribed the city with grants to hire them. The women weren't exactly told to lie about their duties, but the grants dictated certain guidelines that the Atlanta Police Department was not going to follow – mixed assignments being primary among them.

No white woman would ride with a black man. The white men really wanted to ride with the black women, but the black women weren't stupid enough to get in a car with them. And there was no way in hell a black man and a white man would ride together.

Maybe there was a reason Atlanta was statistically one of the most violent, criminal cities in America. As far as Maggie could tell, the only thing the black and white male officers could agree on was that none of them thought women should be allowed in uniform.

Meet the new boss. Same as the old boss.

Maggie climbed the twenty-one steps to the headquarters building. The brass doors were a tarnished green. The thin sliver of glass was oily from smoke and sweat. She took one last whiff of fresh air before entering the lobby. As it was outside, the place was packed with men. There was no joking or jive talking. The weight of Don Wesley's murder blanketed the room as palpably as the cigarette smoke that fogged the air.

Even in their grief, they were true to form. None of them moved out of Maggie's way as she pushed through the packed squad room. A shoulder bumped hers. A hand brushed across her ass. She kept her expression neutral, her eyes straight ahead, as she headed to the back of the room.

'Hey, doll.' Chuck Hammond was short for a man. He came up to around Maggie's breasts, which seemed to suit him just fine. 'Jimmy okay?'

Maggie kept walking. 'He'll be here soon. You can see for yourself.'

'Listen, if you need to talk about—'

Rick Anderson saved her. 'Hey, Maggie, you got a minute?'

'Sure.' Maggie felt Chuck's hand on her arm, but she kept moving. She followed Rick as he cut a path toward the back. Everybody liked Rick. He was funny and good-natured and always laughed at everybody's jokes.

He looked over his shoulder to make sure she was still there. 'You holding up okay?'

'Sure,' she repeated. 'Jimmy's great.'

'I wasn't asking about Jimmy.'

Unreasonably, Maggie felt the urge to cry. She couldn't remember the last time anybody had asked her how she was doing. 'I'm good. Thanks.'

'Madam.' He bowed slightly, indicating the door marked ladies. They both ignored the crude drawing of an ejaculating penis taped under the sign.

'Thank you.'

Maggie cracked the door just enough to slide through in case anyone was indecent.

Good thing, because Charlaine Compton had her pants off. She was dabbing clear fingernail polish on the ladder working its way up the back of her pantyhose. She saw Maggie and said, 'I just bought these.'

'I have an extra pair.' Maggie had to turn sideways to get past Charlaine. The women's locker room was an afterthought, a narrow bowling alley of a space meant to store cleaning supplies. There were no toilets or sinks. If they needed to use the facilities, they had to go up a flight of stairs and use the public restrooms.

Maggie spun the combination on her lock. 'Chuck cornered me.'

'Did he touch you?'

Maggie shuddered. 'Rick Anderson saved me before he could.'

'Rick's one of the nice ones.' Charlaine studied her. 'Jimmy okay?'

'He's mad. He wants to catch the guy.' She handed Charlaine the white plastic egg from her locker. 'Don was a good cop. He deserved better than that.'

'True on all points.' Charlaine rolled the pantyhose so she could put them on. 'You shoulda heard my mother on the phone this morning. "Why're you doin" that job when you could get killed? What's wrong with you?"'

Maggie was familiar with the questions. She floated out an idea. 'Maybe they'll let us work some of the leads.'

'Maybe Princess Grace will come scrub my toilet.'

Maggie thought about Gail's suggestion that they work the case together. More like a challenge. Gail knew how to push Maggie's buttons. As awful as it sounded, thinking about helping solve Don's murder was an exciting prospect. But then there was the other component, which was that Maggie would have to turn the name over to Terry. She wouldn't just be giving Terry a name. She would be signing a man's death warrant.

Then again, she could always feed the information to Rick Anderson and his partner, Jake Coffee. They weren't Terry's kind of cops. They actually followed the law. Which brought up another problem. If Terry found out that Maggie had gone behind his back, she wouldn't be anybody's kind of cop. Terry was losing his power on the force, but he still had enough pull to keep her behind a desk or, worse, make her work night shift at the jail until she either got stabbed or quit.

'Good morning, ladies!' Wanda Clack squeezed through the half-open door. She had a big smile on her face that dropped the minute the door shut. 'Another cock drawing?' she asked. 'Honestly. Don't these boys have mothers?'

Charlaine asked, 'How was your date this weekend?'

'I told him I'm a cop and he stuck me with the check.' Wanda rolled her eyes. 'Maybe I should tell the next one I'm a stewardess.'

'He'll think you're fast.'

'That's exactly what I want him to think. I haven't been laid in two months.'

The door opened wide.

'Hey!' Charlaine screamed, clutching her pants around her waist.

'Jesus, lady!' Wanda pushed the door closed on the ensuing whistles and catcalls. 'What the hell?'

They all stared at the blonde who'd stumbled into the room. She looked panicked. Her chest was heaving. At least Maggie thought her chest was heaving. Her uniform was big enough to pass for an Indian sari. You could always spot the new recruits by their clothes. They didn't get their uniforms until they graduated from the academy, because most of them washed out before graduation. The guys in the supply room gave the women uniforms that were too large, while the black men got uniforms that were obscenely small.

'Listen up, blondie.' Charlaine buttoned her pants. 'You never open the door all the way. Ever.'

'Uh . . .' The blonde touched her trembling fingers to

her neck. She was clearly on the verge of tears. Maggie was shocked she'd made it through the gauntlet. She looked like a light breeze could blow her right back out the door.

Instead of asking the woman, Charlaine asked Maggie, 'Who's this?'

Maggie shrugged. 'I guess one of the new recruits.'

'Shit, I forgot they were coming in today.' Charlaine sat down so she could load up her utility belt. 'She obviously can't sew.'

Wanda suggested, 'Maybe she thinks she'll get arrested for altering her uniform.'

They laughed. The new girl stared at them like a caged animal.

Maggie turned to her locker and busied herself with her purse, checking the things that she already knew were in there. She'd endured the same kind of taunts when she'd first put on the uniform. It was part of the initiation. If you couldn't make it in the women's locker room, you sure as hell couldn't make it out on the street. At least the jabs you got in here were only verbal. In her first month, Maggie had been spat on more times than she could count and punched in the face by the wife of the man she was arresting for domestic battery.

'Where you from?' Wanda asked.

The new girl obviously wasn't sure if the question was meant for her.

'Yeah, you,' Wanda said. 'Where you from?'

'Atlanta.' Her voice was like money, so it wasn't surprising when she said, 'Buckhead.'

Wanda gave a low whistle. You didn't find a lot of cops from the wealthiest section of town. 'Hoity-toity.'

Charlaine slapped Maggie's leg for attention. She held out her hand, and Maggie helped leverage her up from the bench. Charlaine told them, 'Y'all've got five minutes before the colored girls get the room.'

The palaver of male voices filled the space as she cracked open the heavy door.

Wanda kept her arms crossed, demanding of the new girl, 'So, Hoity-Toity, what're you doing slumming it here?'

'Just ...' The woman kept wringing her hands. 'Working.'

'Working.' Wanda had an ice pick for a tongue. She kept staring at the woman, obviously checking all the boxes that listed why she hated her. Tall, with strawberry blonde hair and a model-perfect face. Big blue eyes. High cheekbones. Even without lipstick, her lips were cherry red. She had a couple years on them all, but there was something fresher, younger, more feminine about her.

Wanda asked, 'You here to meet guys? 'Cause I can tell you right now, ain't none of 'em worth knowing.'

The woman said nothing, but her eyes told a story. She was going through her options, chief among them being to open the door and run away screaming.

'Go on.' Wanda nodded toward the door. 'You wouldn't be the first gal to call it quits before roll call.'

'I'm not quitting.' The blonde seemed to be speaking more to herself. 'I'm not here to meet men. I'm here to do a job. And I'm not quitting.'

Wanda grunted. 'We'll see about that, Hoity-Toity.'

Her voice got stronger. 'Yes, you will.'

Maggie felt bad for the girl. She asked, 'What's your name?'

'Kay—' She seemed to change her mind. 'Kate Murphy.'

'Kate Murphy?' Wanda echoed. 'We got our own Irish Spring here—"manly, but I like it, too!"'

Maggie smiled at the joke. Wanda sounded just like the woman in the commercial.

'I'm not—' Kate shifted, nearly losing her balance. Her shoes were too big. Her pants were coming unpinned. She was swallowed in a sea of navy-blue wool. Still, she said, 'I need this job.'

Maggie studied Kate Murphy. She was obviously scared, and there was no denying the desperation in her voice, but she deserved some credit for not backing down. Especially since Wanda was in her cop stance, which even Maggie found intimidating.

Wanda seemed to notice this, too. She moderated her tone, but only slightly. 'Don't wear the dress socks they gave you. Franklin Simon has wool ones, two for a dollar, that'll keep your feet in your shoes. Find a stapler for your pants. Those pins ain't gonna hold, especially if you have to chase somebody, and believe me, you're gonna have to chase somebody, or fight somebody off, and with that figure, it'll probably be one of those monkeys on the other side of the door.'

Kate looked at the door.

'Eyes back this way.' Wanda wasn't done. 'There's a tailor on Carver Street does alterations without copping a feel. He's a Jew, but he's reasonable.' She winked. 'Just don't stare at his horns. Makes him nervous.'

Kate seemed even more terrified than before.

'What, you're afraid of Jews?' Wanda was giving her the business again. 'You gotta problem with them?'

Kate gave a slow half shrug. 'As long as they keep their hooves covered.'

Wanda huffed a laugh. She patted Kate on the shoulder as she headed for the door. 'Good one, Hoity. If you're still here by Friday, I'll buy you a drink.'

The door cracked open, Maggie saw a bunch of male faces trying to see if there was something interesting behind the door.

She looked at her watch. 'We'd better hurry before the colored girls get here.'

Kate glanced at the curtain splitting the room in half. She seemed horrified. 'It's segregated?'

'They change back there. They can't wear their uniforms to work.'

'Why?'

Maggie felt her eyes narrow. She couldn't tell if this doe-eyed look was an act or not. 'You ever talk to a black person in Buckhead don't have to come through the back door?'

'Well, I—'

'Cops aren't welcome in the neighborhoods where they live, even if they've got the same color skin.'

Kate looked back at the door. 'Why don't you have a curtain, too?'

Now Maggie was certain she was playing some game. 'Because they put one up first.' She felt the need to warn her. 'Seriously, though, if you get caught back there, they'll kick your ass. I mean it. They're mean as hell. Even Wanda won't mess with them.'

'Oh—okay.'

'Toilets are upstairs,' Maggie said. 'It's a tight squeeze, only two stalls. Don't spray your hair in front of the mirror unless you wanna get knifed. I'm Maggie, by the way.'

Kate said nothing. She just stood there gripping the strap of her purse like she wanted to strangle it. Or use it to strangle herself.

Maggie asked, 'You got a combination lock?'

Kate shook her head.

Maggie held open her locker. 'Put your purse in here. Get a lock after work. There's a sporting goods store on Central Ave. near the university. Wear your uniform and they'll give you the lock for free. Actually, wear your uniform whenever you can. You'll get free coffee, free food, free groceries.'

Kate put her purse on top of Maggie's. 'Is that legal?'

'Anything's legal if you can get away with it.' Maggie slammed the locker closed. 'Welcome to the Atlanta Police Department.'

6

Kate sat at the last table in the back of the squad room, wedged between the woman who was hateful to her and the woman who was only marginally less hateful.

Maggie Lawson. She was about Kate's height, with dark hair pinned into a bun on the top of her head, brown eyes, and a pretty face that would've been prettier without the uniform. Of course, the latter might be said for Kate, so she should probably be more generous. Maggie had been helpful in a begrudging way. Kate wondered if the next time she saw her purse, the wallet would be empty.

Then there were Clack and Compton – the other two. Both short. One thick-waisted, the other thin as a rail. They bleached their short hair and wore heavy makeup, as if they were desperate to prove that they were still women. They hadn't even bothered to introduce themselves. Kate had seen their last names engraved on the silver bars pinned to their uniforms.

She had to think all the way back to junior high school to recall a time she'd felt so despised by a group of women. Kate had been an early bloomer. She'd had curves before anyone else. She'd developed breasts before anyone else. She'd got her period first of all her girlfriends. And then she didn't have any girlfriends, and the boys wouldn't stop staring at her.

Which was pretty much what was happening now. Despite the fact that she was wearing the police equivalent of sackcloth, every man in the room found some excuse to turn around and look at her. Never in the history of civilization had so many pens been dropped so repeatedly.

She ignored them all, even as she prayed that she would get partnered with one of them. The bigger and stupider, the better. Kate knew how to handle men. It was the women she was worried about. This job wasn't a lark. A police officer had been killed this morning. If Kate got partnered with Lawson, Clack, or Compton, it was clear that she was on her own. And the vulgar woman who stood with her feet planted apart and had a gait like a horse leaving the barn would be proven right – Kate wouldn't make it through the first week.

She clasped her hands together so she would stop wringing them. There was the usual split-second panic when she didn't feel her wedding ring. Two months ago had marked the second year since Patrick's death. He had been gone longer than Kate had known him.

She wondered what Patrick would make of her current situation. There were probably two answers to the question. The Patrick she had married was different from the Patrick who'd written her letters from the jungle. He was six weeks into his tour when he started sounding like a different, darker version of the boy she'd married. He was obsessed with the new guys who shifted in every week to replace the ones who were sent home in body bags. They called them FNGs, which took Kate some time to figure out because there was no scenario in which her husband was going to write the word 'fuck' in a letter to his wife. As if she'd never listened to a Richard Pryor album.

Fucking New Guys.

Kate could never comprehend Patrick's hatred of the FNGs. He excoriated them. He railed against the very idea of their existence. They came in with their fresh faces and sense of purpose and photos of their girls tucked inside of their helmets. No one wanted to know their names. Why bother when most of them wouldn't survive the week?

That was Kate. That was why they didn't introduce themselves to her – the fucking new girl.

She straightened her hat on the table, surreptitiously taking in her fellow female officers, the way they sat on the edge of their seats with their knees spread and elbows on the table. Kate felt like a prim schoolmarm with her legs crossed and her hands folded in her lap.

She was one of eight white women in patrol uniforms. The other white women stood against the wall by the locker rooms. They smoked incessantly and wore tight miniskirts with skimpy tops that left nothing to the imagination. At first, Kate thought they had been arrested, or were waiting to be arrested, or perhaps looking for customers, but then she figured they must be undercover officers because, as bad as this place seemed, she doubted they let prostitutes stand around listening to the morning roll call.

At the very least, she assumed prostitutes had better things to do.

She turned her attention to the opposite side of the

room. There were eight black patrolwomen across the aisle – the colored girls everyone was so worried about. The concern did not seem unfounded. There was something terrifying about the women, the way they stared straight ahead, shoulders squared, all business. As a group, they were intensely separate. This explained the curtain. They had walled themselves off from the world before anyone else could.

In the front half of the room, the men were similarly segregated by skin color, though their ranks were higher in number – probably fifty altogether. Patrolmen sat with detectives in street clothes that would've been slightly more stylish ten years ago. Nearly all of them had long sideburns and shaggy mustaches. They wore their hats inside and held their cigarettes between their thumbs and forefingers. The smell they gave off was overwhelming. Sweat, tobacco, and far, far too much Old Spice.

Kate tried not to think about what it had been like to walk among them. She'd been literally man-handled; her breasts, her bottom, even the back of her neck had been touched by some stranger. She'd never in her life been so roughly treated. Something about putting on the uniform had turned her from good girl to bad. It was as if they were telling her: come into our territory, play by our rules.

One of the men a few tables away tried to catch Kate's eye. She quickly looked down, gripping her hands tighter. She forced out a slow breath, trying not to choke on the cigarette smoke that permeated the air. No more daydreaming about Patrick. No more strolls down memory lane.

She had to do this.

A low murmur went through the room. A fat white man with a bulbous red nose took the podium. Captain Cal Vick. He had interviewed Kate this morning and warned her to keep her breasts strapped down so she didn't give anybody a heart attack.

Vick rapped his knuckles on the podium. 'All right, settle. Everybody settle.' The noise wound down like a music box. 'Let's start this off with a prayer for Don Wesley, may he rest in peace.' Everyone bowed their heads. Kate averted her gaze to the floor.

Don Wesley. She was driving to work when she heard about him on the radio. The fifth police officer murdered in the last three months. According to the news reporter, the Atlanta Shooter had struck again. There was a five-thousand-dollar reward. Listeners were urged to call the police department with any information.

Kate had started to sweat while she navigated the downtown streets. She had wanted to pull over to the nearest pay phone and call her family to let them know that she was all right. Then she had realized how foolish that would be. They would hear the details the same as Kate and know that she was safe. The reporter had given the victim's name, said that he was unmarried and had served with distinction in Vietnam.

And still, Kate had fought the need to call her mother. Only when she considered how the conversation would go did Kate push herself to keep driving. The only reason to call her family was to tell them that she had changed her mind. That she couldn't do this. That she wanted to move back home. They would be disappointed with her. Not that they would say it, and of course on some level they would be relieved, but they would be disappointed, which in some ways was worse than any 'I told you so.'

So Kate had not pulled over at the nearest phone booth. Instead, she had pulled into the marked lot by the police headquarters building. She had gotten out of the car. She had walked the three blocks up the street. And then she had reported to Cal Vick so that he could wonder aloud if Kate's breasts were too large for her to safely run down the street.

Vick said, 'Amen,' and everyone chimed in. 'We'll get through roll call, then Sergeant Lawson will run down what's the what.'

Kate glanced at Maggie, guessing by her bare ring finger that Sergeant Lawson was a male relation.

Vick continued, 'Before I start, I wanna make sure every single one of you peckerheads is out there with his eyes open. Nobody goes out alone today. Nobody runs off trying to play cowboy. We get this dirtbag together. You hear?'

None of the women answered, but all the men shouted, 'Yes, sir.'

'This ain't gonna be a repeat of six months ago. Am I clear?'

'Yes, sir,' they repeated.

Kate glanced around. Everyone seemed to know what had happened six months ago except for her.

Vick started the roll call. 'Anderson?'

There was a gruff 'Here,' followed by another name, then another.

Kate shifted in her chair, trying to keep her flashlight from stabbing into her side. She shifted again and the handle of the nightstick jammed into her thigh. Kate moved again, and several people turned to stare. Her new leather belt was creaking, announcing her every move.

She looked at Maggie, then Clack, then Compton, and realized their knees were apart to more evenly distribute the weight from the belts. Kate carefully uncrossed her legs. She inched her feet away from each other. Her face burned with embarrassment. She'd kept her knees together or legs crossed since she was old enough to sit up on her own. Maybe there was another way. Or maybe these women had something in them that Kate did not.

She couldn't think about that. If she admitted that she was different, she would have to admit that she wasn't cut out for this. Frankly, she wasn't cut out for much of anything. She hadn't the patience for being stuck in a classroom full of children. She hadn't the training to be a nurse. Her father had gotten her three different secretarial jobs in a row, but Kate had been unable to keep any of them. Her typing speed was laughable. Her dictation was atrocious. She could fetch coffee and look pretty, but there were plenty of younger girls who were willing to do that for a hell of a lot less money than a grown person could live on.

The police force had to pay women the same salary as men. They had to give you benefits and a pension. They had to train you, such as it was. Perhaps most importantly of all, they had to let you do your job. Kate had worked her ass off at the academy. She'd studied more than she ever had in college. She'd practiced looking people directly in the eye. Raising her voice. Standing her ground. She'd worked on not apologizing when someone bumped into her, not explaining herself in restaurants when her order was wrong or asking for forgiveness before gently complaining to the dry cleaner that he'd ruined her favorite blouse.

'Wake up.' Maggie bumped Kate's elbow. Everyone had their spiral notebooks out. Kate's was in her purse, which was in Maggie's locker.

Vick said, 'Terry, you wanna take over?'

Kate studied the new man behind the podium. White, as with everyone else in charge. He had a thick neck and squinty eyes that scanned the room. Sergeant Terry Lawson, she presumed.

He unfolded a sheet of paper and read haltingly. 'The suspect is a black male. Afro, long sideburns and mustache. Approximately twenty to twenty-five years of age. No distinguishing tattoos or birthmarks.' He looked up, making sure he was being followed. 'Five-ten, maybe six foot. Dressed like a hippie. Levis and a red shirt. He wore gloves. Black gloves. The weapon was a Saturday night special.' Terry paused again as they all recorded the details into their notebooks. Even the blacks were taking notes. Suddenly, they'd all come together.

Terry said, 'Chipper?'

Chip Bixby. Kate recognized him from the academy. He and a man named Bud Deacon had been responsible for teaching them how to shoot. Both men had worn matching red ties, seemingly for the sole purpose of telling the women that the only rule in handling a gun was not to shoot the men wearing red ties.

'Gentlemen.' Chip waited for silence. 'The Shooter carried a weapon similar to the pistol in my hand.' He held a handgun over his head that looked nothing like the revolver Kate had been issued. 'This is a Raven MP-25 from the original Ring of Fire. Twenty-five-cal semi with a blowback action. Holds six in the mag and one in the chamber. A piece of shit, this gun. Jams all the time. American made, so what's their excuse?'

'No excuse!' a drunken voice called. Jett Elliott. Kate recognized him from the shooting range. He was sitting in the front row, listing to the side. The man beside him held a hand at his back to keep him from toppling over.

'Okay.' Terry took over again. 'This Raven handgun is the type what took out Don Wesley. Chip's has the wood grain grip. The one that killed Don had imitation pearl. Anybody not familiar with this weapon, come up after and take a look. I want the real deal in my hands by close of business today. That sound like a plan?'

There were nods around the room.

Terry said, 'Since all of ya'll are wondering, I'm gonna make it easy for you and lay out what happened straight from Jimmy's statement. I don't want no gossip after this. Nobody pimpin' to no damn reporters.'

Jett spoke up again. 'Nobody pimpin' to Reggie, neither.'

There were mumurs of agreement around the room.

Reginald Eaves, Kate assumed. At the academy, she'd heard a lot of whispers about pimping to Reggie, which she gathered meant reporting infractions to the commissioner.

'Jett's right,' Terry said. 'Everything I tell you stays in this room. No pimpin' up to nobody.'

'Damn straight.' This came from the man sitting beside the drunk. They were strikingly similar with their cheap suits and bad haircuts. Kate wondered if they were twins, then decided they were both stamped from the same blue-collar machine that had spit out Cal Vick and Terry Lawson.

'All right, quiet down,' Terry said. He bent down his head and read from the report again. 'Last night around three in the a.m., Officer Don Wesley and Officer Jimmy Lawson received a report of a possible break-in at the C&S Bank, Five Points, off of Whitehall Road. They went to investigate. Officer Wesley was on foot, checking the back entrance, while Officer Lawson, also on foot, checked the front.'

Kate felt Maggie stiffen beside her. Another Lawson. The place was crawling with them.

Terry folded up the paper. He rested his elbow on the podium like an old man telling a story. 'Jimmy finished securing the front and called in a false alarm. He was maybe ten, fifteen feet away from Don in the alley behind the bank when out of nowhere, this black brother rounds the corner. Brother fires. Twice. Don takes both in the head. Jimmy goes for cover. He squeezes off three shots, but the brother hoofs it. Jimmy has to stay with his partner.' He paused. 'Your partner's safety is your first priority. Right?'

Staunch, manly echoes of 'Right' bounced around the room.

Beside Kate, Maggie put down her pen.

Terry said, 'We're gonna shut this city down today, gentlemen. Nobody does any business until we get a name.'

There were whoops all around.

Terry banged his fist on the podium. 'We're gonna shake the monkeys outta the trees. We're gonna knock some heads. We're gonna get this asshole.' The bang turned into a drumbeat. Some men had joined him, hitting the tables. 'Am I right?'

There was an eruption of noise – banging on tables, stamping the floor, calls for blood. Kate wondered if this was what halftime inside a football locker room was like.

'All right. All right.' Vick took Terry's place behind the podium. He calmed them with his hands, lowering the tone. 'Jimmy's working with a sketch artist, so we'll have something to release to the press and TV news.' Vick raised his voice over the rumble of disgust. 'Check your usual places for the Raven, see if anybody's pawned it or tossed it.' He stared over the crowd, expectant. Everyone turned to look at the young man standing in the back of the room. He was handsome, with an athletic build, and long sideburns that framed his square jaw.

Vick asked, 'We miss anything, Jimmy?'

Jimmy shook his head. His eyes scanned the crowd, settling on Kate first, then Maggie. Or, technically, on the back of Maggie's head. She was the only one in the room who had not turned around to look at Jimmy.

She obviously sensed Kate's scrutiny. Maggie nodded toward Jimmy. 'Brother.' She nodded toward the man at the podium. 'Uncle.'

Kate mumbled, 'I'm sorry for what happened.'

Maggie stared ahead.

'All right.' Terry held up two sheets of mimeographed paper. 'I got your assignments. They'll be posted on the board.' He stacked the pages together. 'This is serious business out there today, gentlemen. No chicks riding with dicks. Except you. New girl.' Kate's heart jumped in her chest. He was pointing at her. Everybody was looking. 'You're with Jimmy.'

There were some wolf whistles and laughs. Kate felt her face turning red.

'That's enough,' Terry said. 'Get to work. Remember, no cowboys.'

Kate turned to Maggie, hoping for help. 'What should I—'

Maggie stood up and walked away.

Clack and Compton hadn't abandoned her, but Kate was under no impression they'd stuck around to help.

'Jimmy-boy,' Clack said. 'Lucky you.'

Kate tried, 'I didn't ask—'

'Do yourself a favor, sweetheart. Put a towel down if you let him fuck you in the back of his squad car.'

Kate followed Jimmy Lawson across the parking lot, feeling like the walking embodiment of a Keystone Kop. She had to shuffle her feet to keep them from slipping out of her too-large shoes. Her nightstick slapped her leg. The hooks on her belt dug into her sides. She kept having to tip back her hat on her head so she could see. She felt as if her every move was being scrutinized, though the crowd around her seemed intent on leaving, not watching the FNG to see what mayhem would befall her.

Despite Jimmy's quick pace, he walked with a pronounced limp. She wondered if he'd been injured in Vietnam. She doubted she'd find out his life story. He hadn't spoken one word to her, just nodded toward the door and started walking. Kate had prayed to be partnered with a male cop. She should've been more specific. Jimmy seemed to be the only guy on the squad who wanted nothing to do with Kate.

He stopped to talk to a group of men. Kate recognized Jett Elliott and his seatmate as well as Captain Cal Vick, Chip Bixby, Bud Deacon, Terry Lawson, and a handful of other men who could easily be mistaken for extras in a Sam Peckinpah movie. They showed Jimmy great deference, which was strange considering they all had at least two decades on the younger man. Maybe this was because Jimmy's partner had been shot. Or because they were drunks making an effort to appear sober.

Kate didn't know what to make of their drinking and she was hard pressed to care. Instead, she thought of all the things she'd left in her purse. And then she wondered how she was going to retrieve her purse at the end of the day. Maggie hadn't told her the combination to the lock.

'Let's go.' Jimmy spun his key ring around his middle finger. The keys made a clinking sound every time he caught them. The noise corresponded with his limp as he made his way toward one of the last cruisers left in the lot. The white Plymouth Fury mirrored the early morning sun. The red and blue Atlanta Police Department badge on the door was faded to almost pink and baby blue.

Jimmy popped the trunk so he could secure the shotgun over the spare wheel well. He told Kate, 'Check the car.'

She had learned basic patrol procedures at the academy. Kate knew how to take apart a back seat, replace a flat tire, and top off a radiator. She'd even learned how to pump gas into the tank, which was the only thing Kate learned at the police academy that had truly shocked her father.

She inspected the inside of the car as instructed, checking for weapons or personal belongings that had been left behind. It was important to ascertain that there was nothing in the back seat that an arrestee might find and use as a weapon. The flimsy chain-link fence was the only thing separating the front of the car from the back. A knife or even a sharpened plastic fork could be easily jammed through the diamond-shaped openings.

Jimmy pulled on a pair of leather racing gloves as he watched her. 'You gonna take all day?'

Kate locked the back seat into place with her knee. 'Ready.'

He unclipped the transmitter from the back of his belt, then climbed behind the wheel. He had to angle his leg because of his bum knee. When he shut the door, he gave Kate a challenging look, daring her to mention the injury.

Kate unclipped her transmitter. She rested it in her lap as opposed to between her legs, as Jimmy had. 'I'm sorry about your partner.'

'Why? You didn't know him.' He turned the key in the ignition. 'Write this down, 'cause I ain't gonna repeat it.' He put the gear in reverse, but didn't move the car. 'Where's your notebook?'

'In my—' She cut to the point. 'In the locker room.'

Jimmy slammed the gear back into park. 'Go get it.'

Kate felt her cheeks burning again. 'It's in somebody else's locker.'

'Motherfucker.'

Kate flinched at the word. She didn't know why. She'd certainly heard it before.

Fortunately, Jimmy didn't seem to notice her reaction. He leaned over and opened the glove box. Instinctively, Kate pulled away from him. He glared at her as he dropped a spare notebook on her lap. 'First rule is, don't leave your fucking notebook.'

She flipped the cover open to a blank sheet, but she didn't have anything to write with.

'Christ.' Jimmy took a pen out of his pocket and threw it in her direction.

Kate missed the pen. Of course she missed it. She leaned

down to retrieve it from the floor just as he backed up the car. The brim of her hat slammed into the dash, sending a slash of pain across her forehead. Kate felt something close to a swoon. Her vision blurred. Her stomach curdled.

Jimmy pulled out onto the road. 'Write that down,' he said. 'Never forget your notebook.'

Kate sat up. She pushed her hat back on her head. She was still seeing pricks of stars, but she clicked the pen, started writing: *Never forget your notebook.* She felt like an idiot, but she looked to him for more.

He said, 'Rule number two: you type all the reports. I'm not here to do paperwork. That's why you write down every single fucking thing that happens. Mark the time, what the weather's like, what people look like, how they sound – they crackers or hillbillies? Southside or West?' He paused, waiting for Kate to finish. At least that's what she thought he was doing. She couldn't help but notice that his eyes never went above her chest.

'Rule number three: I'm the boss of this car. I say where we go, when we stop, where we stop. If you gotta pee every ten minutes, you bring a cup to piss in. I don't wanna hear about it. Got me?'

Kate kept her head down, thinking if she just kept writing, the words wouldn't matter.

'Rule three, section A, I always drive, and you shut the hell up about it.'

Kate didn't have to write that one down.

'Four: Ask. Tell. Make. You *ask* somebody to do something. They don't do it, you *tell* them to do it. They still don't do it, you *make* them do it.'

Her hand was cramping. She could barely keep up.

'Number five: forget rule number four. It don't matter. You're not talking to anybody. You're not looking at anybody. You stay in the car when I get out and you still be in the car when I get back in.'

Kate looked up. This was the exact opposite of what they told her during her training. You never left your partner's side. Even Jimmy's own uncle had said as much during roll call.

Jimmy seemed to read her mind. 'I don't care what they taught you. There's different rules for men and women. You go out into the street, you're my responsibility. I can't look after me and look after you at the same time.'

She stared down at the point of the pen pressing into the white notebook paper. 'You don't find it possible that I can look after myself?'

He laughed, but not because he thought it was funny. 'Look at this shithole.' He waved his hand out the window. 'You think you can handle yourself outside this car?'

Kate felt her eyes go wide. She'd been too busy writing to notice the scenery had changed. They were smack in the middle of the projects. Young black men were clumped around the street corners. Scantily clad girls strolled the sidewalks. She suppressed a shudder of fear. They were the only white people around.

'Capitol Homes,' Jimmy announced, as if it wasn't obvious they were in a government housing project. 'Look behind you.'

Kate turned. The gold capitol dome shadowed the complex.

He said, 'Funny thing, ain't one of those windows

looking this way. They all look toward downtown, where the money comes in. They don't see the filth and the trash the city shits out behind them.'

Kate took in her surroundings. Scores of two-story brick buildings dotted the complex. There were no trees, nothing on the lawns but red Georgia clay. Children who should have been in school were playing outside, their bare feet kicking up dust. The temperature was low, but people had their windows open. She saw old men sitting on front stoops. Women leaned out the windows to yell at their kids. Litter was everywhere. Graffiti. Condoms and needles collected around the drains in the street.

And the smell. The stench was indescribable.

Jimmy slowed the car to a crawl. 'You get a whiff of that?'

Kate tried not to gag. The air burned her eyes and nose, cut into her pores. Sweat, urine, rancid food. Kate didn't know what the odor was, but she would never forget it as long as she lived.

He said, 'Roll down your window.'

Kate didn't want to, but she grabbed the handle. Her hand was sweating so badly she couldn't get the lever to turn.

Jimmy leaned across her and cranked down the window. He yelled, 'Romeo, get your ass over here.'

A black man sauntered over, his fingers tucked into the waist of his pants. He was dressed in wide yellow bell-bottoms and a vivid green shirt. The buttons were open so low that Kate could see the hair trailing down from his belly button. And then she saw it closer, because he was standing so near that Kate's shoulder almost touched him.

Jimmy said, 'Stop fuckin' around, Romeo.'

The man finally leaned down and stuck his head through the open window. Kate pressed her spine so hard into the seat that her handcuffs pushed apart the vertebrae.

Romeo asked Jimmy, 'Whatchu want, honky?'

'You hear about Don?'

'What's that?'

'Don't dick me around,' Jimmy warned. 'Tell me what you know.'

'I know y'all lookin' to do some beatin' today.'

'You wanna be my first?'

Romeo winked at Kate. Like Jimmy, he seemed incapable of looking at anything higher than her chest. 'Shit, man, you know I don't know nothin' about that. I'm just a bidness man goin' 'bout my bidness.'

Jimmy lightened the pressure. 'You got your ear to the ground.'

Romeo nodded his head. 'That might be true.'

'You get me a name, I'll give you a coupla passes.'

'I'm gone need more than a coupla somethin'. My black ass'll be toast folks find out I'm helpin' you crackers.'

Jimmy's face was stone. 'Whatta you want?'

'I'll thinka somethin'.'

'You get me that name, you better think fast. I don't leave no open tabs.'

'I hear ya, brother.' Romeo turned his attention to Kate. She held her breath. The odor off him was foul – something sickly sweet, like burned candy. He showed her a row of gold teeth. 'You a foxy little thing.'

To Kate's horror, Jimmy said, 'She is, ain't she?'

'Blonde hair. Pretty white skin. Got them fine, full lips.

I liked to feel me some a them lips. You ever suck a chocolate creamsicle, baby?'

Jimmy chuckled. 'I bet she ain't.'

'Lemme show you, baby.' Romeo's face got closer. Kate moved so far away that she was almost in Jimmy's lap. 'Why don't you pucker up them fine lips for me, gal?' Romeo's shoulder moved. She could tell his hand was touching the front of his pants. 'Come on. Open up that sweet mouth for me.'

Kate willed herself not to look down. Not to breathe. Not to scream.

'Do you recognize that burned-cotton-candy smell?' Jimmy asked, like Kate was sitting in a classroom instead of about to be raped. 'That's heroin. They put it in a spoon and cook it to a boil with a lighter.'

Romeo's tongue darted out. 'Got-damn, you the whitest white bitch I ever seen.'

'They pull the liquid into a needle then shoot it in their veins.' Jimmy said, 'That right, Romeo?'

Romeo wouldn't be distracted. His hand was doing things below the window that Kate didn't want to know about. 'You just stay there just a little minute more and I—'

Jimmy hit the gas. Romeo slipped out the window. Kate was flung back against the seat. She struggled to turn around, to get her bearings. Jimmy was laughing so hard that he had tears in his eyes.

'You stupid bitch,' he said. 'Holy shit, you shoulda seen your face.'

Somehow, Kate managed to sit back in her seat. She clenched her hands in her lap, tightened her jaw so hard that her head ached. She hissed out, 'You asshole.'

'Asshole?' Jimmy kept laughing. 'You cringe like a nun when I say "motherfucker" and now you're calling me an asshole?'

'Asshole.' Kate practically spit out the word. She was shaking. Her fists would not unclench. A volcano raged inside of her.

'I'm the asshole?' Jimmy swerved the car into a sharp turn. He slammed down the brakes. Kate grabbed the dashboard before she hit it again. 'Let me tell you, sister – what happened back there? That's why you don't belong out here.'

She stared at him. He wasn't laughing anymore.

'Why'd you let that pimp talk to you like that? What are these for?' Jimmy grabbed at her flashlight, her nightstick, her gun. 'These for show, girlie girl? You like the way they make your hips look?'

'Stop.' Kate tried to push him away. He was made of stone. Nothing would move him. She started to panic. 'Please.'

'Shit,' Jimmy muttered, finally returning to his side of the car. 'Better it comes from me than some pimp raping your ass.' He stared at Kate with obvious disgust. 'Go on and cry. Get it out so I can take you back to the station.'

Kate would gouge out her own eyes before she cried. 'What the hell do you want from me?'

'What do I want?' Jimmy leaned over again, crowding her against the door. 'I want you to get out of my car and take off that fucking uniform and go find a husband and have some kids and bake pies and play house like a normal fucking woman.'

Her fingernails cut into her palms. She struggled to

102

bring air into her lungs. 'Get away from me.'

Jimmy leaned closer. 'Why don't I drive you back to Romeo? He'd cut your slit open like a fish. And then he'd pump you with H and toss you back into the street until you'd suck a fucking dog to get that needle in your arm.' Kate tried to turn away. Jimmy grabbed her face with his hand. 'I watched my partner's head explode. I got bits of his brain in my eyes and teeth. I tasted his death in my mouth. You think you can handle that? You think you can come out here every day knowing what death tastes like?'

Her throat filled with sand. He was almost on top of her. Her face was covered in his spittle. His fingers dug into her cheeks.

'Can you?' he demanded.

From somewhere deep inside, she found the courage to ask, 'Can you?'

Jimmy wrenched away his hand. 'You got no fuckin' idea what you're talkin' about.'

Kate touched her face. She could still feel his fingers digging into the flesh. 'What is this?' she whispered. 'What happened?' She wasn't talking to Jimmy. She was asking these questions of herself. 'What gives you the right to talk to me like this – to treat me like this – just because you don't want me here?'

Jimmy shook his head like she was the stupidest person on earth.

Kate pushed open the door. She got out of the car.

'Where are you going?'

Kate started walking. The smell wasn't so bad. She could deal with it. The capitol dome would guide her back to police headquarters. She had a spare key in a magnetic box over the back tire of her car. She would drive to the hotel, get her things, and then go to her parents' house. There was nothing her family could say that would be worse than what she had just experienced.

Jimmy got out of the car. 'Where the hell are you going?'

Kate took off the hat. She unbuttoned her shirt collar. The temperature was just under forty degrees, but she was burning up. She breathed through her mouth, pulling great gulps of filthy air into her lungs. Jimmy was right. The awful women in the locker room were right. Her mother was right.

She wasn't cut out for this.

'Hey.' Jimmy grabbed her arm. She shook him off. He grabbed her again and spun her around. 'Just stop a minute, okay?'

She punched him in chest. He wasn't expecting it. He stumbled back on his bad leg. Kate knew exactly what to do next. It came to her like breathing: she kicked his leg out from under him.

Jimmy looked stunned. He slammed flat on his back into the ground. The air huffed out of him. Dirt clouded up.

'You asshole!' Kate wanted to kick his head in. 'I *had* a house. I *had* a husband. I had a *life* before all this, you fucking animal.'

He tried to sit up.

She shoved him back down.

'What the hell is—'

'Shut up.' Kate leaned down to get in his face the same as he'd done with her. 'If my husband were alive, he would kill you. Do you know that? He would wrap his hands around your neck and strangle the miserable life out of you.'

Jimmy stared at her, his eyes wide with surprise. He didn't have a comeback, couldn't seem to find the words to cut her with, so he just shrugged, as if to say, *So what?*

It pulled the rage out of her. It brought her back to her senses.

Kate saw that an audience had gathered. Men, women, and children. They'd probably never seen such a show. She had certainly never been a part of one. Kate had never hit anyone in her life. Even at the academy, they'd only let them punch padded dummies.

So what?

Jimmy was right. Patrick wasn't going to save her. No one was going to save her. Wasn't the point of this idiotic experiment to prove that Kate could save herself?

Why had she remained silent when Romeo first leaned into the car? Why hadn't she told Jimmy to stop? Why hadn't she *asked, told,* then *made* them stop? Kate had an arsenal at her disposal – her back had been aching from her belt the moment she'd loaded it: The heavy flashlight with its four D-cell batteries. The metal nightstick with the rounded tip. The revolver with five bullets in the cylinder.

Any one of them could've been used to stop either man, and Kate had just sat there like a helpless simpleton.

Jimmy sat up. He brushed the red clay from his pants. 'What happened to your husband?'

She looked down at him. He was kneading his thigh to work out a cramp. 'None of your goddamn business.'

'You got a mouth on you, lady.'

'Shut up.' She turned on her heel and headed toward the car.

Jimmy asked, 'Where are you going?'

'Back to work.'

'That's it?' He laughed at her again, this time with surprise. 'After all that, you're just going back to work?'

She turned around. He was still on the ground rubbing his knee. 'Yes.'

He held out his hand. 'Help me up.'

'Help yourself, motherfucker.'

The crowd of spectators cleared a path as Kate walked to the car.

8

Fox felt that tickle in his throat that came from smoking too much. He took a swig of bourbon from the pint he kept in the glove box. Just enough to wet his whistle, as his father used to say.

He hated that his father was on his mind so much lately.

But it wasn't his father, really. It was his mother. The two were indelibly linked, the yin and yang of Fox's life. Black and white. Dark and light. She had been a kind woman. Always forgiving. Always looking to keep the peace. That these qualities had made her a victim was a fact that Fox had a hard time accepting, even all these years after her death.

He still missed her. When he was growing up in juvie, when he was stuck in the Army, when he was fighting in the jungle, when he was breathing or walking down the street, every day of his life, he missed her.

Maybe that was why Fox was drinking too much. Smoking too much. Watching Kate Murphy too much.

He had never killed a woman before. Sure, he had slapped around a couple when they got out of line. But he had never killed one. Fox didn't know what was making him hesitate. The evidence against Kate was clear. Fox had pages and pages in his clipboard. She was a liar. She was a charlatan. She didn't belong.

So why didn't he just shoot her?

Dragging it out was not Fox's style. Quick and painless, that was how he had always done it. He was an executioner, not a murderer.

How it usually worked was like this: The target presented itself. Fox studied it. He tracked it. He kept a detailed log on all the reasons why the target should be eliminated. Or not. Occasionally, after a few weeks of surveillance, he decided that the target should not be removed. There were redeeming qualities, extenuating circumstances. Of course, sometimes the information yielded a definitive yes. In those cases, Fox acted quickly. He studied his clipboard. He picked the right place and time. He shot the target in the head. No muss. No fuss. That's how it was with rabid animals. You had to take them out fast before they infected other people.

Kate Murphy was not an extenuating circumstance. She embodied the rabid animal. She was the cancer that needed to be cut out. Somewhere deep in her soul, she probably knew this. That was the way most of them were. By the time Fox came around to take care of business, they had already accepted what was coming.

So why wasn't Fox acting?

There was no point in continuing his surveillance, because he already knew when Kate was with her family, when she was alone, when she was at her most vulnerable. He should put her down just like the others and move on to the next targets.

But Fox couldn't.

He could only drink too much and smoke too much

and drive around too much and make too many notes on his clipboard.

Gluttony, Fox the Senior would've called it, using that tone of voice that indicated Fox was a piece of shit that had gummed into the treads of his shoe.

Fox hoped it was gluttony, because the alternatives would've pissed off Senior even more. Greed. Sloth. Wrath. Envy. Pride. Lust.

Lust.

Fuck yes, he lusted for Kate Murphy. Every man who laid eyes on her did. One more reason she didn't belong on the city's payroll. On the streets. In the grocery store. Anywhere an unsuspecting man of good character might see her.

Unfortunately, being lusted after was not a redeeming quality. If anything, it made Kate even more irredeemable. How could Fox in good conscience leave her out in the world where she could do more harm? Just entertaining the thought showed an unprecedented lack of discipline.

And like that, there was Fox's father back in his head again.

Senior was the kind of man who valued discipline. Or at least he claimed to. Every lesson he gave Fox had something to do with self-control, doing the right thing. He never talked about how hard it was to stop somebody else from doing the wrong thing.

Lesson one: Do as I say, not as I do.

Senior was a Navy man. Four years was all he lasted. He had gone to college. Another four years down the drain. He had gotten married and fathered a son and lucked into a job at the factory, which took him into what was left of his miserable life.

Senior insisted that he had done everything that a man was supposed to do. Was it his fault that wasn't good enough anymore? There was nothing wrong with Senior. Hell no. It was the system. It was the machines. It was the pushy broads. It was the uppity blacks. It was the lying Jews. It was the greasy Italians. It was the world turning upside down so that nobody really knew their place anymore.

The factory job was beneath Senior. He made that clear to Fox. He made it clear to Fox's mother when she was beneath him, too. He was a better man than this. All of this. The walls were thin. Fox heard them at night: the way Senior took out his disappointment. The way his mother begged for mercy.

Fox begged for mercy, too.

Not for himself. For his mother. For Senior, too, because why was it that all the lessons Senior was trying to teach Fox disappeared the minute the bedroom door was closed?

Lesson two: Never hit a girl.

Fox was twelve years old, just a kid, the first time he realized what was really going on in the next room. He felt powerless. He tightened his fists. He tensed his muscles. He thought about jumping out of bed and saving his mother. Like Superman. Like Spider-Man. Like any man worth his salt.

Lesson three: It's a man's job to protect the weaker sex.

That same year, the old man took him to see a dentist. Too much money, but the teeth were literally rotting in Fox's head. The office building was the tallest Fox had ever seen. Six stories of concrete and glass. Floor-to-ceiling windows that sparkled against the sun like diamonds.

110

Fox had never been in an elevator before. He stood at the back of the car with Senior. A woman got on. She was made up to be pretty, not pretty in a natural way. Her perfume smelled like too much candy. She was wearing a furry white coat. Fox remembered the way his nose tickled from just thinking about how soft the coat might be, because you would want to put your face in something like that – the coat, not the woman. Okay, maybe the woman, but Fox was at the age when those kinds of thoughts made him nervous.

The bell dinged. The elevator doors opened. Fox started to leave, but Senior grabbed him by the collar. Fox croaked like a frog. Senior smiled at the lady in the white coat. Fox was of the opinion that there was more to the smile. Not flirting, because his father didn't punch above his weight, but a sort of 'Please excuse my son's ignorance,' because Fox still had a lot to learn.

Lesson four: Ladies always go first.

Fox was recording everything on his clipboard by then. Not Lessons, but Facts. The date and time to begin with. Then the number of blows at night. The number of apologies during the day. The way his mother struggled to muffle her screams. The way his father pushed her to let them out. The way Fox used to press his face to her stomach when she hugged him, and he'd smell washing detergent on her dress and sometimes onions if she was in the middle of making dinner.

Fox took another sip from the bottle. The familiar anger scratched at his chest, begging to be let out.

His mother had died exactly one month before his thirteenth birthday.

There were times before she died when she was happy.

Fox didn't have actual pictures of these moments, but his memories were photographic. His eyelids were like a slide carousel. He could blink and see images of her doing the things that brought her pleasure. Baking cookies. Letting Fox lick the batter off the spoon when she made a cake. Ironing Senior's shirts.

She had actually smiled when she ironed Senior's clothes.

And she had stood up to him. Fox didn't know where she'd found the strength. Like every bully, Senior only had to be backed down once. He raised his hand to correct her, and she gave him this wilting look that sent his hand back down to his side. His bullying days were over. Yet again, the world had turned upside down. Fox's mother forgot her place. Or maybe she remembered it. Maybe for her, the world was finally right side up again. Life had dragged her back by the collar the same way Senior had grabbed Fox in that elevator.

Please excuse my wife's ignorance. She's still learning.

Why was Fox thinking about this now? Why was he sitting in his car drinking and thinking about the way his mother had finally found her ability to fight back?

Because of Kate Murphy.

Kate was the answer to a lot of his questions lately. He was watching her too much. Thinking too much. Letting his mind consider the options too much.

Like his mother, Kate was a fighter. She had knocked Jimmy Lawson to the ground right in the middle of the goddamn projects. Fox had laughed when it happened. He had known from the beginning that Kate was different.

He hadn't expected to like it.

9

Maggie drove past Mellow Mushroom pizza on Spring Street. Her stomach grumbled, but she saw the cops eating inside and decided to go somewhere else. She could always skip lunch and grab a coffee from one of the diners. Or she could keep taking mindless calls for the rest of the day while the boys ran up and down the city bashing in heads.

The radio had been buzzing all morning with hot tips that turned out to be nothing. Even the black officers were in on it, urgently sending units across town only to find out the guy who was going to talk wasn't talking anymore or was lying about what he'd said in the first place.

This latter situation didn't cause the problems you'd think. One of the things that had disheartened Maggie the most about being a police officer was the constant lies that people told; not the bad guys, but the regular citizens who were supposed to be helpful. They gave false names, false jobs. They lied about where they worked, what car they drove, where they lived. That they did all of this for absolutely no reason was as maddening as it was alarming. These were the same eyewitnesses who put men in jail every day.

Eyewitnesses like Jimmy.

The report Terry had read during roll call this morning was a load of bull. Maggie had nearly bitten off her tongue trying to keep quiet. Fifteen feet away? As in, Officer Jimmy Lawson was standing ten, fifteen feet away when Officer Don Wesley was shot in the head?

Maggie had seen the dried blood on her brother. The only way Jimmy could've been sprayed like that standing ten or fifteen feet away was if Don had been shot with a bazooka. Jimmy was either lying to save face or lying for the sake of lying. And he was going to get away with it because no one on the force – especially Terry – wanted to hear that their darling golden boy had screwed up.

Golden Boy.

The sports reporters had called Jimmy Lawson Atlanta's Golden Boy. He was still in junior high then, but Friday night football games were the most important entertainment in town. At the beginning of the season, there was always a pullout section in *The Atlanta Journal* that highlighted all the up-and-coming players around the state. Jimmy's picture had been on the front page. Maggie still had the article somewhere. Probably in the scrapbook she'd kept on him since his first game.

Maggie heard the sharp blast of a siren. She waved, recognizing Rick Anderson and Jake Coffee as they passed her on the opposite side of the street. She'd seen them twice today, which wasn't unusual, as their beats overlapped. What made their presence noteworthy was that none of the guys were sticking to their beats today. They were barely sticking to their zones.

Contrary to Cal Vick's warning about cowboys, they'd all declared open season on the population. Maggie had stopped counting the radio requests for paddy wagons when the number reached ten. There probably wasn't a black man in Atlanta who wouldn't be fingerprinted by the end of the day. The mayor would be wise to stay in his office.

'Hello,' Maggie mumbled to herself. She tapped the brakes, slowing the car.

There was a suspicious-looking man walking down the street. Young, white, clean-cut. None of the things that belonged in this neighborhood.

He was wearing a long coat that was meant for a taller man. The hem hit just above his brown loafers, showing spindly ankles with no socks. His hands were tucked deep into the pockets. His shoulders were stooped. Maggie couldn't pinpoint it, but there was something about the way he was walking that didn't sit right. She slowed the car to a crawl, trailing behind him like she could sneak up on the guy in a twenty-five-hundred-pound police car.

The man didn't turn around. He didn't run. He didn't pick up his pace. His hands stayed fisted in his coat pockets, but that could be because of the wind. Or because he had something in one of his hands. A gun? Not this kid. Maybe a bag of weed or an eight ball.

Maggie whooped the siren. He didn't jump, which irritated her because it meant that he knew she was there, and if he knew she was there, he should've turned around.

And he sure as hell should not have kept walking.

She punched the gas and pulled a few yards ahead of him. By the time Maggie got out of the car, the guy already had an annoyed look on his face, like he had every reason to be in the street wearing a raincoat he'd probably stolen off a homeless man.

Maggie blocked his path. Up close, she changed her estimation. Not so clean-cut. Not so innocuous. She snapped open her holster. She rested her hand on her revolver. 'Did you see me behind you? Did you hear the siren?'

'I assumed you were—'

'Shut up and listen to me.' That got his attention. His jaw tightened. He gave her a hostile look. Maggie said, 'Very slowly, I want you to use only the tips of your fingers to pull your pockets inside out.'

He moved quickly. She pulled her revolver, cocked the hammer.

He gave her a weak smile. 'Really, Officer, this is a misunderstanding.'

Just the sound of his voice sent up all kinds of flags. He might have been unshaven, but his accent shouted rich white Yankee. 'Yeah. You misunderstand who's in charge here. Pockets. Slowly.'

He used the tips of his fingers to pull out the pockets. A used Kleenex fell to the ground. A penny. Loose tobacco. His hands were empty. He was probably a little younger than Maggie. His hair was trimmed well above the collar, sideburns short. The peach fuzz on his chin made his round face look younger.

She asked, 'You got any ID on you?'

He shook his head. His eyes looked down, but there was nothing meek about him.

'What's your name?'

'Harry Angstrom.'

'You think I've never read John Updike?' He started to respond, but she stopped him before he could lie again. 'Let's call you London Fog, all right?'

He glanced up, then quickly looked down again. She thought that he was looking at his feet. He was actually looking at her gun.

She said, 'Why don't you unbutton your coat for me, London Fog?'

'I don't—'

'Unbutton your coat.'

'Lady, you don't want me to—'

She used her cop voice. 'Unbutton your coat *now*.'

He took his time, starting at the top. The coat was shabby, definitely not the kind of thing this kid would have hanging in his closet. When the third button opened, she saw his hairless white belly.

'Stop.' She had definitely seen enough. 'Where are your clothes?'

He didn't answer, just kept looking down at her gun.

She slid her revolver back into the holster. Her hand rested on the grip. 'You're a student at Georgia Tech.' He looked up, surprised, but it didn't take Perry Mason to notice that the university was just across the interstate. 'You came over here for some fun. You met a date. You drank too much, maybe smoked too much?'

He kept his expression neutral.

'She wanted to renegotiate the price? She robbed you?' Again, he didn't respond. 'She took your clothes so you would be too embarrassed to file a police report.' Maggie held out one hand like a magician. 'And here we are.'

He looked down at the ground again. She saw his tongue dart out between his teeth.

'You're lucky she didn't stick a knife in you, you know that? Or worse if her pimp had shown up.'

He kept staring down.

'Look at me.' She waited until he complied. 'You live on an island called Georgia Tech that's surrounded by a sea of ghettos. They didn't tell you that during orientation? You can't see where the grass stops and the dirt starts?'

There was a subtle shift in the way he was looking at her. Maggie got a weird tingle at the base of her spine. She'd obviously hit a nerve, which opened up a whole new side of this kid that she wasn't inclined to give a pass.

He was glaring at her like he wanted to strangle her.

She glared back like she wanted to shoot him.

The stalemate was broken when another siren whooped. Maggie waved away the cruiser. She assumed it was Rick and Jake seeing if she needed backup.

She was wrong.

Jimmy jumped out of his car the minute the wheels stopped turning. 'You need some help?'

'I got it.'

Jimmy kept coming.

Maggie made her voice low as she told London Fog, 'I know what you look like. I know where you go to school. I know where you live. Don't think you're getting away with something here.'

He opened his mouth to object, but she talked over him.

'I ever – ever – see you out here again, I'll haul you down to jail wearing exactly what you're wearing right now. You hear me?'

'Yes.'

Jimmy thumped the guy in the shoulder. 'Yes, ma'am, asshole.'

'Yes, ma'am.' He smiled at them both. 'Have a good day, Officers.'

The kid's tone was ice-cold. Jimmy shoved him hard. 'Get outta here, shithead.'

The kid didn't argue. He started down the street. Maggie felt her bad feeling get worse. London Fog wasn't running away. He'd returned to his previous leisurely pace. His hands went into his pockets. He didn't look back.

The worst thing you could do in front of a cop was show that you weren't afraid of them.

Jimmy said, 'What are you doing letting that asshole go?'

'You're the one who—'

'You've got your gun cocked in your holster. That's your gut telling you to take this guy in. Why didn't you listen to it?'

Maggie uncocked the hammer on her revolver. She snapped the safety strap closed. 'What am I gonna arrest him for, being naked under his clothes?' She looked at the cruiser. The new girl was sitting in the passenger seat. 'She didn't quit yet?'

He shrugged off the question, giving Maggie an expectant look. 'She's not so bad.'

'No,' she told him, because she knew how Jimmy's brain worked. 'I'm not gonna take her.'

'I need to follow up on some leads.'

'You can do that with her sitting in the car just like I'm sure you've been doing all morning.'

'No,' he insisted. 'I can't.'

'You heard Cal and Terry this morning. Nobody's supposed to ride alone today.'

'You're alone.'

'Because I don't matter.' She pointed out the obvious. 'Jimmy, you barely escaped with your life last night.'

'I'm fine.' He flattened his hand to his leg.

'You're limping worse than I've seen in years.' She looked down at his hand. He was trying to hide the dark spot just below his pocket. 'Are your pants wet?' She leaned down. 'Is that blood?'

Jimmy pushed her away. 'Dammit, Maggie. For once in your life just do what I fucking tell you.' He waved for Kate to get out of the car.

'I said no.'

'I didn't know that word was in your vocabulary.'

Maggie felt her nostrils flare. This was the third time today that somebody had thrown that in her face. 'You shut up.'

'Or what?'

Kate was a few feet away. She wouldn't look at either of them. 'I'll wait in the car.'

'*Her* car,' Jimmy ordered.

Maggie waited until Kate had closed the door. She told her brother, 'You're an asshole. You know that?'

'So I've heard.' Jimmy rubbed his jaw. His fingertips brushed his sideburn. She thought about the piece of Don Wesley that their mother had found on his face this morning.

She asked, 'What happened to your radio?'

'It's right here.' He pointed to his back. The transmitter was so new it practically gleamed.

'I mean your radio from last night.'

There was a flash of alarm in Jimmy's eyes.

'You didn't call it in when Don got shot.'

120

His left shoulder went up in a shrug.

'You lied in your report. You weren't standing any feet away. You were right beside Don when he got hit. Inches, not feet.'

Jimmy's face drained of color like water from a can of greens.

Maggie stepped closer, crowding his space. 'You got splattered with his blood. I saw it, Jimmy.'

'Stop being dramatic.'

'It was all over you.'

'And?'

'You jumped for cover, but you didn't shoot back.' Maggie should've stopped, but she kept going. 'I checked your gun this morning. You never fired it.'

'You checked up on me?'

'You lied about what happened because you didn't wanna admit that you froze, which makes you a coward who let a cop killer get away.'

She waited for Jimmy's anger to erupt. It didn't. Instead of yelling at her or sticking his finger in her face, or pushing her to the ground, he just nodded.

Or almost nodded.

He gave a small movement of his head, a barely perceptible acknowledgment that what she was saying was the truth.

Maggie was speechless. Knowing Jimmy had screwed up and seeing him admit it were two different things. She couldn't think what to say.

Jimmy looked out over the interstate. 'He's still dead.' His voice went up a few octaves higher than usual. 'No matter what happened, what I did or didn't do, he's still dead, and the guy who murdered him is still out there.'

She stared at her brother. For once, he looked back at her.

This time, it was Maggie who looked away.

He said, 'You need to listen to your gut.'

'I don't need—' She figured out a second too late that he was offering advice, not criticizing. Still, she was a Lawson same as he was. 'I don't need you telling me what to do.'

'I know, kid.' Jimmy chucked her on the chin, then limped back to his car.

10

Maggie felt numb as she drove around the city. She couldn't seem to right herself. All morning she'd been spinning like a top over Jimmy. He was a liar. He was a bad cop, a bad partner. He'd crapped out under fire. He'd let Don die. Her mind had run through all kinds of horrible accusations.

Now that Jimmy had basically agreed with her, she didn't know what to do with her anger. The worst part was that Maggie had really hurt him. Not that she hadn't set out to do that very thing in the first place, but Maggie and Jimmy had an unspoken agreement that they would only inflict surface wounds. Death by a Thousand Cuts was the motto under the Lawson family crest. What she'd done to Jimmy in the street had violated that code. She'd gone too far, cut too deep.

And Kate Murphy had witnessed the whole thing. How she felt about the exchange was a mystery. The new girl hadn't said a word since Maggie had gotten into the car. She had just sat there thumbing through the pages in her notebook like she was cramming for a test. She would probably go back to the station tonight and tell everybody she'd heard Maggie curse her brother in the middle of the street. For once, Jimmy had been the quiet one. Cop 101: When someone is screaming at you, keep your tone low and reasonable.

He'd sandbagged her.

Maggie slowed for a stoplight. The dry cleaner was just around the corner. She looked at her watch. It was close to noon. She'd used the bathroom at a chicken restaurant before the run-in with Jimmy, but she asked Kate, 'You gotta pee?'

'Yes.'

She'd answered so quickly that Maggie guessed she'd had to go for a while. 'Jimmy wouldn't stop so you could go?'

'I didn't presume to ask him.'

Maggie bristled at her clipped tone. She glanced over. Everything about this new girl set her on edge. She didn't have a hair out of place. Her posture was perfect. She had her legs neatly crossed. She kept her radio transmitter in her lap like a diamond-encrusted clutch.

Maggie said, 'You think you can hold it until the shift's over? That's only another five and a half hours.'

'Absolutely.'

'Tough gal.' As soon as the words were out, Maggie wanted to scour her mouth with lye. She sounded just like her uncle Terry. If there was anything she feared about this job, it wasn't the hardness or the lack of dating prospects – it was looking into the mirror one day and seeing her uncle Terry staring back.

Maggie said, 'I'm sorry.'

'About what?'

She didn't know what to say. The point of being silently judgmental was that it was silent.

Maggie turned into the dry cleaner's parking lot. 'An

Italian guy owns this place. It has the cleanest bathroom – maybe the only clean bathroom – within twenty blocks. The next closest is a place called Ollie's. Owned by an old Pollock. It's a bar, so don't go in after five if you're alone. There's a chicken joint in the other direction. Not the best, but it'll do in a pinch.' Maggie put the gear in park. 'I'll show you when we're out again.'

'Thank you.' Kate bolted from the car.

Maggie watched her trot toward the building at a fast clip. The new girl was harder to read after three hours on the streets. Three hours with Jimmy. Maggie wondered how long it would take before the two were going out. Kate was an attractive woman. Jimmy was a handsome man. You didn't need Barbara Cartland to write that story.

Maggie clicked the mic on her radio. She called an out-of-service and gave their location. Long after dispatch had given her the okay, Maggie sat in the car thinking about what Gail had said this morning. Jimmy hadn't called in the shooting. Dispatch had heard about it from a doctor at Grady Hospital. Even if Jimmy had been in a full-on panic, there had to come a time when he snapped out of it and realized he had to do something. He'd carried Don Wesley all the way to the hospital. Why hadn't he taken two seconds to call it in? Somebody could have met him halfway. Even for a stubborn ass like Jimmy, it didn't make sense that he hadn't called for help.

Unless you took into account the fact that he'd lost his radio.

Maggie pushed open the car door. She was thinking herself into circles again. And the bigger question about whether or not to meet Gail at the restaurant was still hanging out there.

She scanned her surroundings as she walked toward the building, her head going back and forth like the glass on a copy machine. She checked the entire front section of the dry cleaner's. The floor-to-ceiling plate glass wasn't for show – it was for safety. She drove by here at least twice a day in her cruiser and could see everything going on inside without having to stop.

The bell over the door rang. Warm, wet air enveloped her as she entered the building.

'Officer Lawson.' Mr. Salmeri flashed some teeth under his pushbroom of a mustache. 'I take it the other lady was with you?'

'Yeah.' Maggie looked around. Kate had already disappeared into the back. She was probably suffering from uremic poisoning. She'd have to wait another two minutes. Even with practice, that was about how long it took to remove your equipment, your belt, your other belt, your pants, pantyhose, and, unless you'd already started peeing yourself, your underwear.

Salmeri offered, 'I'm sorry for your loss. Officer Wesley was a stand-up guy.'

'Don was a customer?'

'No one can beat our police discount.'

'You're very generous,' Maggie said, because she knew Salmeri laundered uniforms for half the force. She also knew that no money ever changed hands.

'I've got some of Officer Wesley's things.' He pressed the button on the rack of clothes and sent them spinning around. 'He was just in here last week.'

'You don't have to—'

'Here we go.' The spinner stopped. Salmeri lifted a bunch of clothes, all still in their plastic bags. Don's uniform. A couple pairs of bell-bottomed pants. A bright blue button-down shirt, the pointed collars nearly touching the embroidered breast pockets.

'That's flashy.' Kate came out of the back struggling with her belt, trying to fasten it back around her hips. 'Is it Jimmy's?'

Maggie laughed at the suggestion. 'Jimmy's wardrobe is black or navy, unless it's summer, then it's gray or navy.' She looked at Salmeri. 'You sure these are Don's?'

Salmeri laid the clothes flat on the counter. He pulled up the bag, then checked the paper tag pinned to the inside collar. 'Wesley,' he showed her. 'He was a sharp dresser. Brought a lot of interesting clothes in here.'

Maggie looked at the other clothes hanging on the spinning rack. Don's weren't the only flashy duds. 'Mr. Salmeri, I don't want to put you on the spot, but you see a lot of people in here. Not just cops and businessmen.'

He nodded. 'This is true.'

'Maybe you see people who make their living in nontra-ditional ways?'

He smiled. 'I'm Italian, sweetheart. You can talk to me about pimps.'

Maggie smiled back. 'I want you to know if you heard something, you could tell me. I could send it up the line. No one would have to know where it came from. I would protect you. And there's a reward, so . . .'

Salmeri was still smiling. He put both his hands over hers. 'You know, sweetheart, I see your car outside my window two, three times a day. You come in here and smile with your pretty face, and it lights up the whole joint. And yet I am always thinking to myself, "Why doesn't that girl let me do her dry cleaning?"' He stopped her from answering. 'I figure it's because you don't think it's right.'

Maggie wasn't going to pick sides. 'I do all the laundry at my house. I know it's not easy. And it sucks even more when you know you're doing it for free.'

He laughed, but still said, 'It never hurts to have a police officer for a friend.'

'You don't have to buy me, Mr. Salmeri. I'm just doing my job.' Maggie was aware that Kate was watching her intently. 'We should get back to work. Think about what I said.'

'Hold up.' Salmeri pulled out a cigar box from under the counter. He opened the lid. There were lots of small plastic baggies inside, the kind that dealers used for drugs. Apparently, Salmeri used them to hold items he'd found in people's pockets.

'Here.' He handed Maggie a clear bag with the name *Wesley* scrawled across the front. Inside were two quarters, a dime, and a black matchbook with four matches left.

'Dabbler's,' Maggie read off the matchbook cover. The script had a swoosh under it like the old Atlanta Braves logo. No phone number. No address. She asked Salmeri, 'You ever heard of the place?'

'Sorry. Never heard of it or seen a matchbook from there before.'

'Do you have a Yellow Pages I can look at?'

He pulled a thick phone book off the shelf behind the counter. 'Just came last month.'

Maggie thumbed to the *D*'s. She traced her finger down the lines. No Dabbler's was listed. She would have to ask around to see if anybody knew the place. Businesses popped up all the time around the city, and the only way you could get their address was through an official request to the phone company or by running into someone who happened to know.

'Sorry.' Salmeri had been watching her intently. 'Maybe they're new?'

'Maybe.' Maggie closed the phone book. 'Thank you.'

'I'll keep an ear out for you,' he offered. 'You're right. People say things around me. Maybe I can make some discreet inquiries.'

'Very discreet,' she told him. 'Don't get yourself into trouble.'

He put his hand under the counter. Maggie knew he kept a shotgun there. 'Did I mention I'm Italian?'

She took the matchbook and left the coins. 'I'll wave the next time I drive by.'

He gave a formal nod of his head.

Maggie looked at the matchbook as she walked out the door. There were no indentations where someone had scribbled a phone number or written a name. She could ask Jimmy about the bar, but then he would want to know why she was asking. Going through formal channels to the phone company would alert Terry. She knew one person who worked for Southern Bell. Whether or not she could reach out to him was another matter.

Kate said, 'I thought you told me everything was free.' She was still fidgeting with her belt as she trailed Maggie outside the building. It was a puzzle she had forgotten how to put back together.

'It can be. Up to you whether or not you take it.' Maggie spun her key ring around her middle finger, catching the keys and letting them go. She did this three more times before saying, 'Your clips are upside down.'

Kate groaned as she switched them right side up. 'Thank you.'

'When you go to the toilet, leave your Kel and your baton in the sink – never your gun. Lift the belt off the metal clips. Put the clips in your pocket – same pocket every time. Pull your shoulder mic plug out of your transmitter jack. Hold the plug between your teeth so it doesn't drop into the toilet. Undo your belt, then take it into the stall with you and hang it on the hook on the back of the door, or if there isn't a hook, put it on the back of the toilet.'

All she asked was, 'Kel?'

'Kel-Lite. Baton.' Maggie tapped her flashlight, then her nightstick. 'Did you make sure your gun was secure before you took off your belt?'

'Secure?'

'Stop repeating everything I say.' Maggie pulled the revolver out of Kate's holster. The hammer was flat against the firing pin. She showed it to the woman. 'You know how this works, right?' She pulled back the hammer with her thumb. 'You have to cock it if you want to fire a bullet.'

'Right.' Kate sounded like she'd heard this before, but it was just coming back to her. 'During training—'

'You were told not to shoot the guys in the red tie.' The joke was older than Maggie. Chip and Duke used to make it. She guessed Bud Deacon had taken up the reins now that Duke was gone. 'Just remember: PCP. Pull, cock, point.'

Kate got a funny grin on her face. Maggie had never caught the innuendo before.

'It's not so funny when the other guy manages to shoot

you first.' Maggie showed her how to do it, pulling the revolver, cocking the hammer, pointing the muzzle out in front of her. 'It really should be SPCP, but nobody snaps their safety strap.'

'You do.'

'Because I don't want my gun falling out if I have to chase somebody.' She indicated Kate's holster. 'Try it, but point toward the ground. And not at me.'

Kate's lips moved as she checked off each step. The gestures were slow and jerky, more like the robot from *Lost in Space*.

Maggie tried to keep the irritation out of her voice. 'Go home tonight. Take all the bullets out. You know how to do that, right?'

Kate nodded.

'Make sure the cylinder is empty, then practice pulling your gun. Cock the hammer with your thumb at the same time as you pull. That's why the cylinder needs to be empty, in case the gun goes off. Bullets go through walls and floors. They go up into the air and they come straight back down. This is the most important part: Never rest your finger on the trigger. Rest it to the side. That's called the trigger guard. Only touch the trigger when you're going to shoot.'

'The instructor showed us that.'

'So, you're ahead of the game.'

Kate laughed. The sound came deep from her belly. She started to reholster the weapon, then remembered to uncock the hammer. 'Any more advice?'

Maggie had a lot of it, but she wasn't sure she should waste her time on Kate Murphy. Wanda had called it this morning.

Irish Spring wasn't going to last the week.

131

11

Fox sat at the bar with his Southern Comfort and a half-empty bowl of peanuts. He stared at the smoked mirror behind the bottles of liquor. Fox wasn't a vain man. He was looking at the space behind him. The place was almost empty. It was a seedy bar like any seedy bar: dark interior, black vinyl on the booths, dark tiles on the floor, black walls that sucked in the faint glow of light from the neon liquor signs.

Not that the décor mattered. The patrons only came here for one thing.

A man in a business suit was sitting at a small table in the corner. He had the desolate look of a mid-level manager and an untouched shot of Jack in front of him. A homeless guy was a few tables over. He stared solemnly at the wall. In front of him was a bottle of rotgut and an oily-looking shotglass. His arm moved in two directions: up or down. Glass to mouth. Glass to table. Glass to mouth. Glass to table. The only variation came when the glass was empty, but he used his other hand to perform the task of refilling.

Just like Senior, only Senior would've had his hat on; his way of saying he was only stopping in for a drink when everybody in the joint knew he'd been there for hours.

The door opened. Sunlight scythed through the crack. Fox narrowed his eyes, but didn't look away.

Another guy in a suit. It was coming up on lunchtime. The place was going to fill up soon.

The new suit sat at the bar a few stools down from Fox. He lifted his chin in a nod.

Fox didn't return the gesture.

Instead, Fox pushed his glass toward the bartender. The guy was good at his job. He'd already figured out Fox wasn't a talker. The drink was poured, a new napkin was offered, and the bowl of peanuts was topped off without mention of the weather or sports or whatever bullshit small talk these guys excelled at.

Fox thought if he had to do a job like this, in a place like this, he might end up putting a bullet in his head.

There was a handgun under his jacket. Raven MP-25. Six-shooter, semiauto, pearl grip. A Saturday night special. He'd spent an hour this morning cleaning it, making sure it wouldn't jam again. He probably should've tossed the gun, but he'd always been sentimental. Even during the war, he had his talismans. Lucky socks. Lucky undershirt. Lucky gun.

That's where he'd gotten his nickname, during the war. Fox, as in 'crazy like a—' not Fox as in Foxy, which another grunt had been called. The women swooned over him until his face got burned off, and then they swooned for a completely different reason.

The door opened again. Fox blinked away the sunlight. Another guy in a suit. He joined the original suit at the bar, giving Fox the same nod.

Fox shook a cigarette out of his pack. He checked his pockets for his lighter.

The bartender placed a book of matches by Fox's glass as he talked to Suit the Second. 'What's up with this weather?'

Suit Two responded, but Fox gave not one shit about the weather.

He gripped the matchbook in his hand. Just looking at the suits, long sideburns and flared pants and slouched shoulders made his blood simmer. Fox had spent a lifetime distinguishing himself from his father, but he had to think that Senior would've shared his hatred of these new age pussies who made their money with their mouths instead of with their hands.

Not too long ago, this city had been filled with men who built things from the ground up. Factories churned day and night. Trains rushed up and down the tracks. Eighteen-wheelers roared toward all points on the compass. Now, every bit of cash that flowed through Atlanta came in on a wire. Foreigners clogged the sidewalks outside shiny new office buildings. Tiny cheap cars flooded the roads. Fox would sometimes look up at the skyscrapers, the new hotels, and wonder what the fuck was going on inside. How did these guys in two-hundred-dollar suits make so much money sitting behind a desk all day?

And why was it that men like Fox were expected to answer to them?

The world had turned upside down again. Nobody knew their place anymore.

Fox knew his place. He had a mission, which was all that mattered. It was his job to put the world back where

134

it belonged. If he didn't, there would be collateral damage. The last time Fox had slacked off, he'd found himself standing by his mother's grave watching her cheap pine coffin being lowered into the ground.

Never again.

Job number one: Kill Jimmy Lawson.

Two to the head, just like the other one. Then Fox could move on to the next target.

But which target?

Fox looked down at the matchbook. The curly logo reminded him of the curve of Kate's neck when she bent over to look at her notebook.

Fox couldn't think about Kate now.

But then he was.

Kate sitting in the squad car. Kate taking notes. Kate calling in a job on the radio.

Kate in his bed.

There it was, like a picture. Kate laid out on his white satin sheets. Her hair crazy wild. Her arms and legs splayed. Fox wouldn't know where her creamy white skin stopped and the sheet started. He wondered what she would smell like. Taste like. Feel like.

Because who would know? She was going to die anyway. What was the harm in getting a little pleasure out of her before she was gone? Fox knew Kate would be wanting it. An oversexed girl like that was probably used to all kinds of nasty things in bed. Fox would probably have to take her somewhere quiet so nobody would hear the filthy words that came out of her mouth.

Good thing Fox had already soundproofed a room in his basement.

Another sign of the plan taking shape. Last weekend,

Fox had no idea why he was soundproofing the room, but he trusted that thing that sat at the back of his brain and figured out options. Even as Fox laid the rows of batting and insulation, he could feel the plan working through the strands of his mind. Sure, part of him knew he was still going to kill Kate Murphy, but somewhere else, Fox was thinking there was no reason he couldn't have a little fun first.

It was true that he had never killed a woman before. Maybe there was a different way to do it. Maybe there was an option that got them both what they deserved. Sort of like bribing the executioner so he made a clean cut with his ax.

Lesson five: A man prepares for all contingencies.

Sunlight cracked through the open door. Two more suits entered the bar. They took the two stools between Fox and the other suits. They mentioned the weather again. It was agreed for the second time in as many minutes that it was getting colder every day. Talk turned to the game this weekend against Alabama.

Fox tuned it out, though he was interested in the game. One thing being a grunt taught you was to always keep your focus.

He wanted to look through his clipboard, to relive the last month of reconnaissance. But you couldn't take a thing like that into a bar. People would stare. Even in this kind of place. Fox didn't need it anyway. Today's details were fresh in his memory.

Capitol Homes. Techwood Homes. Bankhead Homes. Carver Street. Piedmont Avenue. Jimmy had taken Kate to almost every shithole in Atlanta.

But this bar was one shithole Kate could never see.

Fox was inside Jimmy's head now. He knew how a man like that would behave. Jimmy had gotten rid of Kate almost an hour ago. He had done this for a reason. He wanted to lick his wounds. Or to have somebody else lick them for him.

In some ways, Fox was glad. He wanted Jimmy away from Kate when his time came. She didn't need to see that side of Fox.

At least not until he was ready for her to see it.

12

Maggie stared aimlessly out the window as she drove the cruiser along Ponce de Leon. The city was already locking itself down. There were no girls on the streets. The pimps were probably whiling away their time in lockup or getting the crap beaten out of them behind the jail. She guessed London Fog was the most exciting thing that was going to happen to her today. So far, they'd given a warning to a jaywalker and broken up a fight over a sandwich.

Beside her, Kate shifted in her seat. She moved stiffly, trying to get comfortable. Maggie could've told her it was no use. There were no shortcuts. You just learned to live with the pain.

Despite her better judgment, Maggie offered some advice. 'You're gonna be bruised tonight. It'll look like some guy went at you. Hips, legs, back. It's all the equipment. Don't complain where anybody'll hear you.'

'Of course not.'

Maggie felt her eyes narrow. 'I'm trying to help you.'

'Gosh, I hope you know how much I appreciate it.'

Maggie ignored the haughty Buckhead tone. What did she expect, for Kate Murphy to fall to her knees and thank her? She tried to remember what it was like to ride with Gail Patterson that first day. Maggie had known enough to tailor her uniform ahead of time, but like Kate, her hat had been too big and her shoes were roomy enough to rent out space. When Maggie wasn't bored, she was terrified, and thanks to Gail's sharp tongue, even when she was bored she was still slightly terrified.

She asked Kate, 'You got any questions?'

Kate thought for a moment. 'What happened six months ago?'

Maggie knew what she meant, but she still asked, 'What?'

'During roll call, Captain Vick said we're not going to have a repeat of six months ago.'

'The Edward Spivey trial.'

'Oh, the man who was found innocent of killing that police officer.'

Maggie chewed the tip of her tongue. She replayed Kate's words, trying to analyze their meaning. No one she knew talked about Edward Spivey as an innocent man. No matter what the jury said, they all knew he was guilty.

Kate said, 'He almost went to the electric chair. I wonder what happened to him?'

'He lives in California.' Maggie forced her hands to loosen around the steering wheel. 'What else? What other questions?'

Kate had the wisdom to move on. She took out her spiral notebook. 'Where do I hand in my notes?'

'You type them up and hand them in to the watch commander's secretary within forty-eight hours of the end of your shift, sooner if something big happens.'

Maggie hadn't asked her about her morning with Jimmy. 'Did something big happen?'

Kate flipped through the pages. 'We visited Capitol Homes. We visited Techwood Homes. We visited Bankhead Homes. We spoke with an intoxicated gentleman on Carver Street. We visited an unnamed woman in an apartment off Piedmont Avenue.'

'That's where Don lives. Lived.'

'Oh. Well, she wanted to know if Jimmy had the keys to a Chevelle parked out front.'

'Classy.' Maggie took a left onto Monroe Drive. 'Did you get anything out of anybody?'

'I stayed in the car, but Jimmy didn't seem like he had much luck.' She closed the notebook. 'I failed typing in high school.'

'Most of us wouldn't be here if we'd passed.'

Silence filled the car. They had the volume down on their radios so that only the occasional staticky signal interrupted the sound of wind rushing in through the open windows.

Maggie said, 'You can get carbon paper from the supply officers. There's two typewriters on the top floor that we can use for reports, but there's always a line and the colored girls go first.'

'Why?'

'Ask the colored girls.' Maggie leaned her elbow on the open window. She wasn't sure why she kept talking to this woman when nothing she said would matter in a week's time. Still, she told Kate, 'It's easier to go to the library. You can rent time on a typewriter for ten cents an hour. It's cooler at the downtown branch. You still live in Buckhead?'

Kate seemed reluctant. 'The Barbizon Hotel off Peachtree.'

Maggie felt a stab of jealousy. Irish Spring was a regular Mary Tyler Moore. 'Not with your folks?'

She shook her head.

'How's your mother feel about you being a cop?'

'Concerned.'

Maggie laughed at the obvious understatement. 'She'll never forgive you. Stop waiting for it to happen.'

Kate turned her head toward the roadside. They were in a hippie section of town. The houses were painted every color of the rainbow.

Maggie asked, 'What's your father do?'

'He's a gardener.'

Finally, things were making sense. Kate had grown up in Buckhead, but she had to have a job just like the rest of them. 'He work on one of those big estates?'

'Yes. We lived over the garage.'

'Like Sabrina.' Maggie had always loved that movie. 'What'd you do before?'

'Secretarial work. I hated it.'

'What made you sign up for the job?'

'Stupidity?' Kate turned around the question. 'What about you? Why'd you sign up?'

'To piss off my family.' She figured she might as well go through the list. 'Charlaine joined because her husband's a drunk and she's got three kids to feed.' Maggie slowed the car for a stoplight. 'Wanda joined because she saw an article in the paper about female motorcycle cops.'

'Wanda Clack,' Kate clarified, like she was just putting together the names. 'I saw that article.'

'There were lots of articles,' Maggie said. 'Wanda

wanted to ride a Harley. They told her, "Sure thing, little lady. Sign on the dotted line." '

'I was given the impression that the motorcycle instructors don't train women.'

'Your impression was correct,' Maggie confirmed. 'She's handling chicken bones just like the rest of us. Only time she sees a bike is when some jackass hops on one to speed away from her.'

'What are chicken bones?'

'Pointless calls where you get there and it's just two idiots fighting over something stupid.'

'Like a sandwich,' Kate noted. So, at least she'd been paying attention.

They took a right at Ansley Mall onto Piedmont Road. Maggie waved to a couple of cops who were sitting in their cruiser eating a late lunch. They had at least five grown men jammed into the back seat. They were big guys. They had to turn sideways to fit.

Kate asked, 'Where are we going?'

'The Colonnade Restaurant.' Gail had told Maggie to meet her there if she was interested in following a lead. At this point in the day, Maggie was interested in following anything that made her feel like a cop instead of a babysitter.

'The Colonnade?' Kate repeated. 'Isn't that the place where mothers take their gay sons on Thanksgiving?'

Maggie had no idea what she was talking about. 'I don't think they allow gay people. Lots of cops eat there.'

Kate got that funny smile on her face again.

'We're not going to eat, anyway. I need to meet up with somebody.'

'A friend?'

'A PCO. Plain clothes officer. She's trying to track down the name of a pimp we can talk to.' Maggie accelerated to pass one of those funny-looking foreign cars. 'The place where Don was killed – Five Points – that's a main drag for hookers. Maybe one of them saw something. If she did, then we'll need to get permission from her pimp to talk to her, otherwise she won't give us the time of day.'

'So, we need to talk to the pimp before we can talk to the streetwalker who works for him.' Kate nodded slowly. 'Aren't we supposed to be looking for the weapon that was used in the crime? The Raven MP-25?'

'The boys will look for the gun.' Maggie didn't mention how much trouble they would be in if they crossed paths with the men who were working that side of the case.

Kate asked, 'PCO. Is that like a detective?'

Maggie was getting tired of all these questions. 'Only men are detectives.'

Kate must've caught her tone. She looked out the window and kept her mouth shut.

The scenery had changed from hippie hangouts to whorehouses. Piedmont was dotted with massage parlors, head shops, and stores that sold marital aids. Maggie felt a flash of trepidation about Kate meeting Gail. Not that Kate acted like she was better than everybody else. She just sounded like it. Hell, she looked like it, too. Her nails weren't bitten to the quick. Her hair was shiny and full. She'd probably picked up her rich accent going to school with all those Buckhead kids, but still, next to Kate Murphy, Gail would sound like she was trying to clear the swamp from her throat.

Then again, maybe Maggie's concern was misplaced.

Gail could light up with laughter, but you had to remember that the thunder was never far behind.

She warned Kate, 'Lookit, don't get clever with Gail. Don't ask her a lot of stupid questions. Actually, don't ask her any questions. She's got a temper you don't want to see.'

'Like the colored girls?'

'That's exactly what I'm talking about.'

'What?'

Maggie stared at her.

'Okay.' Kate let out an exasperated breath. 'Gail is the PCO we're meeting?'

'PCOs work in sex crimes. They pose as prostitutes.' Maggie turned onto Cheshire Bridge Road. The massage parlors gave way to strip clubs and pawnshops with peep booths. 'Gail catches all those suits who come down from Buckhead looking for strange.'

'Sounds exciting.'

'Beats chicken bones.'

'Indubitably.'

Maggie slowed to make the turn into the Colonnade Restaurant parking lot. There was a hotel in the back that rented rooms by the half hour. Gail was standing beside the front office smoking a cigarette. Her blonde wig was tilted to the side.

Maggie flashed her headlights.

Gail took one last hit from her cigarette before pushing away from the wall. She walked over on spindly high heels. Her eyeliner was smudged. She'd chewed off most of her lipstick. Maggie wanted her to look prettier, more sophisticated, but all she saw was someone who was being slowly beaten down by life.

Gail leaned down and rested her arms on Maggie's open window. The car filled with the odor of whiskey and cigarettes. 'Jesus Christ, mama.' She was looking at Kate. 'How'd you get through roll call without them boys eatin' you alive?'

Kate stared blankly at the other woman. Maggie could practically see her playing Gail's words back in her head, trying to cut through the South Georgia twang. She finally answered, 'Golly, I guess I'm just lucky.'

Fortunately, Gail missed the sarcasm. 'Shit. I had a face like that, I'd be married to Keith Richards and popping out a brat every year.' She winked at Maggie, then told Kate, 'Take off your hat, sweetheart. Lemme see is that blonde for real.'

Kate stiffened her shoulders.

'Suit yourself, China Doll. Not like I told you to drop your pants.' Gail turned her attention to Maggie. 'I got a girl says she might have some information if we can clear up an outstanding for a dime bag.' She nodded back to the hotel. 'She's turning a trick. Shouldn't be but another five minutes.'

'Great.' Maggie tried to talk while holding her breath at the same time. Gail wasn't just tipsy. She was downright drunk. Her words were slurring together. She obviously had to lean against the car to keep herself from falling over.

Still, no amount of liquor could dull Gail's perception. She studied Maggie. 'Whass goin' on?'

Maggie shook her head. 'You got an idea where this girl's gonna lead us?' With hookers, it was always better to know the possible answer before you asked the question.

Gail said, 'I got some ideas, but my dough's on a new one they're callin' Sir She.'

Kate barked a laugh.

Both Maggie and Gail looked at her.

'Sorry,' Kate apologized. 'It's funny. Circe?'

Maggie struggled to keep the grin off her face. Kate had obviously misheard the name. Or worse, she assumed Gail was too drunk or too stupid to know the difference.

Maggie decided Kate deserved some hazing. 'You should know this, Murphy. Black pimps use names from Greek mythology. Whites use Roman gods.'

Kate practically guffawed. 'Are you serious?'

'Hell yes, she's serious.' Gail snapped her fingers. 'Why ain't you writing this down, gal?'

Kate took out her notebook. She shook her head as she wrote.

Gail said, 'Jesus Christ. Girl ain't learned a thing. You even go to them classes at the academy?' She opened the car door so Maggie could get out. She didn't bother to lower her voice. 'What the fuck is she talking about?'

Maggie couldn't answer without cracking up. She motioned Gail to follow her away from the car. 'Was I ever that green?'

'You were born wearing a badge and don't you forget it.' Gail put her hand on Maggie's arm to steady herself. 'Lissen, this whore we're gonna talk to, she ain't exactly reliable.'

'Are they ever?'

Gail coughed. Her lungs sounded wet. 'Problem is, she just about fucking hates me. I can't blame her. I've been bustin' her balls pretty hard lately.'

Maggie wondered if Gail was talking literal or figurative. 'Why?'

''Cause she knows better'n sitting around all day sucking cock and shooting speed.'

'Speed?' Maggie didn't like the sound of that. Speed freaks could cause a lot of damage. 'She been using today?'

'We'll get her settled down.' Gail rifled her bag, probably looking for a cigarette. 'I'm just sayin' it might take some prying.'

Maggie remembered how Gail pried. Usually, a nightstick was involved.

'Shit, I'm outta cigs.' Gail looked up from her bag. 'You really should start smoking.'

'You make it look so glamorous.'

'I didn't love you so much, I'd pop you one for that.' Gail grabbed Maggie's arm. She had almost lost her balance. 'You know, even if we get a solid name outta this slut, you're gonna need to talk to the colored girls about getting permission to work in Coon Town.'

Maggie ignored how quickly this whole thing had fallen onto her shoulders. 'I'll get it from them.'

'Good girl. We'll take my car. You shouldn't be driving your cruiser in CT anyway.'

She had a point. CT was what everyone called Colored Town. The area wasn't exactly welcoming to white officers. Even the blacks were nervous about taking calls there after dark.

Gail said, 'If China Doll's still around, this'll be a good lesson for her.'

Maggie didn't want to think about what kind of lesson Gail had in mind. 'You ever hear of a bar named Dabbler's?'

Gail reared back in horror. 'How the hell do you know about Dabbler's?'

'I'm a cop. I know about everything.'

Gail shook her head, recognizing her own line.

'You know where it is?'

'Hell no, I don't know where it is. And don't you try to find out, you hear?' She nodded toward Kate. 'Especially with China Doll over there. They'll peel the flesh right off her.'

'Don ever mention it?'

'Of course he didn't. What the fuck is wrong with you?' She looked disgusted by the thought. 'This is taking too long. I'm gonna get some smokes from the restaurant, then go knock on the door.'

Maggie started to follow, but Gail waved her off.

'Just keep an eye out.'

Maggie leaned against the car. She watched Gail walk toward the Colonnade. Maybe Don had gotten the matchbook off a suspect. Considering Gail's reaction to the place, that made sense. Cops were always taking things off suspects. Maggie had yet to walk onto a murder scene where some homicide detective wasn't going through the victim's wallet looking for cash.

Her bigger concern was Gail's drinking. She was always a little lit, but this was different. She'd never been sloppy on the job before. Maybe there had been more to her relationship with Don Wesley than she was letting on.

Kate's door opened and slammed shut. She still had her notebook out. 'She's lovely.'

Maggie said nothing.

'Maybe she'll let me buy her a drink.'

Maggie ignored that, too. She watched Gail inside the

restaurant. She was banging her fist against the cigarette machine.

Kate said, 'Can I ask you something serious?'

'I guess it's possible.'

Kate took the remark in stride. 'You already have this Circe's name. Why do you need to trouble a prostitute for it?'

Maggie bit her bottom lip. She couldn't remember the last time she'd troubled a prostitute. 'Because everybody lies. What you do is ask a bunch of people the same question, and if they all give the same answer, or most of them give you the same answer, then it's probably as close to the truth as you're going to get. And since I'm in the mood to give you the benefit of my wisdom, you need to go easy on Gail.'

'Because of her temper?'

'Because what you see when you look at her isn't who she is.' Maggie turned, making sure Kate was listening. 'That stuff they teach you at the academy, what you learn from the books – none of that matters out here. How you learn to be a cop is by watching other cops. Everything I know about the street came from Gail.'

'Such as?' Kate held up her pen and pad.

Maggie's mind went blank, but then she remembered, 'There are always exceptions, but pretty much it's like this: White people tend to kill white people. Black people kill black people. Black men rape black women. White men rape white women.'

Kate said, 'Therefore ... ?'

'*Therefore,* don't be scared going into bad places. You're probably in more danger in your own neighborhood.'

'That's comforting.'

'Golly, isn't it?' Maggie could do sarcasm, too. 'You could do worse than having Gail Patterson back you up.'

'I'm certain you're right.'

Maggie gave up. She had better things to do than kick Kate Murphy off her high horse.

Gail was walking across the parking lot to the hotel. She tapped a pack of cigarettes against the heel of her palm. Her trajectory wasn't that straight. Maggie wondered if she'd grabbed another drink in the restaurant.

Kate asked, 'What about the Shooter?'

'What's that?'

'The man who killed Don Wesley last night.' Kate clarified, 'Your brother said he was black, right? I'm assuming Don Wesley was white.'

Maggie walked to the front of the car. Gail had reached the hotel. 'Like I said, exceptions.'

Kate obviously wasn't satisfied by the answer. Still, she closed her notebook and joined Maggie. They both leaned against the hood of the car. It took a few seconds for Kate to get comfortable. Her hat kept slipping down to the bridge of her nose. She couldn't get her nightstick and Kel-Lite out of the way at the same time.

Maggie scanned the area, making sure Gail wasn't about to be ambushed. The hotel consisted of four two-story buildings with four rooms on each floor. The parking lot was shared with the restaurant. The buildings were as run-down as you'd expect. Some of the windows were broken. Others had plastic taped over them. Chips of paint had fallen off the siding. The structures were depressingly similar to the Lawson home.

Gail lit her cigarette as she walked past the first

building. She stopped at the second building, second door, lower level. She was a good fifty yards away, but Maggie had a straight line of sight. Gail's fist went into the air. The door opened before she could knock. A surprised-looking man in a suit stood in front of her. They were both silent for a moment, then the man scampered toward the parking lot.

Kate said, 'Jimmy told me that if anybody ever runs away from you, you should chase them.'

'He's not running away from us. He's running home to his wife.' Maggie kept her eyes on Gail, who was watching the man, too. She looked annoyed, and then she looked startled as a high-pitched scream filled the air.

Maggie had her revolver in her hand and was running toward the hotel before she knew what was happening. Her brain put it together on the fly. Someone inside the room was screaming like a banshee. The whore came into view. Her mouth was opened wide. She was naked from the waist up and high as a kite. A tourniquet was still tied around her arm. She kept screeching as she tackled Gail to the ground. Her arms started flying. She wind-milled her fists into Gail's face.

'Stop!' Maggie screamed, rushing toward the women.

The whore didn't stop. Gail's face was bloody. She was barely fighting back.

Maggie jumped over a pothole. They were still thirty yards away. 'Stop, goddamn it!'

The whore looked up. Her breasts were small, like a second set of eyes. She seemed shocked to find Maggie gunning for her. For Maggie's part, her only shock was that Kate Murphy was keeping pace beside her. She had her elbows locked, gun straight out in front.

'Fan out!' Maggie said, pointing Kate to her right. 'Don't let her run.'

But of course she ran. The whore weighed the odds and ran to Maggie's right, figuring Kate couldn't catch her. Not exactly a genius-level deduction. Kate had already lost a shoe. Her pants were coming unhemmed. One of her sleeves had unrolled so that it flapped behind her like a pennant.

Still, Kate chased after the whore full on as the bare-chested woman headed into a service alley between the hotel and the restaurant.

Gail was already up and running after them. 'Thass'a dead end,' she slurred. Blood streamed down her face, but she was running so hard that Maggie struggled to keep up. 'I'm gonna fuckin' kill that cunt.'

They both rounded the corner into the alley. The whore had started screaming again. Kate was still chasing her. They were each locked in their own kind of tunnel vision. Kate's hat had slipped down to the bridge of her nose. She probably couldn't see more than three feet ahead. Neither of them had yet to notice that there was nothing but a cinder-block wall at the end of the alley.

'Stop!' Maggie warned. 'Murphy, stop!'

'Chrissake,' Gail hissed. 'Doesn't she know you're supposed to bend your arms when you run?'

'There's a wall!' Maggie yelled. 'Kate! There's a—'

It was too late. Both the whore and Kate saw the wall, but by then momentum had taken over. They slammed into the cinder block. Kate staggered on her feet for an almost comical few seconds before falling straight onto her back.

Gail reached into her purse. Instead of pulling out a

gun or a set of cuffs, she grabbed her radio receiver. Maggie didn't know what she was going to do until she did it.

'Stupid bitch!' Gail brought the plastic brick down on the whore's face. Blood sprayed the wall.

The whore slumped to the ground.

'You think you can beat me?' Gail kicked the woman in the stomach. 'And then you run from a cop?' She kicked her again. 'Fucking whore!'

Kate was still on the ground. She was too scared to move. She had her hands up like she expected to be next.

Gail didn't even see her. Her rage had caught up with her. She kicked the whore again. 'Are you fucking stupid?' She kicked her again. 'Are you?'

'Gail,' Maggie tried, because sometimes it worked.

'Shit.' Gail wiped her mouth. Blood was smeared down her chin and neck. Her nose was crooked. There was a wild look in her eyes. Adrenaline did that. Fury. Pain. It was all there, all working to ramp her up. 'I still got my teeth?' She gave Maggie a bloody grimace.

Maggie didn't know how to answer. All she saw was red. 'Yeah.'

'Well, thank God for that.' She noticed Kate was still on the ground and pulled her up by the arm. 'Good going, Sheep. You chased somebody into a brick wall.' She looked at the wall. 'Cinder block. What the fuck? Same difference.'

Kate was breathing too hard to respond.

'You all right?' Gail brushed the dirt from Kate's uniform. 'You okay, Sheep?'

Kate tensed as Gail slapped at her clothes.

'Look at this one,' Gail told Maggie. 'You'd think she

sprinted a mile instead of chased a doped-up whore down an alley.' Gail rattled off another cough. 'Some advice from me sweetheart: you bend your arms when you run. All right?'

Kate nodded furiously.

'All right?' Gail repeated. 'You look like a goddamn sheep when you run.'

'Okay.' Kate's hand was clutched to her chest. She looked terrified.

'You.' Gail prodded the whore with the toe of her shoe. Maggie wasn't sure how she'd managed to keep on the high heels while she was running. Gail's feet were bloody where the straps had cut into her flesh. She didn't seem to notice as she pressed her foot into the whore's shoulder. 'Come on, bitch. Don't make me hit you again.'

Maggie said, 'Let me—'

Gail held her back with one hand. 'What's the name, sugar? What's the name you got for me?'

The whore turned away, curling against the wall. Her hands covered her bare breasts. She was pathetic to look at. Her bleached hair was lank and filthy. Her skin was the color of flour. Her waist was a spindle. Her ribs stuck out like pickets.

'You gotta name for me?' Gail repeated. She was seeing the same things as Maggie, but that only ramped up her anger rather than dialing it down. 'What's the name, sweet-heart? Give me the name.'

'Violet.'

'I know *your* name, dipshit. Remember we talked about this? I need to know the pimp what's running gals on Whitehall. I got some questions for him.'

Violet shook her head. She wouldn't look up.

'You want me to kick you in the kidneys?' Gail pushed the tip of her shoe into the girl's back. 'You wanna be pissing blood for the next two weeks?'

The girl didn't answer. Gail reared back her leg.

'Wait!' Kate screamed. Her hands were out in front of her, palms down. There was a panicked look in her eyes. 'Just wait, okay?'

'Wait for what?' Gail asked.

Kate didn't have an answer.

'Do you even know what we're doing here?' Gail took one step, then another, until Kate was backed into the wall. 'Don Wesley's dead, lady. Somebody killed him, gunned him down like a fucking dog in the street, and then went after *her* brother.' She jabbed her thumb toward Maggie. 'This whore you're so worried about is hiding a cop killer. A cop killer who could be out there right now murdering more of our boys.' She thumped Kate on the side of the head. 'Has your three fucking minutes on the job got you thinking like a cop yet?'

Gail went to thump her again, but Maggie caught her hand.

That was all it took. Like all bullies, Gail just needed somebody to call her on it.

She turned away from Kate. Black tears smeared her mascara. Her jaw was clenched so tight that Maggie was reminded of Jimmy chewing his breakfast that morning.

Gail said, 'All right, darlin'. I'm all right.'

Maggie let go of her hand.

Gail paced out the width of the alley, once, twice. She obviously had a conversation going on in her head. She kept nodding. And when she wasn't nodding, she was shaking her head.

Then she stopped.

Gail steadied her hand on Maggie's shoulder. She slipped off one high heel, then the other. Then she turned. Then she jumped up into the air and landed with both feet on the whore's leg.

A crack of splintering bone shot up the alley.

'Fuck!' Violet grabbed her leg with both hands. She rocked back and forth on her side. 'Oh, God! Oh, Jesus! Oh, fuck!'

Maggie went numb. She couldn't even feel her own heart beating in her chest. Kate slumped back against the wall. Her face was ashen.

Gail got down on her knees. She rubbed the whore's back like she wasn't the one who'd put her into so much misery. Her voice took on a maternal tone. 'Just tell me the name, darlin'. Tell me the name and we'll leave.'

Violet's body shivered with pain. 'What name?'

'Don't play me like that, Vi.'

'I ain't—'

Gail pressed her hand into the whore's broken leg. Really pressed it.

Violet howled like a dying animal. Gail didn't let up. If anything, she pressed harder. Maggie saw the indentation in the flesh. She imagined the shards of bone clashing like forks thrown into a drawer. And then she had to open her mouth just enough to take in a deep breath so she didn't throw up.

The screaming wouldn't stop.

Maggie took another breath. Then another. She tried to think of a song from the radio. *Tapestry*. Lilly's thin voice singing about Smackwater Jack and feeling like a natural woman. Anything that might take the edge off the screaming.

Gail slowly released the pressure. She was patient. She waited for the screaming to die down. She stroked the whore's back again. Her voice was still gentle when she asked, 'You listenin' to me?' Her hand went to the break, fingers a few inches from skin. 'You listenin'?'

'Yes!' Violet yelled. 'Yes!'

Gail's hand rested on the girl's hip. 'There's some whores working the Five in the early hours, right? Some older girls on Whitehall?'

She hesitated, but only for a second. 'Yeah.'

'Who's runnin' them?'

The whore said nothing.

Gail asked, 'Do you think I wanna hurt you?'

'He'll kill me. He'll fuckin' kill me.'

'Sweetheart, you oughta be more worried about me right now than anybody else.' Gail's hand traced down the girl's leg again, hovering over the break. Violet's skin mirrored her name. Bruises covered her body. From the johns. From the needles. From cutting herself out of boredom or spite.

Gail's hand went flat to the leg. 'One more time?'

'She,' the girl whispered.

'What's that?'

'Sir She.'

Kate's head snapped around.

Gail asked, 'Where's this Sir She operating out of?'

'Huff Road,' the whore said. 'West Side.'

'Good girl.' Gail stood up. She wiped her hands on the front of her shirt. 'You want me to call anybody for you?'

'No.'

'Suit yourself.' Gail started back up the alley. She was still barefooted. Her soles left bloody prints until the red clay stanched the cuts. Her hand reached into her purse. She shook out a cigarette.

Maggie's brain struggled with the memory of how to make her legs move. She walked slowly so she wouldn't catch up with Gail. Kate followed, the loose leg of her pants making a sweeping sound with every step.

'What was that?' Kate whispered, the words slurring together worse than Gail's. 'Whawashat?'

'Just let it go.'

'She beat that girl. She—'

'Let it go.' Maggie adjusted the mic on her shoulder, shifted her utility belt back in place. She tried not to think about the spray of blood when Gail's transmitter hit the girl's head. The howl of pain. The black and red blister on the whore's arm where a needle had broken off and caused an infection.

Kate reached the cruiser first. Instead of getting in, she threw her hat onto the hood. She pressed her palms to the metal. She leaned over. Her head dropped.

Maggie said, 'If you're going to throw up, go inside the restaurant.'

'I'm not going to throw up,' Kate answered, but then she heaved. There wasn't much. A single stream of bile came out of her mouth. Maggie watched it travel down the front of the car, past the grill, then drip onto the asphalt.

'Go inside the restaurant.'

'I'm not—' Kate heaved again. She must have had a light breakfast. Her stomach worked like a cat bringing up a hairball.

Maggie walked toward Kate's missing shoe, which was about ten feet from the cruiser. She bent down to retrieve it. She glanced inside the restaurant. Gail was talking on the pay phone. The dining room was empty.

Kate gave one last heave. She looked up at the sky. She took a deep breath. Finally, she wiped her mouth with the back of her hand. 'What time is it?'

Maggie resisted the lecture; officers were always supposed to wear a watch. 'It's a little after two.'

Kate laughed so loudly that the sound hurt Maggie's eardrums.

'I've only been doing this for six hours?' Kate kept laughing. 'How can it only be six hours?'

'Cheer up.' Maggie placed Kate's shoe by her hat. 'Only two and a half more to go.'

Kate's hand went to her stomach, but she didn't heave again. She turned and sat on the hood of the car. There was some vomit in her hair. A red line slashed straight across her forehead where the rim of her hat was supposed to be. A matching line cut across the bridge of her nose, probably from hitting the wall.

Maggie said, 'You know you're going to have to clean that off my car, right?'

'It would be rude not to.'

'That was speed.' Maggie explained, 'The whore. She must've been shooting up when Gail knocked on the door. It winds them up and that's how they spin down.'

'Lovely.' Kate stifled a yawn. 'I could just go to sleep. I'm serious. I can barely keep my eyes open.'

'Adrenaline crash.' Maggie felt like she was teaching a class. 'It's great when you first feel it. You breathe faster.

Run harder. And then your head starts to swim. You get tunnel vision. You forget to look around, see what's coming up.'

'My hat was—' Kate didn't bother to finish the sentence. She reached for her shoe. She didn't have to untie the laces to slip it on.

Maggie checked the restaurant. Gail was off the phone now. She was sitting at the bar. 'Let the equipment hit you.'

'What?'

'Your belt.' That was why Kate had kept her arms straight. 'You can't stop your equipment from hitting you. Just let it happen.'

Kate put her head in her hands. 'Of course. That makes perfect sense.'

'It's not always this bad.'

'Oh, good. I was worried.'

'Gail was close to Don.' Maggie withheld the details. You didn't say anything to one cop that you didn't want every single other cop on earth to know. 'She respected him. We all did.'

Kate kept her head in her hands. 'How can I be so hot and so cold at the same time?'

'Shock.'

'Shock. Yes. Of course.' She finally looked up. Her color was coming back. Her lips were a lighter shade of blue.

Maggie asked, 'You want a drink?'

'I want about twenty.'

Maggie was debating whether to go inside the restaurant or drive to a liquor store when she heard the wail of an oncoming siren. She saw the bright white blur of an

Atlanta police cruiser darting down the road. Then another one. Then another.

'Where are they off to?' Maggie mumbled.

There was a long, low tone that sounded like a telephone button being pressed.

Kate said, 'That's the emergency signal.'

Maggie was already turning the dial on her transmitter to the emergency channel. There was a burst of static. Then a man screamed for help.

Maggie's heart stopped. There was something familiar about the man's voice.

Kate whispered, 'Who was that?'

Maggie turned up the volume. Static chopped the man's voice into unintelligible pieces. The transmitter wasn't receiving. She couldn't tune in the channel.

'Ten—' Static. 'Twelfth and—' More static, then a garbled 'Lawson. Repeat—' Static.

Kate said, 'I think he said Lawson.'

Maggie jogged toward the road. She furiously scanned the dial on her transmitter, trying to get better reception. Another cruiser whirred past. She tried to flag it down as she ran into the street.

'Shit-shit-shit,' she cursed, holding up the transmitter as high as she could. She spun around, searching for a sweet spot.

And then she found it.

'Dispatch?' Terry's voice was filled with panic. 'Dispatch? All cars. Repeat, all cars. Jimmy's been shot.'

13

Maggie ran through the Grady Hospital emergency room. She had to shove people out of the way. There were at least two hundred cops here, and none of them seemed to be doing anything but keeping Maggie from her brother. She despised herself for wanting her uncle Terry. He'd sweep all of these assholes out of her way with a wave of his hand.

'Maggie?' Rick Anderson caught her arm. 'He's all right.'

'Where—'

'This way.' Rick took hold of her hand as he led her through the crowd. His palm was clammy. It was the same as this morning: people parted for him. They nodded their heads. They stared at Maggie. Rick kept glancing back over his shoulder to make sure she was okay. Maggie knew he was being nice, but his calm deliberativeness set her on edge.

Finally, they reached the back corridor. Rick pushed open the door. The wing had been closed down after a chemical spill. Most of the lights were off. Yellow tape still crisscrossed the locked door where the accident had happened.

Rick led her down the hallway. 'They put him back here because it's quieter.'

'What happened?'

'He took a bullet in his arm. Went straight through. No big deal. Doctor says he's gonna be fine.'

Maggie slipped her hand from Rick's. She wrapped her arms around her waist, pretending to be cold. 'Where did it happen?'

'Ashby Street over in CT.'

She knew the area. That was two blocks from the address Violet had given them for Sir She. 'He was alone? You can't go into that area alone.'

'Jimmy's a big boy,' Rick said. 'He was talking to a snitch. Some old woman went nuts. Thought Jimmy was gonna arrest her son. So she shot him.'

They stopped in front of the nurses' station. Two women in white caps were sitting behind the counter. One of them saw the uniforms and said, 'He's in the last room on the right.'

Maggie told Rick, 'Thanks. I've got it from here.'

He seemed reluctant to let her go, but mercifully, Rick wasn't rude enough to stay where he wasn't wanted. He crossed behind the nurses' station, going through the door-way that led back into the main emergency department.

Maggie slowly walked down the dark corridor. Suddenly, she wasn't in such a hurry to reach her brother. She stared at the light pouring from his room. Chemical smells swirled through the air. She ignored the biohazard signs and dirty buckets. The soles of her shoes snicked against the sticky floor.

Out of nowhere, Maggie remembered the first time she'd visited her father at the mental hospital. She was ten or eleven. She was terrified. Her legs were shaking. Her heart beat like her blood was running dry. Hank was in the lockdown ward. People were yelling at the top of their lungs. Maggie had felt like she was going through a fun house at the carnival. Each room she passed had an open door and beyond that doorway was some new horror: a crying man restrained in his bed, another man sitting in a feces-covered wheelchair, yet another man standing in the middle of the room, his gown wide open, a wet, degenerate look on his excited face.

All the while, she was terrified that there would be some sort of mix-up and they'd lock Maggie on the wrong side of the cage door.

She put her hand to the wall. She steadied herself. Now wasn't the time to be emotional. She wasn't at the mental hospital. She wasn't going to be locked up. Jimmy was fine. He'd been shot, but by a frightened old woman, not a cold-blooded assassin.

Maggie tried to make her expression passive as she rounded the door into Jimmy's room. She found him sitting up in bed. His shirt was off, and maybe the rest of his clothes because he tugged up the sheet when he saw his sister standing there.

'Jimmy,' was all she could manage. A large bandage was wrapped around his upper left arm. Rick had said the bullet went straight through. That meant no damage to the bone. No surgery needed. Yet, still, Maggie's heart felt like somebody was straining it through a sieve.

'Jesus.' Jimmy winced as he sat up. His good hand kept the sheet firmly around his waist. 'You call Mom?'

Maggie shook her head. She'd forgotten about everybody until this moment.

He said, 'I'll get Uncle Terry to call her.'

'What happened?' Maggie wanted confirmation. There had been too many lies lately. 'Tell me the truth.'

He stared at her, his face unreadable. Jimmy's waters didn't run deep. He was strong, and on a good day he was silent, but Maggie had always been able to tell what was on his mind. Jimmy made sure of it – whether he was angry or annoyed or all right, which was basically the extent of his emotions – everybody had to know.

But now, she had no idea how her brother felt.

She repeated, 'What happened?'

Jimmy finally relented. 'I got a snitch runs guns over on Ashby. I figured whoever killed Don wouldn't throw away the gun. Money is money, right? If we're lucky, we find the gun, maybe it's got prints, and if it's got prints—' He shrugged. His face contorted in pain as the muscles in his arm twitched. 'Christ, that hurts.'

'What happened?'

'You gonna keep asking me the same question over and over again?'

She figured the answer was obvious.

He absently scratched his jaw. 'I might've gotten a little aggressive with the snitch. His mother, she's old, blind as a bat. I knew she was in the next room. I didn't know she had a howitzer stuck down her girdle.'

'She pulled a .375 and all it did was nick you?'

'A .44,' he told her. 'And who told you I was nicked? Near about ripped my arm off.'

Maggie didn't know why she was surprised Rick had lied to her. 'You should've taken backup.'

Jimmy scratched the top of his head. Then the side of his face. Pain medications always made him itch. Whatever drug they had given him was clearly taking effect. He had a sleepy look on his face. His eyelids were half-closed.

She said, 'I'll go call Mom. Terry won't tell her the truth about anything.'

'Don't go.'

Maggie waited. And waited. 'What is it, Jim? I need to call Mom.'

Jimmy took his time collecting his thoughts. He absently scratched his neck, then his head again. She was about to leave, but he stopped her with a question. 'Remember when you were little and Mom used to make me take you to the pool?'

Maggie felt sucker-punched by the memory. She'd loved going to the pool with Jimmy. Lilly wasn't born yet. Maggie was still his baby sister. She had glowed under his watchful eye.

He said, 'You used to like bugs. Do you remember that?'

She nodded. Jimmy liked them, so Maggie did, too.

'Remember how I used to tell you I'd caught a bug, only when you came over to see it, I'd squirt water in your face?'

She laughed before he could. 'Yeah, I was pretty retarded. Not much has changed, right?'

Jimmy wasn't laughing. 'I shouldn't've scared you like that. I'm sorry.'

Maggie stared at him. She wondered if they had given him too many pills. This wasn't her brother. 'You feeling all right, Jimmy?'

'I should've protected you, Maggie.'

She shrugged it off. 'It was just water.'

'Not then.'

She didn't have to ask him when. Maggie looked down at the sheets on the bed. They were wrinkled. She smoothed them out, tucking in the side.

He said, 'Seven years.'

'Eight,' she told him. 'It was eight years ago.'

'It wasn't your fault.'

Maggie pulled the sheet tighter, tucking the corner under the thin mattress. 'I'd better get back to work.'

'Maggie—'

She was already heading for the door. 'Get some rest, Jimmy. You're not yourself.'

14

Kate watched Maggie Lawson leave her brother's room. Instead of heading toward the exit, Maggie crossed the hall. Kate was surprised to see her go into the women's restroom. She had assumed Maggie had a bag strapped to her leg so she never had to leave her car. Kate could have advised her to hold it a bit longer. The bathroom was as filthy as a gas station's.

Maybe she needed a minute. Kate had only known Jimmy for a few hours and she'd been almost as panicked as Maggie when the call came in. Kate's reasons were slightly different. It was too close to Patrick. They were roughly the same age. They both had that same stoic sense of duty. And until someone had told her otherwise, Kate had been convinced that they had both gotten killed for it.

She checked her watch, then remembered she'd lost it somewhere between the squad car and the hotel behind the Colonnade. Kate put her hand to her back. The muscles had officially turned into a solid block of concrete. She tried to catalogue her injuries but quickly gave up. There was no number high enough. She had guessed right this morning about the metal hooks digging into her sides

– the blisters on her feet certainly took her mind off the pain. And the bruises on her hips. And the goose egg on her forehead. Of course, all of that paled in comparison to the constant sensation of knives stabbing into her spinal cord. She finally grasped why they all stood with their feet spread apart. The equipment belt might as well be carrying dumbbells. If Kate didn't open her stance, she would either fall down or double over.

That was, if the smell didn't knock her out first. The stench in the Grady Hospital emergency room reminded her of the housing projects she'd visited this morning. Kate didn't know how people lived this way. She guessed you could get used to anything if you didn't have a choice. Like most Atlantans, she never thought about Grady other than in terms of gratitude – she was equally as glad the hospital was there for the poor as she was secure in the knowledge that she would never have to be treated there herself.

The publicly funded facility could probably benefit from more paying customers. Almost a century of dirt was ground into the cracked tiles on the floor. The ceiling was stained dark brown or missing altogether in places. Doors were sealed with hazard tape. Broken equipment was piled into every corner. The lighting was deplorable. The flickering fluorescent bulbs gave her a headache.

Or maybe her head hurt because she'd smacked into a cinder-block wall.

'Kaitlin?'

She turned instinctively, not considering how improbable it was that someone from her old life would be in Grady Hospital. The doctor who'd called her name was tall with jet-black hair that grazed his collar, piercing green eyes, and the most delicate eyelashes she'd ever seen on a grown man.

He said, 'Fancy meeting you here, Second Base.'

His voice was deep and sonorous, in no way familiar. And then she read the name stitched onto his white lab coat. 'Tip?'

They both smiled at the nickname, though the last time Philip Van Zandt had begged Kate for just the tiniest bit of sex, he'd been a foot shorter and absent any facial hair. Now, he looked more like Burt Reynolds.

And Kate looked like Soupy Sales.

She'd seen as much in the bathroom mirror. Her hair was a mess. Her skin was splotchy. She'd borrowed a pair of scissors from a nurse and chopped off the dragging leg of her pants. God only knew what her breath smelled like.

Philip had obviously taken all this in, but still, he told her, 'You look fantastic.'

Kate laughed so loudly that she had to cover her mouth with her hand.

'I'm serious,' he insisted. 'That uniform . . . the bruise on your forehead . . . the vomit in your hair . . .'

Now she really laughed.

'May I?' Philip picked a twig off her sleeve. And then a speck of concrete. 'I heard you were a cop. I couldn't believe it.'

'You shouldn't.' Kate tried to smooth down her hair. 'I'm not sure how long I'll last.'

'I've never seen you give up on anything.'

'A lot's changed in ten years.'

'Nine,' he said, and the light banter fell away. Philip

170

stared at her thoughtfully. She watched his eyes scan her face. He clearly liked what he saw.

Still, Kate asked, 'What?'

He shook his head. 'How is it that you're even more beautiful now than before?'

Kate was saved a response by the sudden eruption of laughter from a group of policemen at the end of the hall. She startled, but the men were too far away to hear what Philip had said. At least she hoped they were. Their faces looked familiar.

Philip seemed to sense her discomfort. 'Let's go some-where quiet.' He gently cradled his hand under her elbow as he led her behind the nurses' station. Kate felt a swell of emotion. After half a day on the job, she had forgotten what it felt like for a man to treat her like a woman.

And Philip Van Zandt was certainly a man now. There was none of the tentative fifteen-year-old boy who'd thought he'd hit the jackpot during a game of spin-the-bottle in Janice Saddler's rec room. He was tall, grounded, self-assured. There was something about his broad shoulders that made her want to wrap her hands around them.

Not that Kate would ever be so forward with a married man.

She knew about Philip's life since he left Atlanta the same way she knew all the gossip about everyone from her parents' social circle. Through no effort of her own, Kate had picked up stray bits and pieces during dinners and cocktail parties. Philip had been sent to boarding school at sixteen. He'd graduated from college with honors. He'd gone to medical school up north. He was doing his residency as an orthopedic surgeon. He'd moved back to Atlanta six months ago and was living in his parents' guesthouse. He was married, but his wife lived abroad while she finished her master's degree. They were both hoping to start a family soon. Philip would eventually join his father's medical practice.

Still, polite society dictated that Kate go through the motions. 'When did you get back?'

'Six months ago.' Philip stopped in the doorway of a supply room. 'How are your parents?'

'They're well. You're married?'

'Marta. She's spending a year abroad to work on her master's.'

'Kids?'

He smiled, likely because he'd been to his share of dinners and cocktail parties, too. 'I heard about your husband.'

A lump rose in her throat. Kate had been flirting. Patrick was dead, and Kate was flirting.

Philip said, 'He was a lucky man to have you, even if it was for a short time.'

His hand was still on her arm. Kate gently pulled away. She said, 'I should probably—' just as Philip said, 'Are you here for—'

They both stopped. Kate had been talked over by Jimmy all morning, but she indicated that Philip should go first.

'I was wondering if you were here because of that cop who was shot? James Lawson?'

'Jimmy,' she supplied. 'I worked with him this morning.'

Philip's eyebrows went up. 'How was that?'

For some inexplicable reason, Kate felt herself circling around the Lawson clan. 'Not so bad. I'm still learning.'

Philip looked dubious, but the truth was that once Kate

172

had stood up to Jimmy Lawson, he'd turned almost bearable.

'Well.' Philip had a sly smile on his face. 'I guess he's not so different from people you've met.'

Kate shook her head. She didn't understand the smile.

'Your mother still has her art gallery, right?'

She felt he was speaking in a code she couldn't quite decipher. 'Your hints are too subtle for me.'

Philip pulled her deeper into the supply room. He kept his voice low. 'I've been here for eighteen hours.' He didn't make her fill in the blanks. 'I treated Jimmy Lawson when he brought in his partner this morning.'

Kate gathered from the air of intrigue that there was more to the story. 'And?'

Philip seemed to lose his nerve. She caught a glimpse of the unsure boy she'd met all those years ago. 'It's nothing. Just that I treated him.'

'That's not all.' Kate playfully punched him in the shoulder. 'Come on, Tip. Spill.'

He shook his head. 'Never mind.'

'Just a little bit?' She pitched her voice to a breathy whisper, imitating the same begging tone Philip had used when they were alone in Janice Saddler's bathroom. 'Just a tiny little bit? Please?'

Philip laughed good-naturedly. 'I dunno, Second Base. I wouldn't want to traumatize you.'

If there was one thing Kate was certain of, it was that she was beyond traumatizing. 'A pimp masturbated in front of me this morning and I chased a nude prostitute this afternoon.'

'Completely nude?'

She gave him a look.

'All right.' Philip stood up straighter. He was a real doctor again. 'You're sure about this?'

She nodded.

'Wesley was clearly past saving by the time we got him on the table.' Philip paused. All traces of his earlier lightness were gone. 'But he was a cop, and he was young. They worked on him for half an hour before giving up. The entire staff was there. Lawson was in the next bed. He was wounded, but he wouldn't let us treat him. He wanted Wesley taken care of first. And then when Wesley was pronounced—' Philip stopped again. 'Lawson was so bereft that I had to sedate him.'

Kate chewed her lip. Jimmy was so tightly coiled it was hard to imagine him unraveling like that.

Philip said, 'I'm ortho, so Lawson was my case.'

Kate remembered Jimmy's limp. 'What was wrong with him?'

'Let's start with Wesley's head wound. The killer was standing roughly ten feet away. The bullets entered here in a fairly tight formation.' Philip put his finger just above his ear. 'The trajectory – that's the path the bullets take – went this way.' He traced a line across his face to the opposite cheek. 'So, the path of the bullets went downward, which means we can assume the muzzle of the gun was pointing downward, which means that—'

'The person who shot him was taller.'

'Exactly,' Philip agreed.

Kate felt a lightness in her chest. She'd been so consistently wrong all day that it felt wonderful to finally be right about something.

Philip continued, 'Wesley was about my height. So, one explanation could be that the shooter was taller.'

Philip was at least six-two. 'That's pretty tall. Did you tell that to the police? Nothing was said during roll call this morning.'

'They don't exactly trust medical science,' Philip admitted. 'The point is, either a seven-foot-tall guy shot your Mr. Wesley twice in the head, or there's another, more plausible explanation.'

Kate was all out of brilliant deductions. 'Which is?'

'Wesley was on the ground, on his hands and knees, when he was shot.'

Kate felt her stomach twist at the thought. The image was something out of *The Godfather*. But then she recalled, 'That's not what Jimmy's telling people.' She hadn't taken notes during the briefing, but she knew the pertinent details. 'Jimmy was at the front of the building. He walked around to the back. Don was there. Jimmy didn't say anything about him being on his knees. The shooter came around the corner and fired. He was ten feet away, which is the same as what you just told me. Don was hit. Jimmy dove for cover. He fired back three times. The bad guy's gun jammed, so he ran away. Then Jimmy carried Don all the way here.'

'That's what Lawson said?'

'To the best of my recollection.'

Philip nodded her out of the room. 'Follow me.'

He led her through a door behind the nurses' station. Jimmy had been sequestered away from the regular patients. Kate had thought the other side was run-down, but the main emergency room was a sty. Homeless people were lying on the floor. Garbage cans overflowed. Gurneys were filled with blacks whose faces were so ashen they almost looked white.

Philip noticed her dismay. 'You wouldn't believe how many residents apply to this place every year. Stabbings. Shootings. Suicides. Murders. It's the greatest show on earth.'

Kate held her tongue, thinking she'd again missed one of his peculiar jokes.

'Here we go.' Philip stopped in front of a light box. He flipped through some files on the table below and pulled out an X-ray. 'This is what I wanted to show you.'

He snapped the film onto the light box. She saw the name *James Henry Lawson* etched into the black. His birthday was underneath, then the words *Left Femur.* The bone looked like something out of an Operation board game.

'See these?' Philip asked.

Kate followed his finger as he pointed out black spots peppering the bone. There were dozens of them, some merely specks, a few as large as a dime.

Philip explained, 'Most of these were superficial, but some went deeper. I've got him on antibiotics in case there's an infection. I couldn't get all of the pieces.'

'Pieces of what?'

'Bone, mostly. Some teeth. Hair.'

Kate still didn't get it. 'Hair on his leg?'

'Not Lawson's hair.' Philip made his voice low again. 'Wesley's. Some slivers of his skull were embedded in Jimmy's stomach and chest, too.'

Kate stared at the X-ray, trying to process the information. She couldn't understand how pieces of Don Wesley had ended up in Jimmy's leg and abdomen. 'What am I missing?'

'Wesley's head was in Lawson's lap when the gun went off.'

'He was ducking down?'

Philip's puzzled expression matched her own. 'Didn't you see *Deep Throat*?'

'Of course I didn't.' He'd finally managed to shock her. 'Are you crazy?'

He did something funny with his mouth. 'But you know what it's about?'

Kate struggled to hold his gaze. Her cheeks were on fire, which she guessed was as good an answer to his question as any.

Philip said, 'So that's why his head was in his lap.'

'But that's a movie. Real people don't do that.' She lowered her voice to a whisper. 'Especially two men.'

'Oh, sweetheart.' Philip visibly struggled against the urge to laugh. 'What do you think men do?'

Kate had never really thought about it, but then she did. 'Really?'

'Really.' Philip turned off the light behind the X-ray. 'Like I said, not so different from the guys you've met at your mother's gallery.'

Kate simply could not get the two things to jibe. The gay men at the gallery were flamboyant and witty and charming. To say that Jimmy was unpolished was being generous. 'It doesn't make sense. Jimmy stared at my breasts all morning.'

'He's gay. He's not dead.'

Kate took the compliment, mostly because she couldn't think of a rejoinder.

He said, 'Good thing Wesley's mouth wasn't full when it happened.'

'Philip,' she chastened. He shouldn't joke about it. 'This could end Jimmy's career.'

'It could end his life.' He wasn't exaggerating. They both knew what happened to homosexuals. 'Don't worry. No one will hear it from me.'

'Me either.' Kate didn't think anyone would believe her. She still couldn't believe it herself.

'Murphy!' Maggie stood at the end of the hallway, flapping her hand like she was developing a Polaroid. 'Come on! Let's go!'

Kate told Philip, 'I'm sorry. I need to—'

'Go do your job.' His smile showed his perfect teeth. 'I'm happy for you, Kaitlin. The work suits you.'

Again, Kate didn't know how to respond. Even a goodbye seemed superfluous considering the conversation they'd just had. All she could do was walk away. Kate felt Philip's eyes following her. She was still so astonished that she couldn't even feel pleased.

'Who's that?' Maggie asked.

Kate struggled to switch gears. Did Maggie know about her brother? The way she'd yelled at Jimmy before didn't indicate any closeness. And Maggie didn't come across as particularly open-minded. She categorized everybody. The colored girls. The Italian dry cleaner. The Polack bar owner. Irish Spring.

Kate said, 'I knew him in junior high school.'

'He's good-looking.' Maggie asked, 'Is he Jewish?'

Kate feigned ignorance. 'I think so. He's married.'

'Too bad,' Maggie said, though Kate didn't know which part she thought was the problem.

Frankly, she was too tired to care. All Kate could do was follow Maggie toward the door. This required going

178

through the waiting room. People were packed in so tightly that some patients were sitting on the floor. Just when Kate thought she was getting used to an odor, a new one would pop up. Toddlers were barely clothed. Diapers were full. Desperate faces stared back at her. She trained her sights ahead, thinking she might as well be walking on Mars.

She was reminded of Patrick's letters from his first week at boot camp. He wasn't so thrown by the military setting as the customs of his fellow soldiers. Black, Hispanic, American Indian, even some Asians. Patrick had grown up in a neighborhood surrounded by his own people, the same as Kate. He went to their restaurants. He went to their church. He worshipped their God. He'd never met anyone who didn't vote for Kennedy or think that Nixon was a pig. His fellow soldiers had been as foreign to him as the Vietnamese.

Kate wondered what Patrick had made of the letters she wrote back. She'd tried to keep them full of shopping and family anecdotes and whatever gossip she picked up over drinks at the Coach and Six. She mentioned nothing of the searing loneliness and fear that rocked every single moment he was away. Kate wondered if she would even have the guts to tell him the truth now – if she could write Patrick an honest, awful letter about her day. The housing projects. The harsh way people spoke to her. Her crushing lack of confidence. How when Gail Patterson slammed her radio transmitter into Violet's head, Kate's initial reaction wasn't repulsion but bloodlust.

She'd wanted to hit Violet, too.

She'd wanted to beat her. Kick her. She'd wanted to punish her for the hell she'd rained down. The absolute terror Kate had felt when she saw Maggie pull her gun.

The sharp, stabbing pains of the equipment on her belt beating into her flesh. The blind panic from not being able to see anything beyond the rim of her hat. The jarring shock of slamming not just into a wall, but into a filthy, scrawny whore who still had the remnants of her last customer dripping down her legs.

The impulse to harm had passed as quickly as it had come, but the memory lingered.

Maggie asked, 'You okay?'

'I'm terrific,' Kate quipped, because this job had turned her into an animal who couldn't show weakness. 'Was Jimmy hurt during the shooting?'

Maggie gave her a curious look.

'He was limping.'

'Football injury. His knee got wrecked in high school.' She pushed open the door. 'I guess it's acting up because of carrying Don.' She assured Kate, 'He'll be fine in a day or so.'

The smell of fresh air made Kate's eyes sting. She looked up. The pole lights were on. The sun was sinking like a stone.

Maggie asked, 'Where's your car parked?'

'What?'

'Your car,' Maggie repeated. 'Where is it parked?'

Kate had to think hard to jog her memory. 'In the lot off Central.'

'I'll drop you there and leave the cruiser at the motor pool.'

'What?'

Maggie stopped walking. 'I'm taking you to your car. The shift is over. It's time to go home.'

Kate stared at her, disbelieving.

And then she burst into tears.

15

Kate sat on the couch with a martini on the table beside her. She was in her parents' living room. She was wearing a patterned shirtdress with princess seams and the pearls her mother had given her on her wedding day. She was freshly showered. Her hair was washed and draped around her shoulders. The lights were turned down low. Her feet were in a bowl of warm Epsom salts. She held an ice pack to her forehead. A heating pad was shoved down the back of her underwear. The cord hung like a tail between her legs. Six aspirin and a Valium were working their way through her system. Every time Kate got an inkling that she might live, she remembered what her life was like and wondered if it was worth the effort.

She would not go back tomorrow. She simply couldn't.

So why had she brought all of her uniforms for Mary Jane to tailor? Why had Kate hunted and pecked around on her father's typewriter for two hours writing up her daily report?

The fact that she had begged her mother's maid to clean and mend her clothes served as a shining example of why Kate should not be doing this job. She was not Sabrina living with her father over a wealthy man's garage. She had grown up in the main house with the Larrabees. Kate's father was a respected psychiatrist. Her mother owned a renowned art gallery. Her grandmother had been a professor of chemistry back in Holland.

Kate was just as sheltered as Patrick had been. She had only ever met people like herself. She went to their restaurants. She went to their social clubs. Did the police force even have a club? Kate didn't know and she frankly did not care. She didn't belong with those people, with their coarse language and constant criticisms. Thinking of them as 'those people' was proof enough.

But with whom did she belong? Most of her friends were all married and raising children now. Their lives were interesting, but only to other married women with children. The two single girls Kate had kept in touch with from college were both living in New York, much to the scandal of their mothers.

Philip Van Zandt had gone to Columbia. Kate wondered if her friends had met up with him while he was in medical school. Surely there would have been a letter. It was the sort of thing you did when someone from your crowd was in town. You threw a cocktail party. You asked them to drinks. You made them feel welcome. And with a man as handsome as Dr. Van Zandt, you did a lot of other things that would further scandalize your mother.

Kate let her head drop back on the couch. She moved the ice bag to her eyes. She let her memory conjure Philip's charming grin and strong, broad shoulders. He seemed so damn sure of himself. Kate could not remember the last time a man had looked at her the way Philip had. Hell, she couldn't even recall the last time a man had made love to her. The night before Patrick had shipped out was one she tried to block from her mind. She had driven down from Atlanta and met him at a seedy hotel outside the army base. Kate had still been so desperate and angry. Patrick was drunk. The entire ordeal was sloppy and mean and neither could look at the other afterward.

Since his death, Kate had gone on a grand total of two dates. One ended in a handshake, the other in a chaste kiss, and then word got around to all the bachelors who knew Kate's girlfriends that she wasn't worth the dinner and drinks and no one asked her out again.

She bet Philip Van Zandt would not let her leave on a handshake. Just the thought of him made Kate's legs tremor.

'Darling?' The overhead lights came on.

'Oma?' Kate blinked to clear her vision. She felt a tinge of guilt, as if her grandmother could read her lustful thoughts. Not that Oma would disapprove. She was Dutch; there wasn't much that disturbed her. 'Is something wrong? I thought you were out with Mom and Dad.'

'By great coincidence, we all developed headaches at the exact same moment.' Oma walked gracefully into the room. Her graying blonde hair was pulled into a loose chignon. Her light eye makeup brought out the blue in her eyes. She was wearing a dress Kate might find in her own closet, though somehow, the style looked better on her sixty-five-year-old grandmother than it did on Kate.

Oma sat in the chair beside the couch. 'Will I hear stories about your first day?'

'I'm not sure you'd believe them.'

'Try me.'

Kate dropped the ice bag from her forehead. Oma didn't comment on the dark bruise. Instead, she drank the rest of Kate's martini.

'Kaitlin, is that you?'

Kate suppressed a cringe at her mother's voice. She had wanted so badly to be gone when they returned from supper.

Liesbeth frowned. 'Put your knees together, dear. Anyone could see straight up your dress.'

Kate forced herself not to obey.

Oma offered, 'I think a young woman should open her legs as often as possible.'

Liesbeth ignored the observation. She sat on the couch beside Kate. Like Oma, she was dressed for a night out. Her skirt was light blue. The matching sheer blouse had flowing sleeves that ballooned from her delicate wrists.

Kate always felt reduced next to her mother. She imagined Oma gave Liesbeth the same feeling. They were like Russian nesting dolls, only rather than fat babushkas, they were diminishing blonde replicas carrying on the Dutch maternal line.

Liesbeth primly crossed her legs, setting a good example. She took a cigarette from the box on the coffee table. 'Why are the lights on in the basement?'

'Mary Jane is tailoring my uniforms for me.'

'She has the evening off.'

'I've offered to pay her.'

'That makes it all right, then.' Liesbeth's Dutch accent was always more pronounced when she was being sarcastic. 'I can't imagine a seventy-three-year-old woman would want to be in bed at a reasonable hour.'

'You're right. I'm sorry.' Kate shook her head when

her mother offered her a cigarette. She'd smoked her throat raw after Patrick died. Just the thought of the taste made her queasy. 'I'll apologize to her.'

'And pay her as well.' Liesbeth lit her cigarette. She studied Kate through the veil of smoke. 'You've been crying.'

She had not asked a question, so Kate did not offer an answer.

'This bruise on your head? The blisters on your feet? I hesitate to guess what the heating pad is for.'

Kate didn't know where to begin. The projects. The prostitute. *Deep Throat* – a movie she had a sinking suspicion her far more cosmopolitan grandmother had seen. She thought about the way Jimmy had pushed her around this morning, and how Maggie had said the uniform could get you anything for free, but then refused to take advantage of it herself. Then there was Gail Patterson. Never mind the beaten-down prostitute. Kate knew how to run. The only reason her arms were straight was because she was trying to keep herself from being flayed by the equipment around her waist.

She asked her grandmother, 'Have you ever seen a sheep run?'

Oma laughed at the idea. 'Have I ever seen a sheep run?' Her accent was heavier, too, though this was likely the result of too many martinis. 'I once knew a Flemish girl who kept sheep.'

Kate smiled. Oma's jokes often began with a Flemish girl. She had an Amsterdammer's arrogance about the Dutch-speaking region of Belgium.

'Shush with your Flemish girls.' Liesbeth put her cigarette in the ashtray. She walked over to the bar. 'We saw the afternoon *Journal*. Had you met the police officer who was murdered?'

'No.'

'I'm relieved to hear that.' Liesbeth used the tongs to put ice in the martini shaker. 'I hope they get the right person this time. The paper mentioned Edward Spivey. His life was ruined by that trial. He had to move to the other side of the country.'

'Justice always prevails.' Oma turned to Kate. 'Isn't that right, dear?'

Kate nodded, though she wasn't sure how she felt. She had gathered that no one in uniform thought Edward Spivey was innocent, whereas most of the people Kate knew assumed that the police had tried to frame him for the crime. 'Where's Daddy?'

'In his greenhouse.' Liesbeth poured a generous splash of vodka into the shaker. 'He's worried about his orchids. There's something wrong with the heater.'

Kate hadn't technically lied to Maggie Lawson. Her father was passionate about gardening.

Oma asked, 'How are the people at work? Did you make any new friends?'

Kate would have laughed if she'd had the energy. 'They're fantastic. It's like Seneca Falls without the organization or camaraderie.'

Oma frowned. 'I'm sorry, dear. Were they mean?'

Kate felt like she was back in junior high again, crying to her grandmother about the cruel girls on the bus. Though Maggie and Gail and the rest of them weren't exactly cruel. At least not to Kate.

She said, 'They're all just really tough. They walk around in armor.'

Liesbeth noted, 'I imagine they have to.'

'No, that's not what she means.' Oma crossed her hands in her lap. 'Sometimes, women with a little bit of power can be much harder than men. Especially on other women. They have to distance themselves from the weakness of their sex. Yes?'

Kate looked at her mother. She generally disagreed with whatever Oma said.

For once, Liesbeth didn't offer her opinion. She held the shaker between both hands as she mixed the martinis. Ice clanked against the stainless steel. Her sleeve had fallen down. Kate saw the tattoo on the outer side of her left forearm. The letter *A* followed by five numbers.

Oma asked, 'Are you attempting to punish the ice?'

Liesbeth stilled the shaker. She put two glasses on the coffee table and filled each one. 'Kaitlin, did you eat all of the olives?'

'Of course she did. She loves olives.' Oma offered Kate's empty glass to fill. 'I told Margot Kleinman that my granddaughter was a police officer. You would think I had told her you were an astronaut.' She raised her glass to Kate. 'It's wonderful you've found a way to help people, darling.'

Reluctantly, Kate picked up her glass. She met her grandmother's gaze, then her mother's, then downed half the drink.

'That's lovely,' Oma said, meaning the martini. She told Kate, 'It's very important for your life to have meaning. Even on the days it makes you unhappy, you still need a purpose.'

Liesbeth sat on the couch. She stroked Kate's hair

behind her ear, then rested her hand on Kate's shoulder. 'It's nice that you're wearing your pearls.'

Kate stared at the cigarette smoldering in the ashtray. She was probably six or seven the first time she'd noticed her mother's tattoo. She was in the bathtub getting her ears scrubbed. '*What's that?*' Kate had asked. '*Nothing, schatje. Hold still.*'

'Darling?' Oma asked. 'Are you tired? Should we leave you alone?'

'No.' Kate rubbed her mother's hand. 'Please don't.'

'Will you tell us about your day?' Oma waited expectantly. 'Was it so terrible?'

Kate smiled at her grandmother. Oma's dress was long-sleeved, covering the tattoo that was on the inside of her left arm. Same letter, different numbers. As with Liesbeth, she'd been sent to Auschwitz, but when the Nazis had discovered that Oma was a professor, they'd sent her to Mauthausen, a so-called 'bone-grinder' camp designed to work intellectuals to death.

Liesbeth said, 'You're very distracted. Did something bad happen today?'

Kate held on to her mother's hand. 'Nothing happened,' she lied. And then she figured that since she was lying, she should put her heart into it. 'Work wasn't that bad. My feet don't hurt any more than when I've danced all night. And this' – she indicated her forehead – 'is because I've apparently forgotten how to look where I'm going when I wear a hat.'

Oma leaned back, smiling. 'I suppose the worst part is having to get out of bed before ten. I can't imagine.'

'*Moeder,* you're always up before I am.' Liesbeth seemed more relieved than Oma. She took one last smoke before extinguishing her cigarette. 'I know because half the coffee is always gone.'

'It's very good coffee. How can I stop myself?'

Kate wasn't sure if it was the Valium or the heating pad, but she finally felt her muscles begin to unknot. The room had taken on a lightness that hadn't been there before. She tried to think of something else to tell. 'I think the most galling part is that I never realized how smart I am about things that have absolutely no consequence in the real world.'

Neither her mother nor her grandmother objected to the observation.

'I'm not used to feeling so stupid.' That, Kate understood, was the rock she had been forced to push uphill all day. People had talked to her like she was an idiot because in many ways she *was* an idiot. 'I don't know how to talk to strangers. I don't know how to stand up for myself. Apparently, I don't know how to run. I even had to be told how to go to the bathroom.'

Both looked confused.

Kate couldn't find a way to make it sound funny, so she chose not to explain. 'There are just all sorts of practical things that I've never had to deal with. I've never felt so out of place.' Kate drank her martini, so she didn't see the look exchanged between her mother and grandmother. 'The least you could do is pretend to be surprised by this revelation.'

The look was exchanged again.

'Of course you'll learn,' Oma soothed. 'This job – it's good to help people, yes? To give back?'

Kate nodded, though she couldn't think of one damn thing she'd done all day that contributed to the well-being

189

of anyone, least of all herself. 'You're right. Of course you're right.'

Oma said, 'I remember that nice police captain who spoke to us when the Temple was bombed.' She put down her drink. 'We were all very worried, of course. We'd never met a police officer here except to ask directions. He was very serious. One of our crowd, surprisingly. When was that? Fifty-six?'

'Fifty-eight.' Kate had been eight years old when the Temple on Peachtree Street was nearly destroyed. They lived close enough that they heard the dynamite explode.

'Those fools thought we'd be there on a Sunday,' Liesbeth said. 'But maybe they weren't so stupid. They got away with it.'

Oma was never one to dwell on the negative. 'The point I am making is that the police were very helpful. They made us feel safe again.' She smiled so sweetly that Kate felt her heart breaking in two. 'And now you are making people feel safe, Kaitlin. What a gift you're giving the world.'

Kate knew there was a prostitute on Cheshire Bridge Road who would certainly disagree, but she smiled for her grandmother's sake.

Liesbeth asked, 'It makes things easier for you, yes?'

She meant after Patrick. Kate supposed what she had done today was better than staying in bed all day and crying over something that would never change. Sitting right in front of her were two sterling examples of women with the strength to carry on past unspeakable tragedies.

And the tragedies did go unspoken. Neither her mother nor grandmother ever talked about what had happened to them during the war. They refused to dwell on their losses. Kate knew facts, but not details. Oma had lost her mother and father, a brother, her husband, and a son. Liesbeth had lost her family, too. She was barely a teenager when she was transported to the camps. Each had assumed the other was dead until the Red Cross managed to reunite them after the liberation.

And here they sat trying to comfort Kate as if her aching body and bruised ego were of any consequence.

Kate told her mother, 'Yes. You were right. It's good to have something to do.'

'Something *useful*.' Oma raised her glass in another toast. 'I'm very proud of you, darling. This is unconventional, what you're doing, of course, but always know that your family is very proud of you. You've made us very happy.'

'You have,' Liesbeth agreed. 'Though we would've been equally as proud had you kept that last job as a secretary.'

'*Hoe kom je erbij,*' Oma muttered. 'She was an awful secretary.'

'She wasn't that bad.'

'*Ze is te slim voor dat soort werk.*'

'*Moeder.*'

The two women switched to their native tongue. Kate tuned them out. She understood only half of what they were saying. As with most Americans, Dutch sounded to her more like a disease of the throat than an actual language.

Kate leaned forward so that she could dry her feet. Her back twinged with the movement. Her vision swam. Suddenly, she was so tired that she could barely stay upright. The clock over the fireplace showed it was almost eleven o'clock. The thought of driving home was too much. Kate could stay and sleep in her old room. Mary Jane would have her uniforms ready. She could use her mother's makeup. Or, if she was lucky, Maggie would open her locker and Kate could retrieve her purse.

Her purse. It was only through divine intervention that Kate had been able to drive her car tonight. Years ago, Patrick had stuck a magnetic key box under the wheel well or she'd still be sitting in the parking lot off Central Avenue. Kate would have to get a combination lock. She would pay for it because it didn't seem right not to. They probably had some locks at the pro shop inside the tennis club. She could borrow one from her father until she had time to go.

With a start, Kate realized that she was really returning to work tomorrow. She wasn't going to quit after her first day. How had that happened? Certainly through no conscious effort of her own. Her grandmother wasn't a quitter. Her mother had never given up. Their blood flowed in Kate's veins. Compared to what they had survived, the Atlanta Police Department was a walk in the park.

She could do this.

She *had* to do this.

As if on cue, Mary Jane came into the room with Kate's uniforms neatly folded in her arms. 'I got the stain outta the one, but you can probably see where I had to stitch the tear in the sleeve.'

Kate began, 'I'm so sorry that I . . .' Her voice trailed off.

Philip Van Zandt was standing behind Mary Jane. He

was wearing a charcoal-gray Hickey Freeman suit with a light purple shirt. The hair on his chest showed beneath his unbuttoned collar. His pants were closely tailored to his body. The legs gently flared out below his knees.

He said, 'Good evening again, Mrs. Herschel. Mrs. De Vries.' He was showing off. He pronounced Oma's name like he were riding a bike along the Herengracht. 'I'm afraid I gave Mary Jane a fright knocking on the basement door.'

Kate knew exactly why he was knocking on that particular door. All her friends knew she had moved downstairs when she turned fourteen because her parents could no longer endure Kate's giggly slumber parties. Besides that, her car was in the driveway and almost every light was on in the house.

'All right.' Mary Jane had never been one for tension. She put the uniforms on the sideboard. 'I'll be off now.'

Kate said, 'I'm so sorry I kept you up this late.'

Mary Jane waved away her concern, but Kate felt awful as she watched the old woman shuffle toward the back stairs.

Philip gave the maid a slight bow as she passed him. 'Ladies, my apologies for coming so late unannounced, but my mother was at the club tonight and it seems she may have picked up your lipstick by mistake.'

He held a tube of lipstick in his hand. The item was the sort of thing you'd find in a corner store. All the women knew this. Philip knew this. Yet he pretended he was performing a remarkable act of chivalry.

Oma was always game for deception. 'Yes, that belongs to me. Thank you, Philip. You're so thoughtful to return it.'

Liesbeth wasn't so easy. 'I forgot to ask your mother how your wife is doing. I believe she's studying in Israel?' She turned to Kate. 'Philip is married now.'

'Yes, I know,' Kate said, just like she knew if she tried to stand up, the heating pad would pull her back to the couch like a slingshot.

'Israel,' Oma echoed wistfully. 'Philip, have you seen Dr. Herschel's stamps from the Hapoel Games?'

His smile said the mere thought delighted him. 'I haven't had the pleasure.'

'If you could?' Oma held out her hand. Philip helped her stand. While his back was turned, Kate yanked the heating pad out from under her dress. The noise was awful, like a sash being pulled through a belt loop.

Philip turned toward her. He looked at the heating pad on the couch. He looked at Kate.

Kate looked at the floor.

Oma said, 'I'll find the stamps. Liesbeth, get some fresh ice from the kitchen.'

Unusually, Kate took her mother's view. 'It's very late, Oma. I think Philip must have work in the morning.'

He held open his arms. 'I have the whole day off.'

'Really?' she asked, because what was he doing here? It was one thing to share a harmless flirtation, but this was taking it a step too far. 'Maybe you should spend the time writing a letter to your wife.'

'I've already written two. I told her all about seeing you today.'

'You saw each other?' Liesbeth's voice went up suspiciously. 'When was this?'

'At the hospital,' Kate answered, then because she didn't want to tell her mother that another police officer had been shot, she lied, 'Philip was giving me information about a case.'

Philip winked at Kate. 'Your daughter is quite the detective.'

'She tends to figure things out quickly.' Liesbeth held a fresh cigarette between her fingers.

Philip leaned down with a light. 'I'll have a gin and tonic, Kaitlin. Extra ice.'

'*Lieverd?*' Oma called from the hallway. 'Can you help me in the study, please?'

Liesbeth stabbed her cigarette into the ashtray. 'Your father will check on you before he comes to bed.'

'Thank you,' Kate said, though they both knew that her father was likely asleep by now. 'Philip won't be staying long.'

'I'm sure.'

'Good evening, Mrs. Herschel.' Philip bowed as she left, the same as he had with Mary Jane. He told Kate, 'Such a lovely woman.'

Kate warned, 'You shouldn't vex her.'

'The tactic seems to be working well for me with her daughter.'

'It's really not.' Kate grabbed the ice bucket as she headed toward the kitchen. She pushed through the swinging door. She leaned against the counter. Her hands were shaky, but not because of Philip. She was exhausted. It was late. And he was married.

'I should look at that bruise.' Philip stood a few feet away. The kitchen door swung silently behind him. He certainly liked to make an entrance. 'How did it happen?'

For a change, she told the truth. 'I ran directly into a wall.'

He didn't laugh. 'Did you lose consciousness?'

'No.'

'See stars?'

Kate crossed her arms over her chest. 'What's the point of this?'

'I'm a doctor. This is an exam. Did you see stars?'

She relented. 'Yes.'

'Feel dizzy?'

She nodded.

'Were you nauseated?'

She nodded again.

'Threw up?'

'A little.'

'Get up on the counter.'

'Philip, I—'

'You could be concussed.' He put his hands on her waist and lifted her up. 'Your back feels like it's on fire.'

The heating pad. 'It's where I store my vexation.'

Philip laughed. He kept his hands on her waist. 'Did you take something?'

'Aspirin and Valium.'

'Are you on any other medication?'

'No.'

'Birth control?'

She hated herself for blushing. 'Yes. But not for—'

He held up one finger in front of her face. 'Follow.' She tracked his movement back and forth. 'Let me check your eyes.' He pressed at the lids. 'Look up.' She did as she was told. 'Now down.' Again, she complied. 'Tell me if anything is tender.' He palpated her face and neck with his fingers. 'Open your mouth.' She opened her mouth. 'Open your legs.'

'Why?'

'So I can run my hand up the inside of your thigh.'

She gasped, because she'd blindly complied and that was exactly what he had done.

Instead of clenching her knees together or slapping him away, Kate sat perfectly still. 'You are a married man in my father's house with your hand up my dress.'

'Only halfway up.' He gently stroked the inside of her thigh with the tips of his fingers. His touch was like a butterfly fluttering against her skin.

Kate started to sweat. 'Philip, stop.'

He stopped stroking her, but he didn't remove his hand. His palm rested against the inside of her leg. His skin was hot. He looked at her mouth. 'Do you still taste like strawberries?'

Kate had difficulty finding her voice. 'That was lip gloss.'

'It was delicious.' He started stroking her thigh again. 'You're so beautiful, Kaitlin. Do you know that? You're perfect.'

'Philip,' she managed. His touch was unbearably tender. She felt a tremble working through her body.

'You were the first girl I ever kissed who wasn't my cousin.'

Kate pushed his shoulder. 'Why do you joke about everything?'

'Because it's funny. I'm a married man in your father's house and I'm standing here with my hand up your dress.'

Maybe if it hadn't been Kate's father and Kate's dress, she would've seen the humor. 'I asked you to stop.'

'Do you really want me to?'

197

Kate didn't know what she wanted. 'What about your wife?'

'My wife is for making babies. You're for fucking.'

The sting was unexpected. 'That's an awful thing to say.'

'Trust me, one is a lot more fun than the other.'

'Why would I trust you?'

'You shouldn't.' Philip's hand moved higher up her leg. His fingers brushed against her.

Kate's breath caught. She could feel him through the thin cotton of her underwear. He knew exactly what he was doing. Everything melted away under his touch. There was nothing but the firm pressure of him moving between her legs.

'That's good?' He watched her face as he stroked up and down. 'You can feel that?'

Kate nodded. God, could she feel it.

'It's good?'

She gripped his shoulders. The muscles moved beneath her hands. She wanted to kiss him. He wouldn't let her. She tried to pull him closer. He wouldn't come. He just kept staring at her, gauging her reaction as he touched her.

'Hey, your vexation is even hotter down here.'

'Shut up,' Kate breathed. She was quivering. The feel of him was almost too much.

Philip kissed her neck. Kate wanted to be devoured by his mouth. His lips were so soft. His face was so rough. She reached for his belt, but he stopped her. She tried to pull down her underwear. He stopped her.

'Philip—'

'Shh.' The sound of his deep voice pulsed through her

body. She was so close. 'Will you do me a favor, Kaitlin?'

She nodded because she was breathing too hard to answer.

'Knock on my door,' he whispered. 'Will you knock on my door?'

She shook her head. He was making her crazy.

'Like the song. Knock three times. Okay?'

'For what?'

'For me to fuck you.'

His hand moved ever so slightly forward. Kate's nerves ignited. She was on the edge. His mouth was still at her ear. His tongue. His teeth. Every sensation reverberated between her legs. She didn't know what he was doing anymore. She was too consumed by want.

He said, 'Only when you're ready. But soon, okay?'

Kate couldn't answer. She was almost there. Her body throbbed with anticipation.

He backed off the pressure. 'Okay?'

'Yes,' she whispered – begged. 'Yes.'

Slowly, Philip took away his hand. His wet fingers dragged across her skin. He tenderly kissed her forehead.

Kate opened her eyes. 'What are—'

'Shh.' His thumb traced along her lips. She could smell herself on him. 'Soon, okay?'

He knocked three times on the counter, then turned and walked away.

16

Fox sat in front of his television. He was drunk and he was pissed off. Too pissed even to watch Kate, which meant that he was only punishing himself.

He deserved the punishment. He had failed.

It was the sort of thing that would've happened to Fox Senior – sitting in a bar with a bunch of faggots while some woman was doing his job. Or at least trying to do his job. Sheer luck was the only thing that had kept Jimmy Lawson above ground. Fox had heard it on the police scanner. The old woman had used a .44 magnum. Jimmy's arm had taken the bullet when it should've been his head.

Fox was not going to shift blame. This wasn't like the first time, when Fox had turned the corner onto the alley and found Don Wesley on his knees going at it with Jimmy Lawson. Any man would've frozen in that kind of situation. And the gun had jammed. And Lawson had jumped behind a Dumpster and Fox had left because a good soldier knew when to retreat.

Today was not the same. Fox had been squarely in the wrong. Jimmy wasn't on his way to the bar, looking for some queer to lick his wounds. He was looking for the man who had put down his faggot partner.

That was all it took. The plan no longer sat in the back of Fox's mind, working through the options, spitballing images of Kate Murphy to keep him on the hook.

The plan was going to happen.

Part one: Jimmy couldn't just be killed anymore. He had to be used, because Fox had to prove to himself that he was back in control.

Part two: The pawn would be sacrificed for the queen.

Fox put down his drink. That was the important part. He needed to be clearheaded for this. He could no longer sit idly by waiting for lightning to jolt the thing from the back of his skull into the front. Fox knew all the options. He had to figure out the best way to combine part one and part two into an executable plan.

The sooner the better. One thing Fox had learned during the war was that once a man knew he was marked, he started acting smarter. He noticed his surroundings. He took precautions. He varied his routine.

Fox liked routine. He needed routine. Routine had always served him well, no matter what target he was hunting.

He picked up his clipboard and paged back through his log.

Friday of last week. Wednesday of last week. Monday of last week.

He went back farther. Another Friday, another Wednesday, another Monday.

The same pattern the week before.

Kate's visits to her parents were like clockwork. Fox guessed that made her a good girl, inasmuch as a filthy Jewess could ever be thought of as good. She always dressed up for her visits. She never wore pants. Most nights, she stayed over at their house, which made things more complicated but also gave Fox more options.

Anybody who knew Fox knew he liked options almost as much as he liked routine.

Option one: The thicket of shrubs near the basement window to Kate's bedroom. The bed was a single, probably from her childhood. There were posters on the wall (the Beatles, which he could forgive her for; Paul Newman, which he could not). Soft pink sheets. Matching walls. A dark purple blanket she draped over the bed when it was cold. The bathroom door was always left ajar. A nightlight made it possible for Fox to track the rise and fall of her chest. He timed her breath using the second hand on his watch. If he was lucky, she got up in the night and he would see through the sliver of light Kate's nightgown. White cotton. Almost transparent. When there was a full moon, Fox could see the darkness of her secret places through the thin material.

Option two: The mudroom by the kitchen. They usually left the light on, which meant Fox could stand at the door and see inside the kitchen. Kate always carried the dinner plates to the sink. Sometimes she would stand there watching the water run. Other times, she would sit at the kitchen table and talk to her grandmother.

Grandmother. At first, Fox had thought she was the mother and that the mother was an older sister. He'd finally had to knock on the door and pretend he was taking a survey for the phone company in order to ascertain the relationship.

The mother had invited him in. The grandmother had joined the conversation shortly after. They had served him coffee and cookies and Fox had asked to use the restroom because just being that close to women who looked like Kate made him hard as a rock.

Option three: The fallen tree in the front yard. Fox had sat behind it just that night and watched Kate walk up the curving sidewalk to the front door. She moved like a cat. 'Languid' was the word. Sexy as hell. She was wearing high-heeled shoes that flexed her calves in such a way that a lesser man would've put his hands down his pants to relieve the pressure.

Fox had walked away because he had fucked up too many things today to think that he could remain in control.

Punishment number one: He didn't get to watch her change for bed.

Punishment number two: He didn't get to watch her wrap the purple blanket around her shoulders and lie down.

Punishment number three: He didn't get to relieve the pressure in his pants as he watched the rhythmic movement of her chest.

1638: Talked to doctor in hospital ER (P)
1718: Cried in car parked outside police station (P)
1901: Closed curtains at hotel (P)

Pressure.
This wasn't the first time a Jew had caused him trouble.
When Fox was nine years old, a Hebrew family bought the house three doors down. The Feldmans moved in one weekend, then by the next, everybody had a For Sale sign in their front yard. Two houses sold, then word got out and nobody could sell anything for a reasonable price.

Senior told Fox he had seen this kind of thing before. One Jew moves in, then the property values plummet, then the rest of the Jews swoop down like vultures.

Lesson six: Never trust a Jew.

As with many of Senior's predictions, this one hadn't come to fruition. No one could afford to walk away from their mortgages. The Jews hadn't swept in. There was just the Feldmans and the animosity that bubbled up and down the street.

Still, Fox always thought of Hebrews as vultures. Not theoretically, but in a literal sense. They were all dark with black hair and dark eyes and beaked noses. Feldman's wife was plump and shifty-looking and all the kids scattered when she went to the mailbox because everybody knew a Jew could curse you.

The eldest daughter was a different story. Rebecca Feldman was dark, too, but she wasn't plump. She was curvy. Her lips were a perfect red bow. She wore shapely skirts that showed her hips. And sweaters. Not a man on that street didn't look forward to autumn, when Rebecca Feldman wore her tight sweaters. She did it on purpose. They all knew that. She teased them. She toyed with them. And they couldn't do a damn thing about it without bringing down the law.

Lesson seven: All Jewesses are promiscuous whores.

The first time Fox got hard was when he saw Rebecca Feldman in one of those sweaters. He didn't know what was happening. He ran home to his room. He hid under the covers. He sweated like a maniac because he thought the Jew had cursed him.

And then his hands had worked to relieve the pressure, and all he could think about after that was what he wanted to do to her. Peel off that sweater. Slide down that skirt. Fox wasn't sure what would come next, but he knew instinctively that the Jew had to pay for what she did to him. Because Fox was out of control. In those moments when he ran to his room and ducked under his sheets, the Pressure was in charge.

And now the same thing was happening all over again, only this time, the Jew was Kate.

DAY TWO
TUESDAY

17

For the second time in as many days, Kate pushed her way through the thick throng of men in the squad room. She ignored the leers. She crossed her arms over her chest to keep the groping to a minimum. Unfortunately, she couldn't cover her ears.

'Baaah!' they bleated. 'Baaaaah!'

Of all the nicknames that had been trotted out yesterday, from Irish Spring to China Doll, why was this the one that was sticking?

Someone tipped his hat to Kate. 'Hello, lamb chop.'

Her smile turned into a grimace.

'Baaaah!'

Finally, the door. Kate was careful not to open it too wide. From the frying pan into the fire. Wanda Clack was sitting on the bench loading up her utility belt. She saw Kate and let out a 'Baaah!'

Kate plastered on her smile, held up her hands in surrender. She didn't know how much longer she could do this. She was dying inside.

Wanda said, 'Lookit you with your uniform. I'd have to think twice before I called you a man.'

'Thank you very much.' Kate smoothed down the shirt,

which was still blousy. She'd asked Mary Jane to leave more room than usual.

'You get that Jew to do it?' Wanda laughed. 'He didn't poke you with his horns?'

Kate knew better than to tell the truth about herself. The last thing she needed was another mark against her.

The door opened. Maggie slid in. She raised her eyebrows, seemingly surprised that Kate was here.

Kate felt her leg being slapped.

'Lend me a hoof, Sheep.' Wanda held out her hand. Kate didn't know what to do but to help leverage her up. Wanda gave a loud groan as she stood. The equipment around her belt creaked. 'Well, I gotta say, after what happened yesterday, none of us thought you'd show up again.'

Kate tried for jocularity. 'Surprise!'

'You said it.' Wanda winked at her before she edged like a crab out the door.

Kate smiled at Maggie, but she was busy dialing the combination on her locker. 'Good morning.'

Maggie yanked open the lock. 'How'd you get home last night?'

'Spare key.'

'Magnetic box under the wheel well?'

'How did you know?'

She tossed Kate her purse. 'That's what the victim usually tells me when I'm taking a stolen car report.'

Kate held her purse to her chest. Could she leave? Would it be that easy? Could she just turn around and leave?

Maggie asked, 'You get a lock or do you need to use mine again?'

At least Kate had done one thing right today. She held up the lock she'd taken from her father's suitcase.

Maggie studied the lock with great disapproval. Still, she opened a locker three down from her own. Number eight, right beside the curtain the colored girls had put up.

'Thank you.' Kate didn't really need anything from her purse, but she opened it anyway as she walked across the room. Everything was in there – makeup, gum, a few tampons, some change that she shouldn't let float around. She unbuckled her wallet. She checked the cash compartment, but not for her money. Her wedding photo rested among the bills.

Patrick was dressed in a dark blue suit and tie. His hair was neatly combed. Kate was wearing a white knee-length dress with a peplum that fluttered loosely around her hips. She remembered her pearls kept catching on the light shirring at the sweetheart neckline.

They had been married at the courthouse by a judge and not by a priest at the Cathedral of Christ the King, which was why Patrick's parents had not attended the ceremony. Kate had always assumed that she was agnostic like her parents; which fact still didn't allow them entrance into the gentile country club. She'd gone to temple as a child because it made her Oma happy. She'd gone to bar mitzvahs for the camaraderie and cake. She enjoyed an occasional Shabbat and preferred Christmas to Hanukkah, but there was no way in hell she would dishonor what had happened to her family by getting married in a Catholic church.

'Everything in there?' Maggie asked.

Kate looked up.

'I didn't take your money.'

'I didn't think you had.' Kate closed the wallet and shoved it back into her purse.

'You're with me again today.' Maggie rested her hand on her revolver. 'Is that a problem?'

'I'm delighted.'

Her eyes narrowed. 'If you want lunch, take some cash with you. Lipstick is okay, but nothing dark. You got your notebook and pen?'

Kate tapped her breast pocket.

'Did you turn in your reports?'

'First thing.'

'Get your citation book. We're skipping roll call today.' She slammed her locker closed. 'Meet me on the back stairs in five minutes.'

Kate gathered she was not supposed to ask for details. 'Yes, ma'am.'

Maggie slipped out the door. No one else came in. Kate had never been alone in the locker room before. She glanced at the area behind the curtain, wondering just what was back there. More lockers, she saw. There was a stack of Negro magazines at the end of their bench. A small table with a glass vase was tucked into the corner. There was only a single flower, a daisy, but it looked fresh.

Something bumped against the door and Kate nearly jumped out of her skin. She didn't know which would be worse – being here when the colored girls came or being late meeting Maggie on the stairs.

She took some cash from her wallet and pocketed her lipstick, which was absolutely too dark but what was Maggie going to do, arrest her?

Kate put the lipstick back in her purse.

She quickly figured out why Maggie had disapproved of the suitcase lock. The shackle barely fit through the slot in the locker door. She had to force it closed. The tiny key could easily slip out of her pocket. Kate felt certain she'd feel it. Her hips were black and blue from the Kel-Lite and nightstick beating into her yesterday afternoon. She was shocked she'd managed to get to sleep last night.

Of course, she had been shocked by a lot of things last night, none more so than the mind-blowing thirty seconds it had taken for her to finish what Philip Van Zandt had started. She'd never had a man touch her down there before. Patrick thought it was kinky that time they did it standing up in the foyer.

'Dear Patrick,' she silently composed in her head. 'Thank you for your last letter. I have been very busy myself. I met a colorful pimp yesterday morning. I watched a whore get tortured. I helped resolve a dispute over a sandwich. I let a near-stranger finger me in my mother's kitchen. Hope you are not the same . . .'

The door opened. Kate panicked. The colored girls were here. There were four of them. They glared at her. She put her head down and tried for a quick exit. They didn't make it easy. They crowded together so that she had to push her way through.

'Sorry . . . sorry . . . ,' Kate apologized. They were worse than the men. Her hat was tipped. Her shoulders were bumped like she was traveling through a car wash. A foot came out to trip her. She barely managed to stumble into the outer room.

'Baaah!' a fat cop screamed in her face.

Kate's good humor was spent for the morning. She had no idea where the back stairs were, but she assumed 'back' meant to the rear of the room. There was an exit sign over a door. Kate made her way toward it. The going was easier. Most everyone was taking their seat for roll call. She wasn't sure how this would work. If Kate wasn't checked in by the duty officer, did that mean she wasn't technically working?

'What took so long?' Maggie stood at the bottom of a set of large marble stairs. She didn't seem to expect an answer. 'Come on.'

There was nothing to do but follow her up the stairs. Kate concentrated on her feet as she climbed. Her shoes were still slipping even though she was wearing two pairs of her father's socks. Her hat kept falling down over her eyes. She bumped it up. It slid back down. She bumped it up again.

Maggie said, 'You're allowed to take off your hat.'

Maggie's hat was still on, so Kate left hers in place. 'Is your brother all right?'

'Look up.'

'What?' Kate looked up. She was one step away from running straight into a towering black woman. There were two of them standing at the top of the stairs. They had identical uniforms and identical tightly shaved Afros. Their name badges read DELROY and WATSON. They stared openly at Kate.

Delroy said, 'She sure is white as a sheep.'

'Uh-huh.' Watson nodded in agreement. 'You'd think she'd'a learned after yesterday to look where she's going.' She reached out with one hand and knocked the hat off Kate's head.

Maggie grabbed Kate's arm to keep her from retrieving her hat.

'Listen up, Sheep.' Delroy used a pointed finger to explain, 'You look left, you look right, you look up, you look down.'

Watson finished, 'You do the hokey-pokey and you turn yourself around.'

They both clapped.

'That's what it's all about.'

They both laughed, but Watson kept her eyes zeroed in on Kate. 'We ain't jokin' here, White Sheep. You gotta know everything around you all the time. That's the only way you're gonna stay alive. You feel me?'

'I feel you,' Kate mumbled, sounding like the whitest Jew who had ever taken a wrong turn out of Buckhead.

'She *feels* me,' Delroy told her partner. 'You hear that?'

Watson tried to imitate Kate's accent. 'I feel you, lovey.'

Delroy went for a Thurston Howell. 'Thank you, ma'dear. Might I *feel* you later after we share some cock-tails at the club?'

'We don't have time for this.' Maggie nodded toward a closed door. She let Delroy and Watson go ahead of them. Then she nodded for Kate to retrieve her hat.

Kate did as she was told, offering a cheerful 'You're full of nods this morning.'

Maggie was already in the room, which was another storage closet. This one was actually used for storage. Metal shelves contained pens, folders, staples, notepads.

Maggie nodded for Kate to shut the door. As usual, Kate did as she was told. She had to assume there was a reason Maggie had been so tight-lipped about meeting these women. The curtain in the dressing room wasn't the only thing that separated the colored girls from the whites.

Delroy asked, 'We gonna do this in front of the Sheep?'

'She won't talk,' Maggie said, which Kate took as a compliment. 'I need a favor.'

Delroy twisted her lips to the side. 'Go on.'

'There's a pimp I need to talk to. Name's Sir She.'

'Sir She,' Delroy repeated. 'Tranny pimp works outta CT?'

'You know him?'

'Heard of him,' Delroy said. 'We've dealt with a coupla his girls. Got the shit kicked outta 'em for not turning in their money.'

Watson added, 'He wears these white boots, got gold tips on 'em. Tore this one girl up so bad she won't never pee straight again.'

'Where's he live?' Maggie asked.

'He's renting rooms in a boardinghouse off Huff.'

Maggie nodded for the umpteenth time. 'Good. That's what we got off a witness yesterday.' Kate noticed that Maggie didn't volunteer how they had gotten the information from Violet. 'Anything else?'

Delroy said, 'Boardinghouse is run by a freaky Portuguese chick. Old as dirt, but I wouldn't cross her.' She turned to her partner. 'What's the house number, eight-fifteen?'

'Eight-nineteen.' Watson wrinkled her nose. 'Damn old biddy looks like she got spiders in her hair.'

Maggie asked, 'Portuguese? What's a white woman doing living in CT?'

'You crackers gonna let some damn foreigner live in your backyard?'

Delroy trotted out her snooty accent again. 'She used to live up near the shopping mall, but the noise was atrocious!'

'Better,' Kate admitted. She'd really nailed the intonations.

Maggie held out her arm and physically pushed Kate out of the conversation. 'Are any of them carrying?'

'Sir She don't carry. The one you gotta worry about is the big-ass mother works for him. Fat as a whale. Crazy as a loon. Matter-fact, both of 'em are tetched, from what I hear. But the big one is just flat-out-mothah-fuckin-crazy, knowhattamean?'

Delroy gave Kate a meaningful look. 'He's got a thing about white women. Don't like 'em. And that's for real, Sheep.'

Watson looked at Kate, too. 'He likes 'em good enough when he's cutting 'em up. Keeps a switchblade on him. Pulls it out like magic and the next thing you know, half your face is hanging off the bone.'

Kate willed herself not to shudder.

Maggie asked, 'But no guns?'

Watson shrugged. 'I told you we ain't never met the brothers. They're new in town, been here maybe five, six months.'

Delroy said, 'No time to bring a welcome basket, you dig?'

Watson said, 'This is just shit we heard about him.'

Delroy added, 'It's good shit, but it's still shit.'

'Okay.' Maggie crossed her arms over her chest. She waited.

Watson stared at Delroy. Delroy stared at Watson.

Watson said, 'Sir She runs old whores off Whitehall.'

Delroy said, 'That's where Don Wesley got shot.'

'Where Lawson's brother almost got shot, too,' Watson reminded her partner. 'She must be looking for a gal saw something, maybe wants to see if she can get her to talk.'

'Girl won't talk without the pimp's okay.'

They both continued to stare at each other in silence. Finally, Delroy nodded. Watson nodded, too.

Delroy told Maggie, 'Give us until lunchtime. We'll make sure you got passage into CT after that. Straight to Huff and back. That's all we can guarantee.'

'Deal.' Maggie didn't offer her thanks. 'What've you got for me?'

Watson was obviously prepared. 'Black girl got raped two nights ago over in Midtown. All night long. Thirteen years old. Ended up in the Grady ER needing stitches. We think one of yours did it.'

'I've got a sister that age.' Maggie bumped Kate's arm, indicating she should write this down. 'You get a description?'

Watson answered, 'Better than that. Name's Lewis Windall Conroy the Third. Twenty-one years old. He's a student over at Georgia Tech. Originally from Berwyn, Maryland, where my people tell me he's already got one sexual assault complaint off a fourteen-year-old that his daddy took care of.'

Kate looked up. Maggie's lips were parted. Kate had never seen her caught surprised.

Maggie asked, 'He lose his clothes?'

'Why you ask that?'

Maggie didn't answer.

Watson pulled a thick brown wallet out of her back pocket and handed it to Maggie. 'Cocksucker musta been stoned outta his mind'. His clothes were right there on the floor, but he grabbed her granddaddy's raincoat and bugged out.'

Maggie flipped through to the license. She stared at the photograph. 'Shit.'

Kate looked over her shoulder. The man was college-aged with a round face and wispy blond hair.

'I knew something wasn't right about him.' Maggie told the women, 'I had this asshole yesterday morning, but there was nothing I could keep him on.'

'Well, now you got something.'

Maggie checked the rest of the wallet. There was a picture of an older couple, probably his parents. She stopped on a student ID from Georgia Tech.

Watson said, 'The girl's daddy took the money.'

Delroy added, 'Ain't gonna buy her cherry back, but it paid for the pain medication.'

'That's not what I'm lookin' for.' Maggie pocketed the student ID and the license. She tried to hand back the wallet. 'There's two credit cards in there.'

Delroy didn't like that. 'He's not a thief.'

Maggie put the wallet on one of the shelves. 'We'll pick this guy up. The girl willing to testify?'

The women laughed at the very idea.

Maggie said, 'What do you want me to do, Del? I can't arrest him off nothing.'

'Find something,' Delroy ordered. Kate heard the edge in the woman's voice. 'You had to interview that girl in the hospital, explain to her why she can't get her cooch wet until the stitches come out, you'd be over there right now dragging this baby-raping motherfucker outta calculus.'

'All right,' Maggie agreed. 'But his daddy's obviously connected. Even if I lock him up, he'll be out in less than twenty-four hours.'

Watson looked at Delroy again. Kate wondered if they were telepathic.

Delroy said, 'You get him back on our side of town. We'll take it from there.'

'Okay.' Maggie didn't seem concerned with what they'd do to him. 'I'll talk to my guys and put the details in your locker.'

'You do that.' Delroy told Kate, 'And you, little Sheep, look where you're going next time.'

The meeting was concluded. There was no small talk or asking after each other's parents. Maggie nodded for Kate to open the door. They left the storage room, but instead of going back toward the stairs, Maggie headed down the hall.

Kate almost ran into her when she stopped.

Maggie turned back around and called, 'Del, you know a place called Dabbler's?'

Both women sputtered with laughter. Delroy said, 'Dabbler's? Girl, you crazy.'

They were still laughing as they walked down the stairs.

Kate asked, 'Are we going to see Circe?'

Maggie didn't acknowledge the joke. 'Didn't you hear what they said? After lunchtime. We've got at least four hours until we're cleared.'

'Cleared for—'

Maggie walked down the hall. Kate had no choice but to follow her. She rested her hand on her revolver the same way Maggie did. She tried to keep pace, but her shoes made it hard for her to do more than shuffle along.

'Put away your notebook.' Maggie was back to sounding annoyed.

Kate clicked the pen, closed the notebook, and returned both to her breast pocket.

'Don't put anything about that guy in your report.'

'Why?'

'Because we don't have a warrant or any evidence.'

'That doesn't bother you?'

'It doesn't bother you that a grown man can rape a thirteen-year-old girl and get away with it?'

Kate didn't know what to say. This wasn't a philosophical question around the dinner table. There was a real man out there who had raped a real little girl.

Maggie said, 'Get used to putting your notebook in your back pocket. The spiral will burn a hot spot on your chest in the summer.'

Kate didn't point out that Maggie kept her notebook in her breast pocket. Instead, she tried to lighten things up. 'You think I'm still going to be around by summer?'

Maggie didn't answer.

'Dabbler's. That's from the matchbook, right?'

Again, she didn't answer.

Kate figured she might as well get all of her questions out of the way. 'How do you know those two women?'

'Night school.'

'College?' Kate heard the surprise in her voice. 'I mean—'

'We all answered that ad in the back of the comic book where you draw the turtle.'

'That's not what I meant.'

Again, Maggie didn't respond. They'd reached another

set of steps. Marble, grander than the back set. Maggie took them two at a time.

Kate gripped the railing as she followed. She couldn't spend another day acting the part of an ill-trained puppy. She told Maggie, 'Stop. Please.'

Maggie waited at the bottom of the stairs. She looked at her watch.

'Have I done something wrong?' Kate knew how stupid the question sounded. 'I mean, obviously I'm doing everything wrong, but is there something specific I've done to make you mad at me?'

Maggie remained silent.

'Is it because of the Sheep sobriquet?' Kate realized that she might not be the only one humiliated by the episode. 'I'm sorry. I should've just let my equipment hit me. I'll know better next time.'

'Sobriquet.' Maggie looked down at Kate's feet. 'What size shoe do you wear?'

'Eight,' Kate lied before she remembered this wasn't Saks. 'I mean nine and a half.'

'You can borrow a pair of Jimmy's old shoes. They'll fit better than what you have.' She nodded toward the door. The gesture was turning into a tic. 'We'll go by my house. You can't come in.'

'Your house?'

'My house. Where my brother and I live.' She talked to Kate like she was a child. 'We'll go by my house to get some shoes that actually fit your feet, and then we'll go to the diner on Moreland Avenue. We're supposed to meet Jimmy there in half an hour. We're going to work on some files with him until around lunchtime. And then we'll go to CT with Gail in case I need backup and you're still trying to figure out how to tie your shoes.'

Kate didn't know which question to ask first. 'Files?'

Kate watched Maggie's back as she walked through the empty lobby toward the glass doors. There were two options here: she could follow Maggie or she could jump on her back and beat her with her fists.

Kate let herself enjoy the fantasy behind curtain number two for just a few moments. It was such a wonderful fantasy. But despite what Philip thought about her purpose in life, Kate knew she wanted children one day.

Yet again, she followed Maggie out the door.

18

Kate had never been to Cabbage Town before, which she gathered was not to be confused with the pejoratively designated CT of Colored Town. The southeastern section of the city was literally on the other side of the railroad tracks. She couldn't recommend the place. The area was blighted by abandoned houses and factories that had fallen into disrepair. She assumed the usual culprits were to blame: the oil crisis, high unemployment, and the worst stock market crash since the Great Depression. Public services seemed to stop at the tracks. Garbage cans were overflowing. Potholes pocked the streets. This seemed like the sort of tough area where the Lawsons would live. The people of the Southside were on their own.

Through her rolled-down window, Kate took in a large red-brick warehouse with crumbled smokestacks reaching to the sky. The painted letters on the side were faded. She made out the word 'National' and wondered if this was the pencil factory where Leo Frank had worked. Sixty years ago, the Jewish industrialist had been wrongfully convicted of murdering a young girl. A lynch mob had kidnapped Frank from prison and strung him from a tree. Photos were taken showing his stretched neck. Pieces of

Frank's clothing were sold as souvenirs. Among the mob were a former governor, a retired superior court judge, and several police officers. They were never tried for his murder, and likely pleased with what followed: roughly three thousand Jews pulled up stakes and fled the state.

Kate had heard about Frank as a child. His story was one of those 'this is how they tried to kill us/this is how we survived' lessons they taught at the Temple. Kate couldn't recall, but Philip Van Zandt was probably in the class, too. He was in all of her classes before he moved away. Until that spin-the-bottle game, she had never given him a second thought. He was just one of those awkward, pimply boys who lurked in corners.

And he could continue to lurk, because Kate hadn't completely lost her mind. She had to assume that last night was the result of some kind of temporary insanity. She'd been tired. Her ego was bruised. Her defenses were down. Kate was the daughter of a psychiatrist. She had read her share of Freud. There was no better word to describe what she'd allowed to happen in the kitchen than adolescent. She was a grown woman. A widow. Philip had a wife. He was going to give her children. He had made it crystal clear that Kate was only good for one thing.

And as far as Kate was concerned, Philip Van Zandt could go knock on his own damn door.

The car's tires thrummed against the bridge spanning I-20. Kate looked down at the light traffic on the freeway. Women, mostly. At this time of day they were either heading to the grocery store or going home after having dropped their kids at school.

Maggie spoke for the first time since they'd left the

225

building. 'East-west highways get even numbers. North-south ones get odd numbers.'

Kate had no idea what she was talking about, but she nodded anyway.

'Auxiliary interstates get three digits. The first digit is even if it's circumferential, odd if it's a spur. If the number is divisible by five, that means it's a major artery.'

'How fascinating.'

'You need to know this stuff, Kate. What if you're pursuing a suspect and he gets on the highway?'

Kate stared longingly out the window. The car was going too fast for her to safely jump out.

'Do you know your radio codes?'

Kate sighed as loudly as she could. 'Code twenty-four: demented person. Code twenty-eight: drunken person. Code thirty: driving under the influence. Code forty-nine: rape. Fifty: shooting. Fifty-one: stabbing. Sixty-three—'

'Okay.' Maggie turned onto a side street. Kate noticed that the houses had changed. They were grander, or at least they had been at some point in the distant past. A few Victorians, a handful of Queen Annes, and lots of little Craftsman bungalows lined the broad streets.

Kate asked, 'What's this area called?'

'Grant Park.'

Kate had been here once before. She was on a class field trip to visit the Atlanta Zoo, which was one of the most depressing things she had ever seen in her life. The animals lived in filth. There was a gorilla who sat alone in a concrete cage and watched soap operas all day.

Looking out the car window, Kate didn't see that the neighbors had it any better. The blight from Cabbage

Town extended into Grant Park. Windows were boarded over. Yards were overgrown jungles. Cars were up on cinder blocks.

Maggie said, 'Just like Buckhead, right?'

Kate didn't trust her ability to filter sarcasm.

The car slowed. Maggie pulled into the opposite lane, then glided to a stop in front of a rambling Victorian. Kate smiled. The old house reminded her of a dollhouse her father had bought her. The siding was light blue. The trim was crisp white with black edging around the windows. All the scrolls and cupolas were accented in a darker blue. There was a wraparound porch and a Juliet balcony over a grand porte cochere.

'It's beautiful.'

'Yeah,' Maggie agreed. 'Too bad I live in the piece of shit next to it.' She pushed open the door. 'Stay in the car.'

Kate was glad to have permission. She watched Maggie walk toward the neighboring house. The most generous thought she had was that the Victorian had good bones. Everything went downhill from there. The large turret bubbled out like a growth. Plastic covered most of the windows. Paint peeled from every piece of wood. Broken stones crumbled from the foundation. An ugly metal carport that belonged on an Airstream spanned the bottom of the driveway.

Kate heard a screen door open and bang close. A lanky man in a tracksuit came out of the nicer house. Kate guessed he was around her age. He wore a headband and white sneakers. He stopped at the bottom of the stairs and stretched back and forth. She supposed he was a jogger. Kate saw scores of them around the park these days. There was something on a chain around his neck that she couldn't make out. He kept glancing over his shoulder at the Lawson house. Kate couldn't tell if he was nervous or looking for someone.

'Hey, asshole!' Jimmy yelled. She assumed he was talking to the neighbor. He limped across the front porch. His injured arm was stiff at his side. 'Mind your own goddamn business!'

The neighbor did a very good job of turning a deaf ear. He sprinted up the driveway. His arms were bent at the elbow, which Kate understood was an excellent way to run.

'Murphy!' Jimmy was talking to Kate now. 'Help Rick.'

Kate had no idea who Rick was, but she got out of the car. Delroy and Watson would not have approved. Kate had been so distracted by what was going on in front of her that she'd forgotten to look behind. There was another Atlanta Police cruiser parked on the street. A uniformed man was opening the back door. He was tall with a thick mustache and hair as black as the leather gloves on his hands. She saw at least five file boxes inside the car.

'Rick Anderson,' the officer told Kate, and she realized that he was the only cop since Maggie who'd bothered to introduce himself. Even more surprisingly, he shook her hand.

'Kate Murphy. Very nice to meet you, Mr. Anderson.'

He seemed embarrassed. 'Everybody calls me Rick.'

'Get the boxes.' Maggie had sneaked up on both of them. She looked as angry as she sounded. 'We're going to do it here.'

Kate didn't bother to ask for details that would never

come. She held out her arms and took a box. Maggie took two and Rick grabbed the remaining ones, plus two bags marked EVIDENCE.

Rick said, 'You're looking nice today, Maggie.'

Maggie asked, 'Is this everything?'

'Everything I could find.'

Maggie told Jimmy, 'I thought we were doing this at the diner.'

'We're here. Why would we go somewhere else?'

Maggie was already on the front porch. She stopped before going in. Kate saw her eyes follow the jogger as he ran up the street.

Jimmy demanded, 'What are you looking at?'

'My dick of a brother.' Maggie disappeared inside.

Kate couldn't begin to decipher the exchange. She stepped gingerly up the stairs. All she needed was to fall through one of the rotten treads. Rick was more trusting. He bounded up two at a time, then stopped in front of the door so that Kate could precede him.

Cigarette smoke wafted out of the house like a genie's hand beckoning them indoors. Kate looked down at her feet as she tried to acclimate. Her eyes started to water. Her throat was burning. And then she looked up because she'd met her limit today for almost running into things.

The word 'depressing' came to mind as Kate took in the interior of the house. Everything was painted dark gray, from the walls to the ceiling to the trim. The wooden floors were in disrepair. The fixtures were little more than bare bulbs. The décor was right out of *All in the Family*. Yellow and orange flowered couch. Ugly reclining chairs. A cigarette-scarred coffee table.

'Goddamn, lady.' Jimmy was standing in the foyer. His eyes went to Kate's chest. 'Did you have them knockers yesterday?'

Kate lifted the box higher. She blushed, but not for the reason everyone was obviously thinking. She couldn't look at Jimmy without thinking about the X-ray Philip had shown her.

'In here.' Maggie sat at the dining room table. Even with the large floor-to-ceiling windows, the place had the feeling of a tomb. She stated the obvious. 'The light's shitty and the windows are painted shut.'

Kate tried to think of something positive. 'Your anaglypta is in beautiful condition.' They all stared at her. She played back her words in her mind and figured she deserved it. 'The wallpaper.' She nodded toward the embossed paper on the walls.

Jimmy said, 'My dad painted over it.'

'You're supposed to.' Kate felt the heat of their scrutiny. 'I'll just be quiet.'

'My favorite words from a woman.' Jimmy limped around the table. He was wearing black pants and a white button-down shirt. The sleeves were rolled up. The open collar had shorter points than was the fashion. Kate had never met a gay man who wasn't a stylish dresser. She wondered if Philip was being truthful. He certainly enjoyed shocking her. But then, why would he lie about something like that?

'Sit.' Maggie pointed at the chair across the table. She had a file open in front of her. A yellow legal notepad and pen were at her elbow.

Kate saw that Maggie's belt was hanging on the back of the chair. She took off her own belt and did the same.

The sensation of weightlessness was recherché, which thought she kept to herself.

'Keep your mic plugged in,' Maggie mumbled. Her head was bent over a file.

Kate put the transmitter in her lap as she sat down. Both Rick and Maggie had the volume low on their radios. The crackling noise had become so constant that Kate barely registered it anymore.

Rick took off his gloves. 'Maggie has Ballard and Johnson. You take Keen and Porter.'

Kate reached for the file Maggie offered, though she had no idea what was expected of her.

Jimmy said, 'Just write down anything that seems weird.'

'Excellent.' Kate was still clueless, but she felt it was better to agree. Maggie slid another legal pad across the table. Kate took the pen out of her pocket. She supposed she could doodle until someone asked her why the hell she wasn't doing what she was supposed to be doing.

'We'll split along with the girls.' Rick tossed folders in front of Jimmy as he spoke. 'K&P evidence log. Duty sheet. Dispatch calls.' He scooped the rest of the folders out and held them. 'I've got B&J.'

Jimmy chuckled. 'I could use a BJ.'

Maggie glowered at her brother. 'Shut up, Jimmy.'

Kate felt her cheeks flush. She didn't know what to do but open the file in front of her. Her stomach churned at the photograph: an eight-by-ten color close-up of a dead man. At least she assumed he was dead. His eyes were open. His graying black hair parted like a curtain across his forehead. In the center was an almost perfectly round hole.

Jimmy nudged her arm. 'You never seen a dead man before?'

'Of course she has.' Maggie sounded livid. 'Jesus.'

'Jesus yourself, gal.' Jimmy leaned his chair back on two legs. 'What's gotten into you?'

'We were supposed to do this at the diner.'

'So?' He bounced in his chair as he threw a pen at his sister.

Kate turned to the next picture. Another man. Another bullet hole. The photos they had been shown at the academy were black-and-white. Some of them were photocopies. They were nothing like the Kodachromes she held in her hands.

'That's Porter?' Maggie asked Kate.

Kate turned the photo over. *Porter, Marcus Paul.* The name was familiar, but she couldn't place it. Still, she told Maggie, 'Yes. Porter.'

'When was he killed?'

Kate had to give herself time to process the question before she figured out how to answer it. Bad photocopies or not, she'd read a police report before. She flipped past the photographs and found the incident report. 'September twelfth.' Two days before the anniversary of Patrick's death. That was enough to jog her memory. Two police officers had been murdered execution-style behind a department store on September 12th.

Kate scanned the names on the boxes: Mark Porter. Greg Keen. Alex Ballard. Leonard Johnson. Now she remembered. She'd read about all the men in the newspaper.

They were reviewing the files of dead police officers.

Maggie clicked her pen. She wrote as she talked. 'Ballard

and Johnson were killed – what was that? – three weeks before?'

Kate picked up her pen and followed Maggie's lead, making note of the victims' names and the dates of their deaths. She flipped to the coroner's report. 'Both died from gunshot wounds to the head.'

'Start with the incident report.' Maggie made a column, so Kate made a column. 'What solves a crime is the connections – how is the victim connected to the killer?'

Kate wrote *Porter* at the top of one column and *Keen* at the next.

'There's no such thing as a coincidence.' Maggie tapped her fingers for emphasis. 'If anything sticks out, then write it down. It doesn't matter how stupid it sounds. Let us know.'

'Yeah,' Jimmy said. 'Don't worry about looking baaah-d.'

Kate glared at him. He was sitting so close that she could feel the heat from his body. She didn't understand this man. Regardless of the secret he was hiding, Jimmy had been shot yesterday. Twenty-four hours before that, a man who was likely his lover had been murdered in front of him. The same murderer had tried to kill Jimmy. How could he sit there so casually making jokes?

Rick asked, 'You got any beer?'

Jimmy stood up. He rested his hand on the back of Kate's chair, then the wall, as he limped into the other room. The clock by the door showed it was just after nine in the morning.

Which had absolutely nothing to do with Kate.

She glanced through the personnel files. Just the basics – date of employment, previous experience, marital status.

There were no witness statements, but she found a few notes taken during interviews with family members and friends.

Maggie said, 'You always have to start over with him.' She was talking about Jimmy. Her tone had an air of resignation. 'No matter what you do the day before, no matter how much you prove yourself, he hits reset the next day.'

'Like an amnesiac,' Rick said.

They both looked at him.

'Like when you hit your head.' Rick stood up. 'I'll go check on Jimmy.'

Kate waited until he was gone. 'Can you please tell me what we're doing here?'

'We weren't supposed to do it here.'

As usual, Kate was slow on the uptake. Maggie was embarrassed about her house. And for good reason. Rather than make it worse by offering false platitudes, Kate asked, 'What are we looking for in these files?'

Maggie sat back in her chair. She tapped her pen on the table as she studied Kate. 'I think the Atlanta Shooter is the same guy who murdered Don Wesley and tried to kill Jimmy.' She stopped tapping her pen. 'And Jimmy agreed with me last night, but today he thinks I'm an idiot.'

Kate had to make some leaps to understand what she was saying. 'The Shooter killed these men? Porter and Keen and Ballard and Johnson?'

'The M.O.'s are identical.' Maggie paused. 'An M.O. is—'

'Modus operandi. Yes, I know. They were all killed in the same manner.'

'Right. So, we need to study the details of both sets of

cases. Then we can compare them to what happened to Jimmy and Don. At least what Jimmy is saying happened.'

Kate prayed that her expression didn't give her away. She had a better idea about what happened in that alley than Maggie did. 'Well, Don was shot twice, correct? And these other men were shot just one time?'

'Correct,' Maggie agreed. 'But there are lots of divergent facts. Neither Porter nor Keen were ever partnered with Johnson or Ballard. They were all in the same zone, but they didn't socialize. Detectives who are smarter than us have already combed through these files and they didn't find anything that connected any of the victims.'

'Why do they need to connect?'

'Because . . .' She searched for an explanation. 'Let's say that all the victims were Vietnam vets.'

'My two guys were.'

'My two guys weren't. But if they were, then maybe they were part of a veterans' group. Or they met at the VA hospital. Or served together.' Maggie shrugged. 'If we find out how they all knew each other, then chances are they all knew somebody else.'

'You mean the killer?' Kate finally got it. And now she understood why Maggie kept asking about the bar where Don Wesley had gotten those matches. 'Or if they all hung out at the same place, like a bar, then that would be a connection.'

'Exactly. But if that place from the matchbook was a cop hangout, more people would know about it.'

'That's the first time you've told me I'm right about something.' Kate didn't let Maggie spoil the moment. 'Can't you just call the phone company and get the address?'

'It doesn't work that way. There's not a central number

to call. You have to file a formal request. And Salmeri's Yellow Pages is a month old, same as mine. If the bar had been open when these other guys were murdered, then it would be in the book.'

Kate nodded. 'Fair point. So, we're going through these files to connect these four shootings to Don Wesley's death?'

'Right,' Maggie agreed. 'Sometimes with two cases, it's hard to spot the connections. If you throw in a third case, your odds get better. Only, we need to prove that the third case belongs.'

'And we do that by finding the connection that ties them all together.'

'Right. Do you read?'

'Of course I read.'

'I mean books. Stories.'

'Yes.'

She tapped the file in front of her. 'Look at it like a thriller novel. Michael Crichton. Helen MacInnes. Whatever. It's a story, and we have to figure out the ending before anybody else does.'

Jacqueline Susann was more Kate's speed, but she got it. 'Okay.'

'Good.' That was obviously the end of the lesson. Maggie leaned over the pages in front of her.

Kate flipped back to the incident report. Whoever had done the typing relied entirely on police codes. Thankfully, Kate hadn't just been showing off before. She had memorized all the signals and APCO codes from her textbooks.

She turned to a fresh sheet of paper and translated the timeline.

At approximately 3:15 a.m. on September 12th, a 10-79 (anonymous call) came in to dispatch reporting a possible 20 (break-in) at Friedman's Department Store. The caller said a masked man with a crowbar had been spotted trying to pry open the door. Central station verified no signal 10 (alarm triggered). Officers Greg Keen and Mark Porter 10-4'd (acknowledged). The officers 10-23'd (arrived on the scene) at 3:35 and took a 50 (left their car) to check the building. At 3:55, they called a 4 (all clear) and requested a 29 (meal break). The break was 10-4'd. At 4:45, dispatch requested a 10-20 (location). Officers were apparently still 10-7 (out of service) and it was assumed they were still 29 (eating). At 5:00, 5:05, and 5:10, dispatch reached out again. A possible 10-92 was filed (transmitter out of service). And finally, at 5:15, Officers Pendleton and Carson were sent to check for Keen and Porter at their last known location. A 63 was called immediately (officers down).

Kate reread her work. She turned to a new page and wrote down *Friedman's Department Store.* She underlined the words twice. The store was on Decatur Street. Jimmy Lawson and Don Wesley had been in an alley off of Whitehall, which was the south-southwest leg off Five Points.

Connection.

Next, she tackled the autopsy. Kate made more notes, but she wasn't sure whether they would be helpful to anyone but herself. The report was very convoluted. She wasn't a doctor. The drawings were not helpful. The coroner had a shaky hand.

The similarities were: Both men had grit on the knees of their trousers. Both had been shot point-blank range in the center of the head. Both had eaten hamburgers within an hour of their deaths.

The differences were: Mark Porter's right middle fingernail was split to the bed. Greg Keen had blood in his left ear but Porter had none. The heels of Mark Porter's shoes were worn at an odd angle. His left shoelace was untied. His front teeth were broken, posthumously, as he fell face-forward into the cobblestones that lined the alley.

Kate studied the family statements, which mostly contained anecdotes about the dead men, stories they'd told about catching bad guys. Frankly, they came off as big fish tales, but considering all Kate had seen in the last day, she probably should take the stories at face value. Keen was a hunter. Porter hated the outdoors. They had both served in Vietnam early in the conflict. Keen was Navy. Porter was Army. Their employment records were anodyne. Neither one of them was under review. Neither was up for promotion.

She found it unbearably depressing that the sum total of their lives came down to these scant pieces of paper.

Kate looked at the photographs again. She was better prepared for the images this time. She already knew what had happened. The shooter had been approximately six inches from the targets. The men were on their knees.

Kate thought about that. To be forced onto your knees. To look at a gun pointing at your head. To see the finger pull the trigger. To watch the explosion of the bullet coming out of the chamber. She could not imagine the terror.

Both men were married, though Keen was separated. Their wedding rings had been catalogued in the autopsy report. Both of their wives had called them good husbands, honorable men. Who had gone to their houses and knocked on their doors?

Kate knew what that part felt like, at least. You knew why they were there the minute you saw them. The rest was theater. You said the line 'Yes, may I help you?' as if your brain did not know. As if your heart was not already in your throat.

'What is it?' Maggie asked.

Kate shook her head. She made a show of studying the photographs. Only the first few were hard to look at. The close-ups of the backs of the men's heads. Each bullet had made a perfect hole in their foreheads. The exit wounds were another story. The skulls were fractured out. Chips of white bone were stark as teeth in the bloody mass that showed brain and tissue. Those pictures were almost unreal. Kate was looking into a man's skull, but for some reason her mind convinced her that it was fake.

Maybe that was why she was able to see the scratch on the back of Mark Porter's neck. Kate held up the photo so she could better see. Was it a fingernail scratch?

One time, Kate had scratched the back of Patrick's neck in the heat of the moment. He'd thought it was funny the next day, but she had been mortified.

Had Mark Porter's neck been scratched by his wife, or was he doing the same thing that Don Wesley had been doing to Jimmy when the murder took place?

Kate felt herself shaking her head. That was too much of a coincidence. The Shooter had obviously made the emergency call about the burglar behind Friedman's. Porter and Keen were lured there. As far as Kate knew, there was no directive in the manual that required you to fellate your partner after giving an all clear.

There was a scaled drawing of the crime scene in the back of the folder. Kate studied the diagram. The artist could teach the coroner a thing or two. The lines were steady and the objects were clearly defined. Everything that was within a radius of fifty feet from the bodies was marked with a number on the drawing. There was a legend in the corner. Kate scanned the recovered objects: cigarette butts, pieces of broken glass, hypodermic needles, squares of tinfoil, a bent silver spoon, the keys to the cruiser parked on the street, a piece of broken fingernail.

A thought occurred to Kate. Her face got so warm that she felt the need to lean her head in her hands so that Maggie would not see. If Keen and Porter had oral sex, and the result of the completion was not at the scene, then where else would it be?

She flipped back to the autopsy reports. Kate folded up the pages so that Maggie wouldn't see her focusing on the separate lines that read GENITALS. The word 'unremarkable' was listed for both men.

She flipped back to the sections that listed stomach contents. Both victims had partially digested hamburgers and French fries that the coroner estimated were consumed an hour before death. Nothing else was listed. Kate wasn't even sure it *would* be listed. Was that the sort of thing you could see inside a person's stomach?

'Wait a minute,' Kate said.

'What?'

'Did your guys have anything in their stomachs?'

Maggie nodded. 'Burgers and fries.'

'My guys requested a meal break right around the time we assume they were murdered, but the coroner estimates that they ate dinner at least an hour before they died.'

She showed Maggie the two reports. 'Hamburgers and fries.'

'The only place they could get hamburgers that time of night is at the Golden Lady. It's a strip club off Peachtree. All the night-shift guys eat there.'

'Connection.' Kate wrote *the Golden Lady* on her list. 'So, why did they request a meal break when they'd already eaten?'

'Why would they call a meal break at all?' Maggie explained, 'Night shift pays double. You don't clock out for meals. Nobody checks up on you, because the brass is asleep.' She nodded toward Kate's paperwork. 'What else?'

'Were your guys lured to the scene?'

'Yes. There was an anonymous call reporting a break-in. No alarm.'

'Same with mine. Did yours request a twenty-nine?'

'Their last contact with dispatch was to call the scene clear and request a meal break.'

Kate felt the hair go up on the back of her neck. 'They were forced on their knees?'

'Yes.'

'They were shot in the foreheads?'

'The weapon was eight to twelve inches away, superior angle, so the guy was standing over them, holding the gun down.'

'That's what I have, too.'

'Twenty-five caliber?'

'Twenty-five caliber,' Kate confirmed. 'Anything unusual on the diagram of the scene?'

Maggie flipped a few pages in her notepad. 'Cigarette butts, drug paraphernalia, a pair of ripped women's underwear.' She looked up and shrugged. 'You could find that on any street in Atlanta right now.'

'What about the car keys?'

Maggie flipped to a different page. 'Ballard had them in his front left pants pocket.'

'My diagram has the keys fifteen feet away from Mark Porter's body.' Kate suggested, 'Maybe he had them in his hand because he was walking back to the car?'

'You're supposed to loop the ring around your middle finger.' Maggie pulled out her own keys and showed Kate. 'That way they can't be knocked out of your hand.'

'Their cruiser was around the corner, a good fifty feet away.' Kate shrugged. 'I always take out my keys when I'm closer, but that's anecdotal.'

'Tell me what you see.' Maggie spread two photos in front of Kate. Ballard and Johnson facedown in an alley. As with Kate's victims, the backs of their heads were blown open. Their legs were at awkward angles. Their arms were wide. The equipment on their belts was spread around. The transmitters clipped to the backs of their belts were spattered in blood.

Kate asked, 'What am I missing?'

'Look closer.'

Kate leaned over the pictures. She studied the bodies the same way she used to study those puzzles that ask the viewer to spot the things that are different. She went back and forth between the two. Left shoe. Left shoe. Right shoe. Right shoe. She did this all the way up to the radio transmitters. 'Oh.'

'What about your guys?'

Kate found the corresponding photos for Keen and Porter. Different angles, but roughly the same images:

two men facedown on the ground with the backs of their heads missing. She spotted the same discrepancy Maggie had flagged. 'My guys have their shoulder mics unplugged from their transmitters, too.'

'That doesn't happen by accident.'

'No,' Kate said. The jack was almost too narrow for the plug. She assumed it was designed that way so that the cord didn't easily pop out.

Kate stared at the photographs so long that her eyes burned. Something else was bothering her. She just couldn't put her finger on it.

'Look at the way their arms are spread.' Maggie pointed to each picture. Every victim had his arms at the same angle. 'When you arrest somebody, you make them lace together their fingers and put their hands on the top of their heads.'

'Right.' Kate knew exactly what she was talking about. Their hands must have blown apart when the bullet passed through their skulls. 'Do you think the Shooter forced them to request a meal break, then unplugged their mics?'

'They didn't unplug on their own.'

'But the request for a meal break is a twenty-nine. These guys had a gun pointed at their heads. Instead of asking for a twenty-nine, why didn't they request a sixty-three, officer needs assistance? The Shooter would never know the difference.' Kate answered her own question. 'Unless the Shooter knew the police codes.'

They both thought about that. The Shooter knew police codes. He knew procedure. He knew the routines.

Maggie raised her voice, calling, 'Jimmy?' She waited in vain for a response. 'Jimmy?' She pushed herself up from the table. 'Where the hell is he?'

243

Kate followed Maggie through the humid kitchen, then out to the carport. Jimmy and Rick were in metal lawn chairs under the shade. Terry Lawson and Bud Deacon sat on the hood of a brown Impala. Jett Elliott was behind the wheel, but he was obviously passed out. Chip Bixby leaned against a cord of wood. Cal Vick was beside him. They all had beer cans, even Jett. Empties littered the ground. Kate was not surprised they were all friends. They were the same type of jerks, evidence of which was likely soon forthcoming.

Terry glanced up, but he was obviously in the middle of a story. 'So, then what happens? Kennedy gets shot and the only thing standing between us and that fucking commie brother of his is an Arab with a twenty-two.'

'Good thing he knew how to use it.' Chip tipped his beer can. Kate could see the skin on the back of his knuckles was broken open. She suppressed a wave of nausea, but not because of the violence. At the gun range, Chip had pressed against Kate's back as he showed her how to hold a gun. There weren't enough hot showers in the world to rid her body of the memory.

'No offense, sweetheart.' Terry was talking to Kate. He held a cold can to the back of his hand. His knuckles were bleeding. 'I know you people put those Kennedy bastards right up there with the Pope.'

Kate bristled. 'I'm not Irish. I'm Dutch.'

'I bet you are.' Cal Vick gave a suggestive laugh that turned into a hacking cough.

'Steady.' Chip slapped the man on the back.

Terry picked up where he left off. 'All I'm saying is people don't take power. You give it to them. Look at what's happening here. Mayor Hartsfield traded his soul

244

for the airport and the stadium. Then Massel, that fucking kike, takes over and forces MARTA up our asses.'

Chip muttered, 'Moving Africans Rapidly Through Atlanta.'

Terry lifted his beer in agreement. 'Now we get this spearchucker in a three-piece suit sitting behind the desk and suddenly we're taking shots in the street.' He told Kate, 'You weren't here six months ago, sweetheart. You don't know what it was like.'

'Fucking Spivey,' Chip muttered.

Edward Spivey. Kate heard the name echo in her head.

Bud held up his beer can in a toast. 'To Duke Abbott. Best damn detective this squad ever had. He deserved better than he got.'

'Duke Abbott,' they all intoned.

Terry leaned back and knocked on the windshield. 'Jett? Wake up, you sad shit.'

Jett stirred, but he was too far gone to do anything but roll his head to the other side.

'Let him sleep it off.' Vick slurped beer from the rim of his can. 'Lookit, boys, I gotta call back from California. Spivey's still living there. Coupla D's ran him down for me. He was on a church retreat last night. Twenty people saw him.'

'You believe 'em?' Bud asked.

Vick shrugged. 'Plane schedules won't work putting him in Atlanta around dawn and back in California by the time the detectives knocked on his door.'

'Them D's black or white?' Chip asked.

Vick shrugged again. 'Sounded white, but who can tell with them Hollywood types.'

'Queers and freaks,' Bud muttered.

'Lookit, Spivey don't matter.' Terry slapped Bud on the shoulder. 'We're gonna get this one. We'll fry him up like a chicken.'

'Damn straight,' Vick agreed, though he didn't seem troubled that half his detective squad was drinking in a carport rather than searching for a cop killer.

'So we catch 'em,' Bud said. 'So what? Some lawyer gets him off? And then the next day, another cop gets shot. Then another.'

'Them's the times, boys,' Vick said. 'Ain't none of that bullshit ever woulda happened if the good guys was still in charge.'

'Damn straight,' Chip agreed. 'We kept 'em in line.'

'Kept this city working,' Terry added.

Kate worked to keep her expression neutral. She wondered if this was the sort of talk Leo Frank heard before the lynch mob dragged him toward the tree.

'Shit.' Bud tucked his hand into the waist of his pants. 'When I was coming up, there wasn't a nigger in Atlanta didn't look down when you passed by. Now they're struttin' around like they own the place.'

'They *do* fucking own the place.' Terry threw his empty can into the yard next door. 'What crawled up your ass, Olive Oyl?'

Maggie had her arms crossed. 'I need to talk to Jimmy.'

'About what?'

'About—'

'Nothing.' Terry talked over her. 'I didn't let you bunk off roll call so you could sit around the house with your girlfriend all morning.'

'I'd sit around with her,' Bud offered.

Chip belched. There was genial laughter from all the

246

men but Rick Anderson. He gave Kate an apologetic look. Then he finished his beer.

Jimmy threw his empty into the side yard. 'Dutch.' He was looking at Kate. 'That's Holland, right?'

'The Netherlands.' Terry answered before Kate could. 'I was stationed in Amsterdam back in '45. Them gals all looked like her. Tall, blonde, fucking stacked. They see the uniform, you don't even have to snap your fingers. They're already asking, "How high?"' He shrugged a shoulder at Kate. 'No offense, doll.'

'None taken,' she said, as if he hadn't just accused her mother and grandmother of being whores.

Terry asked, 'It took, what, five days for you guys to surrender after the Nazis started dropping bombs?'

Kate chewed the inside of her cheek.

'There were some Dutch sailors in the Pacific.' Chip crumpled his empty can and lobbed it into the yard. 'Crazy bastards. Sank more ships in a week than the entire Allied forces. Brits said it was uncouth, but fuck 'em.'

Terry said, 'A Dutch ship fished my brother out of the Pacific. Too bad they didn't bring him home.' He sat back on the car, seeming to reflect. 'My tour in Amsterdam was at the bitter end. All over but the shoutin'. Krauts bombed the shit outta that city. The ordnance they used – I don't know. So fuckin' precise. You'd walk by a building and look through the window and there was nothing inside. No floors. No studs. No joists, even. Just brick outside and an empty shell inside.'

'That wasn't from bombing.' Kate was aware that her tone was terse, but she couldn't stop herself. 'The Nazis cut off supplies. People were starving to death. It was the

247

hardest winter on record. They dismantled the buildings for fuel.'

Terry started shaking his head before she was even finished. 'I was there, sweetheart. They were bombed to hell and back. Half the city was gutted.'

'It's called the *Hongerwinter*.' Kate hit the syllables as hard as she could. 'Over twenty thousand people starved to death.'

'I read about that.' Maggie glanced nervously at Kate. 'Audrey Hepburn did an interview. She was there when it happened.'

'Audrey Hepburn's English, you ditz.' Terry grabbed another beer. 'You wanna talk about people starving, you shoulda seen those camps.'

Bud mumbled something Kate forced herself not to hear.

Terry said, 'You could see the bones underneath their skin. Hollowed-out eyes. Teeth falling out. No hair. Dicks shriveled up. Tits hangin' down like sandbags.' He popped the top off his beer can and threw the ring into the yard. 'They were begging us for food, but you couldn't feed 'em. They had to have those what-do-you-call-its when the doctor puts the needle in your wrist?'

'IVs.' Kate's voice was shaking. Her legs were shaking. Every part of her was shaking.

'Yeah, IVs.' Terry stared at his beer can. 'Me and one of my buddies, we saw this old chick – she got ahold of some bread or something. We tried to stop her, but two seconds after she swallowed it, she just dropped to the ground. Started having a seizure. Foam coming out of her mouth. Pissing herself. Doc said her stomach exploded.'

'Jesus,' Rick mumbled. 'I thought Nam was bad.'

Bud spit on the ground. 'Guadalcanal was bad. Nam was a walk in the park for you pussies.'

'Damn straight.' Chip raised his beer in agreement. 'Give me a gook over a Nip any day.'

Rick stood up. He went into the house. The door closed behind him.

No one said anything for a few moments. Kate looked down at the broken concrete. Tears blurred her vision. She saw her grandmother on the ground clutching her stomach. She saw her mother begging for bread. Terry was a brutal man, but he'd painted too vivid an image. Kate needed to get out of here so she could collect herself.

She told Maggie, 'We should go back to work.'

'Work,' Terry echoed. 'That what you doin' in there, tough gal?' He was talking to Maggie. His expression had turned dark. His tone had a knife behind it. 'You following up on those Shooter cases?' He grinned at the surprised look on Maggie's face. 'I know what you been up to, sweetheart. You smooth-talked Rick into getting those files. Dutch over here flashed her tits to make your brother look the other way.'

Kate tasted blood on her tongue. He wasn't going to get to her. She wouldn't allow it.

Terry said, 'You think you found something twenty detectives can't spot?'

'It helps if you're sober.' Maggie dodged the half-empty beer can he threw at her head. The metal hit the wall with a hard thump. 'We found something.'

'Yeah?' Terry chided, 'Come on, tough gal. What'd you two geniuses find?'

Maggie seemed to hesitate. 'Their radios were unplugged.'

Jimmy's head turned. 'What?'

'All four of them. Their radios were unplugged.'

Terry obviously hadn't heard the information before, but he asked, 'So what?'

Maggie explained, 'In both cases, the last call each unit made was for a meal break. And then their radios were unplugged, probably so they wouldn't be able to call out.'

Jimmy asked, 'They took a twenty-nine? On a night shift?'

Terry looked at his watch. 'Three hours of your morning and that's what you came up with? They unplugged their radios before clocking out to eat?' He laughed along with Bud and Chip. 'They were probably taking a shit. Am I right?'

Oddly, Jimmy wasn't dismissive. He told Maggie, 'He didn't talk to us. The guy who took the shots. He didn't talk. He just pulled the trigger.'

'And he slashed their tires,' Terry said. 'Nobody else had their tires slashed, right, Columbo?'

Kate watched Maggie deflate under the scrutiny. She'd been so sure of herself in the house. Kate had felt the same sense of purpose. They were doing something useful. They were trying to accomplish something.

'Go back to parking tickets, sweetheart.' Terry got a fresh beer. 'Another two or three days of us banging up the streets, some asshole will come in begging us to arrest the guy.'

'Better hurry.' Bud flexed his swollen hand. 'My interrogator's starting to hurt.'

Good-natured chuckles followed.

Maggie looked down at her feet. She kept working her

jaw. She was trying to come up with something else, but there was nothing.

'He was dragged.' Unbidden, Kate had said the words out loud. Everyone was looking at her. 'Mark Porter was dragged.' She wanted her notes, but only for a crutch. She'd finally figured out what had been bothering her. 'The heels of Porter's shoes were worn on the back, not the bottom. There was a scratch on the back of his neck, probably from being grabbed. The fingernail on his right middle finger was broken. His keys were found fifteen feet from his body.'

They all stared at her with blank looks on their faces.

Maggie turned it into a story. 'Porter made a break for it. He was grabbed by the collar, which is why he had the scratch on his neck. Porter fell, probably with the Shooter on top of him. He had his keys in his hand. The impact broke his fingernail. He was going for the car but the Shooter stopped him. Maybe Porter was knocked out or at least dazed. The Shooter dragged him back to Keen, put him on his knees, and shot them both in the head.' She answered Terry's question. 'The Shooter is adapting. He slashed the tires because the last time, someone almost got away.'

Jimmy sat back in his chair. He scratched his chin in thought.

Terry muttered, 'Leave it to a coupla broads to zero in on a broken fingernail.'

The laughter was different from before. This time, the men sounded almost relieved.

Maggie held on to the theory. 'In all three cases, they were dispatched out because of an anonymous call reporting a possible break-in.'

251

Terry shook his head. 'You know how many of those calls we get a month?'

'Three,' Maggie said. 'I checked with dispatch this morning. That time of day in that area, they get about three bogus calls a month.'

Jimmy wouldn't let go of his point. 'He didn't talk to us, Maggie. He just came around the corner and started shooting. He was so fast I barely had time to look at him.'

Maggie stared at her brother, almost begging him to understand. 'It's too coincidental. Maybe the Shooter didn't expect you guys to be there when he turned the corner. Maybe he thought he was going to surprise you, but you surprised him.'

Jimmy looked down at his beer can.

Kate knew what he was thinking. The Shooter had been the one who was surprised. He was expecting two cops on foot, not both of them on the ground *in flagrante delicto*. All of the killer's plans went out the window the moment he saw them.

None of which Kate could say to the assembled crowd.

A car horn beeped in the street.

Terry scowled. 'What's that stupid slit doing here?'

Maggie told Kate, 'Go get in the car. I'll be there in a minute.'

Kate didn't ask questions. She walked through the carport. The sun cut into her retinas. She stared at the ground ahead of her. She tried to blink away the stars, then she tried to blink away the awful images that came into her head again. Her grandmother writhing in pain. Her mother begging for scraps of food. Terry Lawson watching the whole thing with a can of beer in his hand.

Kate's chest felt tight. The muscles in her throat tensed. Tears welled into her eyes again. She had to shake this. She couldn't just break down every day. She had to be tougher. Her family was counting on her. They wanted her to be strong.

Kate made herself look up.

Her stomach dropped.

Gail Patterson was behind the wheel of a two-door Mercury. She gave Kate a toothy grin through the open window. 'Hop in, Sheep.'

19

Maggie left by the front door rather than go through the carport. Her hands were loaded down with equipment. The stair treads creaked under the additional weight. She moved fast because she didn't want Terry to ask them what they were up to. Gail was supposed to be out trapping johns. Maggie and Kate were supposed to be writing speeding tickets. All three of them would be in a world of shit if her uncle found out they were going to Colored Town to talk to a pimp about a girl.

She saw Lee Grant jogging up the sidewalk. He was wearing a gold tracksuit with green stripes down the legs. The plastic box for his hearing aid was tucked into his jacket pocket. He was the Boo Radley of the neighborhood – a little older than everybody else, a little quieter, a little strange. When Maggie was a kid, they'd called him Deaf Lee, which turned into Deathly, which everybody thought was no big deal because it wasn't like he could hear you making fun of him.

Lee waved, but Maggie pretended not to see him. All she needed was for Terry to get the wrong idea. He was obviously spoiling for a fight.

'Hey, mama.' Gail pushed open the passenger-side door.

Her eyes were bruised from the whore yesterday, but she still had a grin on her face. She was dressed in her regular clothes. Her yellow skirt was hiked up so she could hold her flask between her legs. She wore matching gold lamé ankle boots with pointy high heels. A vivid blue fedora was tight on her head. Her dry black hair hung like straw around her shoulders.

Gail said, 'Deathly's givin' you the eye. Ain't ya, son?' She turned to Kate in the back seat. 'Maggie's secret boyfriend. Deaf as a doornail.' She raised her voice. 'Ain't that right, Deathly?'

Maggie burned with shame. The only thing to do with Gail was ignore her. She dropped the equipment on the floorboard.

Gail revved the engine several times. 'Hold on, chickies!'

Maggie jumped in before she was left on the street. The car burned rubber as it streaked away from the house. Gail roared with delight. She turned up the radio – Rolling Stones – and lit a new cigarette off the old one.

'Here.' Maggie passed back Kate's utility belt, a pair of Jimmy's old shoes, and one of his hats. 'Sorry about the smell.'

Kate quietly laid the items on the seat beside her. She looked pale and weepy. Terry had obviously pushed her buttons. Or maybe it was the way Bud Deacon stuck his hand down his pants. Or the stench of puke coming off Jett Elliott. Or Cal Vick's inability to look anywhere above a woman's chest. Or the way Chip Bixby had leered at Kate like he wanted to drag her into the woods and ravage her.

Maggie couldn't worry about other people right now. She had her own wounds to nurse. She was embarrassed by her family. Mortified by her house. Terrified that Terry would take the clues she and Kate had scraped together and bust open the Shooter case.

It was supposed to be her and Jimmy. He'd said so last night. They were going to take all the Shooter files and go over them together. Work together. After what Jimmy had said to her in the hospital – apologized, no less – Maggie thought it was all going to be different. For the first time in her adult life, Jimmy was actually going to treat her like a fellow officer.

And then he'd woken up this morning with his same shitty attitude, and Maggie had realized it was all a dream.

Gail whooped as the car fishtailed around a turn. Maggie gripped the sides of her seat. The Mercury Cyclone was an expensive car for a cop. Knowing Gail, she'd probably stolen it from a pimp. Trouble, her husband, had souped up the engine and added a sound system that shook the windows. The seats were uphol- stered in white leather. Red shag carpet was contoured around the dashboard and glued to the ceiling. A pair of dice hung from the rearview mirror. Or mirrors, more precisely. Instead of one, there were six mirrors across the top of the windshield that offered a one-eighty view of everything behind the driver.

Gail took a swig from her flask. There was a wide smile on her face. She was like every cop Maggie had ever met. No matter what came at her, she pretended it didn't matter. This was Gail's one true talent: perseverance. She got up every day and took on the world no matter how bruised and broken she was from the day before.

Maggie wanted to be that way. She strived for that level of self-denial. Unfortunately, the reset button was only passed through the male side of the Lawson line. For

Maggie, everything accumulated. Kate was obviously the same way. She was still staring out the window. Her hand shielded her eyes, though the sun was on the other side of the car.

'Shit.' Gail turned down the music. 'What're you two gals sulking about?'

Maggie silently enumerated the list. Five cops had been murdered. Her brother had been shot. Her uncle was determined to drum her out of the police force.

'Jesus Christ, what a waste.' Gail took a swig of whiskey, then tossed her flask onto the dash. 'Both of y'all need to find a man worth shaving above your knees for.' She playfully pushed Maggie's arm. 'Come on, kid. They ain't so bad once you get their clothes off.'

Maggie thought of another list: Jimmy had kicked her in the teeth. Terry was a raging sadist. Jett Elliott was a disgusting drunk. Cal Vick was incompetent. Bud Deacon and Chip Bixby were practically Nazis. Even Rick Anderson had barked at her when she'd walked back into the house.

Gail said, 'You know ol' Deathly's cute in the right light. Got a Jagger thing going, but not in the face.'

'Gail, please.' Even if Maggie wanted it, there was no way anything would ever happen with Lee. Their families despised each other – the Lawsons because the Grants thought they were better than everybody else, the Grants because they knew that they actually were better. The situation was less like the Capulets and Montagues and more like the Hatfields and McCoys.

'I gotta treat for you.' Gail grabbed a cassette tape from the sun visor. 'This'n's a good one. Trouble's brother recorded it out in LA a few weeks back.'

Maggie fought an eye roll. Trouble and his brother had a side business illegally recording concerts. The quality was always poor. Trouble was a drinker. His brother was a pothead. Most of their tapes captured their own stoned voices singing along with the musicians.

Gail reached back and patted Kate's leg a couple of times. 'I picked this'n just for you, Sulky Sheep.'

Maggie didn't bother checking on Kate again. She stared out the windshield as the sound of a cheering crowd filled the car. Trouble's brother said something about having to take a piss. Gail laughed so hard she slapped the steering wheel. She turned up the volume. No one would mind. They were in Cabbage Town now. The area had been devastated years ago. The brick factories looked as empty inside as Maggie felt.

'Come on!' Gail started banging out the beat on the dashboard. She didn't know the opening lyrics, but she belted out the chorus. '"Poor, poor pitiful me!"' She nudged Maggie. '"Poor, poor pitiful me!"'

Maggie smiled despite herself.

Gail bellowed, '"Poor, poor pitiful me!"'

Maggie shook her head, but her fingers started tapping to the beat. She let Gail's good mood take over. Maybe this was how to do it: listen to a stupid song about feeling sorry for yourself so that you stopped feeling sorry for yourself. The only other alternative was to drink too much or turn into the kind of angry bitch nobody wanted to be around.

Clearly, Kate wasn't thinking along these lines. She was hunched against the window. Her head was in her hand.

And then the chorus came back on and Kate gave a desperate wail.

'Jesus.' Gail turned down the volume. She stared at Kate's reflection in the mirrors.

Maggie did the same. Kate's shoulders were shaking. She wasn't just crying. She was weeping uncontrollably.

Gail asked, 'She ever do this before?'

'No,' Maggie answered, which was partly true. Kate had cried last night when the shift was over. That was nothing compared to her big, gulping sobs now.

Gail said, 'Poor kid. She's really going at it. What set her off? Jett start telling his stupid Irish jokes?'

'Jett was passed out.'

'Had to be something. Did Terry start in with his Helter Skelter bullshit about the coloreds taking over the world?'

'We missed most of it.' Maggie racked her brain. 'The Kennedys. The mayor. Edward Spivey. The war.'

'Bingo.' Gail slowed the car. The wheels hit the broken sidewalk as the Mercury came to a stop in front of the old cotton bag factory. 'Her husband was killed in Nam.'

'What?' Maggie heard her voice go up in surprise. 'She was married?'

'You didn't read her personnel file?' Gail pushed open the car door. 'He got killed in Bang Phuck Mi or wherever the hell.' She threw the driver's seat forward and climbed into the back with Kate. 'Come here, sweetheart.'

Kate practically fell into her arms. 'I'm s-s-sorry.'

'It's all right, mama.' Gail stroked her hair over her ear. She rested her boots on the back of the folded seat. 'Those ass hairs spent half the war in whorehouses and the other half in VD clinics.'

For some reason, this made Kate cry even harder.

Gail rolled her eyes at Maggie, but she hugged Kate tighter. 'That's okay, sugar. Just let it out.' She snapped her fingers at Maggie and mimed taking a drink.

The flask felt half-empty. Maggie unscrewed the cap and handed it back.

Gail took a small portion, then offered the flask to Kate. 'This'll do ya.'

Kate didn't have to be cajoled. She took a healthy drink.

'Don't be greedy.' Gail pulled away the flask. She helped Kate sit up. And then she finished the whiskey. 'You all cried out now, chickie?'

Kate wiped underneath her eyes. Her hands still trembled, but at least her tears had stopped. 'I'm sorry,' she managed. 'I tried not to. I don't know what came over me.'

Gail said, 'We all get that way.' She winked at Maggie, acknowledging that none of them ever got that way – especially in public.

'I'm sorry,' Kate repeated. She straightened her shirt, adjusted her shoulder mic. 'I must look a mess.'

Gail shrugged it off, but she warned, 'Don't ever let those bastards know they got to you. They see you cry, that's the end of it. They'll never take you seriously.'

Kate nodded, but she obviously didn't get it. The hardest battles didn't take place on the streets. They happened inside the squad room. Every time a female officer took a step forward, a male officer felt like he was being pushed back. The guys pounced the minute you showed weakness.

'Shit, you gals don't know how easy you got it.' Gail threw the empty flask back on the dash. 'My first week on the job, every morning I'd open my locker and there'd be a fresh pile of shit inside.' Her lip curled in disgust. 'Terry, Mack, Red, Les, Cal, Chip, Bud – all of 'em took turns trying to outdo each other. They jizzed in my purse.

Pissed in my shoes. Crapped in the trunk of my car. And I leave one bloody tampon on your uncle Terry's dashboard and suddenly *I'm* the crazy bitch.'

Maggie must have heard wrong. She looked at Kate, who was equally perplexed.

'Talk about a smell,' Gail said. 'Middle of goddamn August. Hot as hell. He's lucky I was at the end of my period.'

That was all it took.

Both Maggie and Kate exploded with laughter. Maggie couldn't stop. She grabbed the back of her seat to steady herself. Her stomach cramped. Her throat ached. She couldn't get it out of her head – the look on her uncle Terry's face when he climbed into his squad car and saw the gift that Gail Patterson had left for him. She hoped he threw up a hot stream of bourbon. She hoped he still gagged every time he thought about it.

Gail wiped her mouth with the back of her hand. 'Yeah, they didn't fuck with me after that.'

Tears were streaming down Maggie's face. Kate had her head in her hands again, but this time she shook with laughter.

'All right, gals.' Gail slid toward the door. 'Enough lollygagging. Let's get this show on the road.'

Kate looked at Maggie and they both started laughing again.

Gail sighed as she climbed behind the steering wheel. 'Come on, now. Wind it down.'

Maggie took a deep breath. Her stomach still hurt from laughing. She wiped her eyes. Shook her head.

Gail took off her fedora and wedged it between the dash and the windshield. She lit another cigarette. The

Mercury went into a wide curve as she pulled back onto the road.

Maggie finally managed to stop sputtering with laughter. The trick was not to look at Kate. She wiped her eyes. She settled down into the seat and stared out the side window again.

The scenery rolled by, depressing in its monotony. The abandoned factories gave way to run-down houses, which reverted back to empty factories. Gail was taking the back way to the West End. Jimmy had been in CT yesterday. Maggie doubted he had asked for permission, which was probably why he'd been shot. She wondered what he was really asking his snitch about. Maggie got the feeling that there were things about Don Wesley's murder that no one but Jimmy would ever know.

Gail asked, 'You got any new intel on these mothers?'

Maggie shook her head. She had filled Gail in before roll call this morning: a tranny pimp nobody had ever met and a psychopath henchman who liked cutting white women.

'Listen to me, Sheep.' Gail directed her words to Kate's reflection in the mirrors. 'You know why the colored girls are so high on themselves?'

Kate seemed offended by the question. 'I hadn't given it much thought.'

Gail said, 'Black men. That's why. You hear 'em in the halls, on the street, in the diner. They see a black woman, even one got a face like a shovel, they're all, "Hey, good-lookin". Lemme take you to dinner. Lemme buy you some coffee.' They tell them they're beautiful, flirt with them all the time. You know what I mean?'

Kate looked mystified. The black men in her life were probably all holding rakes or pushing elevator buttons.

Gail said, 'Black girls tune it out, easy. They been hearing that shit all their lives. Now, a white woman hears it, and she's all, "Oh, golly, he must think I'm pretty!"'

Kate's eyes narrowed. Gail had done a pretty good imitation of her froo-froo accent.

Gail said, 'That's how pimps are. They hurl out compliments like it's a business. Because it is. They're in the business of tricking out women.'

'You're saying all pimps are black men?' Kate still sounded haughty, so Maggie took this one.

She framed it as a syllogism. 'Not all black men are pimps, but all pimps are black men.'

Kate raised her eyebrows.

'Stop playing, you two, 'cause this ain't no joke.' Gail checked over her shoulder before passing a truck. She told Maggie, 'Tell her how they trick 'em out.'

Maggie had gotten the depressing lesson off Gail a long time ago. She hoped that Kate paid as careful attention as she had. 'The pimps get the girls when they're twelve or thirteen. They're runaways or addicts or something bad happened back home. The pimps seduce them. They pretend that they're in love with them. They shoot them up with dope. It doesn't take long to hook them. Then they turn them out, or sometimes it's called tricking them out, into the streets.' Maggie shrugged, because it really was that simple. 'The girls have sex with twenty, thirty strangers a day. The pimps keep all the money.'

Gail finished, 'And then when the girls get too old, twenty, twenty-five, the pimp either sells 'em down the road or he slits their throats and tosses 'em in a ditch.'

Kate said, 'Violet's around that age.'

Gail wasn't irritated by the observation. She just

nodded. 'You wait for it, mama. One day you're gonna roll up on a ten-fifty-four and it's gonna be Violet's dead face staring back at you.' Gail shook a cigarette out of the pack. 'You know our objective?'

'Maggie's been incredibly forthcoming.'

Maggie took the dig because she deserved it. 'We're going to talk to Sir She and see if he'll let us speak to his girls.' She told Kate, 'He runs older women like Violet, probably because he's new to town. The area where Don Wesley was shot in Five Points, that's where the hags work.'

'Whitehall,' Kate said. She'd done a good job studying the Shooter files.

'Each part of the Five is divvied up by the pimps.' Maggie tried to frame it in a way that Kate would understand. 'Think of the area as a shopping mall for sex.'

Gail barked a laugh. 'Good one.'

Maggie continued, 'You want black girls? Go down the Marietta spike. There's some Asians down Decatur. Mixed gals are on Peachtree. Prime real estate is north of Edgewood near Woodruff Park. That's your Saks Fifth Avenue. Big money. Pimps are always fighting for that patch. It's where the young white girls work. They get the easy customers – businessmen, lawyers, doctors. The freaks go straight to Whitehall. Think of it as a J.C. Penney catalogue store. The girls are older. Their pimps don't take care of them. The freaks like to beat on women, they're looking for a discount, they don't care so much what her face looks like or how old she is.'

Gail said, 'That's why we wanna talk to 'em. Them gals' lives depend on figuring out who's gonna hurt 'em, who's safe to go with. They watch everybody, see everything. I'd bet my left tit one of 'em either saw something or has a regular she knows for sure's got a grudge against cops.'

Maggie added, 'There's a lot of freaks out there who watch cops. You see them at the station sometimes. They just hang out for no reason. They go to crime scenes. They have police scanners.' As she talked, Maggie felt a weight being lifted from her chest. After reading the Shooter files, she had been worried that the killer might be a cop. The more she thought about it, the more it made sense that they were looking for some freak wannabe. 'Somebody like that would know codes and routines.'

Kate said, 'Or maybe they washed out of the academy or didn't last on the streets?'

Gail couldn't resist. 'You makin' a confession there, Sheep?'

Kate didn't laugh. 'Jimmy said the man who shot Don was black. Wouldn't you notice a black civilian hanging around the station house?' She added, 'I mean, if he's not already there because he's a pimp.'

Gail made a face. 'Depends on the house. The commissioner's moving all the checkers around the board. That's what happened to Bud Deacon. He got moved to an all-black house. He tells 'em to go fuck themselves. They fire him; he sues 'em. Judge puts him back on the job pending the trial.'

'They should've moved Jett Elliott,' Maggie said. 'He doesn't know where he is half the time anyway.'

'Hey,' Gail warned. Everybody knew Jett drank because he had a sick kid. 'Mack McKay's filing a lawsuit, too. Said he was demoted for complaining about a hostile work environment. Wear a coupla tits to work, Mack. You'll see what hostile's all about.'

Maggie smiled at the image. 'Chip Bixby walked out when they put a woman in his unit, but nobody fired him.'

'Chipper's not so bad.' Gail told Kate, 'Back when I was so green I was shittin' shamrocks, I ended up pinned down behind the counter during a bank robbery. Thought I was gonna die. Seriously. I was making my peace. Then from outta nowhere, up pops Chip Bixby, guns blazing. I truck it on out the back while Chip takes the heat. Dumbass caught a bullet right here.' She tapped her collarbone. 'It was meant for me, but whattaya gonna do? Get ol' Chipper drunk enough, he'll show you the scar.'

'I'll put that right on my list,' Kate said, but she was obviously on to something else. 'What about with men? Where do they go for sex?'

Gail looked at Maggie. 'That's what we were talkin' about, sister. They go to Five Points to get laid.'

'I meant sex with other men.'

'Listen to our gal.' Gail sounded proud that Kate even knew such a thing existed. 'The queers go to Piedmont Park. They don't have to pay for it. Lucky bastards.'

'Piedmont?' Kate sounded offended. Her apartment was right up the street.

'Talk to Jimmy about it,' Gail said. 'He's always doing fairy runs with the boys after work.'

'Fairy runs?' Kate was doing the parrot thing again, repeating words. 'What on earth are fairy runs?'

Maggie explained, 'They go into the park and beat up gay men.'

Kate still sounded appalled. 'Jimmy goes to the park and beats up homosexuals?'

'Why wouldn't he?' Gail tapped her cigarette out the

window. 'All of 'em do it. Bud, Mack, Terry, Vick. They're just blowin' off steam. Who cares if a bunch of faggots get their heads knocked in? They shouldn't be doin' that nasty shit anyway.' She took a drag off her cigarette. 'Heads up, gals. We just went from *Bandstand* to *Soul Train*.'

Maggie looked out the window. Black faces looked back. Some were curious. Others were perplexed. All were hostile.

They'd just entered Colored Town.

The area had sneaked up on her. Maggie hadn't noticed the general dilapidation giving way to unpainted shacks and lean-tos. A long time ago, Gail had told Maggie that blacks and whites were separated by rocks. Blacks lived in houses built on dirt. Whites lived in houses built on stone foundations.

Maggie didn't really understand the difference until she saw it with her own eyes. Colored Town crawled through the West Side, which contained Atlanta's last still-operating industrial area. Foundries and factories belched out black smoke. Tanneries spewed rotting flesh and chemicals into Peachtree Creek. There was a constant buzz from the massive power relay stations that dotted the main road.

This wasn't the projects. There was no government housing with on-site management and hourly police patrols. The people who lived in CT either didn't want or didn't qualify for government assistance. They were on their own. They made do with what they had. Bare plywood walls kissed wet Georgia clay. Newspapers plugged holes in windows. The plumbing was so primitive that outhouses dotted the bare backyards. Even in the dead of winter, front doors hung open to air out the odors.

Kate started to cough. The smell wasn't that bad, but

it had a cumulative effect. Maggie had spent her first year on the job coughing up all kinds of disgusting filth. Delia had been appalled by some of the things she'd brought up. Maggie was constantly sick with a cold or the flu. Her doctor told her to quit her job or end up in an early grave.

Gail craned her neck to look up at the houses. They were in one of the residential stretches that specialized in rooms rented by the week. She asked, 'You got an address?'

Kate coughed again before answering, 'Eight-nineteen Huff Road.'

'Shit,' Gail grumbled. 'This is Huff, but ain't a one'a these places got a number.'

Ghetto landlords weren't the only ones who didn't post their street numbers. The problem plagued the city. Most calls, Maggie had no idea whether or not she was in the right location until someone started screaming.

'There.' Kate pointed to a house. 'That must be it.'

She'd picked the nicest house on the block. The windows were clean. The dirt yard was swept. The steps to the porch were stacked concrete blocks that read PROP-ERTY OF ATLANTA WATERWORKS.

As with all of the houses, the unpainted clapboard was weathered brown. The front door set it apart. The bottom part was red, the top was green, and there was a yellow circle around the rectangular window.

Gail asked, 'Where do you see a number?'

'The door,' Kate answered. 'Those are the colors of the Portuguese flag.'

Maggie said, 'The colored girls said the house was run by a Portuguese lady.'

'Well, lah-di-da.' Gail pulled the car over, parking

behind an old truck on blocks. 'Portuguese. Where the hell is that?'

Kate devoted her full attention to putting on Jimmy's shoes. Maybe she was learning after all.

Gail said, 'This part of CT is on the outskirts of an area called Blandtown. We passed through Lightning and Techwood on the way.' She started pointing out landmarks. 'Way over thataway is Perry Homes, which is a shithole you'll see for yourself soon enough. Trains: there's the Tilford Yard and Inman Yard between Marietta and Perry Boulevard. The Howell Rail Wye is what you're hearing. All the trains go through there. It's on the other side of the plow factory. Not wye for Y. Triangular. Don't ask me why.' She seemed to miss her own joke. 'That smell is the meatpacking plant. Place'll turn you into a vegetarian. Found a dead hooker there once inside a cow carcass. That was some sick shit. Wish I still had the picture. You following this?'

Kate nodded. 'Of course. Thank you.'

Maggie got out of the car. She heard the distant rumble of trains roaring through the Howell Yard. The low moan of a whistle pierced the air. The noise was a constant in these neighborhoods. Freight ran night and day through the wye. If you stood still long enough, you could feel the vibrations of the engines through the soles of your feet.

The Portuguese house was in the center of the road. Directly across from it was an abandoned storage warehouse. The red façade was ubiquitous to the city, constructed of slave bricks that had been thrown from Georgia clay in between cotton seasons. The windows were gone. Some of the bricks had been chipped away, exposing the black tar paper behind them. There was a puddle of water on the ground at her feet. Instinctively, Maggie looked up to check for rain. She saw a hand resting on one of the windows in the upper level of the storage facility.

'No, mama, listen,' Gail said from the front seat. She was on the radio calling in their location. She knew the dispatcher, so it took longer than usual.

Maggie forced her gaze away from the storage building. There was probably a kid up there. Or maybe a bum looking for a place to hole up. She pulled the metal clips out of her front pants pocket and hooked them onto her underbelt. She was buckling her utility belt when Kate got out of the car. She held her belt in one hand and Jimmy's hat in the other.

Kate said, 'The good news is that the shoes fit, so thank you very much for that. The bad news is—'

Maggie handed over the metal clips that Kate had left on the dining room table. 'Always put them in—'

'The same pocket. Thank you.' Kate hooked the clips. She was better at putting on her belt today. It only took two tries.

As a rule, Maggie never asked people about their personal lives, but she figured Kate owed her an explanation for the earlier outburst. 'When did your husband die?'

'Two years ago.' She straightened her nightstick. She clipped her transmitter onto the back of her belt. 'I didn't know the details were in my personnel file.'

'They do background investigations. Make sure you're not a communist.' Maggie didn't tell Kate that just about anybody could read your file. 'It's no big deal.'

'Oh, I'm sure.' Kate adjusted her collar. She seemed

ready to change the subject. 'I've been thinking that I'm allowed one really big humiliation each day. Do you think I've hit my quota for Tuesday?'

'You had your reasons.'

'Come on, Lawson. I'd rather you think I'm an idiot than feel sorry for me.'

Maggie smiled. You had to admire her spirit. 'I still think you're an idiot.'

'Of course you do.' She smelled Jimmy's hat. Her face soured.

'No hats today.' Maggie threw her hat into the car. Kate did the same. 'Check your gun.'

Kate unsnapped the strap around her revolver. She pulled her weapon with a surprising fluidity. She ejected the cylinder, then clicked it back into place.

Gail joined them on the sidewalk. A cigarette dangled from her lips. 'She know how to use that thing?'

'I hope we don't find out.'

Kate stuck the gun back in her holster. She was grinning, pleased with herself. 'I practiced this morning.'

'I think I liked you better when you were pathetic.' Gail reached into her purse and opened the drawstrings around the Crown Royal bag where she kept her gun. Her revolver had a pearl handle. The tooling around the muzzle wasn't regulation. She hot-loaded her bullets with extra gunpowder, a violation that just about everybody on the force committed.

Gail told Kate, 'Peepers open, mouth shut. You hear?'

'Yes, ma'am.'

Gail narrowed her eyes. The problem with Kate was that you couldn't tell when she was being a smartass and when she was just being smart.

'Fuck it,' Gail decided. She walked up the dirt path toward the house.

Maggie tapped the leather safety strap on her revolver, indicating that Kate should snap hers closed. She didn't wait to see if her suggestion was followed. If Kate was going to do this job – and it seemed like she was either too stubborn or too stupid not to – then she would have to sink or swim on her own.

The stiletto heels of Gail's ankle boots tapped up the cinder-block steps. The porch was small and sturdy. The boards were painted red to match the door, which gave the unsettling feeling that they were standing in blood. Maggie looked through the narrow window in the front door. She saw a set of stairs leading up to the second floor, but nothing else.

'That's called a Methuselah.' Gail nodded toward an ornate metal box nailed to the right side of the door. The top was angled toward the entrance. Gail clicked her tongue as she gave Kate a bawdy wink. 'Jews use it.'

'Gosh, how interesting.' Kate touched the box with the tips of her fingers.

'Police!' Gail banged on the door so hard that the little window rattled. She told Kate, 'I cracked one open once. It's got paper inside. Funny little squiggles on it.' Gail banged the door again. 'Open up!'

There were shuffling footsteps inside the house. Suddenly, a few wild strands of black and gray hair appeared in the window. Maggie guessed they were looking at the top of someone's head.

'Unbelievable.' Gail kicked the door. 'Open up before I break this goddamn door down!'

Four locks and a chain were disengaged before the door

cracked open. The old woman standing in front of them looked like a Victorian in mourning. Everything was black, from the high lace collar that fanned up her neck to the long-sleeved black dress that touched the tips of her black shoes. She was short, which is why she couldn't look through the window. There was a mole high on her left cheek that gave her a walleyed look. Her long salt-and-pepper hair was spun into a bun on the top of her head. Maggie thought about what Delroy and Watson had said. She could easily imagine a nest of spiders living in there.

Gail said, 'Open the door, grandma.'

'What do you want?' Her voice was deep and heavily accented. She sounded like Ricardo Montalbán – not the female version, but the actual guy from the car commercials. 'I have work to do.'

'So do we.' Gail tapped the police badge on Maggie's chest. 'We need to talk to Sir She.'

The old woman's eyebrows drawbridged up. She was smiling in a way that Maggie didn't trust. Still, she opened the door to let them in.

Gail flicked her cigarette into the yard before entering the house. She took in her surroundings, same as Maggie. Stairs cut through the central hallway that divided the house. To the left was a formal parlor, to the right, a dining room. The kitchen was at the back of the house. Maggie scanned each room. You never just walked into a space without looking for danger. Check the windows and doorways. Make sure you can see everybody's hands. Gail always said female cops added another step: judge the décor and cleanliness so you can make value judgments about the witness and/or perpetrator.

On this latter point, the Portuguese lady was blameless.

273

Her hair was terrifying, but she kept a clean house. Dishes dried neatly in a rack by the sink. The runner down the hallway was straight as an arrow. The floors were swept clean. There were no cobwebs. Maggie guessed the furniture was from the old woman's home country. The parlor contained a colorful, dainty-looking chair and a flowery settee with a curved, carved back. Doilies spotted every surface. There was a solid black tea set on the coffee table. Matching place settings were laid out on the dining room table.

'Bisalhães,' Kate mumbled.

Gail ignored her, which was usually a good idea. 'Who's in the house?'

The old woman gestured up the stairs. 'At the moment, I have three boarders. One is at work. The others—' She shook her head. 'The *paskudnyak* and the *freser*. They think I'm running a *shandhoiz*.'

Gail frowned at the foreign words. 'What the hell?'

'The pimp and his bodyguard,' Maggie guessed. She didn't speak a lick of Portuguese, but the math wasn't all that hard. 'Are they upstairs?'

'They rent two rooms. They do business out of the front one.' She shook her head again. '*Meshugeneh,* the both of them.'

Kate looked wary. 'How *meshugeneh*?'

Instead of answering, the old woman called up the stairs. 'Anthony!'

There was a loud thump overhead. Heavy footsteps banged across the floor. Grit fell from the plaster ceiling. The chandelier swayed.

'What it is, old woman?' An enormous black man stood at the top of the stairs. He was over six feet tall, and at least three-fifty. His head was comparatively tiny, like a joke snowman if the snowman was a knife-wielding psychopath. His eyes settled on Maggie, then Kate, then Gail, then the Portuguese lady.

Gail said, 'Jesus, Tubby. They find you on a meat hook at the butcher shop?'

He wasn't amused. 'Whatchu white bitches want?'

Gail grabbed the railing and pulled herself up the stairs. 'I need to talk to your boss.'

'Go fuck yourself.'

'Every chance I get. You see these uniforms?'

'I see a washed-up old whore and two bitches playin' dress-up.'

'Yeah, well.' Gail didn't dispute the assessment. She stopped a few steps down from the big guy. 'We ain't leavin', Fat Albert, so you might as well mosey on back to the Junkyard Gang.'

There was a flash of silver, a series of clicks, and Anthony was holding a switchblade to Gail's neck. 'You wanna say that again, bitch?'

Gail heaved a wheezy sigh. 'I know you can't see your dick, Lardo, but I'm pretty sure you don't want to lose it.'

He looked down. Gail's gun was pointed straight at his crotch.

She cocked the hammer. 'See how my hand's shaking? That's 'cause it wants to pull the trigger so bad.'

'No need for that, Officer.' There was another man at the top of the stairs. Maggie couldn't see him, but she knew he wasn't local. His accent put him from somewhere up north. He said, 'Anthony, let these women pass. The sooner we find out what they want, the sooner they'll leave.'

Anthony turned sideways. This didn't help matters. Gail squeezed by him first. Maggie sucked in her stomach, but she still brushed up against him as she entered the hallway. She had to pull Kate by the arm to get her through.

Sir She stood in front of an open doorway. He was tall, very thin, with skin the color of river water and a tight Afro that stuck out just past his ears. He had a red and gold scarf tied around his neck. His purple shirt was silk with white pearl snaps. His trousers were twill in a black-and-white herringbone. They were tight enough to show the outline of everything he had underneath.

Maggie thought he was more of a J.J. Walker than a tranny pimp. There was nothing delicate about his features. He didn't hold his hand bent at the wrist or wear makeup. The colored girls were right about his boots, though. They were vicious. Gold pointed triangles shaped the toes. The edges looked needle-sharp. Blood stained the white patent leather.

The pimp zeroed in on Kate. He flashed a crocodile smile. 'Lordy, lordy. You are the most luminescent creature I have ever seen. Your skin reminds me of bone china. And I could wrap both my hands around that dainty little waist.'

So much for warnings. Kate practically preened. 'Thank you.'

Gail rolled her eyes at Maggie. 'You're Sir She?'

His smile melted into a thin, angry line. 'Sir Chic. *Chic.*'

Kate laughed. Maggie knew she would.

'Don't you crackers speak English?'

Gail said, 'Word on the street is you're a tranny fag.'

He cupped his hand to the front of his pants. 'I can prove you wrong right here.'

'Nah, I already got one skinny coon got lost up my cooch. Hurts like hell when I sneeze.' Gail walked into his room. 'Shit, it's Fibber McGee's closet in here.'

Maggie saw what she meant. Compared to downstairs, the pimp's room was a sty. Boxes were stacked everywhere. Trash filled the corners. Stuffing poked out of holes in the furniture. There were two wooden chairs with the backs broken off. They were pushed close enough together that Maggie guessed this was where Anthony sat. His half-empty glass of iced tea was on the windowsill. A baseball bat leaned against the wall.

All Maggie saw was danger. In the right hands, the bat could be more deadly than her revolver. Likewise the broken spindles on the chairs. The glass holding the tea could be turned into a weapon. God only knew what was hidden inside the holes in the furniture or tucked away in the boxes.

Maggie checked outside the window. The abandoned storage facility was across the street. She hadn't seen a gloved hand before. The brick had been chipped away around the window opening so that the granite header could be salvaged. What she'd seen from the street was a piece of black tar paper flapping in the wind.

She turned back to the room. The real danger was standing fifteen feet away.

Anthony grunted as he leaned against the doorjamb. His eyes followed Gail's every move. His jaw was tight. His hands were fisted. Maggie got the feeling he wasn't the type to let things go. The colored girls had warned her that the big guy was crazy, but Maggie had seen up close what crazy looked like courtesy of her father and she always assumed that other people wouldn't know crazy if it bit them in the ass.

In her expert opinion, Anthony looked just like the kind of crazy who could bite their asses clean off.

'All right, ladies.' Chic sat on the couch. He smoothed down the legs of his trousers. 'You gonna stand there and gawp or you gonna tell me why you're here?'

'What the hell.' Gail sat in one of the chairs across from him. She left her purse in her lap, zipper open.

Maggie let Kate take the other chair so she had a reason to stand. She leaned her back into the corner. The window was to her right. Chic was front and center. Gail and Kate were at an angle to where he sat on the couch. Anthony stayed in the doorway. Maggie didn't look at him. She could feel him. He radiated hostility.

Quietly, Maggie unsnapped the safety strap around her revolver. She knew Gail could pull her gun from her purse in under a second, but it would take more than that to bring Anthony down.

'So.' Gail wasn't one for lengthy preamble. 'Whitehall. You're running girls there.'

'Am I?' Chic paused a moment before saying, 'I don't think anybody's running anything. Your storm troopers have jailed just about every working girl in the city.'

'A cop was murdered,' Gail reminded him. 'You can do something about it.'

Chic quipped, 'You think I give a shit about a dead pig?'

Gail braced her hands on her knees. 'Looky here, Sambo. I ain't got time to chase my tail around no tree.'

Kate straightened like a stick had been shoved up her ass.

Chic zeroed in on her. 'Whatchu lookin' at, slit?' He had an accent now, and it was pure street. 'You gonna answer me?'

For a change, Kate had nothing to say.

Chic couldn't push Gail, so he was going to screw with Kate. 'Come up into *my* house staring at me like I'm some kind of bug under a piece of glass. Who the fuck are you, bitch? Staring at me like that?'

Gail didn't move. Neither did Maggie. If Kate was going to keep digging herself into these holes, she'd have to learn how to get herself out of them.

'Well?' Chic demanded. 'Whatchu gotta say, bitch? You want me to make you talk?'

Anthony stirred in the doorway. The floor creaked under his weight.

Kate blurted, 'Your scarf.'

Chic was as surprised as the rest of them. He put his hand to the scarf. 'What about it?'

'I just wondered . . .' Kate's voice shook. 'I wondered if it was Chanel.'

Chic stared at her for a beat. After what seemed like a good, long while, he smiled. 'Of course it is.'

Kate swallowed audibly. Her voice still shook, but only a little. 'It's very stylish. I looked at it for myself.'

He studied her for a moment. 'With your coloring, you should stay away from reds. You're a Winter, right?'

'Autumn, but I've always felt I fall somewhere in between.'

Maggie wanted to bang her head against the wall. If somebody had told her last week that she'd be standing in the ghetto listening to a Yankee pimp discuss the Caygill Color Method, she would've laughed in their faces.

'Christ,' Gail muttered. 'Can we get back to business here?'

Chic raised an eyebrow. 'What business is that?'

'I'm betting one of your girls saw something the night that cop was killed.'

Chic leaned back on the couch. 'Oh, I know at least one of them saw something.'

Gail sat back, too – at least as much as the chair would allow. She was pretending it didn't matter, but they all knew it mattered. 'What'd she see?'

Again, he didn't respond immediately. He smoothed his trousers. He touched the knot in his scarf. Chic had the upper hand now and he was going to enjoy it for as long as he could.

Gail looked at her watch. She looked back at Maggie. She looked at her watch again.

Finally, Chic said, 'It seems to me that a man with such valuable information should get some sort of recompense.'

'All right.' Gail sounded annoyed, but Maggie knew crafting the deal was her favorite part. 'What do you want?'

Chic turned his attention back to Kate. He was flirting with her again. 'What should I ask for, Autumn?'

Kate had worked the streets less than two full days, but she'd obviously been paying attention. 'We can let you work north of Edgewood.'

Gail made a show of being outraged. 'Why don't you give him the keys to the goddamn city while you're at it?'

Chic played right into her hands. 'That sounds good. North of Edgewood.' He looked at Anthony. 'You like that, brother?'

'I like it good.' Anthony nodded his head up and down.

'You'll have to get some better girls,' Gail warned, like she gave a flip what they did. 'Them toothless old whores of yours won't pull in the traffic.'

'I can get some.'

'Two,' Gail told him. 'Stick 'em near the park, not inside. You go anywhere else, you'll end up with your belly gutted, and it might be a cop what does it.' She leaned forward again. 'Now, no more bullshit, Chic. You better give us some goddamn good information. I mean the kind we can verify.'

Chic tapped his fingers to his knee. He was obviously thinking again. And then he decided. He reached his hand into a hole in the back of the couch.

Both Maggie and Gail drew their guns.

Chic said, 'Good Lord, bitches, give me some credit.' He waited for them to lower their weapons. He saw that they weren't going to. He moved slowly, his hand inching out like a stop-motion cartoon.

At first, Maggie didn't recognize what he was holding. It was like reading a clue in a crossword puzzle and seeing the thing in your mind but being completely incapable of translating that image into a word that filled in all the blocks.

But then she knew: Jimmy's radio transmitter.

Chic lofted up the plastic brick like a trophy. 'This verification enough?'

Maggie slid her gun back into her holster. She leaned heavily against the wall.

'All right.' Gail didn't take the transmitter. She lowered her revolver, but she kept the gun in her lap instead of returning it to her purse. 'Tell me where you got that.'

'One of my girls found it in the alley where that cop was killed. Whitehall, C&S Bank.'

'It was just sitting there in the alley?' Gail didn't believe him. 'Where's the girl?'

'I got her hid somewhere. She saw something scared the shit out of her.' Chic looked at Kate, then Maggie, then Gail again. 'Oughta scare the shit outta you, too.'

Gail asked, 'What'd she see?'

'It ain't a what, it's a *who*. And the dude my gal saw sure as shit ain't nothing like the brother you guys put out on the news.' Chic grinned. 'You know, this is some really good shit I'm giving you. I think we need to revisit our deal.'

Gail jammed her gun into the pimp's face. 'Where is she?'

'You gonna Edward Spivey me? Plant some bogus shit in my room and try to put me on trial?'

'I might.'

Chic stared down the muzzle of the gun. 'You listen careful to me, bitch. Either you take that gun out of my face or your dried-out old pussy goes out that window.'

Anthony took a step forward.

Maggie did, too.

He took another step.

She pulled her revolver again. The grip was warm in her hand.

And then two things happened, one immediately after the other.

Kate collapsed to the floor.

The side of Chic's head vaporized.

At least that was how it looked to Maggie. The right side of Chic's face was there one second – eye, cheekbone,

282

jaw – and then the next second, it disappeared in a spray of blood.

Somebody screamed. The window exploded. Or maybe Maggie was just now hearing it, the same as the distant crack of a rifle that reverberated in her ears.

One shot. Head shot.

The Shooter.

Maggie hit the floor. Kate was already there. Her eyes were closed. She wasn't moving. A trickle of blood ran from her ear down her cheek. Broken glass was everywhere. Maggie's hand was empty.

Her revolver was gone.

Gail's chair shattered to pieces. The sound was like another gunshot. Anthony had jumped on top of her. He'd assumed the bullet had come from Gail's gun. He straddled her, pinning her down. The switchblade was in his hand. Gail grabbed his wrist with both hands. Her arms shook as the knife got closer. The blade was inches from her eye.

'No!' Maggie scrambled to get Kate's gun. The revolver was twisted inside her holster. The snap was bent on the safety strap.

Gail gave a bloodcurdling scream. Maggie watched helplessly as the long, sharp blade was driven straight into Gail's eyeball.

The snap finally gave. The strap ripped open.

Anthony sat back on his knees.

That was the last thing he ever did.

Maggie pointed the gun at his head and pulled the trigger.

Her senses went haywire. She felt her finger pulling the trigger but she didn't hear the gun fire. She didn't see

Anthony fall onto his back, but she could tell from the way the floor shook that he was down. Smoke trailed up from the muzzle, but she couldn't smell the cordite.

She heard clicking.

Click-click-click.

Like a set of wind-up teeth.

The gun was empty, but Maggie was still pulling the trigger. She dropped the revolver on the floor. The thud was muffled by the time it reached her ears. Sound came back to her like an approaching siren – first it was so far away she could barely hear it, then suddenly it was loud and heart-stopping.

'Jesus . . . oh, Jesus . . . ,' Gail panted. Her chest heaved as she tried to force air into her lungs. The knife was still jammed into her eye. The handle wavered back and forth like a tent pole.

'Gail?' Maggie crawled over to her. 'Gail?'

'Wha . . .' Gail reached up to her eye.

'Don't!' Maggie grabbed Gail's hand. This wasn't real. It was a drill. None of this was really happening. Maggie didn't really just kill somebody. She wasn't really looking at a knife sticking out of Gail Patterson's eye.

What next? What next?

Maggie grabbed her mic with her free hand. 'Dispatch, this is unit five. Sixty-three times two, my location. Repeat, sixty-three times two – urgent – my ten-twenty.'

Dispatch came back quickly. 'Ten-four, unit five. Help is on the way.'

Maggie dropped her mic. She looked around the room. The carnage was unreal. So much blood. Pieces of bone and cartilage sprayed the couch. Shards of Chic's teeth bit into the wall.

None of this had really happened. These people weren't really dead. Gail was fine. Kate was fine. Maggie had not killed a man. She had not pointed her gun at a man's head and emptied her entire load into his skull.

'Maggie,' Gail whispered. 'Is it bad?'

'No.'

'Is it?'

Maggie forced herself to look at the switchblade sticking out of Gail's face. She was covered in Anthony's blood. A clear liquid seeped from her eye, dragging a line that cut to the pasty white skin of her cheek.

This had happened. All of it had happened.

'It's not so bad,' Maggie lied. The blade was six inches, at least. A third of it went through Gail's eye, another third sunk into her brain.

'Oma?' Kate mumbled. She was coming to. Her hand went to her head. The top of her ear was bloody where the bullet had nicked her skin.

'Kate.' Maggie forced an authority into her tone that she did not feel. 'Kate, get up. Now.'

She sat up quickly, panicked. She looked at Sir Chic. She looked at Anthony. She looked at Gail. Her mouth opened, but only a squeak came out.

Maggie said, 'It's not as bad as it looks.'

Kate couldn't take her eyes off the knife. She knew it was bad. That she didn't say so was a minor miracle.

'Fuck me,' Gail whispered. The panic was taking over. The muscles in her neck stood out like rope as she fought to keep her head from moving. 'It's bad. I know it's bad.'

'You're gonna be—' Maggie's voice caught. She wasn't going to be all right. None of this was all right.

'Don't.' Gail's voice was shallow. 'Don't you goddamn cry, Lawson.'

'I'm not,' Maggie lied. 'I won't.'

'Both of you. I'll take out this knife and stab you myself. You hear me?'

'All right.' Kate had no idea what she was agreeing to. Her pupils were so blown open that she looked stoned.

Maggie tightened her grip on Gail's hand. She willed her tears to stop. She had to keep her promise. The ambulance crew, the responding officers, whoever was on their way – she couldn't let them see her cry. They had to be tough gals. They had to be stronger than everybody else.

Maggie looked up at the ceiling. She took a deep breath and slowly let it go. Her eyes could not find a spot to rest on. She didn't want to see Gail or Kate. She didn't want to see the two dead men whose bodies were already giving off the metallic odor of congealing blood.

She looked out the broken window at the abandoned storage building across the street.

The flapping piece of tar paper was gone.

20

Fox passed the pimped-out Mercury as he walked away from the scene. He plucked Kate's hat from the back seat, leaving Jimmy Lawson's for the rest of her shift.

Flowers.

He knew that Kate's hair would smell like flowers. Not like perfume, but the real thing that grew out of the ground.

Fox let himself consider what it would be like to feel her skin. To bite her with his teeth. To screw her into the ground. To one by one pluck away her petals. To cut himself on her thorns.

He always felt this way after a kill – not satisfied, but craving more.

He owed Kate Murphy. She had led him here. Not that Fox didn't keep his ear to the ground. The police scanner had been filled with chatter since Don Wesley had been taken out. Nobody gave a shit when Fox was killing drug dealers and street scum. Put down a couple of cops, and that got their attention, even if they were the kind of cops who deserved to die.

Still, Fox was getting tired of surprises.

And he was getting tired of correcting his own past mistakes.

Fox had been halfway home when he'd decided he needed to walk the alley where Jimmy and Don Wesley had been going at it. Leaving a kill scene like that was lazy, and Fox was not lazy.

Lesson eight: Always follow the plan.

This was how it happened: You stuck your gun in their face. You made them call dispatch and clock out. You unplugged their radios so they couldn't call for help. You put them on their knees. You made them lace their fingers together and put them on the top of their heads. You pulled the trigger.

Pop.

Pop.

Two men. Two bodies. Two more names off the list.

And then you always checked the scene to make sure you hadn't left anything for the good guys to find.

By the time Fox got back to the alley, the spunk and blood were already drying on the ground. Grid search, just like they used to do for land mines. Fox had paced back and forth and found nothing but the shit you could find on every street in the city.

He now accepted that someone had been there before him. The pimp, obviously. He had a police transmitter in his hand. Jimmy Lawson's transmitter. No whore would've given up that kind of bargaining chip. All any slit ever cared about was sucking cock and stealing some poor guy's money.

The pimp wasn't a nuisance. He was a witness.

Lucky thing Fox had his rifle.

The bullet had clipped Kate's ear because Fox had told

it to. He could taste the blood in his mouth when it happened.

Kate's blood.

Fox licked his lips. The cold wind dried them quickly. He didn't need wind; he needed lightning. The plan wasn't coming together like he wanted. The thing in the back of his head wasn't talking to the front. And the thing between his legs was yelling that it was tired of waiting. Fox was patient, but he wasn't a saint. Tomorrow, all of this had to come together or something really bad was going to happen.

He heard a police siren blaring up the street. They were coming faster than Fox had anticipated. No choice but to duck into an alley. Fox wasn't worried about witnesses in this neighborhood. He was a white man with a cop's hat in his hand and a sniper's rifle slung over his shoulder.

Nawsir-Officer-sir, I didn't see a thing.

The police cruiser zoomed past the alley. Fox's car was parked behind the next row of houses. He knew a back way out. Fox always knew a back way out.

He allowed himself a smile. The ground shook beneath his feet. The trains were rumbling through the Howell Wye.

Trains.

The lightning finally struck Fox's skull. The plan jolted from the back to the front. He saw it now, a living, breathing plan that he could hold in his hand and study from all angles. It was complicated, but brilliant.

And like everything else that had happened this week, it all started with Jimmy Lawson.

21

'You're quitting.' Terry drove with one hand and smoked with the other. 'I'm not playing, missy. Tomorrow. Your resignation on Vick's desk before roll call.'

Maggie said nothing. She had her eyes closed. Her jaw was ratcheted down so tight that she could taste the silver fillings in her teeth.

'Fucking Patterson,' Terry muttered. 'What're you doin' goin' with that crazy slit anyway? You're not a fucking detective. None of you are.'

The taste of blood mixed with the metal. She had cut her cheek in the Portuguese house. Maggie couldn't recall when. The edge of her molars had sliced open the skin like a knife.

A knife.

'You listenin' to me?' Terry slapped her face. 'Open your goddamn eyes.'

Maggie opened her eyes. She stared straight ahead. The car's headlights furrowed through the darkness.

'Un-fuckin'-believable.' Terry continued to berate her. She continued to ignore him.

They wouldn't let Maggie stay at the hospital. Trouble had asked her to stay. Maggie had said she would stay.

Terry had dragged her out by her collar in front of the whole squad.

Gail wouldn't even know she had been there. She was still in surgery. She would never see out of her eye again. That's what the doctors had said. They'd also said she might have brain damage, but what did they know? Gail was joking even before the morphine. She had the paramedics cracking up. They had given her a cigarette and she'd made some comment about the smoke coming out of her eyeball.

Maggie smiled. They used to joke all the time back when they rode together. Gail would tell her stories about old busts, like the bank robber who jumped on the counter, hit his head, and knocked himself out. Or the idiot who was trying to rob a liquor store and ended up shooting off his own hand. Riding alongside Gail, Maggie hadn't just learned how to be a cop. She had learned how to be in charge. For the first time in her life, she had power. People had to stop when she told them to. They had to listen to what she said. They didn't get to argue or talk over her or tell her she was wrong. Or if they did, Maggie wrote down every single word they said in her arrest report so the prosecutor could use it.

And Gail would say, 'Keep on talkin', motherfucker. We got more pens.'

That would never happen again. Gail couldn't be a cop anymore. She couldn't pass the physical readiness test with one eye. She couldn't work the streets or bang up the bad guys. Anthony hadn't just taken away her vision with that knife. He'd taken away her power.

Maybe that's why Maggie could feel no remorse for

her actions. She had murdered a man. She had taken a life.

An eye for an eye.

'Hey, idiot!' Terry snapped his fingers in front of her face. 'I asked you a question.'

Maggie didn't care about his questions. She had answered them all at the scene. She'd told Cal Vick what had happened to the best of her recollection. Not that she trusted her recollections. What happened in the Portuguese house felt so distant to her that Maggie had a hard time believing that she'd actually been there. It was like hearing stories about things she'd done as a child. Maggie didn't really remember the events firsthand. She remembered the stories because she'd heard them so many times. When she was three and she opened all of Jimmy's Christmas presents. When she was five and cut her leg on a rusty nail.

Maggie flattened her palm to her leg. The ridges of the scar were as familiar as her reflection. She knew the story behind the injury, but the pain and the panic and the fear that had likely gone along with it were completely lost.

Terry turned the steering wheel so hard that Maggie had to brace herself to keep from falling. He sped down the driveway and screeched to a stop under the carport. 'Where's your brother?'

Maggie opened the door. She didn't know where Jimmy was. His car wasn't on the street. Back at the Portuguese house, she kept expecting to see him. Her heart lurched every time a new person came into the room. And then she would realize it wasn't Jimmy and a cold wave of disappointment washed over.

Maggie walked up the steps to the kitchen. Delia's back was to Maggie. The ashtray overflowed with cigarettes smoked down to the filters.

Maggie put her belt on the counter. 'Mama.'

Delia didn't turn around. 'You're quitting tomorrow.'

Maggie felt surprised, and then she felt stupid for being surprised.

'I mean it, Margaret.' Delia turned around. Her eyes were red. She looked a hundred years old. 'You'll work with me at the diner. You'll get an office job. You'll drive a damn tow truck. I don't care. You're not going back to that job.'

Terry said, 'That's exactly what I told her.' He wasn't a big man, but his presence sucked the remaining air out of the kitchen. 'Where's Jimmy?'

'He's not with you?' Delia called up the stairs, 'Jimmy?' She waited a second, then called louder. 'Jimmy!'

Lilly yelled back, 'He's locked in his room!'

'Locked in his room?' Terry mumbled. 'What the hell's wrong with him?'

'How the hell should I know?' Delia demanded. 'None of my children give a shit about me.'

Terry went up the stairs. His bad mood lingered.

'I mean it, Margaret.' Delia's voice was a quiet threat. 'No more playing cops and robbers.'

Even if Maggie had wanted to respond, she couldn't unclench her jaw.

'You killed a man. Murdered him.'

Maggie stopped breathing.

'There's blood all over your clothes. On your face. Gail got hurt. She's your friend. I know she's your friend. And look what happened to her. She's handicapped for the rest of her life.' Her voice trilled. 'Her *life*, Margaret. It's gone.'

Maggie forced herself not to look away.

'What's going to happen to her?' Delia answered the question herself. 'She'll lose her job. She won't be able to find another one. Her husband will leave her. What man wants to be with a woman like that? To have to take care of her for the rest of her life?'

Maggie swallowed hard.

'It could've just as easily been you. Did you consider that? That I might be stuck here taking care of you until I die? And then what? Your brother Jimmy has to take care of you? Or Lilly, God help her?' She clutched the counter with her hand. 'Are you just going to stand there staring like an imbecile?'

Maggie found her voice. 'It didn't happen to me.'

'But look what did!' Delia's anger erupted. 'You're a murderer now. Is that what you want to be? A murderer? With blood on your hands?' She grabbed Maggie's arm. 'Answer me!'

Maggie looked down at her mother's hand. The fingertips were stained yellow from nicotine. She told her mother, 'The only regret I have is that I didn't murder him sooner.'

Delia staggered back. She could have been looking at a stranger.

Maggie opened the cabinet under the sink. She grabbed a paper bag from the pile.

'What are you doing?'

'Cleaning up Terry and Jimmy's mess.' She clutched the bag between her hands. 'Isn't that what you want me to do, Mother? Stay here for the rest of my life and clean up everybody's fucking mess?'

294

Maggie walked out the door. The night air was frigid. She didn't bother to turn on the lights under the carport. Her father had installed the fixtures the last time he was out of the hospital. Most of the time, the bulbs flickered like a mirror ball. The kitchen light offered little illumination. For some reason, Maggie wanted to be in the shadows.

Seven hours ago, Terry had thrown a can of beer at her head. Maggie picked it up now. Warm liquid sloshed onto her hand. She dropped the can into the bag. She picked up another can, then another. She didn't intend to count, but she was on fifteen by the time she made her way to the side yard.

Maggie couldn't see where she was going. She stepped on a can. The aluminum cupped around the arch of her shoe. She used her other foot to pry it off. Then she squatted on the ground and resumed picking up cans.

Sixteen. Seventeen. Eighteen.

The bag was overflowing. Instead of going back to the kitchen, Maggie walked across the yard.

Lee Grant's van was in the driveway. She could make out the gold, yellow, and blue bands, the Southern Bell logo on the side. Maggie pressed her hand to the hood. The engine was cold.

She went up the two steps to the side entrance and knocked on the door. And then she rang the doorbell, because she wasn't sure what Lee could hear. She'd said maybe five words to him in the last eight years. He was nervous around Jimmy and terrified of Terry, which meant that he was a hell of a lot smarter than people gave him credit for.

Lee opened the door. His eyes went wide. He'd noticed the blood on her uniform.

'Don't worry,' she told him, feeling self-conscious because she'd forgotten how he looked at people's mouths when they talked. 'It's not mine.'

'Are you all right?' His *r*'s were soft. *Ah you ah-wight?*

Maggie checked her house to make sure no one was outside. 'Is there a central place at the phone company that has numbers and addresses for businesses?'

To his credit, Lee didn't ask her if she had checked the Yellow Pages. 'The billing department.'

'I need the address for a bar called Dabbler's.' She spelled out the name for him, carefully enunciating each letter. 'Can you get it for me?'

'Yes.'

Maggie let herself breathe for the first time in days.

He asked again, 'Are you all right?'

Maggie could remember Lee asking her the same question eight years ago. She was lying on the couch in his mother's kitchen. The air was hot and sticky. His mother wasn't much of a cook. She was a nurse who worked nights. All of their meals were frozen dinners and fast food, which was a luxury nobody else on the street could afford.

Maggie asked, 'Can you put the address in my mailbox? I'm the only one who checks it.'

'I know.' Lee seemed to realize what he'd revealed. He looked out at the street.

Maggie saw the hearing aid tucked above his ear. He wore his old one when he jogged, probably because the new kind was more expensive. She guessed it was fifteen years ago that Jimmy and Lee had gotten into their last fistfight. Jimmy had broken Lee's hearing aid. Lee's father had come to the house and showed it to Delia. He worked for the phone company, too. He was still wearing his lineman's belt. His eyes were blood-shot, which was odd because he wasn't a drinker. Delia had to work extra shifts for three months to pay for a new hearing aid. She'd grounded Jimmy, but Terry had still taken him out on weekends.

'I'm sorry,' Maggie said, but Lee wasn't looking at her and she wasn't sure he had heard.

'Maggie!' Terry yelled.

She jumped at the sound of his voice. Lee heard it, too. He was already shutting the door. Maggie ran down the stairs. She crossed the yard.

'Maggie!'

'What, Terry? What do you want?'

Terry stood in the doorway. Anger burned in his eyes. He was huffing like a bull. Nostrils flared. Mouth open.

Maggie stopped. She had learned the hard way that as bad as Terry could be when he was screaming, it was far, far worse when he was quiet.

He spoke through gritted teeth. 'Get in the house. Now.'

Maggie walked up the stairs. She clutched the wobbly railing. Her legs could barely hold her. The last time Terry got this way, he had beaten her into the ground.

The kitchen had taken on a darkness that wasn't there before. Delia stood in the middle of the room. She held a sheet of notebook paper between her shaking hands. She was swaying. Maggie thought about the knife in Gail's eye, the way the handle had moved back and forth as Gail tried not to blink.

Delia stared at the words on the notebook paper. Everything about her trembled. 'It's not true. Tell me it's not true.'

Maggie could see the blue ink through the white paper. The handwriting was Jimmy's. She took the note from her mother. The first line was so incomprehensible that it might as well have been written in another language.

I am the Atlanta Shooter.

Maggie felt a cold sensation envelop her body.

I killed those guys because I was a dirty fag with them and I didn't want anybody to find out.

Maggie braced her hand on the counter so that she would not sink to the floor.

Don't try to find me or I will kill more people. Maggie—

Maggie read her name twice. She couldn't recall ever seeing her name written in her brother's hand.

Maggie, I'm sorry that I never apologized to you. I should've told you that what happened wasn't your fault.

She studied the signature. He'd written his full name at the bottom – James Lawson. The only letters she could make out were the *J* and the *L*. Maggie knew the mark was made by her brother's hand. She typed all his reports. Every morning before roll call, she watched Jimmy scribble his signature on the dotted line.

Terry said, 'This doesn't leave this room.'

His words hung somewhere over her head. Maggie felt like she could reach up and touch them.

Delia said, 'But the guys. They can—'

'I mean it,' Terry interrupted. 'Nobody hears about this.'

Maggie started shaking her head. 'It's a confession. We have to—'

Terry's hand clamped around her neck. Maggie's feet lifted from the floor. She clawed at his fingers.

'I said no one hears about this.'

Maggie kicked her feet against the wall. Her lungs screamed in her chest.

'This gets out—' He tightened his grip around her throat. 'Them guys find out they been riding with a faggot—'

'Terry,' Delia begged. 'Terry, she's turning blue. Let her go. Please. Please.'

Terry released his grip.

Maggie fell to the floor. She gulped for air. Her throat felt raw.

Delia said, 'It's not true. My boy's not a queer. Somebody musta made him write that.'

'Bullshit,' Terry countered. 'I don't care if you hold a gun to my head, ain't no way I'd say I was a faggot. You'd have to kill me first.'

Delia couldn't let it go. 'Jimmy's out with a new girl every weekend. He's always fighting them off with a stick.'

Maggie rasped the glass out of her throat. She picked up the letter from the floor. 'Where did you find this?' She looked at Delia, then Terry. 'Where?'

Delia answered, 'Terry found it on his bed.'

Maggie was halfway up the stairs before she realized she was moving. She pushed herself to keep going into the hall. She passed Delia's room, Lilly's with her always-closed door, her own room, and then she stood outside Jimmy's doorway.

Terry must have kicked in the door. The jamb was splintered. Wood stuck out like daggers. Maggie ran her fingertips along the sharp ends. They dragged a white line across her skin.

Jimmy's room was painted the same dark gray as the

rest of the house. The hundred-watt bulb in the ceiling fixture gave the space the appearance of a crime scene. He had a full-sized bed that Delia had bought for him when he turned sixteen. There was a dresser they had taken off the sidewalk when the family down the street got evicted. His Dopp kit was open on the top. She saw his razor, his comb, and brush. His aftershaves were lined up in a neat row. This was the only area in which Jimmy liked variety. Pierre Cardin. English Leather. Brut. Prince Matchabelli. Maggie gave him a new kind every year at Christmas.

She went to Jimmy's closet. There was no door, just a curtain that he pulled back. His uniforms were on the left, where she always hung them. His pants were in the middle, then shirts, then jackets on the far right. Jimmy was particular about his closet. He kept the colors grouped together. Navy. Black. Gray. White.

Maggie looked down at the letter in her hand.

I am the Atlanta Shooter.

She heard Terry behind her. He was still breathing hard, probably from coming up the stairs. She asked, 'Where was Jimmy this afternoon? After we left?'

Terry didn't answer.

Maggie started checking the pockets in Jimmy's clothes.

I killed those guys because I was a dirty fag with them. . . .

Delia asked, 'What are you looking for?'

Maggie kept searching the pockets. Nothing. No matchbooks. No more confessions. She did all of Jimmy's laundry. She was constantly finding phone numbers scribbled onto napkins and torn pieces of paper.

Had all those numbers belonged to men?

300

Delia said, 'Maggie, stop. You know Jimmy doesn't like you going through his stuff.'

Maggie couldn't stop. What was she expected to believe? That her brother followed her to the Portuguese house today? That he had almost killed Kate? That he had shot the pimp? And what about the other men – Keen and Porter, Ballard and Johnson? Was she supposed to accept that her brother had murdered all of those men, then come to the breakfast table the next morning and filled up on coffee and bacon and eggs with his family?

And Don Wesley – Don was Jimmy's friend. They were partners.

Maggie turned around. Terry and Delia were standing behind her. She had to talk out the words before they exploded in her head. 'It doesn't make sense. Why would he do it?'

'Because he's a faggot,' Terry answered. 'Can't you fucking read? You're the college girl. It was right in front of your face the whole time, but you had your head too far up your ass to see it.'

'You didn't see it, either.'

Terry backhanded her so hard that Maggie fell against the wall. She put her hand to her cheek. The skin had broken open.

'Fucking mess,' Terry mumbled as he paced the room. The space was small. He could only go three steps before he had to turn back around. 'What the fuck was he thinking?'

No one answered, because there wasn't an answer that made sense. The only sound that broke the silence was the familiar scratch of a needle on a record. *Tapestry*. Lilly

301

had the volume up. She didn't want to hear what was going on.

Terry said, 'This can't get out. Do you hear me? None of this can get out.'

Maggie watched him go from one side of the room to the other. He was more enraged about Jimmy being gay than he was about Jimmy being a murderer.

Delia tried again. 'Maybe Bud and Cal can—'

'No,' Terry stopped her. 'Nobody finds out, Dee. That's it. We handle this on our own.'

'What are you going to do?' Delia sounded terrified. 'Terry, please. Tell me what you're going to do.'

He kept pacing. He was thinking it through, trying to see a way out. Finally, he decided, 'I'm gonna track him down and kill him myself, is what I'm going to do.'

'Terry!' Delia screamed. 'For the love of—'

'Goddamn it!' Terry punched the wall so hard that the plaster bowed.

No one spoke for another moment. *Tapestry* played on. 'So Far Away.'

Terry stared at his hand. The knuckles were already black and blue from work. Fresh cuts had rent open the skin. He flexed his fingers into and out of a fist.

He said, 'I gotta put him down, Dee. He's a Lawson. It's my responsibility.'

'Terry.' Delia was turning his name into a mantra. 'Terry, no. You can't.'

'You wanna trial? Is that what you want?' He looked disgusted by the idea. 'Your cocksucking son pouring out his heart on the stand? Talkin' about how he went queer on all them cops he murdered?'

The color drained from Delia's face.

'You tell Cal Vick this, he'll shoot him himself. Same with Jett, Mack, Red – all of 'em. They'll put him down and nobody'll blame 'em.'

'It won't be like that,' Delia insisted. 'Something's wrong. He wasn't right in the head when he wrote this.'

'You think a jury will buy some kind of temporary insanity?' Terry flexed his hands again. 'You wanna roll that dice, take a chance they won't send him straight to Old Sparky?'

Delia clutched the doorknob to keep herself from falling.

'You wanna go to the state pen and watch 'em strap our boy into the electric chair?' Terry wiped his bloody hand on Jimmy's sheets. 'They put 'em in diapers because they shit themselves. They don't like the guy, maybe they don't wet the sponge enough, so when the switch is flipped, he catches on fire and burns alive.' Terry grabbed Delia's arm. 'Is that what you want for him, Dee? You wanna watch him burn?'

'Oh, God, Terry. Please don't say these things. Please! I can't hear them.'

'You need to hear them.' He looked at Maggie. 'You need to hear 'em, too, tough gal. He may be a dirty queer, but he's still your brother.'

Maggie didn't know what to say. All of this was too much. Her throat was sore. Her head was pounding. This was insane. She couldn't believe it – not any of it. Jimmy wasn't gay, and he sure as hell wasn't a murderer.

'Mom.' Maggie needed to make her see reason. She took Delia's hand. 'He didn't do it. There's no way—'

'No!' Delia pulled back like she'd been scalded. 'Don't you talk to me! Don't you say anything else! You should've never taken that job! It was too much stress on Jimmy!'

The hate in her eyes pierced Maggie's soul.

'This is all on you, Margaret.' Delia's voice got stronger with every word. 'If you'd gotten married, then Jimmy would've, too.' She seemed almost relieved. She told Terry, 'That's it. He couldn't meet a girl and get married. He couldn't abandon us, because no one else would take care of us.'

Terry said, 'I take plenty damn good care of you.'

'I know you do.' Delia rested her hand on his chest. The panic was winding down now that she had figured out who was really to blame. 'I know you do good by us. But Jimmy – he's a young man. He's under a lot of pressure. He just didn't know what he was doing. I'm sure that's it, Terry. I'm sure he can explain.'

Terry put his hand over Delia's. He looked at her in a way that made Maggie's stomach turn. 'I'll handle this, Dee.'

Maggie stared down at Jimmy's note. His confession. His apology.

I'm sorry I never apologized to you.

What did he mean? He'd apologized to Maggie at the hospital just yesterday. The moment was seared into her memory. Jimmy had never apologized to her for anything before. Was there something else he was sorry for? Was there some other thing he'd done that Maggie still hadn't found out about?

Not murder. She could believe her big, strong brother was a homosexual before she could believe that he would kill five men in cold blood.

'You have to stop this,' Maggie told Terry. 'Jimmy

wrote this letter for a reason.'

'He wrote it because he wants us to stop him. You ever think of that?'

Maggie didn't have a response. She hadn't thought of that. She looked at the last two lines. The apology that ignored the apology from the day before.

Was it possible that she was wrong about her brother? Eight years was a long time. The Jimmy that Maggie knew was a grown man now. He went places she didn't know about. He had friends she had never met. Sometimes, he stayed out all night and no one ever asked him questions about it in the morning.

Terry said, 'He'll be a victim. The Shooter got him. I'll make it look the same way, unplug his goddamn radio, break his fingernail if I have to. He'll get a cop's funeral. He'll be buried in the cemetery with an honor guard.' He told Delia, 'You'll get benefits. He'll still be doing his part. That's what Jimmy wants. He knew what he was doing when he left the note on his bed for anybody to find.'

Maggie couldn't accept what Terry was saying. She tried to reason with Delia. 'Mama, you were right. We need to show the letter to people. This isn't our Jimmy. Something's wrong with him.'

Suddenly, the paper was wrenched from Maggie's hands.

Delia tore Jimmy's confession to pieces.

22

Fox lay behind the fallen log and stared up at the big house situated at the top of a meandering driveway. The kitchen light was on. Kate's car was parked on the pad down from the garage. His view of the front porch could not have been better. The ground was cold beneath him. He could feel it pressing into his thighs, curling up to his balls.

Fox shifted. The pressure was getting worse.

The pressure that Kate caused him.

He wished for a night sighter. The infrared detector washed the landscape in green light, making it possible for you to see the enemy while the enemy only saw darkness. During the war, Fox had used a scope-mounted sighter to track his prey. The enemy was clever, but technology eluded him. Sometimes, Fox would follow a man through the dark jungle for hours. The green light tracked his every move. Fox would watch the target pause, check his surroundings, stop for a meal, take a piss against a tree – all without knowing that Fox was watching.

Which was what Fox was doing now, if only for a few more minutes. He couldn't see his watch, but he estimated from the way the moon hung in the sky that one day was slipping into another.

He needed rest. He needed to make sure Jimmy was still where he was supposed to be. And then he needed to go over the plan one more time.

Tonight, Kate would have to go to bed without him.

DAY THREE
WEDNESDAY

23

Kate sat on the front steps to her parents' house. A faint glow of headlights passed through the trees as a lone car drove by. The tips of leggy pines kissed the midnight moon. There was a crispness in the air that sent tiny icicles into her lungs. The pain was almost soothing. She wanted to feel things. She wanted to know that she was still alive.

Kate couldn't sleep. Her head hit the pillow and then without her knowing how it happened, she found herself dressed and walking across the parking garage. She had spent the last two hours driving around town, aimlessly going up one street and down the next. She'd tried to return home, but found herself passing the hotel two, three, four times before she'd finally directed the car toward Buckhead.

The only stop Kate had made was at the Texaco station on Ponce de Leon – not for fuel, but for the slim chance of redemption.

The Lawsons were in the phone book. Kate had dropped a dime into the pay phone. She had dialed the first three digits of the number. And then her hand had frozen as words ran aimlessly through her mind:

I'm sorry I wasn't there for you.

I'm sorry I let Gail get hurt.

I'm sorry you had to kill a man.

I'm sorry . . . I'm sorry . . . I'm so goddamn sorry.

Kate was surprised by the apologies that rushed to mind – not because she hated asking for forgiveness, but because she had never felt so horribly responsible for things going wrong.

Gail might not be in the hospital right now if Kate had been able to help.

Maggie might not have been forced to kill a man had Kate been able to help.

Kate realized at that moment that she had never truly been needed before. Sure, she volunteered to help friends move. She went to house-painting parties. She was a good third wheel. She paid for her share of rounds at the club. Her family loved her. Kate's friends enjoyed her company. Patrick had adored her. She had needed all of them at one point or another, but none of them had ever truly needed Kate.

The sudden realization had felt like a bell ringing in her head. Kate had stared blankly at the graffiti scrawled above the telephone. She wanted a time machine, but not for Patrick. She wanted to go back to the Portuguese house and in that split second before the bullet whizzed past, she wanted to move her head just slightly away.

That was the only thing that Kate would take back.

She didn't regret going to the Portuguese house. She didn't want to time-travel back to Monday morning and erase putting on the uniform and going in to work, or go back even further in time and will herself not to read that newspaper article about women motorcycle cops, or to stop herself from going downtown to fill out the application for the police department, or to prevent herself from not showing up that first day at the academy with her notebook already filled with details she'd copied out of her textbook.

No, Kate would not take any of that back. Her only regret was that she had failed to help her fellow police officers.

This was what she wanted to say to Maggie Lawson: *I am sorry I wasn't able to help you kill that man. I am sorry that we did not get the information from Chic before he was murdered. I am sorry that I could not stop Gail from getting injured.*

I am sorry, I am sorry, I am so goddamn sorry.

In the end, Kate had put the receiver back in the cradle without dialing the rest of the numbers. The sound of the dime making its way to the change slot had reminded her of a pinball machine.

She should've done better. She should've *been* better. The only reason Gail was at that house in the first place was because Maggie needed backup, and she didn't trust Kate to do it. She was right to not trust Kate with her life. Everything they had said about the FNG was true. The China Doll. The Sheep. The worthless Buckhead princess who'd fallen to the floor in a heap when everything went to hell.

In her mind, Kate knew that she wasn't using logic. She hadn't played possum. The fall to the floor was precipitated by gunfire. She'd knocked herself out so badly that she was mildly concussed. It wasn't as if Kate had been given a choice and failed to act. There was no test of courage. No decision to be made. She hadn't seen Chic die. She hadn't seen Anthony attacking Gail. She hadn't seen Maggie stopping him. She didn't remember the bullet clipping her ear. She didn't remember falling. Kate was listening to Gail threaten Sir Chic one moment and the next she was looking around the room and feeling like she had walked into the penultimate scene in *Straw Dogs*.

Kate's first conscious thought when she came to was that she hurt. Her head hurt. Her ear hurt. Her leg hurt where she'd fallen. Her gun was missing. She'd snapped closed the strap when they were outside the house, just as Maggie had told her to. She'd heeded all their warnings about the pimp. She'd even negotiated with Chic, getting him to reveal that he knew something about the shooting. Or at least that he had a girl who knew something. Saw something.

And for what?

They would never find the girl now. Chic had taken her location to the grave. Maggie had literally shot Anthony's head off. There was nothing left of him but a sharp white bone sticking up from his neck like the fin of a great white shark.

For nothing.

Another car drove by. Kate caught the glow of a cigarette. There was a person walking along the street in front of the house. A chill went through her. Then she felt silly, because why on earth would anybody care that she was sitting on her parents' front porch?

Still, she couldn't shake the sensation of being watched. If she was being honest, Kate had felt that way a lot lately – as if a pair of eyes was tracking her every move. Even when she was alone in her apartment or inside her parents' house, she couldn't quell the unsettling feeling that her every move was being monitored. Maybe this came with the territory. Being paranoid was probably a healthy trait for a police officer. And she was a sitting duck on the front porch steps.

Kate stood up. She smoothed down the back of her skirt. She touched her hand to the mezuzah on her parents' front door.

Methuselah, Gail had called it, and then she had winked at Kate because she'd obviously read Kate's personnel file and she knew how Patrick had died just like she knew which box had been checked under 'religion.'

Kate whispered the words her Oma had taught her, 'May God keep my going out and my coming in from now on and ever more.'

The door was unlocked; no one locked their doors in Buckhead. They didn't even know where all the doors were. The front room was dark except for the embers burning in the fireplace. The light was on in the kitchen. Kate heard her grandmother's laughter, followed by the deep murmur of her father's voice.

'Daddy?' she called, but the word got stuck somewhere in Kate's chest. She had no idea why she had come here. When Kate was a child, she would curl into bed with Oma and count the steady beats of her heart. After Patrick's death, Kate had slept by her side for over a month.

She was too old for that now. Too hardened.

What she really needed was a stiff drink.

'Darling!' Oma lit up when Kate entered the kitchen. She was playing cards with Kate's father. Jacob Herschel had two PhDs and a medical degree, but he would have lost everything to Oma had Liesbeth not insisted they play for pennies.

Jacob took off his glasses to study Kate. He'd spent his summers in South Georgia as a boy. He had a soft, southern drawl that always reminded her of Gregory Peck in *To Kill a Mockingbird*.

He asked, 'Is everything all right?'

Kate wrapped her arm around his shoulders. She kissed the top of his head. 'Couldn't sleep,' she told him, which was true. 'I was just driving around and I saw the light on.'

'What a wonderful coincidence.' Oma refilled her glass of sherry. 'I love your dress. Is it new?'

'No. Yes.' Kate sat at the table. She had thrown on the first thing she could find in her closet – a striped yellow, blue, and burgundy dress that cut too low for any occasion that didn't involve a nightclub.

'It's lovely.' Oma touched the material. Her fingers stroked Kate's arm, then held her hand. She told Jacob, 'I'm ready to take more of your money now.'

Jacob put his glasses back on. 'I assumed you were.'

Kate studied her father's features as he shuffled the deck of cards. He looked old, though that was only because Kate always thought of him as the young man who used to throw her into the air and catch her. She imagined her father was always surprised by her face, too. He must still see her as that child he could carry in his arms.

What would Jacob think about Kate's first two days as a police officer? Nothing, if Kate had anything to do with it. She could not tell her father that she had almost died today, that Kate had literally come within an inch of losing her life. Not even an inch. Less than an inch. A millimeter, the paramedic had said.

Kate had refused to go to the hospital. They thought she was brave, but she was really terrified. Jacob Herschel was occasionally at Grady Hospital visiting his charity patients. The way Kate's luck was running, she was certain they would bring her into the emergency room at the exact moment her father arrived for a consultation.

He would not yell at her. He would not rage. He would simply advise Kate to leave the job and find something different that would please her more. Her father was very clever that way. He knew better than to try to order around the women in his life. He never gave ultimatums or put his foot down. What he did was offer advice. He posited what he might do should he find himself in their situation. He subtly pushed them toward his way of thinking.

The technique was brilliant, though it did not take into account that the women in his life were also students of human behavior. Oma always complimented him on the idea, then changed the subject. Liesbeth would tell him he was absolutely right, then do whatever she wanted.

As for Kate, she lied.

'So.' Jacob shuffled the cards. 'What happened to your ear?'

Kate touched the tiny round Band-Aid the paramedics had wrapped around her ear. 'The skin was rubbed raw by that silly hat they make me wear.'

Oma tsked. 'First the blisters on your feet and now this. They should have warned you it was so dangerous.'

'Yes, they should have.' Jacob studied Kate's face as he fanned the cards together. They made a slapping noise that echoed off the marble countertops.

Kate wondered if her father already knew what had

317

happened. There had been early reports on the radio about Gail being injured, but Kate and Maggie were just unnamed officers at the scene. The nightly television news hadn't mentioned their gender. By ten this evening, the radio reporters were referring to Maggie as an unidentified male officer who had saved the life of a seasoned detective and his partner.

'So, ladies.' Jacob started dealing three hands. 'I heard Philip Van Zandt paid a visit to the house last night.'

Kate slid her cards off the table. She had no idea what game they were playing, but felt certain her father was dealing her a shitty hand.

'You know what they call him at the hospital?' Jacob tossed more cards Kate's way. 'Dr. Van Zipless.'

Oma hooted with laughter. 'How wonderful! I love it.'

Kate felt her cheeks ignite. The Zipless Fuck. Erica Jong's much-vaunted no-strings-attached sexual encounter. Kate didn't know which was worse, that her father had intimated the word 'fuck' in conversation or that he had read *Fear of Flying*.

Jacob said, 'I never tell you what to do, Kaitlin, but my advice would be to steer clear of such a man.'

Kate looked down at her cards.

Oma slid some of her pennies toward Kate. 'Here, my darling. The game is no fun without risk.'

Jacob noted, 'Your double meanings are usually more skillful.'

'Oh, my English, Jacob. I have no idea what you mean.' Oma pronounced his name the Dutch way, with a 'y' sound at the beginning instead of a 'j.' She pushed her sherry glass toward Kate. 'Have my drink, dear.'

Kate threw back the alcohol like a cowboy in a Western. Oma stood. 'I found Dr. Van Zandt to be quite charming – much more so than his boring father. I never got to show him your stamp collection, Jacob.'

Kate's father concentrated on his cards. 'I presume there's no double meaning about showing him a stamp collection, Judith?'

'Oh, my. If I were a few years younger.' She went into the pantry and returned with a bottle of scotch. 'Young men are always so eager for instruction.'

Kate searched desperately for a new topic. 'Oma, wasn't Audrey Hepburn born in Brussels?'

'I believe she was born in Elsene.' Oma filled the sherry glass with scotch. She got another glass for herself. 'A nice Flemish girl.'

Kate smiled at the familiar words. And then she drank as much of the scotch as was possible without revealing the bottom of the glass.

Jacob put down another card. 'I always liked the Flemish.'

'Bah.' Oma took his card and replaced it with one of her own. 'Peasants.'

Jacob frowned. He shuffled the cards in his hands. Two minutes in and he was already losing.

Kate sipped the rest of her drink. Her father had worked for the State Department during the war. He'd been sent to Amsterdam after the liberation to do psychiatric triage on the survivors. He'd met Liesbeth during his service, but Kate had no idea in what capacity. The story was that they fell in love at the flower market. Had Liesbeth been a patient? Was she someone he'd simply met in the street?

Unbidden, Kate thought about Terry's words in the carport, the women who threw themselves at soldiers.

'Well.' Oma refilled Kate's glass and topped off her own. 'I suppose the Flemish are not so bad. They tend their sheep and marry their cousins.'

Kate laughed. She was feeling tipsy, but she couldn't stop drinking. Maybe this was what being a police officer did to you. This time next week, she'd be passed out behind the wheel of an Impala.

Jacob said, 'There was a Flemish psychiatrist I worked with – brilliant man.' He laid down another card. Kate realized they had been playing without her. 'His name was Walthere Deliege.'

Oma frowned dramatically. '*Dat is Waals, geen Vlaams.*'

'Oh, I beg your pardon. The gentleman was Walloon, not Flemish. Please excuse my American ignorance.' Jacob winked at Kate. Then he frowned when Oma took his discard.

'How can . . .' Kate let her voice trail off. She hadn't meant to say anything, but it was out now. 'How can awful people be good?'

They both stared at her.

'This woman I work with . . .' Kate stopped herself again. Did she work with Gail? Would she ever work with her again?

'This woman?' Oma prompted.

'This woman,' Kate repeated, then stopped a third time because she didn't know whether to go on. As before, she found she couldn't stop. 'She's vulgar, racist, spiteful, critical, violent, mean.' Kate felt no guilt about saying these things, because she was certain Gail would take them all as a compliment. 'I don't think I've ever met anyone like her. She's just . . .'

Again, her voice trailed off. Kate wondered why she kept talking. She usually held her liquor better. Maybe the stress of the day, the shock, the pain medication – all of it was conspiring to erode her usual defenses.

She looked up. Both Oma and Jacob were paying close attention.

Again, Oma prompted. 'This woman is . . . ?'

'She's awful,' Kate admitted. 'And she's also one of the nicest people I've ever met in my life.' That this was true came as a surprise to Kate. 'I got upset today, and she was so nice to me. It doesn't matter about why I was upset. But she was there, and she was kind.' Kate was aware that she was slurring her words almost as badly as Gail. 'But honestly, she's not kind. She's always saying these things to me – these mean, brutal things – and then I think about them later and I realize that she's taught me something. Not just something, but something useful. Something I need to know in order to do my job. Something that will keep me safe.' Kate picked up the sherry glass again. 'And I think, "How can she be helping me when she's so awful? How can it be that I'm starting to think of this vile woman as my friend?"'

Jacob and Oma said nothing.

Kate finished the drink. She might as well go all in.

She said, 'Then, there's this terrible man. "Coarse" isn't the word for him. He's an asshole.' She gave her father an apologetic look. There really was no other word that better suited Terry Lawson. Or his friends. They were all interchangeable as far as Kate was concerned. 'Anyway, this asshole, he's awful, too, just like the woman, but worse in so many ways because he's so angry about it. He's sexist and racist and ugly and crude. He's the sort of man where you think that it's only a matter of time before he does something violent.'

Jacob put his cards down on the table.

Oma refilled her glass.

'Violence toward me?' Kate asked herself. 'No, I don't feel that way. I feel the threat, though. You know how when you're around a mean dog and he's on a leash, but you know if the leash was released . . .' Her voice trailed off yet again. 'I feel like this asshole man is so angry that if I find myself alone with him, then I'd better be prepared to defend myself.'

Again, Kate wasn't just thinking about Terry. All of them gave off that same threatening vibe. The more they drank, the worse it got, and yet Gail had said that Chip Bixby had once saved her life. How could that be? The man was a repulsive misogynist, but he had risked his own safety to protect Gail.

This was the world Kate lived in now. The old rules simply did not apply. You couldn't judge someone based on their appearance or their accent or by what their father did for a living. Maybe Jett Elliott was really a gentleman. Or Bud Deacon was a God-fearing man. Or Cal Vick wasn't a repulsive letch. Maybe the fault was Kate's for looking at their words instead of their actions.

She tried to explain the dichotomy. 'I feel like if I'm threatened by someone else – a robber or a madman or a killer – that these assholes will be there to protect me. And I feel like I should protect them, too. Inasmuch as I can protect anybody.'

Oma screwed the cap back onto the bottle of scotch.

Kate continued, 'So, I listened to this one particular violent asshole today, and he was disparaging President Kennedy, saying Bobby's assassination was a godsend. Disparaging the mayor, blacks, women, me.' She laughed. Terry had certainly disparaged Kate. 'And yet, he was in the war, too, Daddy. He helped liberate the camps. He freed people from enslavement, from death. He helped them in their darkest hour. In humanity's darkest hour. And I have to assume that in his capacity as a policeman, at some point, perhaps many points, during his day, he helps people then, too. He must do this, right?'

Oma stared down her glass. She said nothing.

Kate shook her head. She couldn't keep track of the words coming out of her mouth. 'How can they be so awful, yet they do these good things?'

No one offered an answer. The silence hung over the table in a dark cloud.

Finally, Jacob said, 'It's one of life's great mysteries.'

'Platitudes.' Kate sat back in her chair. Why had she expected them to understand? She didn't understand herself. And she was tired and she was drunk and she should probably go home before she made even more of a fool of herself.

Kate pulled herself together. She started to stand.

'I once knew a Flemish girl,' Oma said.

Kate smiled automatically, but her heart sank as she sat back in her chair. 'Did she tend her sheep and marry her cousin?'

'No.' Oma stared at the amber liquid in her glass. 'She was from Antwerpen. She came to my school toward the end of what you would call my sixth year.'

Kate held her breath. Her grandmother seldom mentioned her life before Atlanta.

'Her name was Gilberte Soetaers, which would be very funny to you if you had studied your Dutch.' She smiled sadly at Kate. 'Gilberte fit in immediately. The popular girls loved her on sight. And why not? She wore wonderful clothes, very fashionable. Her hair was brown and silky like the mane of a horse. She was exotic to us. Or to me, at least. Her father had rubber plantations in the Congo. My father was an academic. She was privileged. I was not. She was a Calvinist. I was Jewish. I was like you, Kaitlin. My body developed before the rest of them. The girls turned into ice. But after Gilberte arrived, they were far worse. Even my little friend who used to take tea with me. They teased me about my clothes, my hair, my figure, my academics—' She shrugged like it made sense, and it *did* make sense, because that's how girls were no matter where you lived.

Oma continued, 'You will be surprised to learn that the world continued to turn on its axis despite my woes. I graduated. I went to university. I married a wonderful man. He gave me beautiful children. I worked at the school. And then the war came. We were all moved into the Jodenbuurt. We weren't allowed to leave, but—' She stroked her hair. 'The Nazis were so stupid. They didn't think a Jewish woman could have blonde hair.' She glanced at Jacob, and Kate got the feeling her father had heard this story before. 'I would leave the quarter to get food for your *opa* and *moeder*. *Voor oom*—' She looked to Jacob again.

'Uncle,' Jacob provided.

'Yes. Your uncle, he was already away, living with a

couple in Friesland who kindly agreed to take him in. Very nice people. They did what they could.' Oma continued to stare down at the glass. Kate knew the boy had been lost to the war.

'So,' Oma said. 'One day I am looking for food near the Nieuwmarktbuurt. This was a very dangerous area for me. They used the square as a collection point, and of course I could be sent away for not wearing the yellow *jodenster*.' She smiled at Kate, though there was none of the usual mirth in her eyes. 'I was at a shop wondering if I can sneak a piece of cheese into my pocket while the grocer is not looking, and I turn around and there she is.' Oma raised her eyebrows in surprise. 'Gilberte Soetaers, this girl who tortured me for years. And, worst of all, she is with a Nazi soldier.'

Kate put her hand to her throat.

'Gilberte recognizes me. I know this because I see it in her eyes. We are women, but we are still those girls who hated each other.' Oma paused. ' "Friedrich," Gilberte calls. I panic. This is not just a Nazi she is with. This is a German. I look for the door. I want to leave, but he is already standing in front of me. Gilberte says to him, "This is a girl I went to school with." And I am shaking like a leaf. I can't believe it. I'm going to disappear. My family will never know what happened to me. My Liesbeth is already so thin. She can barely rise from the bed. They will die without me.'

Oma took Kate's hand and squeezed it very hard. 'And like this, Gilberte grabs my hand, and I think, "She won't let me go! She is going to turn me in!" And she says to me, very sweetly, "Oh, how happy I am to see you, *mijn zoeteke*." ' Oma sat back, but she still held Kate's hand.

'*Mijn zoeteke*. My sweet, like candy. This is a Flemish phrase; I've told you they speak with flowers in their mouths.'

Kate nodded quickly. She wanted Oma to finish the story.

'I didn't know what to make of it, her calling me this name.' Oma seemed still perplexed. 'And then Gilberte Soetaers, this terrible beast who made me miserable for so many years, tells this Nazi, "Darling, you must give my friend some ration tickets. Look how thin she is."' Even now, Oma sounded surprised. 'So, he gave me many tickets. Too many. We agreed to have drinks soon. We kissed cheeks – all of us. And then I left.'

Oma shrugged. That was it. Her story was finished.

Kate wanted more. 'The Nazi gave you ration tickets?'

'Because of Gilberte Soetaers, we had bread, cheese, milk. It was a *mitzvah*. I made the tickets last three weeks.'

Kate wondered how long it was after those three weeks before they were deported to the camps. 'Did the Nazi know you were Jewish?'

'Of course Gilberte did, but she could not tell him after the fact. He would have murdered her. Or worse, sent her away.' She finished the dregs of her scotch. 'So, that is how horrible people can be good.'

Kate shook her head. 'I don't understand. That was an example, not an explanation.'

'Exactly.' Oma rose from her chair. 'There is no explanation, Kaitlin. Evil people can do good. Good people can do evil. Why does this happen sometimes? Because it's Tuesday.' She looked at the clock. '*Ach*. Wednesday. Much past my bedtime. Good night, my dears.'

She pressed her hand to Kate's shoulder as she walked

toward the door. Kate wanted to stop her, but Oma left without another word.

'Well.' Jacob collected the cards on the table.

Kate could feel her heart pounding in her chest. She asked her father, 'You've heard that story before?'

'Yes.'

'You've nothing to add?'

'About your question?' He shrugged. 'People stink. But then sometimes they don't.'

'All those degrees and I get a fortune cookie.'

He stacked the cards together. 'That policewoman you were with will never see out of her eye again. She was very lucky.' He touched his ear. 'As were you.'

Kate looked away.

'You've nothing to add? Not even a fortune cookie?'

'I didn't want you to worry about me.'

'I'm only worried because you're not telling the truth.'

Kate stared longingly at the bottle of scotch.

Her father stacked the card deck neatly in the center of the table. He took off his glasses. When Kate was little, he'd taught her how to play gin rummy. He beat her all the time until Kate figured out that she could see the reflection of his cards in his eyeglasses. Kate had never told him her trick. Obviously, Oma had never told him, either. She liked winning too much. For Jacob's part, she imagined he liked letting them win.

Kate asked, 'Should I tell you the truth, Daddy?'

'You should tell yourself the truth. I don't matter so much now. You're a grown woman. I can't send you to your room.'

Kate seldom sought his advice, but she really wanted it now. 'What would you have me do?'

He leaned his elbows on the table. He smiled at Kate. 'You are more precious to me than rubies. Do you know that?'

She nodded. If there was one thing of which she was certain, it was her family's love.

'There is no such thing as one city.' He sat back in his chair again. 'You've seen that for yourself these last two days.'

Kate thought he was addressing her earlier question. 'Are you saying people are like cities?'

'I'm saying that your life is very different from the lives that other people live – the girls you went to school with, your fellow officers, the people you help, the people you arrest. For each of them, Atlanta is a different thing. Yet they all take pride in ownership. They all feel that this city belongs to them, and that their idea of the city is what the city should be. And, further, they feel the need to defend it. To protect it.' His smile indicated he knew he was being obtuse, but that Kate should bear with him. 'Your violent asshole, I assume he thinks Atlanta belongs to the violent assholes. Your horrible woman – maybe she thinks it belongs to horrible women. They both feel very strongly, I'm sure. But which Atlanta is the real Atlanta? Is it ours? Is it the one Patrick knew? Does it belong to the blacks now? Did it ever belong to anybody?'

'Daddy, I'm sorry. I still don't understand.'

'Even with my volunteer work at Grady, I will never see the Atlanta that you are seeing. I will never know the people you know. I will never see the places you will see.'

Kate finally got it. Her father was articulating the

thoughts she had been having since she first walked into the station house. 'I'm no longer in my insulated world.'

'Yes,' he answered, and she detected an unfamiliar sadness in his tone. 'I will never understand humanity the way you will if you continue to work this job.'

'If?' Kate asked.

'You know my grandfather fought for the Confederacy?'

Kate nodded.

'And my father and I marched in a rally for Dr. King.'

She nodded again.

'I remember when we returned home after the rally. We had a drink. Such progress! We toasted each other. We patted ourselves on the backs. We did that all right here.' He meant this house, this mansion on a tree-lined street with its chauffeured cars and maids and gardeners. 'Did we know what it was like for Dr. King to return to his home on the other side of town? Did we know what his life was like living in this city, in *his* Atlanta, which was *our* Atlanta, too?'

'You help people,' Kate said. She had always thought of her father as a man of the people. 'You heal their minds.'

'I talk to wealthy men who are afraid of losing their money. I prescribe Valium to housewives who would be better served volunteering at their church.'

Kate didn't like this picture he was painting. 'You saved Mama and Oma. You brought them here.'

'No, Kaitlin. When I got to Amsterdam, the first time I saw with my own eyes what the war was really about—' His voice had turned gruff. He cleared his throat. 'Your mother saved me. I assure you, it was not the other way around.'

329

Kate clutched at straws. 'You have your charity cases at Grady.'

'By the time I see a patient at Grady, he's been cleaned up, he's been medicated, he's been strapped down.' Jacob smiled sadly. 'What was his life like two, three hours before? I only have his patient chart to go by, sometimes the police report. I've never been to his home. I have no idea how he really lives. And I never before gave one thought to the police officer who brought him to the hospital. Who took away the razor before he cut his wrists. Who tackled him to the ground. Who kept him from harming himself and others.'

'I've hardly acted so valiantly, Daddy. I ran into a wall on my first day. I knocked myself out this afternoon.'

He winced, and though she gathered he knew the highlights, she appreciated that her father did not want the details. 'My point is that you see these people in a way that I will never see them. Your experiences are no longer my experiences. I can't guide you any longer because I don't know where you're going.'

Kate thought about the putrid smell of the projects. The pimp who licked his lips as he leered at her. The dry cleaner who let her use his bathroom. The two dead men lying in the upstairs bedroom of the Portuguese lady's boardinghouse.

She told her father, 'It's not all it's cracked up to be.'

'Isn't it?'

Kate couldn't answer him, because she couldn't make sense of it. The job was soul-killing and humiliating and terrifying but on some strange level, it was challenging and, most surprising of all, fun.

She settled on banalities. 'I will always be your daughter.'

'I know that, sweetheart.' He gently cupped his hand to her face. 'Your mother was worried that this job would turn you into somebody you're not. I worried it would turn you into the person you really are.'

Kate wondered why his honesty didn't wound more. 'Is that such a bad thing?'

'I don't know, Katie. People in these high-stress jobs tend to split in two. Part of you will stay the same girl that we know. Another part will break off into a woman we'll never meet who sees these horrible things.'

Kate felt defensive. 'Like Oma? Like Mother?'

'Clever girl. I'll end my suppositions.' The moment was over. His voice took on a lighter tone. 'It is not within a father's purview to find fault with his daughter.'

'Freud?'

'Herschel.'

'That guy,' Kate teased. 'I hear he's fantastic.'

He smiled again. He took off his glasses and rubbed his eyes.

'Good night, Daddy.' Kate kissed her father's head by way of goodbye.

She left through the front door. Her fingertips brushed the mezuzah. She unpinned her hair as she walked down the steps and across the driveway. She had parked in the turnaround down from the garage. Kate leaned her hand on her car and took off her left shoe, then her right. Next, she pulled down her pantyhose and threw everything into the car.

Instead of getting in, she walked down the driveway. Her feet howled with every step. There were blisters on her blisters. Her heels looked like they'd been put through a Waring blender.

Kate took a left at the end of the driveway. There were no cars on the road. No glowing tip of a cigarette. No phantom stranger's eyes following her every move. She looked up at the moon, which offered barely a crescent of light. The path was so familiar that she needed no guide. The first twenty-five years of Kate's life had been defined by this street. Her best friend had lived two doors down before she moved to New York. Her elementary school was six blocks over, her high school seven and a half. The Temple was four streets away. The mall was a ten-minute drive. This was where she learned to ride a bike. This was where the school bus dropped her. This was where she made out with Patrick in the car before she took him up to meet her family for the first time.

The butcher, the baker, the candlestick maker – they were all within one square mile of the exact spot where she stood.

Her father's Atlanta.

No longer Kate's.

She passed Janice Saddler's house. Both her parents were gone now. Car accident. Janice and her brother had sold the house to a young lawyer and his wife.

The Kleinmans'. The Baumgartens'. The Pruetts'.

Their children were grown, but the parents still lived in the grand old houses that had been passed down through the generations. Kate had played on their swing sets, swam in their pools, flirted with their sons, sneaked through their backyards.

She turned left again. The driveway wasn't paved. Pea gravel stuck to the soles of her bare feet. She could barely feel anything now, which she supposed was the best way to describe the current state of her life. When the pain got to be too great, Kate simply blocked it out.

The front porch light was off at the main house. All the windows were dark. Kate traced her hand along a black Cadillac Fleetwood. She walked past the kitchen, the sunken den, the swimming pool, the tennis court.

The guesthouse was originally meant for the help, but those times were gone thanks to civil rights and vacuums and washing machines and clothes dryers and all the other modern conveniences that made it possible to run a large estate without a large staff. There was a small sports car parked in front of the one-story house. The top was down. Kate stroked her hand along the soft leather of the driver's seat.

The porch light was on. There was a faint glow of light behind the front curtains. She heard a record playing inside. As she had in front of her parents' house, Kate rested her hand on the side of the car. This time, she took off her underwear.

She tossed it into the car. She walked up the steps.

Then she knocked three times on Philip Van Zandt's door.

24

Kate's knees felt shaky as she walked across the parking garage under the Barbizon Hotel. Every atom in her body was vibrating at a different frequency. Her lips felt swollen from Philip's kisses. Her breasts were tender from his mouth. If she closed her eyes, she could summon up the sensations of his tongue roaming up and down her body.

She longed to go back to Philip's warm bed, to let him do all those wonderful things to her over and over again, but there was still some small part of Kate's brain that held on to a tiny sliver of sanity. She couldn't wake up next to him in the morning. She couldn't burn his toast or fix his coffee or ask about his plans for the day. She couldn't let herself fall into domesticity.

It felt too much like cheating.

How odd that letting Philip do the things he did to her did not feel like betraying Patrick. The two men were nothing alike. Philip's kisses were more sensual. He had an intimate knowledge of the female anatomy. He was in no rush. He enjoyed every inch of her. When it was time, he did something extraordinary with his hips – an exquisite movement like a spoon dipping into honey. There were no quickening thrusts that ended too soon so that

Kate found herself slipping off to the bathroom to take matters into her own hand.

Kate knew that she had never orgasmed with her husband. At least not like she could on her own. This wasn't a matter of duration, but one of finesse. Patrick brought her to the precipice, which was nice, but there was no final push that sent her over the edge. Kate was certain this would have changed if they'd had more time together. Time to explore. Time to grow up and appreciate what they could offer one another.

As it was, Patrick's pleasure had always been the central issue, which had bothered Kate none whatsoever. She felt good with her husband. Her body responded to him. There were tingles in all the right places and her heart leapt and her body arched up in anticipation. That the obvious didn't follow was something Kate had always assumed was her fault. Not because of Freud, but because she loved Patrick so much that the failure must be her own.

Kate didn't need Patrick for that anyway. Just lying beside him was enough. Feeling his strong arms around her was enough. Hearing the catch in his breath, seeing the look in his eyes – that was more than enough. They were in love, deeply, deeply in love, and his happiness was more satisfying to Kate than anything that could be done to her in bed.

Kate was certain that she would never feel this way about Philip Van Zandt. She would never iron his shirts. She would never lovingly fold his handkerchiefs into neat little squares. She would never press her face to his pillow just to breathe in the wonderful scent of him.

Her father was wrong. Kate wasn't splitting into two different people. She had fractured into three.

She pressed the call button for the elevator. Normally, Kate took the stairs up to the lobby, but she didn't trust her legs to hold her. It was five-thirty in the morning. Bumblebees filled her head. Her body was still pulsing with thoughts of Philip. She needed a shower. She needed a quick lie-down. And then she would put on her uniform and go into work.

The elevator doors slid open. Kate eyed the red velvet bench in the back of the car, but knew she couldn't give in. She pressed the lobby button and thought how strange it was that she was still going to work after what had happened yesterday. If anything, the carnage at the Portuguese house made her want to work more. She needed to prove herself. She needed to make things up to Maggie. She needed Gail Patterson to know that her loss was not in vain.

Freud popped into Kate's head again; the curse of the psychiatrist's daughter. Undoubtedly, the dead shrink would have diagnosed Kate with masochistic tendencies. Or maybe he'd call it penis envy. Why else would a woman want to do a man's job? She wanted her father's attention. She wanted to punish her mother for giving her father things she could not. She was crazy. She was hysterical. Her hormones were imbalanced.

How was it that completely independent of each other, the male cops on the Atlanta police force and an elderly Austrian psychiatrist had reached the exact same conclusions?

They should all consult with Dr. Philip Van Zandt. He was more of a Masters and Johnson man. Which was why Kate was smiling when the elevator doors opened.

And then her smile dropped.

Maggie Lawson stood in front of her. She had obviously been crying. There was a cut underneath her eye. Bruises ringed her neck. She said nothing, but there was such an air of desperation about her that Kate could almost chew it with her teeth.

Kate asked, 'What's wrong?'

'Jimmy's gone.' She blurted out the words like she'd been holding them in for a long while. 'He's missing.'

'Missing?' Kate stepped off the elevator. Mr. Schueneman, the night doorman, eyed her with great disapproval. She wondered how long Maggie had been waiting. She worried that she looked as obvious as she felt. And now she was worried about Jimmy.

Kate said, 'Tell me what happened.'

Maggie took a deep breath before answering. 'I got home last night. Jimmy wasn't in his room. His car wasn't outside. He wasn't at the station. He's not on duty. None of his friends know where he is. Don's girlfriend hasn't heard from him since Monday. He's not at his usual bar. We can't find him. We've looked everywhere.'

Kate tried to focus her weary mind. There was something practiced about Maggie's tone, as if she was reciting a prepared speech. 'We?'

'Terry. Me. We split up.' She kept looking away, not meeting Kate's eye. 'The other guys are looking for him, too. Terry put out a BOLO on him. That's—'

'Be on the lookout,' Kate said. 'Has Jimmy disappeared before?'

'Never.'

'He didn't call or leave a note?'

'No.' She looked over Kate's shoulder. 'He didn't leave anything.'

Kate tried to put together her thoughts. Part of her was still asleep in Philip's bed. 'Are you sure he hasn't gone off with someone?'

Maggie shook her head. 'There's nobody.'

Kate wondered if this was true. If Jimmy Lawson had a man in his life, his family would be the last to know.

Unless there was another reason.

Kate felt her brain finally wake up. 'The Shooter.'

Maggie looked at her now. There was real fear in her eyes. This must be what she was worried about. Not that her brother had run off, but that someone had murdered him and they hadn't yet found the body.

Kate said, 'We'll find him, okay? I'm sure he's fine.' She took Maggie by the arm and led her toward the bank of elevators behind the front desk. 'I just need to change, all right? But I'll make you some coffee and we can talk about this.'

'There's nothing to talk about.' Maggie followed her onto the elevator. 'We just need to find the Shooter. We have to stop him.'

Find the Shooter, not find her brother. She was all over the place.

The doors closed. Kate studied Maggie in the mirrors. She looked awful. Her hair was a mess. Her lipstick had faded. Her uniform was clean, but it was wrinkled, like she'd pulled it from the bottom of her closet.

Maggie said, 'I've already checked the Golden Lady. That's the—'

'Strip club where the four previous victims ate their last meals.' The bell dinged again. Kate got off the elevator. 'What did they say?'

'They haven't seen Jimmy.'

They were back to Jimmy again. Maggie didn't know whom she wanted to find. 'Did you ask about the victims?' Kate turned when she didn't answer. Maggie was standing in the middle of the hall. Her hand was resting on the chair molding. 'Maggie?'

'What?'

'The other victims. Ballard, Johnson, Keen, and Porter. Did you ask about them at the strip club?'

'Yes.' Maggie pushed away from the wall. She was like a toy car. The only way she could move was if Kate wound her up with a question. 'The club manager keeps a running tab so the boss knows who got comped. All four of the victims were there the nights they died. Everyone had the same meal: hamburgers and fries. Those are the only foods on the menu.'

'That matches what the medical examiner found in their stomachs.' Kate slid her key into the lock. 'The club manager was certain that Jimmy and Don didn't go there the night that Don was murdered?'

Maggie had stopped listening again. She was visibly lost in her own thoughts. Her eyes tracked back and forth. The poor lighting in the hallway darkened the bruises around her neck.

Kate opened the door. 'Come in.'

Maggie didn't go in. She was too distracted by the décor. Having seen Maggie's house, Kate could understand.

What she could not understand was the strange smell of cigarettes. No one had ever smoked in Kate's room.

Maggie asked, 'Should I take off my shoes?'

'Of course not.' Kate ignored the smell, which was probably coming from the girl next door. She told Maggie, 'Make yourself at home.'

Maggie sounded suspicious. 'How long have you lived here?'

'A year, maybe.' She indicated the overstuffed chair by the window. 'Have a seat.'

Maggie stayed where she was. 'Did your father help you get it?'

Kate told the first lie that came to mind. 'My husband had an insurance policy.' She glanced at the photo of Patrick on her nightstand. And then she did a double take.

Patrick's dog tags were missing.

They had been there when she'd left last night. Kate could clearly remember looking at the dog tags before closing the door. She leaned over to check behind the nightstand. The space was too narrow to see anything. She wanted to search under the bed, but Maggie already had reason enough to think that Kate was imprudent without seeing her crawl around on the floor in a dress. And no underwear.

Maggie asked, 'What's wrong?'

'Nothing.' Kate rubbed her arms to warm herself. The curtains were open. Kate could've sworn she drew them before she left last night. She got the same chill she'd experienced on her parents' front porch: that now familiar, unsettling sensation that someone was watching her.

'Kate?'

'I'm fine.'

'Are you sure?'

'Of course I'm sure.' Kate changed the subject before the current one got away from her. 'I was just thinking: If the Shooter had done something to Jimmy, we would know by now. You said it yourself: his M.O. is always the same. He kills them when they're on duty. He makes them call in a meal break before their radios are unplugged. He knows that someone will eventually go looking for them. And by virtue of protocol, the first place to look is evident – the last ten-twenty they gave dispatch.'

'That's not how it happened with Sir Chic.'

'Are you certain that Chic was killed by the Shooter?'

'Why else would he be killed?'

Kate could think of a lot of reasons, not least of all because he was a pimp. Still, she picked up from Maggie's line of reasoning. 'We can't be the only ones who figured out one of Chic's girls saw something. Obviously, someone got to the Portuguese house before we did. Or after, since there was plenty of time for him to set up across the street. So, maybe he was following us.' Kate dropped that theory. She didn't want to think about anyone following her. 'Either way, the Shooter was certainly watching Chic when we were all upstairs in the front room. Remember how it happened? Chic held up the transmitter. Gail stuck her gun in his face. Chic was about to talk. You know he was. And the Shooter knew it, too. The transmitter was proof that a witness was there. All that was left was for Chic to tell us what she saw.'

'Jimmy's transmitter.' Maggie had clearly forgotten all about it.

'You know, now that I think about it, what Chic said was strange.' Kate quoted the pimp's words as best she could recall. ' "The dude my gal saw looked nothing like the brother that's on the news." '

Maggie didn't offer an opinion. Her face was pale. Sweat dotted her forehead.

Kate opened the window a crack. Cold air whistled in. 'Chic must have been referring to the police sketch Jimmy

341

made. It's been all over the news. It was on the front page of the evening edition. I don't know the slang, obviously, but it seems to me that a brother is a black man. So, what is a dude? Is that a white man?'

Maggie rested her hand on the chest of drawers. She looked shaky. 'It depends on who you're talking to.'

Kate tried to walk her through it. 'You told me that Gail said that white people kill white people and black people kill black people, so . . .'

Maggie waited.

'What do you remember from yesterday? I mean after I passed out.'

Maggie shrugged. 'I remember everything.'

'Clearly? As in, what everyone looked like?' Kate crossed her arms. Thanks to the open window, now she really was cold. 'Because I've been thinking – for the life of me, I couldn't describe the Portuguese lady. We spoke to her for several minutes. We were in her house. But if you asked me to describe her features to you, I wouldn't be able to.'

Maggie shrugged again. 'And?'

'And if I had seen her at night and she came around the corner with a gun, there's no way I could describe her face. So, maybe Jimmy—'

'That's you, Kate. You've been on the job two seconds. You don't know how to pay attention to things. You ran into a brick wall, for chrissakes.'

Kate replayed the words in her head. It wasn't what Maggie had said, which was absolutely true, it was *how* she'd said it. There was none of her usual irritation. She sounded defensive. And despite the cold air, she was still sweating.

'You're right,' Kate relented. 'Maybe I need some coffee to wake me up.' She took the carafe and walked into the bathroom. She turned on the tap. And she tried to shake the feeling that she was missing something very important.

She raised her voice so Maggie could hear her over the running water. 'Jimmy has been through several traumatic situations in the last few days. He saw Don murdered. He was shot in the arm. Surely he was upset by what happened to you. Maybe he just needs some time alone? To collect his thoughts?'

There was no answer at first. Kate started to repeat the question, but Maggie said, 'That's not what Jimmy does.'

The carafe was full. Kate returned to the bedroom. 'Is there a secret person he might be seeing?'

Maggie studied Kate carefully. 'A secret person?'

Kate made herself busy with the Mr. Coffee. 'I never had a brother, but all my girlfriends who do say they're very secretive, especially when it comes to their love lives.'

'Did he hit on you in the car?'

'Jimmy?' The question was strange. Kate wasn't sure how to answer it. 'I think he was just breaking in the new girl. Isn't that why Terry assigned me to him in the first place?'

'But he flirted with you?'

'Yes.' Kate turned on the machine. 'Of course. I flirted back. He's very charming when he wants to be.'

Maggie's expression had gone blank. Before, she hadn't been able to meet Kate's eye, but now she seemed incapable of looking away.

Kate said, 'Let's work the case, all right? We'll pick up where we left off yesterday. We were looking for

343

information that leads to the Shooter. Let's do the same thing today.'

Maggie's head slowly began to nod. 'We can't find Jimmy, but if we find the Shooter, then we'll know for certain about Jimmy.'

Kate was relieved she was making some sort of sense. 'Is there something else bothering you?'

'What else would be bothering me?' Maggie went on the defensive again. 'Do you have a problem with what I did to Anthony?'

'Absolutely not. You acted in self-defense. You saved us. All of us.' Kate had to stop so she could swallow down the emotions that wanted to come. She was standing in that phone booth at the Texaco again, overwhelmed with the need to apologize. 'If anything, I'm sorry. I failed you. I failed Gail. I should've been more alert. I should've been able to help you when all hell broke loose.'

Maggie looked at the coffeemaker. 'I should've checked the building across the street.'

'You did,' Kate insisted. 'I saw you do it when we walked into Chic's room. Both you and Gail looked at everything, including the building.'

Maggie obviously didn't believe her.

'You told me the first day that you learn how to be a cop by watching other cops. I was watching you and Gail. You both looked at everything.'

Maggie obviously wasn't going to be persuaded. She bought herself some composure by picking a piece of lint off her uniform. 'The boss told us we could have a couple of days off.'

'So?' Kate was standing right by Maggie when Cal Vick told them as much. 'You're not taking off. I imagine Gail would be at roll call this morning if they'd let her out of the hospital.'

Maggie smiled, before she caught herself.

'All right.' The coffeemaker was finished. Kate poured two cups as she spoke. 'The plan is to figure out the Shooter's identity, right? I think that we should go back and talk to the Portuguese lady.'

'Why?'

'We can assume that the Shooter believed Chic was the witness, but there's somebody else in that house who probably knows the whole story.'

Maggie seemed at a loss.

'Didn't you get the feeling that the Portuguese lady is the type of busybody who sticks her nose into every-body's business?'

'We're acting on feelings now?' Maggie shook her head. 'I can guarantee that woman has been interviewed and deposed by every piece of brass on the force by now. That's how it goes when bad shit goes down. There's probably enough paperwork by now to wallpaper this hotel.'

Kate put the carafe back on the burner. 'You told me yesterday that people lie.'

'They do.'

'Then maybe the Portuguese lady lied to the police yesterday.' She tried to make it into a story. 'Look at it this way: Something bad happened to one of Chic's girls. She saw a cop murdered. She got scared. Where do you think she went first?' Kate answered her own question. 'She went to her boss and she woke him up and she gave him that transmitter. And who let her through the front door at that time of night? Who unlocked the four locks and drew back the chain?'

'All right,' Maggie finally relented. 'It's a long shot, but that's all we've got left.'

'Give me a minute to rinse off and change.' Kate collected a fresh set of undergarments. She felt a flash of guilt when she opened her closet door to retrieve her uniform. The rod bowed from all her dresses. Her shoes were boxed two high and three deep and spanned the width of the closet floor.

Kate grabbed one of the coffees on her way into the bathroom. The pipes squealed when she turned on the shower. She tried not to get her hair wet. Stray nerves fired as she washed herself. She looked battered from the waist down. She tried not to think about the gentle way Philip had kissed her bruises.

Kate doubted there was anyone to kiss the bruises on Maggie's neck. There was armor on top of her armor this morning. Was this simply because her brother was missing? Kate felt at her core that there was more to it than that. Had Maggie started to suspect that Jimmy was gay? Was that really why she was looking for him? And it wasn't just Maggie who wanted to find Jimmy. Terry was looking for him, too. The entire force had been alerted with the BOLO. Every cop in Atlanta would be occupied today, whether they were searching for Jimmy Lawson or hunting down the Shooter.

Too bad Kate wasn't a criminal.

She got out of the shower and quickly dried herself. All she could do with her makeup was freshen it up. With any luck, the liquid color corrector under her eyes would ward off any dark circles. Kate had forgotten her panty-hose, but she doubted anyone would notice. She listened for noise in the bedroom as she finished dressing. She wondered if Maggie had fallen asleep. Part of her hoped that she had. Yesterday, Kate thought that Maggie Lawson was one of the smartest women she'd ever met. Right now, she seemed barely capable of making even the most obvious connections.

Kate opened the bathroom door. Maggie was standing where she'd left her. The bruises on her neck were getting darker by the hour. Kate could've sworn there was another bruise coming up around the cut on her cheek.

Kate said, 'We should look at our notes from yesterday.' Before Maggie could ask, she clarified, 'The ones we took from the Shooter cases.'

'Terry has them.'

Kate didn't ask the question she knew Maggie wouldn't answer. 'What about the bar?'

'Which bar?'

'Dabbler's. The one on the matchbook from Don Wesley's pants.'

Maggie had obviously forgotten about the place. But then she told Kate, 'My next-door neighbor works at the phone company. I talked to him about it last night.' Maggie looked for a place to set down her coffee cup. 'He said he'd put the address in my mailbox. We should go there first before anybody finds it.'

Kate wondered who Maggie thought was going to rob her mailbox. 'It's after six anyway. The Portuguese lady might be in a more talkative mood if we give her a chance to wake up. Just put the cup anywhere.'

Maggie placed the cup on top of the machine. 'It's probably another dead end. Gail said it's not a cop hangout.'

'My father always says if you don't know what to do,

just keep moving forward until you figure it out.' Kate slid her feet into Jimmy's shoes. She took her belt off the closet doorknob. The metal clips were in her jewelry box. She saw one of her old watches and put it on. 'Do we need to get in touch with Delroy and Watson?'

'For what?'

Kate hooked the clips on her belt. 'To get permission to go into that part of town again.'

'I shot a man five times yesterday. I don't think anyone is going to fuck with us.'

Kate stared at her. Was that the real problem? Did Maggie feel guilty for taking Anthony's life? Were the bruises around her neck an attempt to quiet the demons?

'I'm fine,' Maggie told her.

'I didn't ask.'

'You're like a book.'

'You know what they say about judging a book.' Kate checked her pockets: lipstick, cash, citation book, notebook, pens. She looped the nightstick through the hook in her belt. She plugged her mic into the transmitter. 'Your neighbor seems nice.'

'He's deaf.'

Handcuffs. Keys. Kel-Lite. Back spasm. 'Gail's half-blind. That doesn't mean you like her any less.'

'His mother's a nurse. She used to give abortions.'

Kate looked up.

'Before they were legal.' Maggie spoke haltingly. 'Girls were in and out of there at all hours. That's why their house is the nicest on the block. She made a lot of money. Are you ready to go?'

Kate started for the door, then spun around and opened the top drawer of her bureau. They had given her a new

348

revolver yesterday because the other one was logged into evidence. Kate dropped the weapon into her holster and pressed the snap closed. 'Now I'm ready.'

There was a glimmer of the old Maggie in the wry expression on her face. 'Check the safety, Murphy. You almost blew your foot off.'

25

Fox could not stop thinking about Kate's hair. He saw it when he closed his eyes. Strands of gold and honey. Silky wisps trailing down her long neck. Cheekbones carved from ivory. Eyes like the most pristine ocean.

All lies.

Light when she should've been dark. Taking an Irish name when she was Hebrew. Presenting one face to the world while she hid her true self behind a mask of normalcy. This was the problem – these frauds who sneaked in under the radar, then by the time you saw them for what they really were, it was too late.

Jews. Italians. Cunts. Chinks. Blacks. Indians.

The old man had been right. The world really was upside down. People really didn't know their place anymore. Fox was doing his part to fix it now, but he couldn't help but wonder what his life would've been like if he had been able to put things right for Senior.

Shoot the greaseball before he could close the factory.

Gas the Jew bitch before she screwed up his unemployment check.

Execute the yellow-skinned bastard before he could steal his job.

Save his mother from Senior's pain.

Because it wasn't his anger that hurt everybody. It was his pain.

After the factory closed, Senior would sit at the kitchen table every night talking about the people who had fucked him over. The kikes. The spics. The slits. The motherfuckers who didn't belong. Senior started reading the Bible. He took to it like a true convert. After years of deriding Fox's mother for her churchgoing ways, he found his calling.

From one man He made all the nations, that they should inhabit the whole earth; and He marked out their appointed times in history and the boundaries of their lands.

Fox was sitting at the table when Senior found the verse. The old man had thumped his finger against the page and given an 'aha' that boomed from his gut. Acts 17:26. God had given Senior a purpose passed down from Adam. His appointed time was being stolen away from him. His boundaries were being redrawn.

And who were the thieves of Senior's time in the sun? The kikes. The spics. The greaseballs. The slits. They fell like dominos, crashing down on Senior's world.

And then they claimed their final victim: Fox's mother.

They were sitting at the kitchen table when she came home from the doctor's office. The Bible was closed. Senior was drinking Jack straight from the bottle and looking for a reason to hit somebody. Fox wasn't going to give it to him. He had just gotten in from school. He was eating the snack his mother always prepared for him: a piece of bread with the crust cut off, a slice of cheese. There was supposed to be a cookie, but Fox knew better than to ask what happened to it.

His mother sat down at the table. Her chair was smaller than theirs. The back was splintered. She always sat on the edge of the seat. Despite a lifetime of smoothing things over, she did not sugarcoat the news. The pain in her stomach was cancer. The tumor was the size of a grapefruit.

They had given her three months. Four if she took it easy.

Senior had started to cry. The first of two times total that Fox had seen the old man break down.

Fox had not cried. He pictured a grapefruit in his mind. He compared it to other known items. A baseball. A softball. His father's fist.

It seemed to Fox more than coincidence that his mother had a cancerous tumor in her stomach the same size as Senior's fist. That was where Senior hit her the most, in the belly. In Fox's head, he imagined the fist compacting the organ until it was the same shape and consistency. He visualized his mother's stomach as a fist. He willed the fingers to open. He begged for God to unclench the tumor and release his mother from the pain.

Morphine was the only thing that could help her now. Maybe two years ago when she first told the doctors about the sharp sensations, or last year when there was blood, something could have been done. But now it was too late.

Fox could not blame the doctors for not believing her. She lied to them all the time. The broken wrists. The fractured ankles. The cuts and bruises and the panic in her eyes when she was told a wound might need stitches. Nobody accidentally slammed the car door on their leg twice in a row. Nobody got a third-degree burn on their arm from accidentally brushing against the eye on the stove. You got the concentric rings seared into your flesh from someone holding you down to teach you a lesson.

If a person lies all the time, how can you tell when they're finally telling the truth? Fox had seen the truth. The way his mother's knees buckled at the sink when the pain cut through. The shaking hands. The shouts of agony when she was in the bathroom. She kept telling the doctors something was wrong, and they kept telling her she just needed some rest.

Fox needed rest. Countless years had passed, and the thought of her suffering still took the breath out of his lungs.

He leaned against his basement door. He closed his eyes and listened. The soundproofing was good. He had to press his ear to the wood in order to make out the rattling of the chains. Jimmy Lawson was still crying. He'd been bawling from the moment Fox took him. He did not beg for mercy. He begged for death. Like the rest of them, Jimmy knew what he deserved. Two bullets to the head, just like Senior.

Or at least like Senior had tried.

The fucker had never done one thing right in his life.

It happened after the funeral. Fox had watched his mother's coffin being lowered into the ground. The day was bitter cold. Fox was freezing. No one had been there to tell him to put on his jacket. He stood in his thin suit by the pile of dirt that had been taken from the earth, tasting the wet clay in the back of his mouth as the wind sliced him in two like a sword.

Senior had cried. The second time Fox had witnessed

this. Big, fat tears rolled down his cheeks. Fox had watched them slap against the tops of his shoes.

Lesson nine: A man always polishes his shoes.

Senior was silent as they drove back to the house. No one was there to greet them. Fox's mother didn't have any friends. Senior's former co-workers were all otherwise engaged. There were some casseroles from the ladies at the church. A neighbor had brought in the milk. There was a pie from the pastor's wife, but no pastor. Just a cold, empty house that Fox had never realized his mother had somehow managed to fill. With her happiness. With her pain. With her fear. With her love.

Senior walked into the kitchen. He sat down at the table. He opened one of the cabinet drawers. He pulled out a handgun. He pressed the muzzle to his head. He pulled the trigger.

Fox was standing right there when he did it. His eyes had locked with Senior's at the last second. As soon as the trigger was pulled, Senior's eye jerked to the side. It was almost comical the way he seemed to be looking out the window and looking at Fox at the same time. The gun fell to the floor. Senior didn't fall after it. He sat ramrod straight in the chair, the same as he had every night for as long as Fox could remember.

Twenty-two caliber. The bullet hadn't exited his skull. It had zinged around inside his brain like a mosquito. Side to side. Front to back. There wasn't much blood. Just a trickle came out of the black hole above Senior's ear. His mouth moved. His throat flexed up something like a bird's caw.

Fox looked at the pie the preacher's wife had brought. The crust was dark around the edges. His mother would've never brought over a pie with a burned crust.

Senior made the caw sound again.

Fox broke off a piece of crust and put it in his mouth. The buttery richness spread across his tongue. Then the singed aftertaste. He reached into the heart of the pie and pulled out a handful of filling. Fox licked the cherry goo from his hand as he walked over to his father. The thought occurred to him that his hand was redder than the bullet wound in Senior's head, and then the disparity was remedied when Fox scooped the gun off the floor, pressed the muzzle to his father's head, and pulled the trigger for the second time.

Lesson ten: A man always finishes what he starts.

The most important lesson. The only lesson that really mattered.

Fox had something he needed to finish soon. Not because there was any rush, but because there was no use drawing it out. Jimmy Lawson was still crying. He would be crying an hour from now or a year from now.

Fox was not a murderer. He was an executioner. There was no pleasure in Jimmy's pain.

At least not much.

Fox pushed himself away from the basement door. He checked the lock. He didn't turn around and go back into the house. He couldn't go anywhere.

Pressure.

Even when he wasn't thinking about Kate, his body was wanting her. Fox held his hand against his stiff cock. He needed time with Kate. Alone time. He couldn't watch her from afar anymore. He had to have her – in his house, in his bed, in his basement.

Fox would keep her until the pressure went away. He

realized he had decided this a long time ago, maybe the first time he saw her. Even then, his brain was working on two plans at the same time. Fuck her. Kill her. Fuck her again.

What was the harm?

No one would ever know what went on between them. Senior was long in his grave, buried beside the rest of the paupers. He would never hear about his son fucking a Jew. He would never know about the control Kate had exerted over his boy.

But Fox would know.

He put his hands to his eyes. The shame hit him like tear gas. The spikes impaling his corneas. The glass in his lungs. The choking, suffocating knowledge that he was in love with her.

Love.

There was no use denying it anymore. The lightning bolt to his skull wasn't the plan clicking into place. It was Kate working her Jew magic. The dirty bitch had turned the tables on him. He had thought he was hunting her, stalking her, but in truth, Kate had already caught him.

Fox was going to take back that control. Kate was going to bend to his will. Maybe she would break. Only time would tell. Fox had to get her alone. That was the most important part. He had to have her undivided attention. He was going to study her. He was going to learn her weaknesses, record her responses on his clipboard so he knew the best way to go at her each time.

This wasn't like Senior going after Fox's mother. Kate wasn't innocent. She was a liar. She was an imposter. She had tricked Fox into falling for her, just the same as

Rebecca Feldman. Just the same as every slit Fox had loved since his mother.

Fox started nodding. Now he understood what had happened. The lightning had not failed him. This was all part of the plan. His brain had been planning this for weeks. The chains were already bolted snug into the rafters. The soundproofing was in place. Fox wasn't out of control. He had been in charge all along.

It was just a matter of bringing them all together.

Here was the plan: Finish the job. Start a new one with Kate.

Fox reached into his pocket and pulled out the dog tags he had taken from her apartment. The metal discs made a familiar click when he rubbed them together.

Murphy.

Patrick R.

His social security number, though he would never pay taxes again.

His blood type, which he'd spilled all over some godless jungle.

His religion, though fuck the Pope for not stopping the war.

Fox looped the chain around his neck. He tucked it into his shirt. The cold metal kissed his chest.

He wondered if Kate's lips would feel the same way.

26

Maggie got lost on her way to CT. She had driven from her house to the West Side a hundred times before, but her brain had checked out and her muscle memory had abandoned her, and instead of finding herself at the Portuguese lady's house, they were stuck downtown in morning traffic.

If Kate noticed, she didn't say. Maggie was glad for her silence. She couldn't understand Kate's transformation. She had gone from being the Sheep to showing the makings of a damn good cop. Maggie had gotten a glimpse of it yesterday when they pored over the Shooter files. This morning, Kate was making connections faster than Maggie could keep up. Every day, Kate seemed to get better at the job.

And every second, Maggie was getting worse.

She was terrified Kate was going to rope-a-dope her into admitting the truth about Jimmy. Not that Maggie knew the truth. Was her brother gay? Was he a murderer? Could she believe one without the other? Were both some kind of cruel fabrication?

Her head was going to explode if she kept asking these circular questions.

Maggie had gotten to the point where she was doing all the stupid things that she looked for when she was confronting a suspect. Her hands were shaky. She was sweating. She couldn't look Kate in the eye. They should drag Maggie out of the car and put her in front of a class at the academy. She was textbook guilty.

And she was so, so tired.

Last night, Maggie had left her mother's house with the thought in her head that she would never go back. She hadn't packed. There was nothing in her room that she needed. She'd grabbed her belt off the counter and walked out the door. She'd radioed a cruiser to come pick her up on the corner. She'd had them drop her at the station. She'd showered in the empty men's locker room. She'd changed into a fresh uniform she kept in her locker.

Everything Maggie did had felt so permanent, but she knew there was nowhere to go but back. She didn't have a place to live. Her car was in the shop. She didn't have a dime to her name. She didn't have a fancy apartment with a white shag rug and more clothes in her closet than there were days left to wear them.

Terry controlled all the money. The idea hadn't seemed like such a bad one at the time. Delia couldn't open a separate bank account without her husband's signature, and Hank cleaned them out every time he got home from the hospital. Delia started giving Terry her checks when they almost lost the house. Maggie started giving him her checks when she got her job on the police force. And when either one of them stepped out of line, Terry yanked the strings on the purse so tight that it strangled them.

There were all kinds of new federal laws that were

supposed to open financial doors for women, but they were still firmly closed in Atlanta, Georgia. There was always a work-around, always some catch that kept the door from opening. Maggie couldn't get a bank account that Terry couldn't access. She couldn't get a car loan without Terry's co-signature. She couldn't get a credit card or rent an apartment without Terry's permission.

Nearest living male's information.

That's what all the forms asked for. Maggie had spent months calling apartment ads in the paper. All of them required a man to vouch for her. Even the sketchy ones. She was too afraid to ask Terry, and Jimmy refused because he didn't want to get caught in the middle.

Jimmy.

Last night, Maggie had started with his friends, banging on their apartment doors, waking their families, all the while knowing Jimmy would not be there. She went to the bar where he sometimes grabbed a drink after work. She called every old girlfriend whose name she could think of. She checked the back seat of his cruiser. She busted open his locker at work. She visited the shooting range. She went to the Grady High School football field. She searched the locker room, the coach's office, the basement where kids sneaked in to make out. She woke up all the managers at the motels along the interstate. She walked through Piedmont Park with a flashlight. She shined her headlights into underpasses and down alleys where she knew gay men went for company. She went to porn theaters and all-night diners.

The despair built with each new parking lot and alley, every frightened, anonymous man who fled at the sight of a police car. Maggie had to find her brother before

Terry did. She didn't know whether or not her intention was to save his life. That felt strangely secondary to locating him. Her primary goal was to get some sort of explanation. Jimmy had to look Maggie in the eye and tell her why he had written that letter.

The letter.

Every single word was seared into her brain. Delia had torn up the paper, but Maggie had transcribed Jimmy's confession into her notebook as soon as she left the house. She'd studied each sentence individually. She had blocked off phrases. She had looked for some kind of hidden meaning. There had to be more to it than the actual words.

Because what was the point?

Even on the off chance that Jimmy really was gay, and Don Wesley and all those other men had been gay with him, then why murder them? Each held a weapon just as powerful as the other. They were like Russia and the United States agreeing not to release their nukes because of mutually assured destruction.

And if Jimmy wasn't gay, then why confess to the murders? What was his motivation? Maybe Kate was right about Jimmy's state of mind. He'd seen Don shot right in front of him. He'd failed to save his partner's life. He'd been shot in the arm by a madwoman. Was Jimmy like those battle-fatigued soldiers who went nuts when they got back into the real world? Was the letter a cry for help?

If that was the case, Jimmy had found the one thing that ensured Terry would put him out of his misery. The only thing he hated more than blacks and liberals was homosexuals.

'Son of a bitch!' Maggie banged her fist on the steering wheel.

They were driving up Third Street, a few blocks from the Georgia Tech tunnel, and there was London Fog traipsing along the sidewalk like he hadn't a care in the world. He was still wearing the old man's overcoat, but this time she saw the legs of his worsted gray pants above the shiny black loafers on his feet.

Maggie swerved the car so hard the engine stalled.

Kate grabbed the dashboard. 'What are you—'

'Him.' Maggie was already getting out of the car. 'That's the rapist who went after that little girl.'

Kate got out of the car, too. 'You're sure?'

'He stole the grandfather's coat.' Maggie pulled the nightstick off her belt. She was talking loudly enough for London Fog to hear, but like the other day, he just kept on walking. 'He raped a thirteen-year-old girl. He stole her grandfather's coat.' She jogged to catch up with him. 'His name is Lewis Windall Conroy the Third. He's from Berwyn, Maryland.'

That stopped him. His hands clutched in his pockets. He still didn't turn around.

Maggie stood behind him. She slapped the nightstick against her palm. 'Get on your knees.'

He didn't move.

Maggie wasn't in the mood for second warnings. She swung the metal baton through the air and slammed it into the back of his legs.

Conroy dropped like a sack of hammers.

Kate gasped. 'Maggie!'

'Get up,' she told the man. 'Get up, or I will hurt you as bad as you hurt that little girl.'

Conroy could only make it to his hands and knees. The baton had knocked the wind out of him. He opened his mouth, but only drool came out.

'I said get up!' Maggie cracked his tailbone so hard that the metal sang.

Conroy screamed. His arms and legs flew out from under him. He fell facedown on the sidewalk.

Maggie gripped the baton. 'You think your daddy's gonna get you out of this, Lewis?' She yearned to hit him again, to hear the crack of bone, the screech of pain. 'Get up,' she repeated. 'Get up, you baby-raping asshole.'

He tried, but his arms would not lift him. He fell flat to the sidewalk again.

Maggie told Kate, 'Help him up.'

Kate looked terrified as she gripped Conroy under the arm. She wasn't strong enough. He offered nothing but resistance.

'Please . . . ,' he begged.

'Use your legs,' Kate said.

'Please, lady.' Like all of them, he sensed Kate's weakness. 'Please, help me. I didn't do anything wrong.'

'Shut up.' Kate let him fall back onto the sidewalk. She asked Maggie, 'What do you want to do with him?'

The question stopped her. She hadn't thought it through.

'Please,' Conroy whined. 'This is all just a misunderstanding.'

Kate said, 'Radio the girls.'

Maggie knew this couldn't go out on the radio. She looked around. There was a phone booth on the next corner. 'Are you okay with him?'

'We'll be fine as long as he understands I'm just as

good with my nightstick as you are.' Kate raised an eyebrow, acknowledging the lie. She was so damn good at this. When had that happened?

Kate asked, 'Do you need change?'

'I've got it.' Maggie shoved her nightstick back onto her belt as she walked toward the phone booth. She was so furious she couldn't get her fists to unclench. Lewis Windall Conroy III. He could walk into any apartment building in the city and rent ten units. He could buy any car he wanted. He could do whatever the hell he pleased.

Except get away with raping a little girl.

The phone booth smelled like piss. Wet vomit splattered the floor. Maggie held the door open with her shoulder as she leaned in. She dialed the station and requested a landline-to-radio transmission. Delroy answered with her call sign. Maggie didn't identify herself or bother with an explanation. 'Corner of Third and Cypress.'

'Gimme fifteen.' Delroy ended the transmission.

Maggie hung up the receiver. The door sprang back on its hinges. She could see Kate standing over Conroy. Her nightstick was drawn, but she held it in front of her face like a Roman candle.

Thirteen years old.

Lilly was the same age. She was pretty and she might even look sexy if she wore too much makeup, but she was still a child who played with her Barbie up until a few months ago.

Maggie looked down at her hands. She made the fingers straighten one at a time. She wanted to be calm by the time she made it back to them. She wanted to think that she wasn't out of control like Terry or a cold-blooded murderer like Jimmy, but by the time she reached Conroy,

364

all she wanted to do was take out her gun, shove it into his mouth, and pull the trigger until it clicked and clicked the same as it had with Anthony.

'How long?' Kate asked.

'Too long. Stand up.' She grabbed up Conroy by the collar. He knew better than to resist. He stumbled like a colt taking its first steps. 'That way.' Maggie kicked his ass to get him started. 'Move.'

Kate was at Maggie's side. Her nightstick was still in front of her face. Maggie pushed it down at an angle so she could get a better swing.

Conroy walked slowly. His head was down. He was looking for a way out. 'Ladies, please. We can talk this through. It's all just a misunderstanding.'

'That girl needed stitches when you were done with her. Did you know that?'

'Is that what this is about?' He sounded relieved. 'For godsakes, I'll pay the doctor's bill. My father will write a check.'

'You're not getting off that easy.'

'Why don't you ask her family? I'm sure they'll accept the money. Trust me, she knew what she was doing.'

'Did she trick you?' Maggie had heard the excuse so many times that it made her stomach turn.

She didn't tell me how old she was. She was mature for her age. She came on to me. She wouldn't stop. What was I supposed to do?

The entire world gave men the responsibility for every-thing in it except for their dicks.

Maggie pulled her nightstick again. 'Pick up your feet.'

He glanced furtively left and right. Now he was looking for an escape.

Maggie pressed the baton to the base of his spine. 'Try to run, asshole. Just give me a reason.'

'I know your names.'

'We know yours, too.' Maggie ignored the panicked look Kate gave her. 'It's gonna be a lot of fun seeing you on the front page of the newspaper beside a photo of that little girl you ripped apart.'

'What do you care?' he demanded. 'She's just some damn little pickaninny.'

'And you're a spoiled little bitch who's gonna take a beat-down instead of going to prison for the next three years.'

They were at the phone booth.

'Get in.' Maggie pushed him. He hesitated. There was vomit on the floor. He didn't want to get his loafers dirty. 'Take off your shoes.'

'What?'

She banged the baton against the phone booth. 'Shoes. Off.'

He slipped them off. There were pennies in the loafers. He wasn't wearing socks. He had probably paid more for his worsted wool pants than Maggie made in a week. She was sick and tired of these wealthy people who floated through life like it was nothing.

She told Conroy, 'Take off the coat. It doesn't belong to you.'

He didn't protest this time. The coat came off. Kate grabbed it before it hit the ground.

Maggie said, 'Take off the rest of it.'

'What?'

She swung the baton back. That's all it took. He ripped open his shirt. The buttons popped off. He unfastened the snap on his pants, slid down the zip. His thumbs hooked into the waist of his underwear.

'No,' Maggie said, not because she didn't want to humiliate him any further but because she didn't want to see him. 'Get in the phone booth.'

He stepped tentatively into the vomit. She hoped it was cold. She hoped he could feel the chunks against the soles of his feet.

Conroy said, 'What are you—'

Maggie pushed the folding door closed. She reached up to the top of the booth. She had to stand on her tiptoes to find the trip lock. The bolt clanged down.

Conroy pushed on the door. It wouldn't budge. 'Let me out.' He started to panic. He put his shoulder into it. 'Let me out! Goddamn it!'

Kate had folded the grandfather's coat. She laid it beside the phone booth. 'Do you think they'll give it back to him?'

'It's not our business.' She jammed the baton back onto her belt. 'Anything else, Kate? Anything you want to ask me, or question me, or drill me on?'

Kate shook her head.

Maggie walked away. She tapped her fingers on her Kel-Lite. Her head pounded with each footstep. Her vision was wonky. She was sweaty and shaky.

Kate's footsteps came up behind her. She followed at a distance. She was giving Maggie some space, which was irritating and demeaning and just like something Kate would do.

The first week Maggie rode with Gail, she'd known to keep her trap shut. She'd taken notes. She'd followed orders. She hadn't asked questions. She hadn't volunteered

367

her opinion every five minutes. She hadn't turned every stupid thing she did into a joke so that she could laugh at herself before everybody else did.

Maggie fished the keys out of her pocket. Her hand cramped. She couldn't loop the ring on her middle finger.

Pulling the trigger. Gripping the steering wheel. Banging on doors. Holding the Kel-Lite. Wielding the nightstick. Wringing her hands and praying to God that her brother was alive. That he was dead. That Terry hadn't found him. That she would never have to see him again.

Maggie stopped in front of the cruiser. Her chest hurt. She wondered if she was having a heart attack.

Kate stood behind her. She said nothing, but the question was loud and clear: Are you all right?

Ah you ah-wight?

Maggie tossed her the keys. 'You drive.'

27

Maggie gritted her teeth the entire way to the Portuguese lady's house. Kate drove like an old woman. She tapped her foot on the brake any time another car got near. She didn't pass anyone. She engaged her signals two hundred feet from the turn. She kept both hands on the wheel in the ten-two position.

Maggie knew an act when she saw one. She had pulled over her share of Kate Murphys. Women like that didn't think the rules applied to them. They ignored stop signs. They pushed the speed limit. They drove with the convertible top down and silk scarves wrapped around their heads to keep their hair from getting messed up.

Gosh, Officer, was I really going that fast?

The cruiser came to a slow stop in front of the Portuguese lady's house. The place looked much the same as the day before. The only difference was the sheer curtain blowing out of the broken window on the second floor. No one had bothered to board it up yet.

Kate got out of the car first. She was first up the sidewalk, first on the porch.

Maggie was fine with letting her take the lead. Let someone else be in charge for a change. Knowing Kate's luck, she would open the door and Jimmy would be standing there. He'd hold out his hands and give her a confession. Cal Vick would promote Kate on the spot. She'd be the only female detective on the force. At the ceremony, she would take a bow and a rainbow would come out of her ass.

Kate knocked on the door like she was the Avon Lady.

Maggie said, 'You need to knock harder.'

'I was under the impression that you wanted me to handle this.'

Maggie said nothing. Every time she thought her hostility was gone, Kate would open her mouth and she would want to punch her all over again.

Kate knocked, this time like she was a kid selling magazine subscriptions.

Maggie asked, 'Where'd you learn Portuguese? You live in Europe or something?' She had probably honeymooned there with her dead husband who looked like Robert Redford.

'Pardon?' Kate looked confused, then she smiled that million-watt smile. 'She wasn't speaking Portuguese. It's Yiddish. I picked up some from my grandmother. Father's side. She's eastern European. *A shande oon a charpe*, it was quite a scandal when they married.'

Maggie was saved asking what the hell she was talking about by the door opening.

There were no bolts and a sliding chain this time. The Portuguese lady stood back from the doorway. She held a candle in her hand. The house was dark; no lights were on. She was wearing the same black outfit as the day before, but the sleeve was torn at the shoulder. Her salt-and-pepper hair hung down to her waist.

Maggie didn't know why. She hadn't bothered to wash it.

Kate didn't speak. She touched the little rectangular box on the doorjamb before walking into the house.

Maggie felt her training rear its head. The rooms were filled with shadows. All the drapes were closed. Even the mirror over the fireplace was covered with a black sheet. She wanted to turn on a light. There was no telling who else was in the house.

The woman walked toward the kitchen. The candle flickered from the breeze. Her feet padded softly against the floor. She wasn't wearing shoes.

Kate started to follow. Maggie grabbed her sleeve.

'Shh,' Kate warned.

Maggie tried to catch her sleeve again, but Kate was already walking down the hallway. All Maggie could do was follow. This was what she got for letting Kate take the lead – an interview where nobody was allowed to talk.

At least the kitchen wasn't as dark as the rest of the house. There were no curtains on the windows. Sunlight streamed into the room. Food of all kinds was laid out on the countertop. Maggie didn't recognize half of what she saw.

The Portuguese lady put the candle on the windowsill over the sink. She nodded toward the kitchen table. Kate sat down, so Maggie did, too. The woman kept her back to them as she fixed two plates.

Maggie let out a long sigh to let everybody know she was not happy. None of this was getting them any closer to finding Jimmy. She'd known this was a stupid idea from the start.

The old woman finished loading the plates. She turned around. The sunlight bathed her face.

A surprised 'Oh' came out of Maggie's mouth.

Stubble covered the woman's face. No wonder she sounded like Ricardo Montalbán. The Portuguese lady was a man.

He asked, 'May I offer you some iced tea?'

'Yes, thank you.' Kate didn't seem surprised by any of this. She took the plates. She set them on the table. She gave Maggie a look of warning similar to the one a mother would give a misbehaving child. 'I don't think we exchanged names yesterday. I'm Officer Murphy. This is Officer Lawson.'

'Eduardo Rosa.' He rested his hands on his hips as he studied Kate. 'Murphy. I'm assuming you married a *shagetz*.'

'I did.'

'Smart girl. Jewish men never shut up.'

Kate laughed very deeply at what was obviously an inside joke.

Eduardo went to the icebox. He pulled out a pitcher of iced tea. He took a tray from the freezer. He found two glasses in the cabinet.

Maggie watched, transfixed. How had she not seen this yesterday? The high collar hid an Adam's apple. The long sleeves covered hairy arms. The floor-length skirt obscured big feet. The biggest giveaway should have been his hands. They were enormous.

Maggie realized, 'You're the tranny pimp.'

'Feh.' He popped the ice out of the tray. 'Pimps are all *schvartzes*.'

Kate snorted into her hand.

'My late husband, Gerald—' Eduardo set the two glasses of iced tea on the table. 'He was in charge of the business.' He pointed to the chair Maggie was sitting in. 'Died right there three months ago. Heart attack. We were together twenty years.'

Kate asked, 'Chic was your son?'

'His name was Lionel. He lived in Detroit with his mother, Lydia. I always liked the dark ones.' There were two more chairs at the table, but Eduardo steadied his hand on the counter and sat down on the floor. 'Lionel was pimping up in Detroit, but he got into trouble. He was always in trouble; *alav ha-shalom*.' Eduardo paused a moment before continuing. 'Lydia asked if I could help. With Gerald gone, we thought he could take over the business down here.'

Maggie rested her chin in her hand so her jaw wouldn't hit the floor. 'Did you give them your real name for the witness statement yesterday? That's sworn testimony.'

'I gave them Gerald's name. Nobody asked me to put my hand on the Bible.' Eduardo looked up at Kate. 'I know you're here for information. Can you get my boy released to me?'

Kate seemed surprised. 'You haven't had the funeral?'

'The coroner won't release the body. We have all the paperwork. Lydia is down there now. They say it will be another week.'

Finally, Maggie could contribute something. 'They have to do an autopsy. It's an important part of the investigation. If they can track the bullet back to the gun that was used, then they might find the killer. And all of it has to be presented at trial.'

'I don't want my son's body mutilated any more than

it already is.' Eduardo's voice was firm. 'I need to do right by him.'

Maggie said, 'I'm sorry, but it's the law. Don't you want us to catch the man who killed your son?'

'Young lady, I know that Lionel was in a very dangerous line of business. Would I be happy if you caught his murderer? Of course. But you must understand that I need his body released so that his mother and I can bury him.'

Kate asked, 'Have you talked to your rabbi?'

He indicated his dress. 'Do I look Reform to you?'

'Maggie? Do you know someone?'

'At the coroner's office?' Maggie thought she knew a girl from night class who was a secretary. 'I can make some calls, but I can't promise anything.'

Eduardo clasped his hands together in his lap. He looked down at the floor. Maggie wondered if he was praying, but she wasn't sure how Jews prayed. Or if they prayed at all.

He finally looked up. 'If you promise to do whatever you can, then I'll tell you what you came here for.'

'All right,' Kate agreed, as if this was exactly what she had planned.

Eduardo began, 'The girl who was there the night the policeman was shot, her name is Delilah. I have no idea if that's her real name. Maybe she likes Tom Jones. Who doesn't? I don't know her last name, either. She was probably fifteen when Gerald found her sucking cock inside the porn theater on Ponce.'

Kate sat back in her chair.

'He worked her hard. That was his reputation. Puritan work ethic.' He gave a one-shouldered shrug. 'Delilah didn't last long, and she was a lot more trouble than she was worth. Gerald sold her off at a loss just to get rid of her. When Lionel came to town, he had to start from scratch. I loved my boy, but he was an *arumloyfer*. Everything had to be handed to him. I said I might know a girl desperate to do anything that was needed. He found her working the Amtrak station on Peachtree.'

'In Buckhead?' Kate's voice went up. She was back to form.

Maggie took over. 'Is Delilah still working Whitehall?'

'I have no idea where she's working. She came here the night of the shooting. Lionel smacked her around. She was supposed to work all night. She gave him the police transmitter. Lionel called me in to look at it. I knew immediately what we had.'

Maggie said, 'A bargaining chip.'

'We were going to wait until the reward got higher. Five thousand dollars.' He huffed with disgust. 'When they caught the last guy, the reward was up to twenty.'

Kate crossed her arms. All of her pleasantness had drained away.

Maggie asked, 'What did Delilah see? I assume you weren't going to let her walk into the police station, tell her story, and collect the money.'

Eduardo asked, 'You'll make the call? You promise?'

'I said I would.'

'I'm trusting you.'

Maggie said, 'You realize that the person who killed Lionel is probably the same man who killed that cop?'

He put his hand to his chest. His voice wavered. 'I understand that, but you must understand that I want my son's body buried in the ground where it belongs.'

Maggie felt his despair as easily as she felt her own. 'I promise you that I will do everything I can to get him released.'

Eduardo nodded. 'The killer was white, not like the black man in the police sketch.'

Maggie felt her heart seize.

'Tall. Muscular. Broad shoulders. He was wearing black pants, a red shirt, and had black gloves on his hands. She didn't notice the shoes.'

Maggie bit her lip to keep it from trembling. Jimmy wore black gloves.

Eduardo continued, 'He had dark hair, cut short. His mustache was trimmed. Long sideburns. Delilah said he looked like a square except for his sideburns.'

Maggie forced her voice to remain steady. 'That's pretty specific. How close was she?'

'She was at the end of the alley. She saw everything. The man came around the corner. He had a midnight special in his hand. Raven MP-25.'

The brand of gun had not been released to the public. 'Was she sure about that? An MP-25?'

'Delilah knows her weapons. Her father knocked over his share of liquor stores.'

'She saw all of that?' Maggie forced some incredulity into her voice. 'She was close enough to make out the gun and the Shooter's face and what he was wearing, and she was still alive when it was over?'

'If I know Delilah, she was under a cardboard box shooting H.'

'She was stoned?' Maggie felt a glimmer of hope. 'That's not what I'd call a reliable eyewitness.'

'She's reliable when there's a knife in her twat.' Eduardo

reached up to the counter. With much groaning and popping, he managed to pull himself up from the floor. 'I'm telling you what we got out of her. I let Anthony handle it. Delilah told him everything she saw. On that, you can trust me.'

Maggie felt sweat rolling down her back. The kitchen was too hot. She was going to throw up if she didn't get out of here soon.

Kate asked, 'What were the two cops doing when the Shooter came around the corner?'

Eduardo turned back to the sink. 'She didn't say. And I've told you ladies everything I know. May *HaShem* strike you down if you fail to carry out your part of the bargain.'

'We will,' Kate said. 'I promise.'

Maggie stood up. She had to get out of this house. 'I'm sorry for your loss.'

Kate said, 'May heaven comfort you.'

Maggie forced herself not to run up the hallway. Her throat was closing up. She pulled at her collar. Her fingers brushed the bruises on her neck. She wrenched open the door and took great gulps of air into her lungs.

Kate put her hand on Maggie's shoulder. 'You all right?'

Maggie shrugged her off as she walked down the stairs. She buttoned her collar. She had told Kate not to trust anybody; why were they trusting Eduardo? He could be lying about the description. He could be lying about the girl who was a witness. The girl could be lying to everybody.

But then how did she get Jimmy's transmitter?

Kate said, 'Well, I guess that was interesting, but I'm not sure that it was helpful.'

Maggie wiped the sweat off the back of her neck. Her stomach was churning. She felt strung out and exhausted.

Kate said, 'We were already considering the fact that the Shooter might be white. And that description – tall, athletic, mustache, long sideburns. Who does that sound like?'

Maggie tasted bile in her mouth.

'Every cop on the police force, that's who. Including Jimmy and your uncle Terry. And all of them wear black driving gloves. Too many Steve McQueen movies, methinks.' She handed Maggie the keys to the cruiser. 'It's probably best if you drive to Dabbler's. I've never been to that part of town.' She opened the car door. 'I'll give Gail credit for this: she was right about those people. I can't believe the way Eduardo talked about that poor girl. I know she's a prostitute, but still. You'd think he was discussing a side of beef.' She paused for a second. 'He? She? Gosh, which is it?'

Maggie walked around the car. She got in behind the wheel. She tried to put the key in the ignition but the ring slipped from her fingers. She blindly reached down to try to find them.

Kate chattered on. 'She, I guess. We ought to reward the effort. That's what I would prefer in his shoes. Her shoes. I couldn't believe it when she opened the door and I saw that beard. Eduardo Rosa. That explains the voice. Yesterday, I kept expecting her to talk about soft Corinthian leather.' Kate laughed to herself. 'I guess we should run her name just to be sure nothing else surprises us. My gosh. I hate to sound arrogant, but one just *expects* more from a Jew.'

'Goddamn it,' Maggie muttered. She could feel the keys but her fingers couldn't grip them.

'I know. I shouldn't be unkind. She's sitting *shivah*. It's actually a beautiful ritual. There are all kinds of rules. You're not supposed to shave or use makeup. She tore her clothes – that's called *kriah*, to signify grief and anger over the death. She was sitting on the floor because you're supposed to keep low to the ground. Though you're supposed to bury the body within twenty-four hours. That's why she's so upset. The mourning should go on for seven days. *Shivah* means seven.'

'Got 'em.' Maggie's cheek bumped against the steering wheel. She winced from the pain. The bruise had its own heartbeat.

Kate brought her rambling to an end. 'Maggie, I'm running out of pointless things to say, so I would really appreciate it if you would give me some kind of response.'

Maggie took the easy route. 'I'll call in about Eduardo Rosa. See if he has a sheet.'

Kate studied Maggie. 'All morning, I've felt like there's something important that you're not telling me.'

'*Gosh*, really?' Maggie mimicked. 'Like that I'm Jewish? Or that I'm a widow? Or that my father is the richest gardener in the history of the world?'

'Yes, all of those are excellent examples of what I'm talking about.'

Maggie jammed the key into the ignition. She started the car.

'Does your throat hurt?'

'Only when I have to answer stupid questions.'

28

Kate stared at the transmitter in her lap. Every other call to dispatch was about a possible sighting of Jimmy's car or a new lead on the Shooter. She had been right about today being a criminal's holiday. Wanda Clack called in a cleared chicken bone and one of the colored girls reported finding a previously reported stolen CB radio, but those were the only crimes that were being solved today.

She leaned her head against her hand. Kate was sitting in the cruiser outside of Dabbler's while Maggie used the pay phone on the side of the building. She had no idea what part of town they were in, let alone if they were still inside the city limits. To say the bar was nondescript was an understatement. Kate supposed that was its own protection. You didn't come here unless you knew what it was for, and if you didn't know what it was for, you probably never noticed it. The brick façade was painted black. The narrow windows were tinted to block out the daylight. There were no neon liquor signs that she could see from the street. There wasn't even a sign on the door.

What gave the place away was the clientele. One after another, well-dressed men in suits got out of their expensive cars and walked through the swinging door. Their hair touched their collars. Their sideburns hugged square jaws. They all had mustaches and they all to a one looked like the gay men with which Kate was more familiar.

That there was a police cruiser parked outside the establishment seemed to have little impact on traffic. Within ten minutes of Maggie getting out of the car, the parking lot was full. Cars surrounded Kate on all sides. Some of the men even smiled at her as they walked toward the building.

So, a police officer wasn't an unusual visitor at Dabbler's. Kate wasn't surprised. You didn't wind up in this part of town by accident. You had to know exactly where you were going. They could assume Don Wesley had visited the establishment at least once. Had Jimmy, too? Was he inside the building right now nursing his wounds? Because he had to be wounded, and not just from the pieces of skull embedded in his leg or the bullet that ripped through his arm. No matter how cavalier he had acted at the house yesterday morning, Kate could not accept that Jimmy Lawson did not feel something for his lost lover.

Or his sister. Maggie had killed a man yesterday. Did Jimmy know that someone had also tried to choke her? The bruises were starker now. Kate could make out the finger marks where a hand had wrapped around Maggie's neck. She assumed that Terry was the attacker. Jimmy could be a self-righteous prick, but she could not imagine him strangling his sister.

Then again, Kate could not imagine Maggie losing her shit, but that was exactly what had happened with Lewis Conroy. Kate couldn't very well say she'd never seen anything like it. Gail had attacked that prostitute. She'd broken the woman's leg, then tortured her. Maggie had not tortured Conroy in the same sadistic manner, but there were some eerie similarities.

Was this what Kate had to look forward to? Was there a fourth person lurking in her psyche who was going to be a violent sadist?

As with everything else that had to do with this impossible job, the situation wasn't completely black and white. Or maybe in the case of Lewis Conroy, it was. That he was a white man and his victim was a young black girl meant a great deal. There was no question of his guilt. Conroy had just as much as admitted to it. He had shown no remorse, even when he was on the ground straining for air. He'd never apologized. Actually, he'd sounded arrogant, like a man arguing with a waiter over a miscalculated bar tab. If you were the sort of man like Conroy, you knew that was an argument you were always going to win.

No wonder they all hated people from Kate's side of town. She was beginning to hate them herself. The sense of entitlement. The attitude. Was that what had set Maggie against her? She'd been enraged after they left Conroy. Kate had assumed she just needed some time to collect herself. Instead, Maggie had taken that time to redirect her vehemence toward Kate.

The radio hummed with another possible Shooter sighting. Kate turned down the volume. She studied the white plastic brick in her lap. If she lived to be a million years old, she would never forget what this thing looked like. Gail had used it as a weapon. Sir Chic had used it as a bargaining chip. Jimmy had left it at the scene of Don's murder.

Kate could guess why Jimmy had left the transmitter in the alley. You couldn't sit with one of these clipped to your belt, let alone pull down your pants with one on. He must have put the brick beside his leg the same as everyone did. Unplugging the jack ensured no accidental transmissions were sent out. And when Don was shot, the last thing Jimmy would have been worried about was his radio.

Maggie had finished her phone calls. She was walking across the parking lot. She weaved between the cars. Her head was down. Her spiral notebook was in one hand. She got into the car. She rested her arm on the door. She stared at the building and did not say a word.

Kate stared at the building, too. She had tried questions. She had tried pointless babbling. Now, she was going to try silence.

Maggie seemed content to let it drag out. She watched the men going into the building. The lot was full, though it was only eleven in the morning. Overflow parking lined the street.

She finally spoke. 'My contact at the coroner's office is going to see what she can do. She's just a secretary. I don't know if they'll listen to her.'

Kate bit her lip so that she wouldn't answer.

'I asked for Eduardo Rosa's rap sheet. Rick said he can leave it at the hospital for us. I thought we could check on Gail.'

Kate couldn't help herself. She nodded.

Maggie hissed out a stream of air between her teeth. 'This is a gay bar, isn't it?'

Kate hesitated. 'Yes.'

Maggie pulled the door handle. 'Ready?'

Kate got out of the car. She clipped the transmitter on her belt. She put Jimmy's smelly hat on her head.

Maggie resumed her silence as she walked between the cars. Her hat was low on her head. She kept her hands down at her sides. Her shoulders were stooped. Kate wondered how little pressure it would take to knock her to the ground. She hoped she didn't find out.

Everyone inside the bar looked up when they entered. There were some curious mumbles, but for the most part, none of the men seemed worried that two female cops had walked through the door.

And none of them were Jimmy Lawson.

Maggie headed toward the bar. Yet again, Kate followed.

The inside of the building was just as dark as it looked from the outside. Men sat close to each other at the tables. They were jammed shoulder to shoulder into the small booths. Linda Ronstadt played softly through the speakers. The song choice seemed appropriate for the crowd—'When Will I Be Loved.'

Kate didn't know what she had been expecting. Lecherous glances, filthy back rooms. For the most part, the men looked like couples who'd met for a drink before lunch. Hands were being held. Arms were draped over the backs of chairs. Glances were stolen across the room. The atmosphere was loose and casual. Barring the fact that everyone was of the same sex, the place felt like every club Kate had ever visited.

Chivalry was not lost at Dabbler's. Two men gave up their places at the bar. Maggie didn't acknowledge the gesture. She sat down. She put her hat in front of her. She looked like she wanted a drink, but Kate was still surprised when she ordered a bourbon neat.

She asked Kate, 'You want one?'

'Sure.' Kate put her hat on the bar.

Maggie stared at the mirror behind the rows of liquor. Her eyes slid back and forth across the room as she checked each face, noted each gesture.

'On the house.' The bartender put two glasses in front of them. He was gorgeous, probably no more than eighteen, and sporting the same long sideburns and thick mustache as the rest of them. 'Is there something I can help you gals with?'

Maggie reached into her breast pocket. She pulled out a photograph. 'Have you seen this man?'

He smiled. His teeth were straight and beautiful. 'Yeah, that's Jim. Is he a friend of yours?'

Maggie put the photo facedown on the bar. 'When's the last time you saw him?'

The bartender narrowed his eyes. 'Is he in trouble?'

'It depends on when you saw him last.'

'Couple of nights ago?' He gave it some more thought. 'It must've been for Don's memorial service. That was Monday night, right?'

Maggie picked up the glass. She finished the bourbon in one swallow.

Kate asked, 'You haven't seen Jimmy since then?'

'Nope. He doesn't usually come during the day.'

'He's a regular?'

'Sure. Everybody loves Jim.' The bartender nodded at a customer, indicating he'd be a minute. 'Is there anything else?'

Maggie asked, 'Have you seen anyone suspicious hanging around here?'

'Other than two Pepper Andersons?' He told Kate, 'I love your hair, doll. The color is dazzling.'

'Thank you.' Kate stroked back her hair. She couldn't help herself. 'There hasn't been anyone here lately who seems out of place? Someone who doesn't blend in?'

'Honey, every man in this place blends in as soon as

385

he walks through that door. That's kind of the point.' He refilled Maggie's glass. 'Sorry I couldn't—' He stopped. 'You know what? There was a guy here yesterday who kind of freaked me.'

Maggie asked, 'What did he look like?'

'Me.' He laughed. 'Except older.'

Kate knew this wasn't much help. When you were eighteen, thirty was ancient. 'Did he say anything?'

'Not really. He was one of those strong, silent types. Good tipper. Drank Southern Comfort. He kept watching the door every time it opened. I got the feeling he was either waiting for somebody or looking for somebody. Of course, that's pretty much what everybody's doing when they're in here.'

'Was he a cop?'

'He wasn't wearing a uniform. He kind of looked like a cop. Or a soldier. We get a lot of vets in here. I think most of 'em aren't even gay. They just got used to being around men over there. They want to feel like they're part of a unit again. Weird, huh?'

Kate nodded like she understood.

He topped off Maggie's drink again. 'Listen, cutie, you're both welcome to sit here and drink all you want, but don't go asking the customers questions. You won't get anything more than what I've told you, and you'd be surprised how many cops higher up the food chain darken our doors. You pickin' up what I'm puttin' down?'

'Yes.' Kate had given up on jive talk after yesterday's debacle. 'Thank you.'

He winked at her before walking away.

Maggie took another drink. Kate tried her bourbon and nearly gagged. He certainly hadn't given them top shelf.

'Let's go.' Maggie grabbed her hat. She walked toward the door.

Kate decided to take her time. She picked up the photograph on the bar. It was a good picture of Jimmy. He was leaning against a car. His shirt was tight across his muscular chest. His chin was tilted up confidently. He was smiling, and Kate hoped that Maggie had taken the picture, that the grin captured by the camera was meant for his sister.

She tucked her hat under her arm as she made her way through the crowded room. She didn't have to push her way out. Men politely stepped aside. They nodded deferentially. Someone even opened the door for her.

She scanned the parking lot for Maggie. She wasn't in the cruiser. She wasn't walking between cars. Kate turned. The pay phones were empty. She was about to go back into the bar when she heard heaving.

Maggie was on the side of the building. She was on the ground, on all fours, divulging the contents of her stomach.

Kate's first instinct was to go to her, to put her hand to her back, to help keep her hair out of the way. But she was the second Kate now, or maybe the fourth, so she just stood there waiting for the nausea to pass.

The passing took longer than she anticipated. Kate's feet started to hurt. She sat down on the curb. She stared out at the debris-strewn vacant lot next door. Someone had abandoned a shopping cart filled with wet pieces of cardboard. Condoms, needles, tinfoil, spoons. The usual detritus that she'd come to accept riddled every part of the city but her own.

Finally, Maggie groaned out what little liquid was left in her stomach. She wiped her mouth with her hand.

Kate looked down at her hat. Jimmy's name was written inside the brim. She had no idea where her own hat was. She'd found her shoes in the back of Gail's car, but the hat was missing.

Maggie sat back on her knees. She was panting.

Kate said, 'I meant to put a sachet in this hat last night. I keep some in my lingerie drawer. They smell like roses.'

Maggie looked out at the lot.

Kate hooked the hat on her knee. She smoothed the legs of her pants. 'My father's a psychiatrist.'

'Goddamn it,' Maggie muttered. 'That makes so much sense.'

Kate smiled, because it probably did. 'He's paying for my apartment. There was no insurance policy. I never claimed my husband's benefits, because I thought if I did, then it would mean he's really dead.'

Maggie turned to look at her.

'I spent last night with a married man. He wants me to come back tonight, but I don't know if I will. Should I? Probably not.'

'Why are you telling me this?'

'I don't know,' Kate admitted. 'You seemed so angry at me before. I thought it was because you knew I was lying. Now, I'm not so sure.'

'Is this some sort of deal? Show me yours and I'll show you mine?'

Kate shrugged. She didn't know what it was.

'Jimmy's gay.' Maggie's tone had a finality to it. 'He wasn't lying about that. I've been fighting it all night, but I don't think he was lying about anything.'

Kate knew better than to ask for clarification.

'On the street, somebody tells you one lie, you just

block out everything else. They can't be trusted.' Maggie cleared her throat several times. She looked like she wanted to spit. 'So if he's telling the truth about something so horrible . . .' Her voice trailed off. She leaned over and spit on the ground. 'I'm sorry.'

Kate didn't know why spitting felt less ladylike than throwing up, but it did. 'Do you want me to go back into the bar and get you a glass of water?'

'All those men in there . . .' She started shaking her head. 'They looked so normal.'

'They *are* normal.'

Maggie looked back at her again.

'You never thought about what your brother did with women. Why would you think about what he might be doing with men?'

'It's all so easy for you. You just decide that this is the way things are, and you go on like it doesn't matter.'

'I can't sit around feeling sorry for myself. I tried that for two years and it gained me nothing.'

'Kate, you cry all the time.'

She laughed, because she didn't think of it as crying. The tears from the last few days were nothing like the ones she'd cried for Patrick. 'You have to get things out. You can't keep them bottled in all the time.'

'That's easy to say when you have choices.'

'You have a choice.' Kate handed her the photo of Jimmy. 'You can choose to love your brother no matter what.'

Maggie cupped the photo in her hand. She stared at the image until a tear splashed onto Jimmy's face. 'All night, I didn't believe him. I know my brother. At least I thought I knew him.'

Kate maintained her silent strategy.

Maggie crumpled the photo. She stuck it in her pants pocket. 'Jimmy confessed to being the Shooter. He killed all those men.'

Kate felt the words travel around her brain. They were like marbles in a wooden labyrinth puzzle, rolling around, looking for the right path.

Maggie said, 'Mark Porter, Greg Keen, Alex Ballard, Leonard Johnson, Don Wesley. Jimmy killed them all.'

Finally, Kate could speak. 'That's not possible.'

'He wrote it down.' Maggie pulled her notebook out of her pocket. 'His confession. I copied it.'

'Where's the original?'

'It doesn't matter.'

Kate took the notebook. 'Of course it matters. What happened to the original?'

'My mother tore it up, all right? Are you going to read it or not?'

Confusion still clouded Kate's brain. She looked down at the letter and silently read the words. She had to go through the note twice before comprehension began to dawn.

I am the Atlanta Shooter. I killed those guys because I was a dirty fag with them and I didn't want anybody to find out. Don't try to find me or I will kill more people. Maggie, I'm sorry that I never apologized to you. I should've told you that what happened wasn't your fault.

Kate was so stunned that she could barely think of a response. 'Jimmy didn't write this.'

'He did. It was his handwriting. His signature.'

'It's not true.'

'I know what you're going to say. I went through the same thing last night.' Maggie indicated the bar. 'He's gay,

Kate. Why would he tell the truth about being gay and lie about being a murderer?'

Kate's mouth opened, but she couldn't think what to say.

'You ask my uncle Terry, the first one is worse than the second. Jimmy might as well have written a suicide note. Tell me why he said any of it if it's not true.'

'Because—' Kate was still stymied. 'Because.'

'Eduardo's description. That's Jimmy. Think about the Shooter: He knows the police codes. He knows police routines and procedures. Don wouldn't be expecting Jimmy to pull a gun. Nobody would. And look at where we are. This is a gay bar where they had a memorial service for Don. You don't have a service for somebody you don't know. Don was gay. They were both gay, and Jimmy snapped, and—'

'Maggie, stop this. You're exhausted. You haven't slept all night. You're jumping to so many conclusions that you've forgotten the facts.'

'I know the facts.'

'Then let's go over them.' Kate laid it out for her. 'Delilah said that the Shooter was wearing jeans and a red shirt. Are you telling me Jimmy changed his clothes to kill Don, then changed back into his uniform before carrying him all the way to the hospital?'

Maggie started shaking her head. 'I don't know. I don't know what to think anymore.'

'Does Jimmy own a red shirt? You said he only wears black, gray, and navy.'

'The whore could've been lying. Or Eduardo was.'

'She told the same lie Jimmy did, then. He said the Shooter was wearing a red shirt and jeans.'

Maggie still could not accept it. 'Jimmy lied about the Shooter. He said he was black.'

'The Shooter was wearing black gloves. That's why Jimmy said he was black. He probably saw the gun, and the hand holding it, and then he dove for cover. After what you and I both went through yesterday, I think it's understandable that some of the details were lost.'

Maggie kept shaking her head. There were tears in her eyes. 'You just have to accept it. We both have to accept it.'

'I won't accept anything of the sort.' Kate finally realized that there was nothing to do but to tell Maggie the truth. Or at least part of it. 'The night that Don was killed, Jimmy got hurt, too.'

Maggie looked dubious. 'I told you he has a bad knee.'

'That's not what I'm talking about. Some shrapnel from the bullet that killed Don was in Jimmy's thigh.' Kate chose her words carefully. Maggie didn't need the details. 'I talked to the doctor at Grady who treated him.'

'Jimmy didn't say anything about shrapnel.'

Kate flailed for an explanation. 'You know how Jimmy is. He's not going to admit he's hurt. He's too tough for that.'

Maggie looked desperate to be persuaded. 'What are you saying?'

'Jimmy couldn't get shrapnel in his leg if he was holding the gun. Ergo, he was standing beside Don when it happened.'

Maggie put her hand to her neck. 'He had blood all over his face and chest. I remember thinking he had to be close when Don was shot.'

'That's right,' Kate agreed. 'He was standing beside Don when it happened.'

Maggie sat up. 'I saw fresh blood on Jimmy's pants. You were there. I was in the street with Conroy. You guys pulled up. I saw the blood, and I asked him about it, and he got really weird.' She grabbed Kate's arm. 'Oh, Kate – are you sure? That's really what the doctor said?'

'You can talk to him yourself.' Kate felt certain Philip would have no trouble spinning a white lie. 'We'll go there now.'

Maggie wasn't listening. She was still picking everything apart. 'I don't understand. Why would he say he killed those people?'

'Stress?' Kate was on shaky ground. This was more her father's area of expertise. 'Maybe at some level he felt responsible because he couldn't save Don?'

Maggie saw another hole in the confession. 'So all those guys were gay? Keen, Porter, Johnson, Ballard?'

'You heard the bartender,' Kate said. 'The force is full of them.'

'But those guys had wives. They had mistresses.'

Kate could not begin to explain. She was only worried about Jimmy now. Why had he written those words? What could his motive possibly be?

She read the letter again. *Dirty fag*. The phrase was something another person would call you, not something you would call yourself.

Maggie said what they were both thinking. 'None of this makes sense.'

'There's always a reason. We just need to figure it out.'

'I've spent all night trying to. There's no reason.' Maggie picked up a piece of gravel from the ground. She tossed it into the weeds.

Kate read Jimmy's words aloud. ' "I should've told you that what happened wasn't your fault." '

Maggie threw another rock. This one went farther. She was trying to hit the shopping cart.

Kate silently read the lines again.

I'm sorry that I never apologized to you. I should've told you that what happened wasn't your fault.

She asked, 'What wasn't your fault?'

Maggie hurled another rock. This one landed closer to the cart. Instead of answering, she searched for another weapon.

Kate looked down at the letter. She had it memorized by now. She stared instead at the cursive words. Maggie's handwriting was better than her own. The pen had bored down into the paper. She could feel the indentations through the back of the page.

Maggie said, 'Eight years ago, Jimmy had this friend named Michael.'

Kate kept her eyes down.

'He was good-looking. Jimmy's friends are always good-looking.' Maggie's sharp, surprised laugh indicated that she finally understood why. 'Michael slept over all the time. I was fifteen. I had a crush on him. He wouldn't give me the time of day.' She gripped a rock in her hand. 'One night, I was asleep and I woke up and Michael was on top of me.' She shrugged. 'I was stupid about that kind of stuff. I didn't really know what was going on, but it hurt like hell and he wouldn't stop, and Jimmy must've heard me scream, because the next thing I know, he's in my room and he's beating the shit out of Michael.'

She glanced over at Kate. 'My mother was there, and my uncle Terry, which was the first time I realized he spent the night sometimes. My sister was five. She slept through it, but she knows about it now. Terry made sure of that.' She threw the rock. It clanged against the metal cart. 'He hangs it over my head all the time. All of them do. It's what they use against me when I forget my place.'

Kate smoothed together her lips. She didn't know what to say. At least now Maggie's rage over Lewis Conroy raping a teenager made some kind of sense.

Maggie said, 'You know, the whole time Jimmy was beating Michael, he kept screaming, "How could you do this to me?" Like he was the one who was hurt. And he *was* hurt. I'd never seen him upset like that before. He was bawling. Tears pouring down his face. Snot dripping out of his nose. He wouldn't talk to me for months afterward, and when he finally did, it was never the same.' She kicked at the gravel on the ground. 'I always thought that it was my fault. Because of what came afterward. Because I had shamed the family. But now I think Jimmy was upset because Michael had cheated on him.' She laughed again. 'He was jealous of me. Or about what happened between me and Michael.'

Kate heard Maggie's words echo in her ears. *What came afterward.*

What had come afterward? The nurse next door?

Maggie took back her notebook and stared at Jimmy's confession. 'The weird thing is, Jimmy apologized to me yesterday when we were in the hospital. He told me he was sorry for what happened. First time he's ever apologized for anything. And I know that he was talking about that night with Michael, because he said "seven years ago" and I told him it was eight, and he agreed.' She shrugged at Kate. 'So why would he say he never apologized?'

'He didn't apologize for what *really* happened.'

'He was doped up on pain pills. Maybe he forgot he apologized.' She closed the notebook. 'That still doesn't explain why he wrote these things. Or where he is now.'

'He could be with somebody you don't know.'

Maggie echoed Kate's earlier words. 'A secret person.'

'He's probably with a friend, Maggie. Somebody who knows about Don and can comfort him.' Kate tried, 'Look at the letter from his point of view. Revealing that he's gay means you won't show it to anybody else. And the part about hurting more people if you come looking for him – he never hurt any of them in the first place. He was trying to push you away.'

'Terry's looking for him.' Maggie's voice went down in distress. 'He's going to shoot him on sight. He told me himself.'

'If you can't find Jimmy, then Terry can't.'

Maggie's desperation was back. 'I don't know what to do.'

'We need to keep doing what we've been doing. Work the case. This is a big break. Don and Jimmy were targeted by the Shooter for a reason. If that reason is because the Shooter hates gay men, then we have a connection.'

'What if Jimmy knows who the Shooter is? What if it's somebody he was with, and he knows the guy is killing people, but he can't turn him in?'

That sounded as good an explanation as any, but it still got them nowhere. 'We can sit around talking conspiracy theories or we can actually start looking into things.'

Maggie said, 'Maybe Jimmy is tracking him on his own. That's what he was doing yesterday when that woman shot him. Maybe Jimmy has a lead and writing the letter was his way of making sure we didn't get in the way.'

Again, Kate could not argue with the theory. 'I don't see how we can get in the way if we keep working the case the same way we've been working it.'

'You mean the files,' Maggie said. 'Terry has them.'

'He doesn't have our brains. And you have yet to notice what an excellent memory I have.' Kate had no problem recalling all the questions she had yesterday after reading the Shooter files. 'Autopsies are public records. Would a doctor censor the documents if he found evidence that led him to believe that the victims were gay?'

'I have no idea.'

'What about your friend at the coroner's office?'

'All she does is type the reports. They don't tell her anything.' Maggie rubbed her eyes. 'Mark Porter was happily married. Greg Keen was separated from his wife. I didn't know Ballard and Johnson. They were married, according to their files. Two kids each. Gail might know more. She's in everybody's business.'

'Then let's go to the hospital.' Kate pushed herself up. She offered her hand to Maggie. 'You get the gossip from Gail. I know a doctor who might be able to answer our other question about the autopsy.'

Maggie stood on her own. 'What if we're wrong and Jimmy's missing for another reason?'

Kate repeated her earlier advice. 'We just keep moving forward until we figure it out.'

29

Fox flicked up his coat collar as he walked through the train yard. He hadn't shaved today. He smelled of booze. He was dressed in his usual camouflage.

Nothing to see here, buddy, just another bum looking for a dry place to hole up.

He had expected to open his front door this morning and find the newspaper screaming up a headline about a cop who had confessed to the most heinous of crimes. Instead, he saw a story about the mayor's new integration plan. Fox's eyesight was good. He stood over the paper, read the first few lines, then quietly shut the door.

An unexpected development.

Fox's plan had depended upon the confession being made public. There had to be a day of reckoning. Jimmy Lawson had to be hunted. He had to be captured by a hero cop. And then he had to be handled by a hero force. One, maybe two men would be selected for the task. Trusted men. Men with steady hands and iron constitutions. Jimmy could not be allowed to tell his story. The force could not handle the shame. This fallen officer had been one of their own. Would they let the world know that they had harbored a murderer, a deviant, in the brotherhood?

No sir. The good men who controlled this city would not let that happen.

Fox knew for a fact that shame was a great motivator. It was why Jimmy had broken so quickly. All Fox had to do was press the gun to Jimmy's head, and the next thing he knew, Jimmy was sitting at the Lawson dining room table with a pen in his hand.

And then the problems started. Jimmy's tears had wet the paper. Fox made him start over. Jimmy's pen had torn the page. Fox made him start over. Jimmy had fucked up so many times that Fox had finally dictated every single word to him.

And then Jimmy had asked for permission to write more.

Who would've guessed the guy gave a shit about his sister?

Fox had been an only child, as were his parents. There were no cousins to play with. The only uncle he ever knew was his Uncle Sam. Fox had never given any thought to what it might be like to have a sibling.

Just one more head for Senior to cuff. One more ass for him to beat. One more hand to crush with the heel of his shoe. Another pair of legs to break.

Because of course it wasn't just Fox's mother. Why just beat on a woman when you could whale on a growing boy?

Fox didn't ask Jimmy what he was apologizing to his sister for. They had time, but not that much time. If Jimmy was sending some kind of code, Fox was worried not one bit. No one would listen to Maggie Lawson. Fox had considered her for a target years ago and decided that she just wasn't worth it. A woman like that would burn herself out on her own. Maggie had brought so much shame onto the family that her own mother couldn't hold up her head when she walked down the street.

What Fox didn't count on was Terry Lawson's shame. Jimmy was his blood. Fox should've known an old soldier like Terry would want to put his nephew down himself.

An unexpected development, but one Fox could put to his own good use. That was what a man did. Other men looked at problems. Fox looked at solutions.

Still, Fox was nervous. Could Kate do her part? Could Fox coax her into his lair?

He felt a breath on the back of his neck. He heard the invisible footsteps sneaking up behind him. He saw the flicker of the leaves that could be the wind or could be a man with a knife who would silently slit Fox's throat, then hide in the jungle waiting for the next white face that came along.

Fox had seen it happen.

They called him Mick.

He had a movie star's features, but he was willing to get his hands dirty. Adaptable. Smart. He learned the ropes. He paid his dues. And then he went in the wrong direction, ignored the right signs, and ended up with his neck cut back to his spine.

Fox had not tracked the killer. He was too much in awe of his work. Mick was ten, maybe fifteen feet away from Fox when his time came. Fox was transfixed by the killer's dance. The elegant tiptoe through the jungle. The graceful swing of the machete. The lissome turn of his head to keep the spray of arterial blood from clouding his vision.

An artist.

That was how Fox was going to be today. He had planned the dance in his head. There was just the matter of leading Kate to the center of the floor.

Walking across the train yard, Fox heard the music start up in his head.

30

Kate tried to ignore the knowing looks she got from the nurse when she asked how to find Dr. Van Zandt's office. If she hadn't felt like a whore already, she certainly did now.

She checked her watch as she walked down the hallway. Kate had allotted herself ten minutes to ask Philip her questions. Gail was in the bowels of the hospital having some sort of test performed. The nurse had said she would be at least half an hour. Kate didn't need to be in a room with Philip for that long. Ten minutes was more than enough time for him to give her a straight answer.

These were probably fool's errands anyway. Gail Patterson wasn't sitting on information that could break this case wide open. She was too smart a cop not to have already put it together if she did. And Kate wasn't certain that Maggie was up to the job. While she could see how Maggie had gotten to the point, Kate was slightly appalled that the woman could think even for a moment that her brother was capable of mass murder.

As to the questions they had for Philip, so what if all the dead men were homosexuals? What could Kate and Maggie do with that information? There was nowhere for them to go. No one to talk to. They couldn't start questioning members of the gay community, because they had no idea who they were. Kate occasionally read an alternative newspaper. Their offices might be a starting point. Or they could go back to the bartender at Dabbler's.

Or they could just run around in circles until they bumped heads and fell down.

Philip's office door was closed. Kate heard the deep vibrato of his voice. He was obviously on the phone. He was probably talking to another woman. Possibly his wife. Kate almost didn't knock, but a couple of snickering nurses walked by and she knocked so loudly that the door shook.

'Yes?' he called.

Kate opened the door. Philip was sitting behind a metal desk. He held a telephone to his ear. Two leather Sled chairs were across from him. A sleek leather couch took up the entire left side of the room. He was wearing a dark blue suit that brought out the color in his eyes and an open-necked yellow shirt that showed the curling hair on his chest.

Kate wanted to turn around and walk back out the door.

'Darling.' He hung up the phone and rose from his chair. 'What a pleasure to see you.'

'I'm here on business.' She shut the door. 'I need to talk to you about sperm.'

'I'd be happy to make you some more.'

Kate silently cursed her verbal idiocy. 'This is serious.'

'Of course it is. I can see that now.' He indicated the couch. Kate sat on the edge of one of the deep chairs.

He said, 'May I ask if you're well? You left in such a hurry this morning.'

'Yes, Dr. Van Zipless. Thank you for your concern.'

He laughed, seemingly more delighted with the name than Oma. He sat behind his desk. 'Now, let's be serious. What is your question, Officer Murphy?'

'Would a doctor lie on an autopsy report?'

His interest was piqued. 'I suppose it would depend on what was found.'

'If a man was homosexual, would there be physical signs?'

'The short answer is yes.' He leaned back in his chair. 'As for your original question, you would likely find traces in the areas you would expect to find traces. If it was ingested within one to two hours of death, it might be found in the stomach. Sperm is high in fat and protein, which takes time for the digestive system to process. Though the caloric value is roughly the same as a can of Tab, which I would like for you to keep in mind.'

Kate caught herself before she stupidly asked him why. 'Let's say that the coroner found traces where you mentioned, or found evidence in the stomach. Would these findings be noted on the autopsy report? Or is that something that would be left off?'

'I would leave them off if they didn't serve a purpose, but then, I am a man of great discretion. Shall I call the coroner for you and find out?'

'You know the coroner?'

'One of them – Artie Benowitz?' He noted Kate's surprise. 'Yeah, that putz. Bottom of his class at UGA. Let me give him a call.' He picked up the phone. 'Candy, could you get me Dr. Benowitz, please?'

He winked at Kate.

She looked at her watch. How had this only taken four minutes? Kate glanced around the office. The couch was longer than Philip was tall. The chairs were so deep that her hamstrings were starting to ache from the effort of keeping herself perched on the edge.

Philip cupped his hand to the phone. 'Do you have names for me?'

Kate took out her notebook. She flipped to the names of the dead officers. 'They were double homicides, so they go together, two and two.'

'I can't hear you. Could you please come sit in my lap?'

Kate slapped the notebook down in front of him.

Philip silently read the list. 'These are the police officers who were executed.'

'Yes.'

He held up a finger and spoke into the phone. 'Hello, Artie? Yes, Van Zipless here.' He winked at Kate again. She wanted to smack him. 'I've got some names for you. I need to know if they were *faygelehs*.' He read the names from the list. At the same time, he reached his hand into his jacket pocket. Kate saw a flash of black silk in his hand.

She lunged across the desk. He snatched back her underwear.

He said, 'Yes, I'll hold.'

'Philip.' Kate struggled to control her voice.

He moved the receiver away from his mouth. 'I found these in my car this morning. Do you know to whom they belong?'

'Give them to me.'

'You don't want them. I wore them on my head as I drove to work.'

Kate held out her hand. 'Now.'

'But they're so silky.' He tucked her underwear down the front of his pants. 'I love the way they feel against my – Yes.' He moved the phone back to his mouth. 'I'm here, Artie. That's great. No sign whatsoever. What's that?' He moved the phone away again, telling Kate, 'Artie took the liberty. Don Wesley is an affirmative. The other four are a no. Anything else?'

Kate grabbed a pen and added Lionel Rosa's name to the list. 'This man was killed yesterday. His mother is trying to get him released. She's already sitting *shivah*.'

Philip sat up in his chair. His voice lost its teasing tone as he relayed the information to Artie Benowitz. There was no more small talk at the end. He simply hung up the phone. 'Mr. Rosa will be released this afternoon.'

'Thank you.' Kate felt relieved. At least that was one good thing she was able to do today. 'Now will you give me back my underwear?'

'Darling, I would like very much for you to come get it.'

Kate gripped her hands in her lap. 'Please try to be serious. I've just seen you do it, so I know it's possible.'

'But I keep thinking of your hand in my pants. I can't concentrate.'

She gave up. 'Where is this going?'

'Why does it have to go anywhere?'

Kate had had her fill of him always answering her questions with more questions.

'Listen to me, Kaitlin.' Philip came around his desk and sat in the chair beside her. 'Will you let me hold your

406

hands? This really requires me to hold your hands.'

She reluctantly let him hold her hands.

He gazed into her eyes. 'I've wanted you from the moment I saw you in Janice Saddler's basement. You were the most beautiful girl I had seen in my life. I carried the memory of your kisses to Jerusalem. I begged my parents to let me return. I wrote our names in the back of my notebooks. "Mr. Kaitlin Herschel." I kissed my hand and pretended it was you.'

Kate laughed, because this was ridiculous even for Philip. 'Then why didn't you look me up when you came back to America? I was still single then.'

He held her hands more gently. 'Because I have a duty to marry a Jewish woman who will raise my children in our faith, so that they will raise their children in their faith, and so on until our people are made whole again.'

Kate slid away from his grasp. 'And what am I in this equation?'

'You are my shiksa without the guilt.'

'I'm as Jewish as you are.'

'Yeah, but you smell better.' He nuzzled her neck.

Kate pushed him away. 'I'm working. I have to be back downstairs in—' She looked at her watch and wondered if the hands had somehow moved backward. Gail was still in the middle of her test. Kate had lied like a cat in a sunbeam all week, but suddenly, the skill abandoned her. 'I only have fifteen minutes.'

'So, kiss me for fourteen minutes. That leaves you plenty of time to get downstairs.'

'Why do I get the feeling you've done that math before?'

Philip shot his cuffs. He showed Kate his digital watch.

407

He pressed a few buttons and a timer came up showing fourteen minutes.

'Philip.'

He started the timer.

She said, 'I should go.'

'But you're not.'

Kate pressed her hands against the seat of the chair. She did not stand.

'Do you know how perfect your mouth is?' He looked down at her lips. 'I think about the color all the time. Is it like roses? Tulips? It drives me mad just wondering.'

She smiled, but not because he was charming. He talked to her like a pimp. Except he wasn't tricking her out. He was turning her feral.

'Here.' Philip took her hand and pressed it to his chest. 'Do you feel my pounding heart? Do you understand the effect you have on me?'

His heart was beating fast. She could feel it through his shirt. Kate moved her hand to his open collar. The skin was hot. She let her fingers travel up to his face. His cheek was rough with stubble. His lips were so soft.

Kate kissed him because she wanted to. She wrapped her hand around the back of his neck. She pulled him close. All because she wanted to.

Philip hardly needed encouragement. He took off her belts with a practiced authority. Kate didn't let herself wonder why he knew how. She concentrated on his mouth, his hands. He went down on his knees in front of her. Kate's shirt came off. He unhooked her bra. She leaned back in the chair. She pressed her foot against his desk. Her head dropped back as he pulled down her underwear.

And then he slowed everything down.

His tongue made soft, lazy circles around her breast, down her stomach. He inched languorously downward until he was gently stroking between her legs. Kate ran her fingers through his thick hair. He was watching her, noting her breathing, her responses, so he could build her pleasure at his own leisurely pace.

'Philip . . .' She thought about his goddamn watch. 'Come on. Please.'

He allowed her to pull him back up. Kate bit his lip. She sucked his tongue. She tried to coax him with her hand but he wouldn't let her. He would not be rushed. He kept the same languid pace until his mouth had set her body on fire. When he finally eased into her, it was with such exquisite slowness that Kate's teeth wanted to chatter. He pulled out by degrees. Her body clenched for him. She felt hollow. And then he pushed back inside and she moaned with pleasure.

'Kaitlin.' His breath was hot in her ear. He kept the same maddening rhythm. 'Do you like the way I'm fucking you?'

Kate dug her fingernails into his skin.

'Do you want me to go slower?'

'No.' He was killing her. 'Please.'

'Are you sure?'

'Philip.' She couldn't stand it anymore. 'Just shut up and fuck me.'

31

Maggie stood outside Gail's hospital room listening to the stray calls coming through her radio. The chatter was soothing. No one was looking for her brother anymore. There had been a bank robbery downtown. Two tellers and a guard had been gunned down. All available cars were dispatched to search for the robber.

Maggie should have been relieved to hear they weren't looking for Jimmy. Instead, she was disgusted with herself. Why had she believed his letter even for a moment? What was wrong with her?

When they were little, Jimmy was always tricking Maggie. He pretended he didn't know where her shoes were. He hid her books or shrugged when she asked if he'd seen her skate key, even though it was in his back pocket. He did that stupid thing in the swimming pool where he squirted water in her face. Every time, Maggie did the same thing she'd done last night: she overrode that nagging in her gut and believed Jimmy not because she was gullible but because part of her could not accept that her brother would ever lie to her.

Yesterday had been one of the worst days of Maggie's life. She had been embarrassed by Terry and his friends.

She had killed a man. Gail had been hurt. Terry had thrown her around like a Frisbee. By the time she'd read Jimmy's confession, Maggie had been like Kate after she hit that cinder-block wall. Shock had taken over. She couldn't think straight. She couldn't see straight. Her brain couldn't grasp reality.

That was the only explanation for why the words of a grieving transsexual and a gay bartender had turned Maggie's doubt into certainty. All night, she had struggled against the contents of Jimmy's letter. Her thoughts kept ping-ponging back and forth. For every yes, there was a but – but he didn't have to, but he dated so many girls, but he was so dependable and honest even to a fault.

Two days ago, Maggie had laid it out to Kate outside of the Colonnade: people lie all the time, but if enough people tell the same story, then you have to accept that maybe they are telling the truth.

Talking to that bartender, hearing him call her brother Jim, watching the way he smiled when he looked at Jimmy's photo – that was proof of one thing. And if Jimmy was telling the truth about that one thing, then it followed that he was telling the truth about the other.

Just like that, Maggie had accepted Jimmy for lost. She had given up on her brother just as quickly as Terry had.

At least Maggie had given up for different reasons. Terry was stricken about Jimmy being gay. Thinking he was a killer was almost incidental. Maggie was the opposite. And now that the worst of all possibilities was removed, the other was one burden too many. Maggie would deal with that later after Jimmy was back home and the real Shooter was caught.

For now, they had to keep moving forward. Kate was

right about that. All they could do was work the case into the ground. Maggie was exhausted, but she couldn't even think about sleep until she knew that her brother was safe.

She heard laughter from inside Gail's room. Bud Deacon, Mack McKay, and Chip Bixby had dropped by for a visit. They were talking football with Trouble, Gail's husband. The men were joking around like they were all friends. Maggie couldn't fault them for their hypocrisy. This was what cops did. No matter who you were, no matter how much everybody hated you, if you wound up in the hospital, you were guaranteed to be paid a call by every cop on the force. They had done the same thing for Jimmy the day before.

And if Terry found him, they would do the same thing at Jimmy's funeral.

He wouldn't listen to Maggie. She had called Terry from the pay phone outside the emergency room. She had told her uncle that she knew for a fact that Jimmy wasn't the Shooter. When Terry had asked her for proof, Maggie had stuttered like a moron. What proof did she have other than a gut feeling and some secondhand information from the Sheep? It sounded like a bunch of he said/she said. Terry didn't trust doctors. Other than fingerprints and blood type, he thought forensics was a load of shit. He didn't deal in nuance. He wanted cold, hard truths. In the end, Maggie's only fallback was to ask him to trust her.

Terry was still laughing when he hung up the phone.

Maggie's transmitter beeped. 'Unit five, Dispatch. What's your ten-twenty?'

She pressed her shoulder mic. 'Dispatch, unit five. I'm at Grady Hospital.'

'Ten-four, unit five. You're requested ten-nineteen.'

'Ten-four.' Maggie let go of the mic. They wanted her back at the station. She didn't want to think about what would happen once she got there. Terry couldn't force her to quit, but he could fabricate a reason to fire her.

She looked at her watch. Kate was two minutes late. She'd practically begged Maggie to meet her here at twelve-thirty on the dot. Hopefully, she was following up on a solid lead.

'What're you doing out here, gal?' Mack was his usual three sheets to the wind. She had to step back so she didn't get a contact high. 'You should be out looking for your brother.'

Maggie bristled. 'If Jimmy wants to be found, somebody will find him.'

'Listen to tough gal here,' Chip said. He looked a hell of a lot better than Bud and Mack, but that wasn't saying much. They were all around Terry's age, but they looked like old men. Too much booze, too many late nights and early mornings. When they first started on the force, that was the only way to do the job. Now that things had changed, they didn't know how to stop.

Bud asked, 'You ever find out why Mark broke his fingernail?'

Mack chuckled at the joke, like Mark Porter's death was inconsequential.

'Yes, I did.' Maggie talked over their laughter. 'We've got a lot of leads, actually. Murphy and I have been working the case all morning. We found a witness.'

'Woo-hoo,' Bud said. He obviously didn't believe her. 'Girlie here found a witness. How about that, Chipper?'

'Guess we'll read about it in the newspaper.' Chip

smirked at the idea. 'Let's get outta here. We ain't got all day to wait for that crazy old slit.'

'No, we ain't.' Mack took his gloves out of his coat pocket. They were black leather, the same as Terry's. The same as Jimmy's. The same as everybody's.

'Detective Tits.' Chip gave Maggie a half-assed salute as they walked away.

Maggie rested her hand on her nightstick. She couldn't summon her earlier rage. Why had she told them anything? How many more mistakes was she going to make today? She'd already broken down in front of Kate. Now, she'd told Bud, Mack, and Chip a lie that they would probably radio in to Terry as soon as they reached their respective cars. How long before Terry tracked down Maggie and asked her what the hell she was doing? That was all she needed to start her afternoon, to take a beat-down in front of Kate Murphy.

'Hey, mama!' Gail yelled from down the hallway. A nurse was pushing her in a wheelchair. A large bandage was wrapped around Gail's head and covered her injured eye. Her hospital gown rode up her legs. She didn't bother to keep her knees together. 'How long you been here?'

'Not long.' Maggie felt the embarrassing urge to cry. Gail was sitting up. She was talking. She sounded like her old self.

'Damn, where'd you get them bruises?'

Maggie shook her head. She didn't trust herself to speak. This was the problem with letting yourself cry: once you gave in, you lost your ability to fight it back the next time.

Gail told the nurse, 'Thanks, doll, I got it.' She took over the chair and rolled herself into the room. 'Trouble!'

414

Trouble was lying in bed reading a car magazine. 'Oh, hey, Maggie. What's up, babe?'

'They had me in some damn machine downstairs. Wouldn't let me smoke for forty-five minutes.'

He rolled out of bed and handed Gail her purse. 'What'd they say?'

'Jack shit, same as they been saying.' She held her head at an awkward angle so she could see inside her purse. 'Did you smoke all my cigarettes, you asshole?'

'I got bored.'

Gail leveled him with a look from her remaining eye.

'There's a machine downstairs.' Trouble scampered out of the room.

'He's driving me batshit.' Gail rolled herself toward the window. 'Won't leave me alone. Keeps fetching me pillows. Filling the pitcher with ice water. You know I don't drink water. What the hell is he thinking?'

Maggie knew she didn't expect an answer.

'This thing sucks.' Gail meant the bandage. 'Can't look down because my eyeball might fall out.' She laughed at Maggie's expression. 'Shit, gal, I been through worse. Talk to me about work. Nobody will tell me squat.'

Maggie tried to put her thoughts together. She had come to Gail for a reason. 'What do you know about Alex Ballard and Leonard Johnson?'

'Not a lot. They were good cops. Hated the shit out of each other. Always fighting.'

Maggie hadn't read that in their files. 'About what?'

'Who the fuck knows?' Gail concentrated on turning her chair. 'Bosses put them together because they're both married to black chicks. Thought they would have something in common. Typical high-handed bullshit.'

Maggie guessed both men being married to blacks was some kind of connection. 'What about Greg Keen and Mark Porter? Were they married to minorities?'

'Not that I know of. Keen's a poonhound, but that comes with the job.' Gail pointed to a folder on the bedside table. 'Rick Anderson left that for you. He had to ditch Jake Coffee to run downtown and get it, which he said twice, so I'm assuming he's expecting you to thank him for it in an off-duty way.'

'I'll put a note on his windshield.' Maggie opened the file. Eduardo Rosa's rap sheet. There were six pages front and back.

'Been like Grand Central Station here all morning.' Gail clamped the brake on her wheelchair. She had turned sideways so she could see Maggie. 'Rick was here, Cal Vick. Les Leslie brought me some whiskey. Red Flemming drank half of it. Your uncle Terry finished the rest. Couple of the colored girls brought me some chocolate. Delroy and Watson. You know 'em?'

Maggie looked up from the sheet. Delroy and Watson. She could tell from the way Gail was staring at her that they'd blabbed about finding Lewis Conroy naked in a phone booth.

Gail asked, 'Did it feel good?'

'When I was doing it,' Maggie admitted. 'Afterward . . .' She shrugged. She knew Conroy deserved it. Even on top of what Delroy and Watson had planned, he deserved it. Still, Maggie felt bad. Not for Conroy, but for herself. She had lost control. She'd never done that before.

Gail said, 'It always feels good when you're doing it.'

'Does it always feel bad after?'

'Every goddamn time.'

Maggie couldn't bear Gail's scrutiny. She looked down at the rap sheet again. Eduardo Rosa's early life was typical to most criminals. Convenience store robberies. Liquor store holdups. A few years in and out of the Big House. On paper, it looked like he'd cleaned up his life. There was nothing recent in the last twenty years. Probably because Gerald had handled the family's criminal exploits.

'Edu-ardo.' Gail pronounced the name phonetically. 'Who's that cat?'

'The tranny pimp.' Maggie closed the file. 'Or at least the pimp's mother. Father. Husband?' She sounded like Kate. 'Remember the Portuguese lady?'

Gail made a face that Maggie deserved. Of course she remembered the Portuguese lady.

'She's really a man. We saw her this morning. She practically had a beard.'

'Holy shit!' Gail laughed so hard her foot kicked out. 'Hot damn!' The chair rattled from her laughter. She looked up at the ceiling to keep from doubling over. 'Oh, Jesus.'

Maggie smiled, not because it was funny, but because she was relieved that Gail could still laugh about things.

'Shit.' Gail wiped her good eye. 'Shit, man. That's a cracker. I think I peed myself.' She told Maggie, 'Really, I think I did.'

'Should I get a nurse?'

'Nah, let Trouble deal with it. He likes that stuff.' Gail stuck her hand into her purse and started blindly digging around. 'Can't believe none of those dipshits picked up on it yesterday. The entire station musta been at that house. Somebody took her statement?'

'She gave them an alternate name.' Maggie didn't go

417

into Gerald and Sir Chic. Gail had had enough fun this morning. 'Did you know Murphy's Jewish?'

'Sure. Wanda Clack told me. Read it in her file.'

Of course she did. 'She's rich, too.'

'No shit.' Gail's penchant for sarcasm had obviously recovered. 'What gave it away – the fancy accent or the car?'

Maggie couldn't bring herself to ask about the car. 'She's been lying about a lot of things.'

'*Oh, gosh,*' Gail mimicked. 'Tell me something, kid: you been sayin' you got them bruises from falling down the stairs?'

Maggie didn't answer.

Gail held up her purse so she could look inside. 'Come over here. Pull up that chair.'

Maggie sat down in front of her. 'You think she'll make a good cop?'

'Murphy?' Gail opened her compact. 'I'm still trying to puzzle that gal out. Closer.'

Maggie leaned closer.

Gail used the sponge to pat foundation on Maggie's cheek. She was gentle, but the pain made Maggie's toes curl. 'Murphy's gotta sink or swim on her own. Nothing we can do for her. She's sharp as a tack, but she's too stupid to know when to be scared.'

'She's scared of Terry.'

'Shit, he ain't gonna hurt her. It's not like she's family.'

Maggie laughed because it was probably true.

'Stop smiling. This is hard work. He clocked ya good.'

Maggie closed her eyes as Gail blended in the makeup around her eye. She couldn't recall the last time someone had taken care of her. Delia wasn't the type to fuss over her children. The few times Maggie had been sick with a cold or the flu, her mother had sent her to her room so no one else would catch it.

Even the day Maggie had come home from next door, Delia had told her to go upstairs and stay in her room. The only person who'd cared about her well-being was Deathly. He had stood by the couch in his mother's kitchen. The cords from his hearing aids were sticking out of his ears. The receiver was strapped across his chest. She had never been that close to him before. He had the kindest eyes that Maggie had ever seen.

'There you go, Miss America.' Gail had finished the makeup job. 'It's not your color, but that's the best I can do.'

Maggie took the compact so she could see herself in the mirror. Gail's skin tone was darker. The foundation was a little too tan. Still, the bruises were covered. 'Thanks.'

'Listen, baby.' Gail dropped the compact back into her purse. 'What went down yesterday. Bad shit happens. That's just how it is.'

Maggie knew she was right, but her gut kept telling her otherwise.

'You killed that fat motherfucker. That was good. I got hurt. That was bad.' She shrugged. 'That's the job. You been doin' it for five years. You're gonna do it another fifty more.' She gripped the arms of the chair. 'You got ice water in your veins, same as me, kid. Ain't nobody on this earth right now I trust more than you.'

'I feel the same way.'

'Good.' Gail nodded. 'That's out of the way. Now tell me about this BOLO on Jimmy.'

Maggie thought about Jimmy's confession, what they'd found out at Dabbler's. Maybe she didn't trust Gail as much as she wanted to. 'He just disappeared.'

'That don't sound like Jimmy.'

She tried Kate's line of reasoning. 'Don was shot right in front of him. Jimmy got shot yesterday. That's two bullets that nearly took him out in two days. I think he needed to go off somewhere and pull himself together.'

'Jimmy Lawson, your brother?' Gail sounded extremely skeptical. 'He don't sulk outta sight. Shit, no man sulks unless a woman can see him. What's the point otherwise?'

'This is different. He's not sulking. I think he really got scared.'

'And he didn't tell you where he was going? Didn't tell Terry or Bud or Chip or any of 'em?' Gail shook her head. 'Nah, kid. I don't buy it.'

'He left a note.' Maggie didn't show her what she'd transcribed. 'He said he wanted to be alone.'

'Did he say why?'

'No.' Maggie kept eye contact. She regulated her breathing. She didn't fidget or shift in her chair.

Gail saw right through it. 'You're lying to me.'

Maggie bit her lip. Even if she wanted to tell Gail, she couldn't. There was too much to explain. Maggie couldn't put herself through it again. And she couldn't tell Jimmy's secret. The gossip would be too irresistible for Gail. Plus Maggie knew from experience that as much as Gail loved to raise hell, she could be extremely judgmental when she caught other people crossing the line.

Maggie settled on telling her, 'I looked for Jimmy all night. He doesn't want to be found.' She grappled for a better lie. 'He said in his note not to look for him.'

420

'What else did he say?'

'That was it: "I'm going away. Don't look for me."
You know Jimmy. He's not gonna write a book.'

'He turn in his papers to the boss?'

'No.'

'He ask for time off?'

'No.'

'He tell your mama he was leaving?'

'No.'

Gail wasn't swayed. 'That's all right, chickie. I lie to
you sometimes, too.'

'I'm not—' Maggie caught herself. She couldn't even
lie about lying.

'You're trying to put together this case,' Gail said. 'You
think you got a line on the Shooter?'

'I don't know anything.'

'Bullshit.' Gail still thought she was lying. 'You asked
me about the cops who got killed. Why didn't you ask
me about Don?'

Maggie said the first thing that came into her head.
'Tell me about him.'

She shrugged, like she hadn't solicited the question.
'He had his demons.'

'Such as?'

'War.' Gail leaned on the arm of the chair. 'It tears
these guys up. They go in thinking it's for God and
country and they come out knowing it's all bullshit – just
a bunch of old generals playing Battleship because that's
the only way they can get their dicks up.'

'I heard Don pushed his girlfriend around.'

'Pocahontas.' Gail snorted at the name. 'Lookit, that
don't mean nothing. All them soldiers come back seeing

the world a different way. Most of 'em let it go, get on with their lives, raise a family. Some of 'em can't do it. Look at your uncle Terry. All that shit he saw over in Europe – don't think for a minute that ain't still with him. Jett almost lost an arm at Midway. Mack was captured in the Philippines. Chip and Red pissed away their souls at Guadalcanal. Who the hell knows what Rick did over in Nam. Point is, they hold on to it, too, but in different ways. That's just how it is.'

'Pocahontas,' Maggie echoed. That was the only thing she had heard. Her gut was telling her not to let it go. Don Wesley's girlfriend was American Indian. Alex Ballard and Leonard Johnson were married to black women. Jimmy didn't have a girlfriend, but he might have a boyfriend. She asked Gail, 'Do you remember Mark Porter's wife from the funeral?'

'Yeah. I think so.'

'She was white, right?'

'White as snow. Short, round, kinda looked like Totie Fields. High as a fucking kite. I saw her going for a toke behind the hearse.' Gail picked up on Maggie's train of thought. 'I know Greg Keen's wife is white, too. If she was black, I woulda heard about it. Where are you going with this, kid?'

'It's just weird that three of them had women who weren't white.'

'You gotta take Jimmy and Don out of the equation. They don't usually work nights. They were filling in for Rick Anderson and Jake Coffee.' Gail rubbed her chin in thought. 'Rick ain't got a gal that I know of, though bless his heart he's tryin'. Jake's girlfriend is all hippie-dippie. Good lookin', though. Kinda has a Marina Oswald thing goin'. Works for some group that's been trying to start a union down at the supermarket.'

'Jimmy and Don weren't the targets.' Maggie had to say the words out loud. She didn't know why she felt relieved. If her brother was going to have a target on his back, she wanted it to be because he was a cop, not because he was gay.

Gail blew out a huff of air. 'So, dead end number ten-thousand-whatever-the-fuck.' She reached into her purse. 'Shit. Where's Trouble with my cigs?'

Maggie shook her head. She was still thinking it through. Rick was one of the good ones. That's what everybody said. He helped the women out. He took up for them when he could. He didn't seem to mind that they were on the job. Jake Coffee was the same way.

So, there was a connection between four of the men at least – six if you counted Don and Jimmy.

They were all men who were bucking the system.

'Am I interrupting?' Kate stood in the open door. She was glowing again, the same way she'd looked when the elevator doors opened this morning. 'I'm sorry I'm late. The conversation took longer than I expected.'

Gail gave a raspy chuckle. 'Hey, mama, where do I get some a that conversation you just got?'

Kate blushed. 'Gail, I'm glad to see you're up and about. I'm so sorry that—'

Gail clicked her tongue.

Kate smiled, but her cheeks were still red. 'Do you mind if I use your restroom?'

'Take your time, darlin'. Looks like you need a sec.' Gail was still chuckling when Kate shut the bathroom door. 'My, my, my. That slick bitch might be a cop after all.'

Maggie didn't care about Kate. 'Gail, what we were talking about before: all of the victims. They stood up to the system.'

'What's that?' Gail was still distracted.

'Ballard and Johnson were married to black women. How did their station house feel about that?'

'How do you think? They put a goddamn noose in Ballard's locker.'

'And Jake's girlfriend. What about her?'

'Shit, she's white as you or me, but she's some kinda communist, trying to start a union like that.'

'And Rick is practically a hippie. He's the only guy I know who thinks women should be on the job.'

Gail rested her chin in her hand. She was giving it serious thought now. 'Porter voted for McGovern. Had a bumper sticker on his car.'

'So did Jake Coffee.' Maggie remembered the teasing he'd gotten at the station house. Cal Vick had revoked his parking pass.

The bathroom door opened. Kate had obviously been listening. 'Greg Keen drove a Toyota. I read it in his file.'

'She's right,' Maggie said. The toaster-sized foreign car got lost in the sea of Fords and Buicks with their extended front ends and beefed-up chassis.

Kate said, 'Keen also had a peace symbol tattooed on his arm. I saw it in the autopsy report.'

Maggie said, 'You didn't tell me that.'

'I'm sorry. The tattoo was on his upper arm, anyway. No one would see it.'

Maggie had showered in the men's locker room last night. There were no curtains, just a pole in the center of a tiled room with shower nozzles all around.

Everyone would've seen it.

Gail said, 'You know, I been thinking about that bullet that took out Sir Chic. Came all the way from across the street. Shooter musta used a rifle. That's – what? – fifty yards?'

'At least.' Maggie hadn't considered the skill involved in hitting such a precise target.

Gail said, 'I fooled around with a rifle once. You gotta know what you're doing. Take wind direction into account. Anticipate where your target's gonna move. It's not like a shotgun, where you just yank the trigger and blow a hole in the fucker.'

Kate said what they all were thinking. 'He could be a cop or a soldier.' This was the same description the bartender had given them at Dabbler's.

Gail told them, 'There's only one gun range fitted out for rifles. It's over by the women's prison. The city owns it, but there are civilians, too.' Gail frowned. She obviously didn't like where this was going. 'Shit, it's what we were saying in the car. The Shooter could be some ex-military jackass hanging around cops. You see it all the time. They can't make it through the academy, so they buzz around cops, picking up the lingo, hearing the stories. You know how we are. Give us a couple of beers and you can't shut us up.'

Kate said, 'That's how he would know the codes and procedures.'

Maggie thought about all the time Jimmy spent at the gun range. He was one of the best shots on the force. Her earlier theory floated back up. Had Jimmy met someone? Was there a man at the range who was good with a rifle?

425

And was the man more to Jimmy than just someone who knew how to handle a weapon?

Kate said, 'I remember at the range that they had targets posted on the wall. It's part of some sort of scoring system.'

'That's Jett's department. He's the rangemaster.' Maggie knew anything she said to the man would go straight back to Terry. She asked Gail, 'Can you call him?'

'Don't trust that asshole. Go down to the range and see for yourself. Murphy's right. The targets are on the wall, plain as day. They got the names written right underneath 'em.' She pointed at Maggie. 'You find out who's the top scorer, then you'll have a good suspect.'

Kate asked, 'Maggie, did you hear the radio? We're supposed to go back to the station. They upped the reward. They've been inundated with calls.'

'You go back.' Maggie stood up. 'Somebody downstairs can give you a ride.'

'I'm not going to leave you alone.' Kate had her hands on her hips. She sounded like a cop until she said, 'Don't be silly.'

Gail said, 'Both of you go. You think they're gonna write you up if you figure out who the Shooter is? Even Terry won't be able to fuck with you.' She grabbed Maggie's arm. 'Only you listen to me, sweetheart. Make sure it's by the book. You don't go handin' this off to your uncle or one of those other dumbasses. It's gotta stand up in court.'

Maggie stared at Gail. This was the closest she'd ever come to saying that Terry had planted the evidence against Edward Spivey. The gun found in the sewer grate. The bloody shirt. The two snitches who put one hand on the Bible while holding a get-out-of-jail-free card in the other.

Nobody seriously believed Terry had gotten that lucky. And the shitty part was that the case against Spivey was solid without the fake evidence. At the trial, his lawyer had used the gun and shirt as misdirection, waving both items in front of the jury while the prosecutor's case disappeared out the door.

'Okay,' Maggie said, a tacit agreement to all that was left unsaid. 'If I find anything at the range, we'll do it the right way. I'll radio Rick and Jake. We'll take it straight up to the brass.'

'Good girl.'

Kate's radio squealed with feedback. Instead of turning down the volume, she covered her ears.

Maggie turned off her transmitter. She told Kate, 'Just turn down—'

'No.' Gail told Kate, 'Turn it up. Turn up your radio.'

Kate adjusted the volume. A familiar long, drawn-out tone came out of the speaker, like someone was holding down a button on the telephone.

Maggie said, 'Change it to—'

Kate was already tuning in the restricted emergency channel.

'Ten-ninety-nine.' Terry's voice was clear as a bell. There was none of the panic from the day before. He sounded steely, resigned. 'Ten-ninety-nine, shots fired at Howell Yard. Confirmed Shooter sighting.'

'Howell Yard,' Gail said. 'That's the railroad tracks over near CT.'

Maggie focused on Terry's voice. He was too calm. There was no fear. No excitement. 'He's got Jimmy.'

32

Maggie swung the cruiser across town. The lights and siren were on, but as usual, no one cared. Cars stopped in the middle of the road. They sped up instead of getting out of the way. Maggie didn't slow for them. She didn't slow for anything – stop signs, red lights, crosswalks. She kept the gas pedal flat to the floor.

'Maggie—' Kate had to shout to be heard over the siren. 'Maggie, slow down.'

Maggie swerved into the oncoming lane to pass a truck. A car was heading straight toward them. She yanked back the wheel at the last minute.

'Maggie—'

'I know my uncle, Kate.' Maggie's throat hurt from yelling. Her palms were sweating. They kept slipping on the wheel. 'I know his voice. He said he was going to give Jimmy a cop's death. That's what he's doing.'

'He wouldn't get other people involved.'

'That's exactly what he'd do.' Maggie wiped her hands on her legs. 'He said he was going to make it look like the Shooter. Give Jimmy a hero's funeral. This is exactly how it would happen.'

'Bus!' Kate screamed. 'There's a bus!'

Maggie slammed on the brakes, banking to the left, sideswiping a Greyhound bus. Kate's window exploded. She covered her head as chunks of safety glass rained down. The car rocked to a stop.

'Kate?'

She still had her arms over her head.

'Kate?'

Slowly, she lowered her arms. Maggie saw it sink in: she wasn't cut into a million pieces, they weren't going to die.

Maggie hit the gas. The cruiser's tires squealed, the car lurched, and they shot up the street.

Kate shook chunks of glass out of her hair. She brushed it off her lap. She still didn't give up. 'I heard everything – what you and Gail were talking about. That all the victims bucked the system in some way.'

Maggie steered into the oncoming lane again. The street was empty on that side. She passed six cars, then pulled the wheel back to the right.

Kate said, 'What if Terry is the Shooter?'

Maggie looked at her, then looked back at the road.

'He gave that whole speech in the garage about how liberals and minorities are ruining the world.'

'You can hear that same speech in just about every squad room in the city.'

'Terry was in the army, right?'

'Marines.' Peachtree was straight ahead. Maggie kept her foot to the floor as the cruiser crested the intersection.

'Shit.' Kate grabbed the dashboard.

The wheels left the pavement.

The cruiser bounced down the road. Maggie's head hit

the ceiling. She fought the steering wheel to keep the tires straight.

Kate waited until she was back in control. 'If Terry's the Shooter, he could've taken Jimmy. This could be part of his plan. Take Jimmy and frame him for the crimes.'

Maggie flew past another car. Then another.

'He could've forced Jimmy to write the note. The end part – the apology. That could've been a code.' Kate's voice got louder. 'Maybe Jimmy was trying to send you a message.'

Maggie couldn't think about it. No matter if Kate was right or wrong, the only thing that mattered was stopping Terry before he killed Jimmy.

They were nearing the Howell Wye. The factories gave way to overgrown lots. The cars in the street were missing wheels and engines. Broken glass cracked under the cruiser's tires.

Maggie heard the trains in the distance. The clack of their wheels, the rumble down the tracks. She slowed down so she wouldn't miss the entrance. The gates to the abandoned yard were usually chained shut, but today they were wide open. Maggie took the turn down the long stretch of gravel road. About a hundred yards ahead were two office buildings, one on each side of the dead-end street, both five stories high. Each took up half a city block.

The wye was two football fields away, but Maggie felt the heavy vibrations through the floor of the cruiser. The shaking got worse as they got closer. The steering wheel clattered. The rumbling trains spread an earthquake through the ground.

The Howell rail yard had been a main artery until the

Tilford and Inman yards merged a half mile up the tracks. The business end had moved upstream, too. Now the wye was nothing but a thoroughfare to the larger yards. The offices were no longer filled with workers. The parking spaces were overgrown with weeds. Maggie had been here on calls before. Every cop in her precinct ended up at the wye at least once a month. The looming buildings and relative remoteness offered cover for criminal enterprise. Drug deals. Violent bums. Dead hoboes. Stolen merchandise stashed in the abandoned offices. Girls dragged inside so the trains would mask their screams.

Murders planned.

Maggie stopped the car. There was no more going forward. At least twenty cops were already here. Their cruisers were scattered like pick-up sticks along the roadway. At the end of the long stretch was Terry. He was surrounded by a group of men. He was putting a team together. They were huddled together between the office buildings, soldiers planning their attack.

She told Kate, 'Stay here.'

Maggie was out of the car and jogging up the street before Kate could object. Mack McKay rushed past two-handing a shotgun. Red Flemming followed with a rifle. She had watched enough training drills to know what was happening. They were setting up a perimeter so the suspect couldn't escape. A helicopter hovered overhead. Bud Deacon was pulling barrier vests out of his trunk. Jett Elliott looked sober as a judge as he pocketed a handful of speedloaders.

Kate ran up from behind. She was breathing hard, but she kept up. Her arms were bent. Her equipment was pounding into her hips and legs the same as Maggie's. She looked left and right. Maggie did the same until they were a couple of yards from Terry. She slowed down so she could hear him.

'There.' Terry pointed to the building on the left. 'The shots came from the third floor. The Shooter's still inside. We've got the back and sides covered. My team will take the front. Any one of you sees Jimmy, shoot to kill.' Terry banged the hood of the car with his hand. 'Let's go! Move it!'

A dozen men streamed toward the building. There was no door to kick in. Once they were inside, they fanned out into two teams to sweep the building bottom to top. Three men stayed in the street, guns ready, in case the target ran out. Rick Anderson was one of them. His face was grave. He barely glanced her way.

Terry screamed into the radio, 'Dispatch, get these goddamn trains stopped.'

Maggie said, 'Terry.'

He spun around. 'What the fuck are you doing here?'

Maggie's revolver was in her hand. She couldn't remember pulling it. She had to raise her voice to be heard over the trains. 'I'm not going to let you kill him.'

Terry wasn't afraid of the gun. 'You let your faggot brother get away and you pull your weapon on me?'

Heads turned. Rick Anderson nearly dropped his shotgun.

Terry said, 'Jake Coffee's dead. Shot just like the others.'

Maggie looked at Rick. She could tell from his expression that what Terry had said was true. He was visibly stricken. She had never seen him in so much pain. 'What happened?'

Rick shook his head.

'Tell her,' Terry ordered.

Rick cleared his throat. He couldn't meet Maggie's gaze. 'I was downtown pulling that rap sheet for you. Jake was patrolling on his own.' He didn't say the words, but the blame rose up like a shard of broken glass between them. 'Chip heard Jake send an all clear on a possible loiter. Then he requested a twenty-nine, same as you found in the Shooter files. Chip came here to check it out and . . .'

Rick wasn't looking at the ground anymore. Maggie followed his line of sight. The body was in front of the building on the other side of the street. The sun bathed Jake Coffee in a gruesome light. He was lying on his stomach. His arms and legs were spread. His head was turned toward the street. A perfect black hole pierced the center of his forehead. His pants had been pulled down.

All she could say was 'No.'

Terry took advantage of the distraction. He grabbed the gun out of Maggie's hand.

Before she could react, he slammed his fist into her face.

Maggie hit the ground hard. Her lungs rattled. Gravel bit into her scalp. Her jaw felt loose. She tasted blood in her mouth.

Terry tossed the revolver to Rick. He stood over Maggie. He raised his fist again.

'Stop!' Kate swung her nightstick. The metal baton cracked against Terry's head. He was dazed for half a second. Then he grabbed Kate by the front of her shirt. Her feet left the ground. He pulled back his fist.

Then for no discernible reason, he let her go.

Maggie saw Kate's shoes gently touch the gravel. There wasn't even a puff of dust.

Terry went down on one knee. He reached for Kate. Maggie's first thought was that the scene was something out of a movie, the guy kneeling in front of the girl as he asked her to marry him.

But Terry wasn't asking for anything. He looked down at his stomach. A large spot of blood flowered open across his white shirt.

The trains were too loud. Maggie didn't hear the gunshots. She saw them. Gravel spit up at her feet. Holes blistered the hood of the car. The three men in the street returned fire. They couldn't pin down a target. Their shots went wild. Rick fired his shotgun into the air. Maggie didn't want to be here when the lead came hurtling back down.

She ran toward her revolver. A bullet zinged into the ground in front of her. Maggie turned back toward the front gates, but another bullet stopped her. Panic threatened to take hold. She didn't have her gun. She couldn't find cover. Kate was crouched down with her arms over her head. Men were yelling. Shots were coming from the teams inside the left-hand building. Confusion rained down with every bullet.

'Kate!' Maggie screamed, running toward the building on the right.

She knew Kate would follow. Maggie jumped over Jake Coffee's body. She didn't stop once they were inside. She ran through the first open doorway she could find. The room was compact, obviously a front office. Filing cabinets were laid on their sides. Paper littered the floor.

Maggie hurtled through the room, Kate close on her

heels. She ran through another open doorway. They were in the main part of the office building. The space was as large as an aircraft hangar. The ceiling was at least twenty feet high. The back wall was fifty feet away. The width of the room was twice that. Rusted metal trestles criss-crossed the air. Hundreds of desks were stacked two and three deep in the middle of the floor. Broken chairs and metal bookshelves lined the walls.

Maggie pulled Kate behind an overturned desk. They pressed their backs against the top. They said nothing for the first twenty seconds. They were breathing too hard. Maggie's heart was flipping in her chest. Her head was ringing. Her jaw still felt loose where Terry had punched her in the face.

She looked down. Kate was holding her hand. Her radio was on. Gunfire from outside echoed through the speaker. Men were yelling at dispatch for help. The helicopter pilot was screaming about taking a hit. Maggie reached behind Kate's back and turned off the transmitter.

'Jake Coffee is dead,' Kate mumbled. 'He's dead. Terry's dead. Anthony's dead. Chic's dead.'

'It wasn't Jimmy,' Maggie told her. She had never been more certain of anything in her life. 'It wasn't him.'

Kate nodded. 'I know.'

Maggie squeezed her hand. There was a lull in the trains. The helicopter's chopping blades started to recede. Shots were still being fired at the front of the building.

They couldn't hide here, not least of all because the men outside might need their help. Maggie looked around the room, desperate for a way out. There were massive windows along the walls. The sun splashed like water across the hardwood floors. The glass panes were broken. The metal frames were cut into squares that were too narrow for escape. And any one of them would offer a clear view for the Shooter if he decided to take out the two cops cowering behind an overturned desk. Their position in the vast, open space was almost worse than the street.

'Over there.' Kate pointed to the back of the room.

Maggie saw another stack of desks in the far right corner. There was a door beside them. Metal. No window. Rusted red hinges. Maggie had never been this far into the buildings. She didn't know where the doorway would lead, or if someone was waiting for them on the other side.

Kate startled like a cat. She crouched down lower. Her hand covered her head. 'Did you hear that?' She was panting again. 'I heard something. From the other office. From the front of the room.'

Maggie reached for her revolver and found her empty holster. She had to use Kate's gun again. She'd been issued a replacement yesterday. Cleaning oil covered the grip. The weapon had never been fired. Was the pin properly aligned? Were the sights true? Would the firing mechanism jam?

There was no easy way to find out.

Maggie tightened her hand around the revolver. She cocked the hammer. Her heart was beating so hard that she felt it inside her tongue. She had to make herself move. Quickly, she turned around and peered over the desk. She checked the doorway at the front of the room.

Empty.

Or maybe not.

There was a shadow across the open doorway. The bright sunlight from the front office windows made the lines crisp. Was the shadow from a filing cabinet? A chair? Another overturned desk? Maggie stared at the shaded area so long that her vision blurred. She blinked her eyes to clear them.

The shadow moved.

Someone was on the other side of the door. He had his back to the wall. And then he didn't. His shadow spread up the opposite wall as he pressed his shoulder to the doorjamb. There was something in his hand. Something long and skinny that looked a lot like a gun.

Maggie stood up before her shaking legs made her slump down. Her heart beat up her neck and into her skull. Every instinct was telling her to hide, but she couldn't give in to emotion right now.

She walked quickly and quietly across the room. If the Shooter was behind the doorjamb, her only advantage was to be to his left rather than straight in front of him. She silently begged Kate to keep her head down, just as she silently begged whatever god was listening to not let either of them get shot in the face.

Maggie heard her shoe squeak against a wooden floorboard.

She stopped. How had she been able to hear that?

The trains weren't running. The floor had stopped vibrating. Someone had halted the rail traffic. The lack of rumble was almost deafening.

Gunshot.

Maggie ducked, but the sound had come from outside. Two seconds later, the shot was returned.

Maggie came out of her crouch. She looked for the

shadow behind the door. He was gone. Or maybe he had fired his gun at someone in the street.

Behind her, Kate gasped.

Maggie swung around. Chip Bixby stood a few feet away from Kate. He had a gun in his hand – a hogleg, an Old West–style six-shooter that could take off a man's head at twenty paces. The gun was pointed toward the ground. Maggie's gun was pointed at his chest.

Chip glared at her until she lowered the revolver. He pulled Kate up by the arm and shoved her toward the rear exit. He waved for Maggie to follow. She did as she was told. Maybe Chip knew a back way out. Maybe they could sneak around to the front of the building and take the Shooter by surprise. Or they could go upstairs and give cover to the men in the street. Even now, Maggie could hear the occasional stray gunfire. Rick was out there. He had lost his partner. Maggie wasn't going to be responsible for him losing his life.

She walked backward toward Chip. Kate had already disappeared behind the rear door. Chip was standing in front of it, his hogleg trained on the only other doorway in the room. His eyes slid back and forth between the open windows and the entrance. Sweat poured down his face. The front of his shirt was stuck to his chest. He waved for her to hurry.

Maggie wanted to run toward the exit, but she forced herself to appear calm. Her revolver was straight out in front of her. She covered the space in front of her. Her eyes narrowed onto the same doorway Chip was drawing down on. She was six feet from the exit when the shadow came back.

This time, the shadow was more than a shadow. The

muzzle of a gun stuck around the corner. Even from a distance, Maggie could see the sights sticking up from the tip of the revolver.

And the black-gloved hand that held the weapon.

Chip grabbed her collar and pulled her behind the door. Maggie fell back against the wall. They were in a stairwell that went straight up the back of the building. The emergency exit. The door to the outside wasn't just locked, it was chained. She pushed as hard as she could. The chains rattled. A crack of light showed. There was not enough space for them to squeeze through.

'Maggie,' Kate whispered. She was already halfway up the stairs. She stood on the landing. Her nightstick was out. She held it low and angled the way that Maggie had shown her. 'This way.'

Chip fired the hogleg. The air rattled with the sound. He ducked behind the door to use it as a shield. 'Go!'

Fear took over. Maggie bolted up the stairs. She heard a bullet thunk into the metal door. The Shooter was coming after them. Vomit roiled into her mouth. She fought back the panic even as her brain was yelling at her to slow down, to think, to be logical. The stairwell was poured concrete. The only light came from the open floors at every other landing. Each new landing would represent a different tomb in which to trap them.

'Kate!' Maggie yelled. She was running straight up. She wasn't stopping.

The hogleg fired again. The boom echoed like cannon fire. The responding pop was a smaller-caliber weapon. Two different sounds. Two different guns.

Maggie rounded the next floor and stopped. She strained to hear something other than the blood rushing through her ears. Kate was still running at least one floor above. There were heavier footsteps on the stairs below her. One set? Two? Three? Everything echoed. Heavy breathing. Scuffing feet. Was it Chip? Was it the Shooter? Was it the mysterious shadow from the doorway?

She crouched with her gun out in front of her. Her finger almost twitched when Chip rounded the corner. He waved for her to keep going. Maggie didn't hesitate. She ran up the stairs. The pop of the revolver echoed in her ears. A chunk of concrete splintered near her head. There was another pop. The air shimmered. The stairs felt like they were crumbling under her feet.

Maggie took the next flight at a crouch. She stopped on the landing and pressed her back against the wall. Kate's footsteps had slowed. She was getting tired. Maggie was the opposite. Her heart was hammering. Her guts felt twisted. She couldn't get her breathing under control. She was going to hyperventilate if she didn't slow it down.

For just a second, she closed her eyes. She concentrated on controlling the air going into and out of her lungs.

Jake Coffee.

Maggie couldn't get the man's face out of her head. The bullet hole that unblinkingly stared back. Rick's forlorn expression when he told her what had happened.

Jake's girlfriend would get the news. His baby brother, his mother and father, his whole family would hear about what had been done to him. Executed in the street. His pants pulled down.

Maggie opened her eyes.

Why were Jake's pants pulled down?

The hogleg went off. The revolver returned fire. They were close. Too close.

Maggie ran up another flight of stairs. She stopped again, straining to make out sounds. There was a slow shuffling from above. Why was Kate going up at all? Had she panicked, or had Chip told her to keep going to the roof? They were three against one with two guns. Why run up the stairs when they could stake out a better tactical position on any one of the floors? Chip had run the SWAT team before he walked away. He taught tactical support at the academy. He knew the procedures better than all of them put together.

Maggie felt her lips part.

Chip knew their routines. He knew all of their codes.

He had been an Army Ranger in the jungles of Guadalcanal.

He didn't take a breath without assessing the tactical advantages.

And he hadn't been right since Edward Spivey walked. Everybody knew Chip was screwing a prostitute when his partner was murdered. The guilt was a heavy burden, but Spivey's acquittal had nearly broken him. Over the last few months, Chip had been showing up at the house unannounced, dragging Jimmy out of bed, sometimes calling Terry to come over, so he could rehash the good old days he'd had with Duke Abbott.

Every cop loved telling stories, but Chip somehow managed to make them sound like checklists. He had the annoying habit of listing things out. Steps he and Duke took to isolate the aggressor. Options they had explored when choosing their weapons. Chip talked about their targets like they were his prey. The deranged husband who took his wife hostage. The bank robber who hunkered down in the back of a Cadillac. The teenager who got high on PCP and chased after his mother with a hatchet.

They were all crazy, Chip claimed. But that was okay. He was crazy, too.

Crazy like a fox.

The hogleg fired, just like it did every time Maggie stopped. Just like it had downstairs when Maggie had tried to break the chains on the locked exit door.

Chip had been first on the scene. All the information about what happened to Jake Coffee would have flowed from his mouth. He had told Terry that the Shooter was in the other building, that the shots had come from the third floor. Meanwhile, Chip had staked out a spot across from the action.

There was no other way to explain his sudden appearance downstairs. Maggie and Kate had come through the front door. The exit was barred, the windows too narrow for escape. The shadow they had seen in the doorway was probably cast by a cop who'd been trying to help. The hogleg had likely stopped him cold, just like the rifle shot had stopped Terry. Maggie could practically see it in her mind's eye: Chip leaning out the first-floor window, aiming down on Terry out in the street.

But why shoot Terry? Maggie didn't have to consider the question for long. In all of Chip's stories, he was the one who always took the shot. He wouldn't let Terry get the kill. They were both the same kind of man, but only one of them could be in charge.

The hogleg fired.

Maggie didn't startle this time. Instead, she gripped her revolver with both hands and pointed it down the stairs.

Chip had lured Jake Coffee to the rail yard, and now

he was trying to get Kate and Maggie up to the roof.

The hogleg fired again. Then the revolver. Or maybe it wasn't a revolver. Maybe it was a .25 caliber Saturday night special.

Maggie heard Kate's footsteps again. She looked up. The light was sharp. Kate was almost to the top. Slowly, Maggie climbed to the next landing. Sunlight. The roof door. She couldn't go down. The only option was up.

She took the last flight of stairs full on. Maggie wasn't stupid enough to think that Chip wanted her on that roof. She would be collateral. It was Kate he was after. Like all the other victims, Kate fit the kill criteria; everything about her said she didn't belong. She was a woman. She was independent. She was a Jew.

Maggie's only chance to save them both was to get a tactical advantage. The stairwell was a deathtrap. She needed to be waiting for Chip the minute he came through the roof door. The afternoon sun would blind him. Her gun would do the rest.

She looked up. She could almost touch it. Blue sky. The flat white asphalt of the roof. She raced toward the open door at the top of the stairs.

And then an arm snared around her neck. Maggie fell back. The warm muzzle of the hogleg pressed against her temple.

Chip said, 'Drop the gun.'

Maggie hesitated.

'Do it.'

She threw the revolver as hard as she could out the door.

33

Kate stood on the white asphalt roof. She could barely catch her breath. The sunlight sent needles into her eyes. She had to cover her face for a moment just to get her bearings. The door was behind her. The rail yard was to her left.

Jimmy was on the ground in front of her.

He saw Kate, and his eyes went wide with fear.

She rushed to his side. Jimmy's hands and ankles were tied together. Sealing tape covered his mouth and was wrapped around his head. She didn't know where to start. The twine around his wrists cut into the skin. The knots were red with his blood. Kate started to pick at the threads.

And then she heard a noise behind her.

Kate turned. Her eyes were still playing tricks on her. She saw a gun flying through the air. A revolver, just like the one she carried on her belt.

Jimmy groaned. His shoulders twitched. He was looking at the gun.

Kate was looking at Maggie.

Chip Bixby had his arm wrapped around her neck. A large pistol was in his hand. Kate had never seen anything like it. The barrel was at least a foot long. He had his finger resting on the trigger guard the same as he had taught them at the gun range.

'You,' Kate said, because she could see it now. Everything that had made her think Terry Lawson was the Shooter could also be applied to this repulsive maggot.

Chip told Kate, 'Thanks for runnin' all the way up here, darlin'. I didn't wanna have to drag you.'

Kate looked at the revolver lying on the roof. It was twenty feet away.

'Go ahead.' His voice held a challenge. 'You think you can reach that gun before I pull this trigger?'

Kate's hand went to her chest. She had to say the words before she truly believed them. 'You're the Shooter.'

'Smart gal.'

'Kate,' Maggie said. 'Get the gun.'

Kate moved because she always followed Maggie's orders. And then she stopped when Chip's finger went to the trigger.

He said, 'You really wanna try your luck?'

Kate felt something trembling against her chest. She realized it was her hand.

He said, 'Take a step back.'

Kate didn't move. She could finally see how Chip had brought all of this into play. He had told Kate to run up to the roof as fast as she could. Obviously, Jimmy was already up here. Now Maggie had a gun to her head. This was no happenstance, all of them standing on this rooftop in this rail yard. They were all exactly where Chip wanted them to be.

Maggie said, 'Don't do this.' Her body was stiff against Chip's. Her fingers dug into the back of his arm. 'You think you're honoring Duke's memory by murdering a bunch of cops?'

'They weren't cops,' Chip hissed. 'They were vermin. Nigger lovers, hippies, kikes, greaseballs, fucking pansies.' His eyes were on Kate, and she knew that she was the kike he was talking about.

She told him, 'I'm just trying to do my job.'

'Bullshit, lady. You don't even know what the job is.'

His disgust was so palpable that Kate felt it like a fist clutching her heart.

Chip said, 'I seen it with my old man. You let one in, they bring another, and another, and pretty soon they're running the show and your whole fucking world's upside down.' He pressed the muzzle harder against Maggie's temple. 'All I'm doing is putting things back where they belong.'

Kate asked the only question that mattered. 'How is this going to end?'

'Ain't you more curious about how it all started?' He showed his small, brown teeth in a smile. 'Think about it, baby. When did this all start for you?'

Kate didn't have to think about it. Her part in all of this began that first day on the shooting range. Chip Bixby had suggestively pressed his body against Kate's as he'd shown her how to hold a weapon. She had been disgusted, but there was no other choice because she had to learn how to use a gun. That initial uneasiness had never really gone away. It followed her to her parents' house. It followed her around town. And lately, that initial disquiet from six weeks ago had grown into a full-blown feeling of paranoia.

The glow of a man's cigarette outside her parents'

house. The smell of smoke in her hotel room. Patrick's missing dog tags.

She said, 'You've been following me.'

'*Watching* you.'

With a sickening clarity, Kate understood the difference.

Watching implied careful attention. Watching meant you noted gestures, recorded even the most inane details. Kate thought about Chip's hands roughly grabbing her hips at the range. The rancid smell of his breath. The stench on his clothes from the chain smoking. The revolting knowledge that the stiffening in his pants would probably be later remedied with Kate in mind.

Was that why he was watching her? Was he gathering more fantasies?

No.

What was happening on this roof was no fantasy. Chip was planning to take her.

'This won't work.' Kate struggled to keep her voice from wavering. 'Those men on the street will come up here eventually. How are you going to explain three dead bodies?'

'I'll tell 'em the truth. I chased all of you up here, but I was just a second too late. Jimmy killed Maggie. And then he knocked you out before I put a bullet in his head.' Chip started smiling again. 'Don't worry, sweetheart, I gotta nice, safe room all ready for you. Ask Jimmy. You can yell as loud as you want and nobody's gonna hear you.'

'I'd rather die than let you touch me.'

'We'll see how you feel in a week, Kaitlin.' He grimaced at the name. 'Ain't that what your mama calls you?'

The breath left Kate's body.

'Put on that white nightgown. Wrap yourself in that purple blanket.'

Kate's hand went to her mouth. She wore a white nightgown when she stayed at her parents' house. The purple blanket was on the end of her bed. There was a window right across the room. She left it cracked open most nights. Had Chip been standing on the other side? Had he watched her sleep?

Kate's heart stopped at one particular memory.

Had Chip been there the night she finished what Philip had started? Kate had left the covers off so she could feel the breeze on her skin. She had been at her most vulnerable. Her most open.

'Oh, God,' Kate whispered. 'What did you see?'

'You think I don't know what a dirty Jew looks like when she spreads her legs?'

Bile rushed up her throat.

'I know you, Kaitlin. I know everything about you. And what I didn't know, I heard from Oma.'

Kate felt punched in the stomach. Oma. How did he know her name?

There was a shout from the street below. Police sirens bellowed in the distance.

Chip obviously heard the sounds, too. He unwrapped his arm from Maggie's neck. 'Get on your knees.'

Maggie didn't move, so he pushed her down. The gun was inches from her head.

'Don't,' Kate begged. This wasn't happening. She couldn't watch Maggie die. 'Please. We can talk about this.'

'Talking time is over.' Chip unplugged Maggie's radio

448

from her transmitter. 'You know what to do, Lawson.'

Jimmy pounded his shoulder against the roof. Maggie looked at her brother. Her jaw was locked. Kate had seen her like this once before. She was resigned to her fate. She was done fighting. She laced together her fingers.

'Maggie, don't.' Kate couldn't let this happen. The revolver was lying on the roof less than twelve feet away. She took a step toward it.

Eleven feet away.

Chip said, 'Hands on the back of your head.'

'Maggie.' Kate took another step.

Ten feet away.

'Hurry up, Lawson.'

Maggie put her hands on the top of her head.

'Don't do it,' Kate pleaded. There had to be something that she could do. Kate took another small step.

Nine feet.

Another step – eight feet away.

Seven.

Kate couldn't stop counting. She always counted when she was afraid. The number of lightning strikes before the thunder. The number of times her heart beat before Patrick's plane disappeared into the sky.

The number of bullets fired in the stairwell as she ran up to the roof.

Kate asked Maggie, 'How many bullets are in his gun?'

Maggie said nothing, but Kate could read her thoughts. This was how it happened. This is what Chip had done to Ballard and Johnson, Keen and Porter.

Kate said, 'I heard six shots that were louder than the others. I counted them.'

Maggie turned her head toward Kate. She was dumbstruck.

'How many?' Kate repeated.

'Six.'

Kate lunged for the revolver. There was nothing graceful about the movement. Her shoulder slammed into the roof as she scooped up the gun.

She was too late.

Chip pulled the trigger.

Click-click.

Kate had been right. His big gun was empty, and her little revolver was pointing directly at his chest.

She said, 'Drop it.'

Chip stared at her for a moment. He let the gun fall from his hand. Kate's eyes followed the weapon as it clattered to the rooftop.

'Kate!' Maggie yelled.

Again, Kate was too late.

She had made the same damn mistake she'd been making all week. Her eyes were looking in the wrong direction. Chip had dropped one gun, but with his other hand, he had reached behind his back and pulled out another.

Kate remembered the weapon from that first day of roll call. Chip had held it above his head for all to see. The Raven MP-25. Six in the magazine, one in the chamber.

'You have one bullet,' Kate told him. 'Unless it's magic, you can only kill one of us.'

'You sure about that count, Kaitlin?' Chip sounded calm. He could have been talking about the weather. 'Sure enough to bet your life?'

'I'll shoot you in the head.'

'I taught you how to use that thing, sweetheart. You couldn't hit the side of a bus with a machine gun.'

'Are you willing to bet your life on that?' Kate struggled to keep the fear out of her voice. Her hands dripped with sweat. She hadn't cocked the hammer. Had Maggie already cocked it? Would she throw the gun onto the roof without the safety engaged?

Chip said, 'Why don't you put down that gun before you hurt yourself?'

'Why don't you kiss my ass?'

Chip took the bait. Kate had his full attention now. 'I been wantin' to grab that ass since day one.'

She held his gaze as she let her thumb travel up the side of the gun. 'I thought you already grabbed my ass.'

'I sure as fuck did.'

She felt the cylinder release, the metal backstrap that scooped underneath the hammer. 'Did you like it?'

'You think I didn't know what you were doing?' Chip was making Kate's mistake, no longer looking for threats. 'Pressing that tight ass against my cock, working your kike magic.'

'I remember that day.' Kate felt the three ridges that scored the top of the hammer. 'You said the person with the most bullets always wins.'

'Oh, darlin', I'm gonna win this.'

'No, you're not.' Kate pulled the trigger.

The hammer was already cocked. The firing pin dropped. The bullet fired.

Chip's shoulder jerked back. His gun went off.

Maggie fell to the ground.

For one heart-stopping second, Kate thought Maggie

451

had been hit, but the bullet had pierced the asphalt a few inches from her leg.

Kate heard a familiar noise.

Click-click.

Chip was pointing the gun at Maggie's head, but Kate had been right. The magazine was empty.

He dropped the gun. He pulled open his shirt. Blood dribbled in a steady stream from his shoulder. The hole was black at the center, just like the holes he had put in his victims. Just like the hole in the roof that had almost been a hole in Maggie's head. The bright red blood cut a line down his torso and pooled into the waist of his pants. His chest hair was gray and splotchy. There was a tattoo of a red fox above his heart.

Patrick's dog tags were around his neck.

Kate stood up. She clutched the revolver in both hands. There was no more sweating. Her skin was cool. She was not afraid or panicked anymore. She was just certain that she was holding the gun that was going to kill this man. 'Take those off.'

'Come and get 'em.' Chip hooked his thumb through the metal chain. He actually winked at her. 'You better be careful, sweetheart. Your doorman sees a badge, he'll let anybody up.'

'Give them back.' Kate's voice was flat. She was dead inside – dead as Patrick. Dead as Chip Bixby was going to be. 'Take them off right now.'

'You really thought you could do this job?'

'I said take them off.'

'Even your own mama don't want you wearing the badge.'

'Shut up,' Kate ordered.

'That's what Liesbeth told me. Her and your granny. I talked to them last week.'

He was lying. He had to be lying.

'Saw them Jew tattoos on their arms. You'd never guess it, right? Coupla blonde slits. Guess Hitler wasn't fooled.' He smiled again. 'Too bad he didn't finish the job.'

'Shut your goddamn mouth.'

'Are you going to finish the job, Kaitlin?' The smile had turned into a grin. 'Nice couch they got in the living room. What do you call that color, turquoise?'

Kate was a statue. Her lungs stopped breathing. Her heart stopped beating. Her finger was frozen on the trigger. She could see Chip on the turquoise couch. Sitting back with his legs spread wide as if he owned the place. Oma and Liesbeth would offer him cigarettes and cocktails, and why? Because they had no idea that a monster had talked his way into their home.

'Do it,' Maggie said. 'Shoot him.'

Kate wanted to. With every ounce of her being, she yearned to pull the trigger.

But she couldn't – not because she didn't have it in her, but because Chip Bixby so obviously wanted her to. Even now, Kate could hear the men on the street. They had heard the gunfire on the roof. They were probably working their way up the stairs, clearing each floor as they made their way to the top.

Chip had obviously heard them, too, and he'd decided he'd rather be killed than taken alive.

Kate put her finger back on the trigger guard. She told Maggie, 'Handcuff him.' When Maggie didn't move, Kate threw down her own set of cuffs. 'We're taking him in.

You and me. We're arresting this asshole and we're going to take him in.'

Maggie didn't move.

'Let's go,' Kate told her. 'You and me, Lawson. Not the guys. Us two tough gals are going to handcuff the great Chip Bixby and throw him in the back of our squad car and take him in.'

Maggie took her time coming around. She reluctantly picked up the handcuffs. 'I get to book him.'

'I wouldn't presume to have it otherwise.'

Maggie clicked open the cuffs. She was nodding now as she worked it out in her head. 'I'll fingerprint him. Take his picture for the papers. Toss him into the cell.'

'May I accompany you?'

'You mean when I put him in the cell?' Maggie smiled. 'Sure. Both of us will throw him in a cell in front of all the bad guys.'

'No.' Chip took a step back. Then another. 'Fuck no.'

'Stop.' Kate's finger curled around the trigger.

Chip kept backing up. 'You two snatches ain't taking me in.'

'Stop.' Kate's voice was stronger now. She was walking toward him even as he kept walking away. 'I'll shoot you again.'

Chip didn't stop. He took another step back, then another, until his heels hit the parapet. He stepped up. He stepped out. He hung in the air for less than a second.

And he was gone.

At first, neither Maggie nor Kate moved. Then they

both rushed to the edge of the building. The scene below was eerily similar to the one they'd found when they arrived. Except this time, instead of Terry Lawson surrounded by a group of cops, it was Chip Bixby with a dozen guns trained on him.

They needn't have bothered. Chip was obviously dead. His limbs were splayed. His skull had cracked open. Blood was everywhere.

'Up there!' one of the cops shouted. Rick Anderson. He had his shotgun on his shoulder.

Kate felt a bout of vertigo come on. She dropped to her knees so she wouldn't tumble after Chip. The revolver fell to her side. 'Oh, my God.'

Maggie ran to Jimmy.

'My God,' Kate repeated. What had just happened? She should have shot him. She should've put a bullet in his head before he jumped off the roof.

Kate laughed. Was she really thinking that she should've killed Chip Bixby before he killed himself? She heard her father's voice in her head: talk about beating a dead horse.

Her father.

Her Oma and mother.

Kate shivered uncontrollably.

Chip Bixby had been in their house. He had sat in their living room, talked to Liesbeth and Oma. He had planned to take Kate away from her family. He had the place ready for her. A room where she could yell and no one would hear her scream. Kate would've been gone. Her family would've lived out the rest of their lives never knowing what had happened to her.

Just like Oma's father and mother, her brother and son. There one moment, vanished the next.

'Kate!' Maggie yelled. 'Kate! Help me!'

Maggie was using her teeth to tear the tape around Jimmy's head.

Kate had to let this go. She had to bury it somewhere safe in her psyche where it couldn't hurt her. Chip was dead. Kate hadn't been his victim. She hadn't been anyone's victim. She was a police officer. She had a gun she'd used to stop a suspect. She and her partner had closed a case. Kate had helped solve a crime that had been haunting the city since before she'd even decided to put on the uniform.

Her uniform. How many times had Chip watched her take off her uniform?

Kate shook her head, trying to rid her mind of the terrible thought. She pushed herself up. She wiped her hands on her pants. She walked toward Maggie and Jimmy to see what she could do to help.

Maggie finally tore through the tape. Jimmy groaned as the adhesive pulled away from his skin. Maggie wrapped her arms around her brother. They were both crying. Neither one of them spoke.

Until Jimmy said, 'I'm sorry.'

'It's all right,' Maggie soothed. She stroked his back, kissed his cheek. 'It's gonna be okay. Everything's fine.'

Kate looked away. She felt tears in her eyes. She didn't know for whom she was crying. Herself? Patrick? Maggie and Jimmy? Her parents? Her Oma? Maybe Kate was just relieved. That was the lie that she would tell herself. She wasn't scared. She didn't feel hunted or violated at the most intimate level possible.

She was just relieved.

'You're okay,' Maggie told her brother. 'You're safe now.'

'Everybody knows.' Jimmy sobbed. Like his sister had a few moments ago, he sounded resigned to the fate that awaited him. 'Just shoot me, Maggie. Just throw me off the roof before they do.'

Maggie was crying, too. 'I won't let them hurt you. They'll have to come through me.'

'It's too late.' He was clearly devastated. 'I'm sorry. I'm so fucking sorry.'

There were loud voices in the stairway. Kate could hear the footsteps pounding up the concrete treads.

'Just kill me,' Jimmy begged. 'Give me the gun and I'll do it.'

'No.' Maggie wouldn't let him go. 'Jimmy, I don't care. I don't care about any of it. All that matters is that you're okay.'

'I'm not okay.'

'Yes, you are.' She held him tighter. 'We'll get through this. We will.'

Jimmy didn't respond. He stared over Maggie's shoulder at the door, waiting for the judgment that was certain to come. There were more shouts echoing up the stairwell as the floors were cleared. Every man on the street was making his way up to the rooftop. Every man had probably heard what Terry Lawson had said to Maggie about his own nephew.

You let your faggot brother get away.

Kate said, 'Chip lied.'

They both looked up at her.

She shrugged her shoulder. 'He admitted it.'

Maggie asked, 'What are you talking about?'

Kate spelled it out for them. 'Chip admitted that he

457

lied about Jimmy right before he jumped off the roof.' She put on her haughtiest Buckhead tone. 'Gosh, you guys were standing right here the whole time. Didn't you hear him say it, too?'

DAY FOUR
THURSDAY

34

Maggie sat in a chair outside Terry's hospital room.

He was going to live.

Maggie couldn't let herself get used to the idea. All day yesterday and through the night, she had let herself think that he wasn't going to make it. The doctors had said it would be touch-and-go for twenty-four hours, and here they were on the other side and Terry was still alive.

Nobody knew what kind of life he was going to have. The bullet had grazed Terry's spine. There was a lot of swelling. Part of the bullet was still in there. There was no way the fragments could be safely removed. They didn't know if he would walk again. He couldn't feel anything below his waist. All that they knew was he could breathe on his own.

Which meant that he could talk.

Not that Maggie had spoken to her uncle. She stayed in the chair outside his room and watched the door. Terry's visiting hours were limited. There wasn't the usual steady stream of cops floating in and out.

Delia and Lilly cried too much to be with him for any length of time. The commissioner had come by, but he'd left five minutes later. Cal Vick stayed a little longer before the nurse kicked him out. Gail had wheeled herself up for a chat, but found out she wasn't allowed to smoke because of the oxygen and wheeled herself back out. There was no sign of Mack McKay, Red Flemming, Les Leslie, or Jett Elliott. It fell to Bud Deacon to tell Terry about Chip. That conversation had gone on for almost an hour. Bud wouldn't look at Maggie when he left the room.

Jimmy had talked to Terry this morning. That was all the information Maggie had. She had pressed her brother for details. Of course she had pressed him. That was what Maggie always did. Only this time, Jimmy hadn't done the thing he always did back, which was yell at her. He just shook his head and told her that everything was fine.

Was it fine? Maggie had been downstairs. She'd heard the murmurs in the waiting room. She'd seen the way some of the other cops looked at Jimmy. All three of them had stuck to Kate's story about Chip's confession, but cops were naturally suspect. She assumed this was the reason that Red, Mack, Les, and Jett were staying away. They had worshipped Jimmy. What did it say about them if Jimmy turned out to be queer? And what did it say about Terry Lawson that his nephew was gay?

Maggie should've been relieved that the men were gone from their lives, but she was furious at them for abandoning her brother. They had mentored him. They had treated him better than they treated their own sons. She would never forgive them for turning their backs on him for something that was none of their goddamn business.

Not that Jimmy seemed bothered by the betrayal. What happened on the roof outside the rail yard had changed a lot of things, but Jimmy Lawson still wasn't the type of guy to pour his heart out.

And about the other thing – well, Maggie wasn't the type of gal to pour her heart out, either.

Kate, on the other hand, had done a complete one-eighty from the fresh-faced newbie who'd opened the locker room door too wide on her first day. She had some kind of liquid steel in her blood. Even when she'd seen the hundreds of pages on the clipboard they'd found in Chip Bixby's car, all she had done was make a quip about how she preferred 'Jewess' to 'kike.'

Who knew what Kate was really thinking when she saw the lists of things that Chip was planning to do to her? Or what she made of the surveillence reports that recorded her every waking hour from the moment Chip had met her on the shooting range? Or the rants he'd scribbled about the kikes and spics and chinks ruining the world while good men like Chip Bixby fought to put things right?

Who knew about anything where Kate Murphy was concerned?

She was such a fucking good liar. Or obfuscator, as Kate would probably prefer. At least she was using her skills for good. The amount of bullshit Kate put into her incident report was breathtaking. Oddly, none of the embellishments were for her own benefit.

Officer Lawson drew Bixby's attention by kneeling on the ground, which gave me the opportunity to move closer to the revolver. Had she not distracted him, I would not have been able to act.

Bixby. Maggie almost wished she'd been there when Terry was told the news. She wanted to see the look on his face. Not just one, but two men in Terry's life had managed to pull the wool over his beady little eyes. And part of her couldn't help but think that it just proved how full of shit Terry really was. He spent every waking hour complaining about the kikes and slits and coloreds and liberals and feminists and everybody else who was ruining his perfect little world. What did he think would happen when somebody like Chip used his words as a call to action?

'Miss Lawson?' The nurse came out of Terry's room. She held the door open for Maggie. 'He's asking for you.'

Maggie didn't know whether to laugh or check the woman's pockets for dope.

'Don't stay too long.' The nurse wasn't joking. Taking care of Terry had obviously sucked all the life from her soul. 'He needs his rest.'

Maggie put her hands on her knees. She pushed herself up. Her body still ached from being thrown around. Her cheek was bruised black. Her neck was blue and yellow. Her jaw popped from Terry punching her in the face.

The lights were off in the room, but the glow of the equipment was enough to see by. Maggie had always felt comfortable in hospitals. She'd been visiting her father at Milledgeville for so many years that part of her thought of it as a second home.

Terry was on an inversion bed to take the pressure off his spine. He was stomach-down. The face cradle offered him a view of the floor. Long straps kept his arms and legs immobilized. Another strap wound around the back of his head. His hospital gown was open. Maggie could see the wings of his shoulder blades. Twelve inches below, there was a large bandage where the bullet had torn into his flesh. A sheet covered the rest.

Someone had painted a blue sky and fluffy white clouds on the tile directly below his face. There was a small mirror attached to an arm on the bed. The glass was tilted to show Terry's eyes and nose, though Maggie wasn't sure whether or not he could use it to see who was in the room.

He said, 'Move closer.'

Maggie couldn't understand him at first. His jaw was pressed into the face cradle. He could barely speak.

'Closer.'

She moved closer. He was staring into the mirror. He could see her.

'Where's Jimmy?'

'He's back at work.'

Terry's nostrils flared. 'He has to quit.'

Maggie didn't respond.

'He doesn't belong.'

'You sound like Chip Bixby.'

Terry's face was already red. His eyes were already bulging. Maggie didn't need the usual clues to figure out that he was furious with her. She felt it in her gut. She felt it with every breath. Every beat of her heart. No matter how much she denied it, she was connected to Terry the same way she was connected to the sounds in her house: the slap of the phone cord, the bang of the cabinet, the crack of the egg in the bowl.

Maggie sat down on the floor. She crossed her legs Indian-style and leaned down just enough so that Terry could see her without the mirror.

She said, 'I want to tell you something.'

He stared straight ahead.

'You were wrong. Don't you want to know what you were wrong about?'

Terry's jaw bulged.

Maggie quoted his favorite saying: ' "People don't take power. Somebody has to give it to them." ' She waited not for a response, but for her words to sink in. 'You were wrong, Terry. I took the power. Kate Murphy took the power.'

He didn't look at her. He didn't look in the mirror.

'I've been sitting outside your room all night thinking about this. Do you wanna know what I figured out?' Maggie didn't wait for an answer this time. 'I don't think you're really racist. Or sexist. Or anti-Jew. Or anti-gay. Or any of that bullshit. I think you're scared.'

Terry still wouldn't look at her.

'You're terrified.' She recalled Chip's words on the rooftop. 'Your whole world's upside down. You don't belong anymore.'

Terry didn't respond, but Maggie could tell her words were hitting the mark.

She said, 'Chip didn't kill those cops because he hated them. He killed them because he couldn't stand the fact that they were changing things. And you made him see that when you planted the evidence against Spivey. That's what set him off. You know it. I know it. Spivey walked free, and two months later, Chip was murdering the same kind of people you blamed for making it happen.'

Terry's jaw clenched so hard that Maggie could see the outline of the bone underneath his skin.

She said, 'And the sad part is that Spivey walked because

of you. The case was tight, but you couldn't leave well enough alone. You couldn't let a judge and jury decide on the facts.' Maggie gave him time to think about what she was saying. 'Chip was paranoid. He was alone. His world was falling apart. And he couldn't handle it. Just like you.'

Terry trembled with rage. His flesh was mottled. Sweat dripped onto the floor beneath him.

'That's what I wanted to tell you, that it was your fault. That the world isn't just changing. It's passing you by.' Maggie smiled. 'Atlanta's still a cop town, Terry. You're just not the cop who's running it anymore.'

He finally broke his silence. 'You fucking cunt.'

Maggie couldn't stop smiling. She loved this too much. She could sit here all day letting out every word he had ever crammed back down her throat and Terry couldn't do a damn thing about it.

He said, 'You think anything's gonna change?'

'I think the whole world is gonna change. For me. For Kate. For the blacks. For the browns, yellows, greens. For you. Especially for you.'

Terry looked at her now. 'You're nothing. You know that? You're the streak in my fucking underwear.'

Maggie saw his hand clench. She couldn't control her body's response. Every time his anger threatened to boil, her chest filled with mercury and her heart shot into her throat.

Terry said, 'Get the fuck out of here.'

'You don't tell me when to leave.' Maggie got on her knees, put her face close to his. 'You're not in charge anymore. Do you hear me?'

'When I'm outta this bed—'

'You feel this?' She rested her hand on the back of his neck.

Terry's breath huffed out. 'What are you doing?'

Maggie walked her fingers down his neck. His skin was cold and dry. 'I know you can feel my touch. It's just everything below the waist that's gone, right?'

'Ma—' He couldn't finish her name. Sweat dripped onto the floor, ran across the painted tile.

'They tell you the bullet's still in your spine?' She kept the pressure light on his neck. 'You're a quarter inch away from pissing and shitting in a bag for the rest of your life.'

'Don't—'

She moved her hand down half an inch. Her finger found the place between the vertebrae at the base of his neck. Her touch got lighter, but she knew Terry would feel it like a jackhammer. 'Tell me you're sorry.'

'Wh-what?' he stuttered.

'Tell me you're sorry.' Her mouth was by his ear. She hoped he felt the spit come out. She hoped his heart was trembling and his nerves were shaking and he was racked with the kind of fear that came when you were pinned down in bed and somebody was behind you doing whatever the fuck they wanted.

Maggie pressed her fingers between his shoulder blades. She could feel the bone of his spine. The incision was six inches away. It would be so easy for her to press her fingers into the wound, push the bullet that quarter inch over.

'Stop,' Terry begged. 'Please.'

'Tell me you're sorry right now or I'll slam my fist so hard into that bullet that it shits out your nose.'

'I'm sorry!' he screeched. 'I'm sorry!'

'Are you sure?'

'Yes.' He was crying. 'Please stop. I'm sorry. Please.'

Maggie removed her hand. She took her time getting up from the floor. She brushed off the back of her pants. She walked toward the door. She turned the handle.

The nurse was in the hallway. She had obviously heard the noise. 'Is he okay?'

'He's fine.'

'I'll get his pain medication.'

Maggie stopped her. 'He told me he doesn't want it.'

'Are you sure? I thought I heard him screaming.'

'That's what he does,' Maggie said. 'He grits it out. You should see him at the dentist. It's awful to hear. He always makes the hygienists cry.'

The nurse had been around Terry long enough to believe the story. 'Well, if that's what he wants.'

'Trust me. I learned a long time ago you don't argue with my uncle.' Maggie smiled at the woman. 'He's a tough guy.'

DAY EIGHT
MONDAY

Epilogue

Kate pulled her car into the parking lot down from the police station. She took the scarf off her head. Her sunglasses went into her purse. She thought about putting the top up on the convertible, but no one was going to steal a car from a police parking lot.

Even if it was a red Ford Mustang.

She grabbed her belt off the passenger's seat. The metal clips were in her front pocket. She looped them on her underbelt then hooked on the utility belt. She clipped the transmitter at her back. She checked her pockets: gum, lipstick, notebook, citation book, pens. She checked her belt: Flashlight on the hook. Handcuffs in the pouch. Shoulder mic threaded up to the epaulet. Jack plugged into the transmitter. Keychain attached to the ring. Nightstick through the metal loop. Holster secured around the belt. Safety strap snapped over her gun.

Her gun.

Kate had shot a man with a gun very similar to this one. She had been aiming for his chest and winged his shoulder, but as her people would say, closeness only counts in taxes and horseshoes.

Not that her people would ever know the truth about

473

what happened on that rooftop. Even if she wanted to tell them, Kate could not find the words to explain how she'd really felt. She had wanted to kill Chip Bixby. Not the first time she'd shot him – that time, she'd just been desperate to stop him. And not just stop him from killing Maggie, but stop him from saying the awful things he was saying.

Kate's white nightgown? Her purple blanket? Her Oma?

The time Kate had wanted to kill him came when she had seen Patrick's dog tags. Rage had consumed her. She hadn't wanted to just murder him. She had wanted to empty her gun into his chest. And then she wanted to fill the holes with burning oil and dance in his still-warm blood.

She had felt dead inside. She had felt capable of anything.

The fifth Kate reared her ugly head. This Kate wanted darkness. Her finger was on the trigger. She was ready to pull back. And then the other Kates took over. She wasn't sure which ones. The daughter? The widow? The cop? The whore?

The real Kate, she wanted to think. The only Kate who mattered was the one who had taken charge on that roof. Her finger had moved from the trigger. Her hand had tossed Maggie the handcuffs. The real Kate was a good person and she was not going to do a bad thing.

Why had that happened?

Because Kate had made a choice.

She had pulled herself back from the abyss. She was not a vigilante. She was not Chip Bixby. Her job was to uphold the law, and that's exactly what Kate had done.

And not just that. She had protected Maggie. She had saved Jimmy. She had saved herself.

Sure, she'd urinated down her leg in the process, but thanks to Philip, Kate happened to have an extra pair of underwear in her pocket.

She locked her car door, which was silly since the top was down, but it was a habit she was trying to develop. Kate scowled as she put on her hat. The band smelled of Jimmy Lawson's sweaty head no matter how many lingerie sachets she stuck in it every night. At least the baking powder had absorbed the foul odor in his shoes.

Small victories.

Kate walked up the sidewalk. The air was crisp. The sun was out. Her nightstick banged against her leg. Her holster dug into the flesh. She wondered if she was going to develop a callus. That seemed like the sort of thing a doctor would know.

'Murphy.' Jimmy Lawson was behind her.

Kate slowed so he could catch up. She asked, 'Good weekend?'

'The usual.'

Kate glanced up at him. Jimmy had never struck her as the funny type.

Maybe he was trying to make changes. Jimmy seemed different from a week ago, and not just because of the bruises that cut into his wrists. The anger that had lived inside him was starting to uncoil. Kate wondered when that had started. No one knew what had happened to Jimmy during the eighteen hours Chip had held him hostage. Jimmy claimed all he remembered was hearing a noise downstairs in the kitchen. The next thing he knew,

Chip was slapping him awake on the roof of the rail yard office building.

There was no mention of the letter.

Which was fine with Kate. No matter how things really went down, she could only hope nothing coiled Jimmy back into that angry person. Maggie needed him. The police force needed him. Though she wasn't certain how long Jimmy would last on the job. Despite what Kate felt was a fantastic performance, there were still rumors floating around the station. She'd thought that the girls were bad at her high school. As Kate had told her Oma the night before, there was no society more viciously controlled by rumor than your local police force.

That was the only detail she had shared with Oma. Kate's picture had been in the newspaper. She let the journalist tell her family what had happened, and thanks to the police commissioner, the journalists did not know much. The truth about Chip Bixby and his nauseating log were going to sit in police storage for the next hundred years. That is, unless Kate managed to move up somehow. She was certain detectives were allowed access to the storage rooms.

Jimmy said, 'Can I ask you a question?'

'It would be my pleasure.'

'The bullets in the stairwell. What made you count them?'

Kate gave a long sigh. 'Tables reserved for four or more. Only six items allowed in the dressing room. Two-drink minimum.' She shrugged. 'I've been counting all my life.'

'Jesus Christ,' he muttered. 'Didn't it ever occur to you that any one of those shots coulda come from Maggie's gun?'

'Absolutely.' She smiled up at him. 'That thought occurred to me the minute I got home. I almost had a heart attack.'

'Are you kidding me?'

'I wish I was.' Kate had been in such a state that she'd stood under a hot shower until the water ran cold. 'I never even considered that Maggie could've fired her gun.'

'Jesus help me, I was saved by Lucy and Ethel.' Jimmy was teasing her. There was no animosity in his tone. He indicated the steps up to headquarters. 'Ladies first.'

'Gosh, thanks.' Kate walked up ahead of him. As usual, there were cops crowded around the entrance. As usual, they didn't part for her to walk through.

Kate turned around. She almost bumped into Jimmy. She said, 'So, I'll see you tonight.'

Jimmy's mouth opened in confusion, but Kate closed it with a kiss.

It wasn't just any kiss. Kate put on a good show. Her hands caressed his neck. Her fingernails scratched his scalp. She literally knocked his hat off.

Kate saw Jimmy picking it up from the stairs as she walked through the tarnished front doors.

The gauntlet through the squad room wasn't as bad as the first day. Kate had learned so much since then. Such as the fact that it was called a squad room.

She ignored the new penis drawing on the door to the women's locker room. Kate cracked open the door and edged in.

Maggie was alone. She stood at her locker. 'You're early.'

'Don't get used to it.'

'I won't.'

477

Kate smiled as she dialed the combination on her lock. Reflexively, she checked her pockets again. She had forgotten to bring cash. Again.

Patrick's photo was in its usual place inside her wallet. Kate touched his beautiful face. Cal Vick had offered to return Patrick's dog tags, but Kate had politely declined. She was going to have to get a new apartment. Kate couldn't go back to the Barbizon, and though her father had told her she was more than welcome, she was too old to live in her parents' basement.

Besides, one look at the footprints outside her bedroom window had convinced her she needed to live in a more secure space. Just thinking about Chip Bixby watching her still made Kate ill.

So she didn't think about it.

Kate closed her wallet. 'I hear they've scheduled Jake Coffee's funeral for tomorrow.'

'Gail wants me to take her. You need a ride?'

Kate thought about the last funeral she had attended. Patrick's remains had been flown to Atlanta from the other side of the world. There were bureaucratic snafus. A freak storm had hit Atlanta. Ten days passed before what was left of her husband finally made its way home. Kate had been so drugged by the time the funeral was held that she barely remembered the coffin being lowered into the ground.

Maggie asked, 'You all right?'

'Absolutely,' Kate fibbed. 'I'll meet you at Gail's so you don't have to make the drive into Buckhead.'

'Buckhead,' Maggie grumbled. 'Listen, just to warn you, Gail's thinking about getting her PI license.'

Kate slapped her hand to her mouth.

Maggie knew what was coming. 'Everything can't be a joke, Kate.'

'Cyclops Investigations?'

'Stop it.' Maggie's head disappeared inside her locker. Her voice was muffled. 'Keeping an eye out for Trouble.'

'Oh, well done.'

'Good morning, ladies!' Wanda Clack squeezed past the door. Her smile dropped. '*Another* cock drawing? Really?'

Kate said, 'I thought the shading gave it an air of realism.'

'I'll bow to your expertise, Mrs. Lawson.'

Maggie said, 'What?'

'You didn't know your partner's dating your brother?' Wanda sat down on the bench. 'They were making out in front of the station house. Half the squad saw 'em.'

Maggie looked at Kate.

Kate shrugged.

'I can't believe it's Monday again. Every fucking week.' Wanda leaned back and opened her locker. She loaded her belt with her nightstick, handcuffs, transmitter. 'I met a stone fox on Saturday. Looked like Al Pacino, but shorter. He took me dancing and dining and then he found out I was a cop and sneaked out the bathroom window. Stuck me with the check!' She huffed a laugh. 'Guess I'm lucky he didn't have a gun taped to the back of the toilet.'

Maggie was smiling the way she did only when she was really happy. 'You could always date a cop.'

'I'll leave that to the young and stupid. Right, Murphy?'

'Absolutely.'

The door opened wide. A terrified young woman stumbled into the room. Her hands were clasped over her breasts. Her hat was down in her eyes. Her uniform was three sizes too large.

'Jesus Christ.' Charlaine Compton came in behind her. She pushed the door closed with both hands. 'What the hell were you thinking? We could have naked women in here.'

The new girl's mouth worked. She looked ready to run out the door. She probably would have if Charlaine hadn't been blocking the way.

Wanda said, 'Lookit her, she's terrified.'

'Like a deer caught in the headlights.' Charlaine feigned sadness. 'Poor thing won't last a week.'

Kate openly studied the new girl. She had dark hair and a wholesome appearance. She was attractive except for the unbridled terror.

Wanda asked, 'What's your name, sweetheart?'

'B-B-Beth Dawson.'

Wanda said, 'She reminds me of that chick from *Laugh-In*. What's her name?'

'Lily Tomlin?' Charlaine suggested. 'Judy Carne?'

'Ruth Buzzi.' Wanda clapped her hands together. 'I'm gonna call you Buzzi.'

Charlaine looked at her watch. 'I gotta call my sister, make sure she didn't stick my kid in her trunk instead of taking him to school.'

'Better get out of here before the colored girls come.' Wanda slapped Kate's leg. Kate helped lever her up. Instead of leaving, Wanda grabbed Dawson by the shoulders. 'Listen up, Buzzi. A word of advice: stay away from Jimmy Lawson. He's Murphy's over there.' She shook the woman like a sack of laundry. 'Trust me. You don't want to fuck with Murphy. She shot a man just to watch him cry.'

Wanda cracked open the door and slid out into the squad room.

Maggie told Kate, 'Vick told me we're partnered. That work for you?'

'Gosh, I'm thrilled.' Kate couldn't help herself. She really was thrilled.

Still, Maggie was shaking her head as she crabbed out through the door.

Kate zipped her purse. She patted her pockets one last time. She slammed her locker closed.

Dawson jumped. She was standing in the corner. Her hands still clutched her breasts. Her hat was so low that Kate couldn't make out the color of her eyes.

Kate said, 'Take your hands off your breasts.'

Dawson moved her hands. Her purse dropped to the floor. She leaned down to retrieve it and hit her head on the doorknob.

Kate willed herself not to smile. 'Do you have a lock?' The woman was too petrified to speak. 'A combination lock?'

Dawson shook her head. She put her hat back on. The brim dipped into her eyes. She pushed it back up.

Kate opened her locker. 'You can use mine today. Get one for yourself by tomorrow. There's a sporting goods store on Central Ave. near the university. Wear your uniform and they'll give you the lock for free.'

Dawson didn't move.

Kate grabbed the woman's purse and threw it into her locker. 'Never open the door all the way or the guys can see in. Don't wear the dress socks they gave you. Franklin Simon has wool ones, two for a dollar, but I prefer cashmere from Davison's. Either way, get something thick

481

that will help keep your feet in your shoes. And find a stapler for your pants. Those bobby pins won't hold. Trust me. You'll end up looking like the scarecrow from *Wizard of Oz*. And speaking of looking, always take in your surroundings. Up, down, left, right, front, back, sideways. You can take off your hat.'

Dawson took off her hat.

'You see this curtain?'

Dawson looked at the curtain.

'The colored girls change back there. They get the room ten minutes before roll call. That's the rule. They don't like it when we're in here and we won't like it if you piss them off. Understand?'

Dawson's head moved like the ball in a typewriter. Somewhere in her brain, she was trying to record all of this information.

Instead of slowing down, Kate went faster. 'You won't get arrested for altering your uniforms. There's a tailor on Fourteenth who'll take care of you. He's Jewish, but reasonable. What else? Oh – toilets are upstairs. It's a tight squeeze, only two stalls. Don't spray your hair in front of the mirror or someone will kill you. I'm serious. We all carry guns. I'm Kate, by the way.'

Kate offered her hand.

Dawson hesitated, then tentatively reached out to shake Kate's hand.

'Welcome to the Atlanta Police Department.'

Acknowledgments

Please keep in mind that Atlanta is not just one city – every experience is unique. While this novel is peppered with real-life details, it is still a work of fiction (which means I made stuff up).

For background on Atlanta during the 1970s, I'd like to thank Janice Blumberg, Dona Robertson, Vickye Prattes, and the lovely and handsome Dr. Chip Pendleton. Thanks to Ineke Lenting, my Dutch translator, for helping me with my Dutch (which is nonexistent except for the swear words I picked up from Marjolein). Iannis Goerlandt and Leen van den Broucke were particularly helpful with all of my questions about Flanders (and to my Flemish readers, whom I adore – my deepest apologies. You are the kindest, most joyful people I have ever met and I treasure the time I've spent with you). Melissa Van der Wagt pronounced some Dutch words for me (no, Melissa, they did not sound just like English). Nanda Brouwer took me to the Joods Historisch Museum in Amsterdam, where Mirjam Knotter very patiently answered my questions. I am particularly grateful to Linda Andriesse at the Hollandsche Schouwburg for her generosity and willingness to speak with me about her personal experiences.

Barbara Reuten, thank you for facilitating both of these meetings. I would encourage anyone interested in the history of the Netherlands during the war to visit and support these vital organizations. Actually, I would encourage anyone to visit the Netherlands whenever possible (and especially Flanders!).

Apologies to railfans for the liberties I took with the Howell Yard Wye. Also, I should mention that *Warren Zevon* was recorded in 1975 but released in May of '76.

David and Ellen Conford were my go-to Jews for all things Yiddish. If a reader finds I'm wrong: *a glick hot dich getrofen!* Laurent Bouzereau: thank you for your Rolodex. Susan Rebecca White: thank you for the Colonnade line. Kitty: thank you for proving that grown women in Buckhead still say 'gosh.' Kat: thanks for you know what, mama. Gillian: this is what I was working on while you were crafting your awesome sweet potato joke. Charlaine and Lee: yes, that's you guys. Mo Hayder: I am sorry so few people die horribly in this one. Next time.

To my editorial team, Jennifer Hershey and Kate Elton (BBF): thank you both so much for your diligence and patience. Writing a novel is like walking a tightrope, and I feel very glad to have y'all as my net. Thanks also to folks at Random House US and UK: Gina Centrello, Libby McGuire, Susan Sandon, Georgina Hawtrey-Woore, Jenny Geras, and Markus Dohle. Victoria Sanders, thank you for putting up with all my crap. Diane Dickensheid, thank you for listening to Victoria put up with my crap. Angela Cheng Caplan, you are a star. More crap to come.

My last thanks always goes to the two most important people in my life: Thank you to my daddy, who while I am in the throes of writing always brings me soup and cornbread and reminds me to comb my hair. To DA, my love – I don't know what I did to deserve you, and I am pretty sure you've forgotten, too.